THE
HURRICANE
SEASON

Other Books by Rosemary Daniell

Fort Bragg & Other Points South

Sleeping with Soldiers: In Search of the Macho Man

Fatal Flowers: On Sin, Sex and Suicide in the Deep South

A Sexual Tour of the Deep South

For Glenys —

THE
HURRICANE
SEASON

Rosemary Daniell

*One of the most brilliant,
loving and unusual
women I know —

And much, much love
to a dear friend —*

WILLIAM MORROW AND COMPANY, INC.
NEW YORK

Rosemary Daniel

Library of Congress Cataloging-in-Publication Data

Daniell, Rosemary.
   The hurricane season / Rosemary Daniell.
      p.   cm.
   ISBN 0-688-08860-0 : $20.00
   I. Title
PS3554.A56H8   1992   92-22943
813'.54—dc20   CIP

Printed in the United States of America

First Edition

1 2 3 4 5 6 7 8 9 10

BOOK DESIGN BY M. C. DE MAIO

For my sister,
Anne,
who is a mother, and knows a mother's heart.
For my children,
Laura, Darcy, and Laurens,
for their part in helping me realize the
upward spiral of the human spirit.

Though addiction and madness saturate my family history—my father was an alcoholic, my mother died a suicide—what follows is a work of fiction.

Hurricane Season

We want the hurricanes to come—
like passion   dark & overwhelming
they break up our dismay   we cannot
think in the midst of them   cannot
recall what might have been.   For this
is it   the essence: the winds
the roar   the spray   like needles
soft with morphine   *blowing out*
our craziness   blowing out our pain.

Mardi Gras: the stranger bares
a breast tattoo radiant—
a tit pierced by gold—
O God of the cobalt
eye   how did this come
to be: that one would
sit   allow the needle
passed through a nipple
next   the ring of metal—
the brute jewel by which
she is forced to her knees. . . .

Mater dolorosa,
the sorrowing mother

PART ONE

Tattoo Beneath a Dior Slip

Your first pain, you carry it with you like a lodestone in your breast, because all tenderness comes from there.
—Jane Bowles, *Two Serious Ladies*

"He's mine, all mine, and he's made me the happiest woman alive!"
—An elderly woman in a nursing home, just after receiving a kitten as a pet

Q.—*Easter O'Brian. Where did you grow up?*

A.—*On a farm a bit north of Mobile.*

Q.—*Were any other members of your family artists?*

A.—*No, none. Well, maybe craftswomen—my grandmother on my mother's side cross-stitched samplers, and made our clothes. She glued collages of magazine illustrations—the Campbell soup boy, the Clabber baking-powder girl, the Bon Ami chick—to the sides of pottery jugs. And once Mother shellacked pictures from the* Ladies' Home Journal *to the kitchen floor. But my father walked across it before it was dry—it was both literally and figuratively, as we say down South, "tacky"! (laughter)*

Q.—*Definitely not a conventional aesthetic upbringing! So—how did you begin painting without benefit of background or art school?*

A.—*There were colors, textures, everywhere—red dirt, pine needles, the waxy magnolia blossoms. Peacock feathers—my grandmother kept the crazy-looking things in the yard with the chickens, which were always fighting with them. Then there were the sunrises,*

13

sunsets. The smell of honeysuckle, the quiver of one perfect drop of honey when you pulled the stamen out. Then I found a book in the Mobile Public Library during a Saturday trip into town— The Lives of the Painters, *or something like that. That was when I first learned that painters existed. . . .*

Q.—*But the actual technical processes of painting, your well-known technical virtuosity—how did you achieve it?*

A.—*Later, as a young married woman in a suburb of New Orleans, I had time on my hands, didn't like playing housewife, or bridge. I walked around the French Quarter, observing the outdoor artists around Jackson Square, the amazing costumes of the transvestites; wandered through galleries, followed the work of the local primitives: a sanctified old black in her white cotton nurse dress, a Cajun who—though he couldn't write his name—carved the night creatures of the bayou. Now and then, I audited a class in religious art history, taught by a Jesuit at Loyola with whom I had made friends. Or took an evening art class at Sophie Newcomb, the women's school at Tulane. But mostly, I just bought paints—I had fallen in love with the colors of acrylics, the possibilities of oils—and painted—at first while the babies were asleep, or my son was at school.*

Q.—*Let's see—you've been married, twice divorced, have three children—what are your children doing today? How has it affected them to have a mother who's a noted regional artist? How did you work out your roles as wife, mother, and painter?*

A.—*Yes, three children—two daughters and a son. My older daughter, Rose, is beginning work on her doctorate in neuroscience; but she's also cataloging the works of contemporary women painters for an additional master's she hopes to get at Johns Hopkins. Her sister, Lily, presently works in the French Quarter as . . . Lily said to me at nine that she had dreamed the house was on fire, but I wouldn't save her because I was in my studio painting. (laughter) Now, we're the best of friends. I'm very proud of them—yes, very proud.*

Q.—*And your son?*

A.—*I'd rather not talk about that.*

Q.—*As for your marriages—*

A.—*The marriages: No, they weren't all that serious, you see. It was rural mores, people didn't have sexual lives or just live together back in the midfifties—yes, we're still the best of friends. Well, no, not with the Cajun who raised redbone hounds, trawled shrimp off a rickety bateau—we weren't really even married, he was just the father of my son, he's dead now, anyway—nor with my first husband, the used-car dealer . . .*

Q.—*When was your painting first recognized?*

A.—*I had moved to Georgia by then, with my second husband, a young gallery owner who had shown my works in New Orleans. There was a competitive show at the Atlanta Cultural Center, the High Museum of Art, it was called then—and my painting—a shaped acrylic with an intimation of body parts—won first place. A fluke, I told my husband. It was the first juried show I had entered. And none of his other clients had even been hung—I hated that. It was the beginning of the end of our relationship. . . .*

Q.—*And then?*

A.—*Three years later, Robert Motherwell came down to judge another regional show. He gave me first place—I never quite understood why, since he's an abstract expressionist. (laughter) But he took slides of my work to New York, where I later visited him, he introduced me around. . . .*

Q.—*Then the commission by . . .*

A.—*Yes.*

Q.—*And now this big prize, this international competition. But why— with this recognition—do you choose to stay in the South?*

A.—*This is where my roots are, my colors, the colors of red dirt and kudzu and azaleas—did you know that kudzu was brought here from Japan, that azaleas, if you eat them, are poisonous? The very red clay beneath which my mother, my grandmothers, are buried. Then there's that delicious grime of the whole city of New Orleans, that heat that gives a peculiar shimmer to the air. . . .*

Q.—*What will you do next? Where will you go with your prize money— what new work will you pursue?*

A.—*A shack at the edge of the bayou. Water moccasins and alligators, swamps and mosquitoes. I'll wait, simmer—see what comes from the colors, the shapes. . . .*

Q.—*As for your notorious images—your frankly sexual, sometimes nightmarish, representations of enormous genitalia, hermaphroditism, even mutilation—what your critics have called "your excessive use of the color red"—do you plan to continue them? And how have those close to you—your children, husbands—dealt with your imagination—an imagination so bizarre that one reviewer called your last exhibition "a literal freak show, a study in aberration"? . . .*

—*Art in America,* January 1976

CHAPTER ONE

WHAT THEY usually mean when they ask that is "How did a nice southern girl like you get so fucked up?"

Just a rebellious kid, I sometimes answer—my Irish blood fighting it out with my Cajun. Like in second grade: The boys drew stick men shooting other stick men with oversized pistols, falling from walleyed horses amid fiery explosions; the other girls colored round green treetops, neat red circles hanging at their edges, in front of two-story saltbox houses like none I'd ever seen near our dirt farm. But I crayoned Mama standing naked over the washtub, the cat giving birth to kittens, a chicken with its head wrung off, hopping around, its neck spurting blood. *Why cain't you be a li'l lady like the other girls?* the teacher boomed, her tight lips, her corseted boobs, her fat, folded arms, swaying ominously above me.

Though I didn't know it then, hers was to become the central question of my life: Today, in 1977, at thirty-nine, I'm still pressed into corners at cocktail parties by broad faces that protest that my best work is "something you do to shock people." Without even trying, I've become that aberration known as a ball-busting female.

True, I've never been one to docilely do as I was told—and *that*, as we all know *down hyah in the Deep Sawth*, is the first prerequisite for *bein' a li'l lady, a good wo-man to a good man.* Indeed, I've often asked myself whether I do the things I do because I'm an artist, or whether I've become an artist in order to do the things I do. The latter is something frustrated husbands and jealous women—as though I had never thought of it myself—have often accused me of. For as everyone in the South and everywhere else knows, women who are achievers—especially achievers in the *ahts*—are: a) crazy, and b) losers—of femininity, husbands, lovers, children. They expect us to all wear bib overalls like Andrea Dworkin, or shave our heads like Betty Dodson did after writing that book on masturbation, or at the very least become bona fide lesbians, and then when we don't, they're angry. The debutantes who've held themselves in check for a lifetime, like overbred horses frothing at the bit, the "good" women who've followed all the rules of martyrdom, the lesbians and man-haters—they're *all* angry at women like me.

But what they don't know is that success, for a southern woman, equals loss equals grief: The price must be paid—usually in flesh. And maybe they're right: Often enough—before I was liberated by therapy, the women's movement, and the pleasure principle—I raked myself over the jagged edges of how and why I sacrificed "everything" to my*self*, that sinful, greedy self that craved—indeed, insisted on—its own life.

It's just that I have—have always had—to know the truth of things. The day the fourth-grade teacher told the class that glass was really a liquid, I squirmed all the way home on the school bus, ignoring the other kids, wild with my own thoughts. When I got off, I ran up the dirt road before the house, through the front door, into the kitchen, where I dumped my books and picked up one of the Welch's grape jelly jars Mama kept for us to drink from. I went out onto the back porch, and with all the force I could muster, shattered it on the back steps. But before the glittery pieces could turn to liquid, my baby sister Musette ran up to kiss me, cutting her feet on the jagged edges. She had to be taken into town for twenty stitches; when she came home, tears still in the corners of her fat brown eyes, alternately sucking her thumb and a sucker shaped like a broom, I had my first inkling of what my curiosity would cost those I loved.

"I swear, I'm goin' through one a those midlife crisises," Musette cried to me over the phone from Mobile last week. "It seems like I'd be relieved—with Mama 'n the kids gone 'n all. But now I wish *I* had a career, a fancy life like yours. . . ." Her unspoken question—why she's still literally back on the farm, while I'm standing here in this elegant room with a woman who—gossip around the Quarter has it—was recently a man; who, at this very moment, is asking me to touch between her legs, stroke her newly carved cunt—is one I have asked myself. But how can I explain to my little sister that I have been stripped of everything *but* the exotic—that at this point in my life, I'm as much a prisoner of pleasure as she is of the once-stringy country town—now clotted with McDonald'ses and Burger Kings—where we both grew up. Or that, as a woman at the sheer edge of forty, I've learned the hard way to *enjoy*: that it's not the past but this moment—no matter how nauseous—that counts.

Just as now, testing out my psyche, its health, I raise pictures from the past: me, nine, kicking at the red dirt with my bare toe, watching the chicken zigzag headless through the yard. Its parts screaming on the cookstove, the faded blue roses in the greasy wallpaper. Mama, her Cutex Wild Rose nail polish chipped, her permanented brown curls awry, trudging back and forth, back and forth, across the floor smeared with the once-beautiful scenes from the pages of the *Ladies' Home Journal*. Daddy, staggering in drunk, yelling and throwing the cat against the side of the icebox. Musette, beating time to his rage with a bent spoon on the tray of the high chair with the decal of the blue bear on the back. Then, later, me sitting beside the oilcloth-covered table, my son Dwayne's Seminole-dark hair feathering my teenage breast, his jet eyes looking up into mine, his mouth sucking at my nipple with all his infant strength, as though through sheer will, he could join our bodies forever.

And Mama—Mama, who worshiped Normal—is dead from it. Till at last, I've learned to let go of the rest in advance: the sturdy, studious daughter, Rose, who—no matter how I want to hold or be held by her—keeps me at arm's length, saying she wants only the relationship of "official biographer." And my bruised and slender youngest, Lily, who—no matter how I long to press her skinny bones, her model's breasts, into my own, to draw her back, safe ("Safe from what?" she would ask) into the flesh that twenty years ago held her as cozy as soup—I in turn hold from me. Yes, husbands, lovers, friends, followers—I let them flow through as though I were a sieve. I no longer have any idea—if I ever did—what love between God and woman, woman and child, woman and man, woman and woman, means.

As the writer Blanche Boyd wrote of herself in *The Village Voice*, I've come to regard orgasm as nothing more than a sneeze—to be sneezed into as lovely and/or interesting a handkerchief as possible. The problem is—that like crawfish étouffée, bananas Foster, and long-stem "Perfection" roses (so delicately, deathly blue!)—beautiful handkerchiefs obsolesce as quickly as Scott tissues, and using them up gets like taking out the trash: twenty-year-old boys with their dewy eyes and cries for mother love, even marriage; beautiful women, with their gladiola-like cunts and rages against men; hard-bellied adventurers with their tales of oil-rig fires and smuggling trips to South America, their demands to be tied up and/or have their backs scratched.

So right now, I ask myself, Which would be more interesting to eat: this flowerlike creature leaning eagerly toward me— or the poisonous labia-pink azaleas that cover New Orleans at this moment? More and more, painting in my studio over Royal Street, I think alternately of colorful ways to get laid—or commit suicide. My best fantasies combine both. Like that of getting into a gutted Chevy with fuzzy dice at the dashboard with six of the blacks who lounge outside their ramshackle frame houses in Elysian Fields, occasionally throwing languid baskets, mostly listening to a loud transistor—then riding out to a place where, their onyx backs and biceps blazing the Louisiana sun, they take out on my white southern woman's flesh all their pent black rage. Maybe one of them would be the same one I saw a policeman beating down with his club in a parking lot while everyone else was turned toward the parade on Canal Street during

Mardi Gras. Yes, like Musette and Blanche Boyd and Mama, I grew up in the southern tradition, connecting sex with violence. To be fucked or killed, protected or abused, loved or hated— what's the difference?

Yet if I believe truly that, why do I ask myself whether *this*—sex with a woman who is really a mutilated man—is all that is left to me? There's a disco song that's popular now, the Village People, I think: "If my parents could see me now, if my parents could see me now. . . ." I've danced to it dozens of times in the sleaziest bars in the Quarter, and all over New Orleans, the rotting and, yes, exotic seaport town where I now live. It rings in my mind as Iris, in an iris-colored dress, fresh violets stuck into a link of her gold chain belt—her Sassooned hair a clear geometric red—pushes me against the refrigerator in the kitchen of this flat in the Pontalba where we are both cocktail guests.

Though I've never met her before this minute, she has just asked me to bed; then, at my hesitation, accused me of thinking her a man. I've countered by asking whether she's really a transsexual, or just a man in drag. "Touch my tits, just touch them . . ." she moans, engulfing me in what smells like a wave of hyacinths.

Well-brought-up southern woman that I am, I acquiesce, press one breast through the lavender silk that, yes, does seem real enough, if a bit too springy, too adolescent, for the fortyish woman she appears to be. And is that a faint feminine mustache or the scars of electrolysis edging her slickly lipsticked mouth?

Still, I record the breast, its texture; drink in her hyacinth, violet, cream. But then, I've always been a sucker for what affects the senses. . . .

At nine, I walked barefoot down the red-dirt roads outside Mobile, loving the warm, grainy dust between my toes, swishing the skirt of my coarse feedsack dress, pretending it was the gown of the heroine of a story set in an English castle. I savored the striations, variations in the soil, from pale salmon to deep sienna to charcoal, and I loved the way, after a hard rain, the auburn dust turned a slick, vivid red, like a raw side of beef hanging in the slaughterhouse, or this sleek red steak tartare I

21

now lift to my mouth on a round of rye, breaking the circle of Iris's, yes, rather muscular, arm.

I could have eaten the clay as well, and sometimes I did. I pried it from the earth with sticks, dug my fingertips into it, patted it into breastlike mounds. I learned not to wait for the rain but to sneak a Mason jar of water from the kitchen, mix it with the red dirt in a beat-up pie tin. There was something terribly satisfying in the plastic quality of the clay, its slipperiness. My first woman lover told me of the dream that confirmed to her her sexual inclination: In it, she lay on a beach, her eyes closed, digging her fingers rhythmically into the warm, wet sand—till the tide had crashed in, matching the contractions in her lower body. For me, the red clay, warm after an Alabama rain, was seductive, earthy—above all, *vaginal*. I understand why Iris, if she was once a man, wanted to become female, to share the way we rise, flowerlike, out of menstrual blood, semen, afterbirth—even the carcasses of the animals we cook. I, too, have long been more comfortable with, even hungered for, shapes and textures that are slick, sleek, damp, fleshy. And there were plenty of those around what we called the home place. For instance, the caviar, black and glistening, poised on another round of rye, that Iris now edges toward my mouth between Revloned fingertips, recalls the great gobs of slick black tadpole eggs that filled the creek each spring.

Everywhere were sensuous shapes: translucent blue soft-shelled crabs, wiggling in the bottom of Daddy's trap. Pale rose salamanders, gliding from beneath wet rocks. The tiny green frogs that fell, like drops of viridian acrylic, with the summer rains—Mama said that when I was two, she caught me popping them into my mouth, chewing, swallowing, smiling. The black snake that slithered beneath the screen door into the kitchen to hypnotize the small gray mice with the sway of his head, then dart to swallow them whole faster than Musette's or my eyes could follow.

And the endless cats: the tom's one yellow eye, wet in his fat, scarred head, his other sewn as shut as though Mama had stitched it on her treadle Singer. His harem of females, who leapt from the hayloft at our footsteps, twined themselves around barn corners, curving tails to match their motion. Newborn kittens mewling in the cloudy sacs the mama cat quickly, rhythmically lapped away with her fuchsia tongue, just as she would the mauve-and-pearl afterbirth.

The satisfying oval of a newly laid egg, warm and shit-smeared, in my palm. The *plop* of cow shit, the arch of her tail. Even a wild rabbit, just after Daddy had whacked the back of its soft neck: the quiver, the twitch of its fluffy body; then Daddy stripping the fur from its purplish flesh, as though he were pulling off its coat.

That's what I liked to think—that he was just pulling off its coat.

When I was six, I ran into Mama and Daddy's room to tell her about the new litter of kittens I had found beneath the porch. Daddy stood beside the bed with his clothes off, his thing sticking straight out, the same purplish color as the rabbit without its coat. Mama lay on the bed, her skin a damp peach; one of her legs was raised at the knee, revealing what looked like a damp, dirty rose. Daddy held her brown curls in his fist, jerking her head from side to side; she moaned, *No, no.* With each motion he made, his thing swayed dangerously near her face, darting back and forth like the black snake just before it struck.

I ran back out before they saw me, and it was then that I had the notion: that I could make things better in the house— persuade Daddy not to hurt Mama with his thing—with something I would make from the clay. All afternoon, I worked in the barn on an ashtray. As I formed the indentation at its side for Daddy's half-smoked Camel, I imagined him smiling, perhaps even pulling me into his lap. At the end of the day, I backed out the barn door, admiring my masterpiece on the ledge where I had set it to dry from an increasing distance. I passed the next day at school in a daze, and that afternoon ran out to the barn to add what I knew would make it the most beautiful ashtray in the world: I pulled from the pocket of my jumper the bottle of Cutex Fire Engine Red I had stolen from Mama's dresser drawer, and painted—carefully, oh, so carefully —an enormous rose, radiating from one side of the ashtray, the indentation forming its stem. For twenty minutes—twice

23

the time recommended on the bottle—I watched it dry, then gingerly carried it across the yard and into the kitchen. Mama was setting the table, a moist glow to her cheeks, as there sometimes was when she had been cooking. "Where you been, girl?" she asked as she laid out the forks. She was cross, but I thought she was the most beautiful woman in the world, just as my ashtray was the perfect artifact. When she turned her back, I set my gift beside Daddy's plate, just above his iced-tea glass. In a minute, I heard his old pickup with the broken muffler, chugg-chugging into the yard.

When he came through the screen door, Mama was walking across the room with the bowls of corn bread and redeye gravy. He yelled something I didn't understand, something about some man down at the truck stop where she worked the 3:00 to 11:00 A.M. shift on Saturdays. As he lurched toward her, he picked up the ashtray from the table without even looking down at it, then threw it across the room. It hit the wall just above Mama's head, and my beautiful rose exploded against the blue roses in the wallpaper, then fell to dull orange crumbs on the picture-smeared floor at her feet. Then Daddy was over beside her, still yelling, and twisting her arm behind her till she dropped the bowl of gravy; the hot mess covered the hunks of my ashtray, melting it down to greasy red clay again.

That dummy Musette began screaming at the top of her lungs, hanging on to my legs the way she did when Daddy was really drunk; but I was watching him grab the neckline of Mama's dress with his fist, rip open its buttons with one motion. As she stood crying in her old peach slip and brassiere, he yelled, "Take 'em off, too, yuh ho'ar!" He bent her arm back around again, then grabbed the butcher knife off the corn-bread plate and waved it while she pulled the slip over her head, undid the bra, and, looking at him in a way I didn't like to watch, stepped out of her peach rayon panties. As she took each thing off, Daddy snatched it from her hand and held it in his fist with the flowered dress.

The next thing I knew, he was nailing her clothes to the wallpaper with the knife, sticking the blade right through the layers of cloth. I stared at the way the roses in her old cotton dress vibrated against the bigger roses in the wallpaper, how the blade stabbing one flower's center seemed to explode it, the peach straps of her underwear fluttering beneath it like the streamers from the birthday popper I had seen in a picture in *Woman's Day*. The blade at the flower's center stuck out like a weird stamen; the blossoms beneath it made me dizzy, as though they were swirling. I felt the way I did sometimes at the Church of God, when I looked up at the stained-glass windows: The flowers against flowers, the drape of cloth against the smooth texture of paper, made chill bumps pop out on my arms. I wanted to cry, it was so pretty.

Daddy looked like a balloon with all the air let out. Mama squatted on the floor, her arms tight around her breasts, her head down as though she were praying. "Look, Mama, look at the flowers in your dress," I called out to her in my head. "Look how pretty they are against the wallpaper!" But I didn't say anything; nobody did.

Then Daddy whispered, "Yuh slut," and after another minute stamped out the back door, and we heard him gunning the motor of the pickup. Mama sat down on the floor with a plop, her arms still tight around her breasts, her legs spread apart, showing the damp, dirty rose. Her feet, still in her dingy pink scuffs, stuck out at either side. Musette kept crying and pulling on me, till I slapped her, and she let go and fell down, too.

While she and Mama sat on the floor crying, just as if they were singing together in church, something inside me hardened. Daddy was nothing, that was clear—no more than the most tick-infested hound dog out in the yard, its scrawny old balls, its ugly tail, hanging down between its skinny legs. But Mama was at fault, too: Mama, with her droopy old breasts, her nail polish always chipped, that damp, ugly thing that grew, like a fungus, between her legs: This was *why*—why Daddy had yelled at her, why he had broken my ashtray.

I would never be like Mama, I decided. My nail polish would never chip, my breasts would never droop, and that neat, hairless fold between my thighs would never—I determined—gape in disarray. I would be as perfect, as sleek, as the bride doll I had pored over in the Sears Christmas catalog. Just as I had created the perfect ashtray, I would create a perfect world, full of perfect things, a perfect self to inhabit it.

As perfect, as self-created, as Iris.

"Well, are you coming or not?" she presses, her glossy mouth making a moue. "If it's a *man* you want, we can get somebody, a ménage à trois. . . ."

I look at her idly: What would a vagina made of the skin of an inverted penis look, taste, smell, like? I had read somewhere—or had I seen it on PBS, one of those journeys into the interior of the human body?—that at the base of the penile shaft in each man lies a minute but perfect womb. And if so, what had become of Iris's womb in miniature?

"*Well?*" she repeats.

I answer by diving into the center of the hyacinths, kissing her Mary McFadden—pale cheek. Long ago, I learned that if I concentrated on shapes, colors, I gained perspective, answers would come to me. Mama could sob: I would examine her ten-cent-store nail polish, the cheap crimp of her home-permanented curls. She would yell at me with that pained twist of her mouth, almost a snarl: I would check out the tacky way her Tangee lipstick drifted upward in the tiny channels above her upper lip. Daddy could twist my arm behind my back, stick his nicotine-yellowed forefinger inside my cotton panties, between my clamped thighs: I would concentrate on the dark sandpaper coarsening the bottom of his ugly chin, the scent of his Four Roses breath.

I already knew I had more control over matter than the actions or feelings of others—that while I couldn't change Mama or Daddy or the way things were in the house, I *could* change colors, textures, grains. Once, as I mixed red dirt to clay, I dumped too much water into the pie pan. When I stirred, the clay was thick, like blood, but too thin to shape. Then I had the idea: Excitedly, I mixed in more water, till the red was thin, almost as thin as water itself, a cloudy sienna fluid. I ran out to the edge of the hog pen, where I remembered an old paintbrush, half-stuck in the Alabama mud. It lay where I recalled it, where indeed it had probably lain, half-submerged, since before I had been born. It was a grimy white with black bristles,

26

its handle rusty where the metal joined the horsehair. When I pried it up, I realized the bristles were stiff, stuck together with black paint. I felt that I wanted to part them more than I had ever wanted anything. But no matter what I did—scraping them against a rock, beating them against the fence to the stupid snorts of the hogs—nothing worked: The bristles stuck. As I threw the brush down, tears heated my eyes. Then I flashed an image, as clear as the sudden parting of the bristles would have been. I saw two broad sticks tied together with one of my shoelaces, their ends feathered with the kitchen knife. The next day, I had my brush, and painted a ragged sun on the dull gray side of the barn.

But I wanted more: If I boiled wild violets, would the water turn the purple of their petals? I tore up clusters of the blossoms, ran into the kitchen, and stuck them into a pot. I filled it up with tap water and set it on the eye of the cookstove. In five minutes, the water had bubbled, but the violets had floated to the surface like blue-black corpses: instead of a deep purple, the liquid was a vague stinky green, smelling of turnips, the vegetable I hated most. As I dashed the repulsive water down the sink, I felt the hot tears again.

Till I recalled the wonderful thing I had seen the week before, when Daddy had let Mama, Musette, and me off in town on Saturday to do some shopping. In Woolworth's, I had held Musette's fat, sweaty hand and walked around the toy department while Mama examined the Pond's face powder, the different shades of Tangee, the celluloid earbobs. And suddenly there it was, right beside the jackstones and yellow-handled jump ropes—the slender tin box with ARTIST'S COLORS written across the top! I lifted the lid gently: Inside lay a half-dozen platelets of hard, clear color; beside the opaque circles, set within its own slender metal compartment, was a narrow brush, its end feathered with fine black bristles. "Duh yuh wont thet colorin' set 'er not?" The salesclerk rose above me accusingly, her arms folded like the second-grade teacher's. "No'm," I lied as I reluctantly replaced the lid. As I dragged Musette behind me toward the cosmetic counter, I felt something akin to the memory left in my mouth by the silver-wrapped Hershey's Kisses Musette and I had gotten in our stockings at Christmas. For months, I

27

had longed for more, and had kept the silver foil, crumpled and recrumpled into metallic balls, in the chifforobe drawer beneath my underwear, where it had finally melted to silver dust.

Now flamboyant fantasies of what I might paint with the paint set danced in my head, and I began to make my plan. The next Saturday, when Mama, Musette, and I came back from town, I hid the stolen Artist's Colors where the silver crumbs had been.

Stealing them was my first, but by far not my last, criminal act. I already knew I was a misfit, an outlaw, and had from the time the teacher had said *Why cain't you color inside the lines, like ev'rybody else?* There was something improper, unladylike, in my interest in colors, shapes, textures; in molding and mixing and making; but most of all, in my desire to *know*. "It's all right for a woman to *look*, but not to *see*," a sister in the Quarter said to me recently. We were in a bar, looking for men to sleep with, but her statement struck me as profound: As a girl, I had daydreamed that I had X-ray vision, could see through heads, torsos, to brains, guts, genitals, that I could read the secret thoughts—as though they were projected on a television screen—of everyone in my class. Back then, it was partly that I hated, felt paranoid, about my classmates, and felt sure they would do me in had I not had this special protective power. But it was also just that the truth of things seemed to me to be their beauty. And I was beginning to realize that other people didn't feel the same way—that I didn't see things as others did, and that my vision was something to keep secret, like the plans for a robbery.

When I was three, my leg went to sleep. As I stood on it, pinpoints of crimson, violet, electric blue—like the fireworks Cudden Jones had set off in the barnyard on the Fourth of July—exploded in my shank. I cried to Mama that it was filled with sparkling colors.

By the time I was nine, the weird things that went on inside my head, the strange things evolving between my thighs, seemed connected. I suspected that the shimmering event that occurred when I touched myself long enough down *there* was

28

somehow wrong, another of my criminal acts. Then, too, colors sparkled through my legs, starting in my belly and thighs, moving through my calves, bursting out my toes. But these colors were fluorescent, more pleasure than pain.

One day, I opened Mama's dresser drawer to stroke the slick red pools of spilled nail polish. In the corner, mixed with her tangle of plastic beads and rhinestone earbobs, her boxes of cake Maybelline and Tangee lipsticks, I saw her old metal compact: Faint pink powder spilled from beneath the round wire mesh, but the top held a dusty cracked mirror. I closed the clasp with a satisfying *click*, dropped it into my pocket, and ran out beyond the cow pasture, where I knew of a smooth, secret patch of ground. Hurriedly, I took out the compact, opened it out on the grass, and pulling my underpants aside, squatted over it.

What I saw looked like a pink yeast roll, or a purse decorated with faint brown hairs a shade lighter than the hairs on my head. I was pleased that it didn't gape, or look scraggly like Mama's. When I levered it with two fingers—just as if I was opening a doll's pocketbook—I saw in the mirror the most beautiful thing I had ever seen, a thing of wonder, like a translucent salamander, or a wet purplish azalea in the side yard in early spring. At the fork of the opening, shaped like a dowsing stick as I held it wide, stood the wormlike projection that quivered as though it were electrified—turning what I imagined to be a shocking fluorescent pink—when my fingertips brushed it beneath my quilts at night. I stuck the tip of a finger inside myself, then into my mouth. What I tasted seemed pink, too— a salty shrimp that somehow brought tears to the corners of my eyes.

Suddenly, I realized that it was that delicate deep pink, that pink that filled my brain behind my newly closed eyes, that Daddy had wanted all those times he had stuck his finger in me, trying to push farther each time. Once when Mama had seen him touching me, she had yelled at him to stop, but I had known by the look on her face that even though I was crying and trying to get out of his arms, it was somehow my fault. And now I knew why—inside me was something so beautiful that it created a magnetic field, that Daddy's fingers had been drawn to it just

29

as Mama's bobby pins had flown to the little painted horseshoe I had found, along with the Hershey's Kisses, in my stocking at Christmas.

I lay back on the grass, my eyes still closed, feeling the heat of the sun on my lower body. I rubbed myself till the colors started, sparkling behind my eyelids, moving down my legs. The tears that ran down my cheeks, into my ears and hair, felt as though they had been heated by the sun.

The next afternoon, I came into the house from the cow pasture, where I had been sitting, watching some pretty silver-and-pink worms crawling in and out of a cow dropping. Mama looked up at me from where she sat sewing. "*Eeas*-ter!" she cried, sounding as though I somehow had wounded her: She wore the same look she had when she had caught Daddy touching me. "Git to yuh room rite now, 'n git thet dress off!"

Puzzled, I pulled my favorite pink-and-white checked gingham over my head—and saw the big blot of vermilion mixed with the green grass stains and a few grains of red dirt. As I stood in my undershirt and pants, fingering the spot, I recalled the trail of red dimes across the picture-smeared floor when Mama had what she reluctantly whispered was "the curse." Then I felt the warm trickle between my thighs for the first time—pleasant and sticky, a satisfying *grab* in my lower belly, like the rhythm of a gospel song. I pulled down my underpants and saw that the dingy cotton had turned a bright, wet red.

When Mama rushed into the room, her fists full of rags, hot blood filled my face as well. I could tell by the look on hers that what was happening wasn't good, no matter how excited we became at school, chattering on the playground about who had "got it" and who had not. As she told me what to do with the rags, I looked down at the flowers in the linoleum until they formed dissecting lines. I was finding out that another good thing was bad—that it, too, had to do with my hidden thoughts, my criminality, the secret of the pink.

"Now git on in thyah 'n soak thet dress in col' water so it won't make a stain!" Mama said angrily, as though she knew my guilt, suspected my thoughts.

*   *   *

If Daddy hadn't killed a rabbit or a couple of squirrels by Saturday, Mama would wring a chicken's neck before church on Sunday.

The decapitated bird would lurch headless through the dirt, a fountain of red jetting where its head had been. When it finally slowed, zigzagging as though it had developed narcolepsy, Mama grabbed it by a wing, threw a rag over the bloody neck; then, holding it at arm's length, marched into the kitchen to throw it into the pot of scalding water waiting on the cookstove. As she pulled it back out a half minute later, its steaming feathers stood awry, like Mama's permanented hair just after she had washed it.

I stood by the sink, the waiting washbasin, to begin the plucking: I loved the little *snap*, the release from the piece of cartilage that held each feather into the damp skin, and especially, I loved to press out the smaller, more tedious pinfeathers—just as later in the afternoon I would enjoy pressing the blackheads from my Cudden Jones' ugly teenage face (an obsession I would recognize twenty years later, reading Sartre's essay "The Hole").

When all the feathers were gone—the chicken naked and uncomfortably human-looking—Mama would let me stick my fist into the hole at the fat end of the hen to pull out the entrails. "This hyah is the clo-a-ca!" I told Mama brightly. I had learned the word from the big dictionary on the stand at school. "It's why chickens don't have but one hole." Mama looked up for a second with a disturbed look on her face, then—as though she hadn't even heard me—went on stirring the corn bread for the dressing.

Thinking *translucent*, another word I had recently learned, I pulled out the lavender-and-pink guts. If the hen was about to lay, I discovered a partly formed egg, its shell a delicate membrane. Rolling it gently back and forth in my palm, watching the yolk shift from side to side within the tender sac, the viscous fluid, I looked for the red smear that indicated a baby chick.

"Gimme thet aig!" Mama finally said. "How we gon' put it

31

in the gravy if you keep playin' with it?" She held up the pieces
of the hen's hacked carcass, throwing each into a brown paper
sack full of salted flour, shaking them angrily, then throwing
them, one at a time, into the iron skillet full of bacon grease
sizzling on the cookstove. As I watched, I thought of the
chicken, only an hour before pecking at corn or other chickens
in the yard, and imagined the crackling sounds to be its final
screams of protest.

Why weren't they like the schmoos in "Li'l Abner" in the
Sunday funnies, I wondered, just loving to be killed and eaten? I
liked to watch textures change—the once-feathered, squawking
hen to crusty, salt-scented hunks of meat; thin beige liquid to
thick brown gravy; runny egg batter to crunchy corn bread;
hard little peas to soft green spheres. Every week, at the store,
I begged Mama to buy Jell-O chocolate or butterscotch pudding
mix, just so I could stand at the stove, feel the weight tugging
at the wooden spoon as I stirred, the thin liquid magically turning thick and creamy. But though she would only accede to my
pleas occasionally, she would, every other week, bring home a
big white lump of margarine, accompanied by a bright yellow
capsule. I itched to tear open the cellophane, plop the fat into
her cracked mixing bowl, and, blending the capsule in with both
hands, watch the gelatin oblong first break, then release into
the pristine mass streaks of bright orange that gradually paled
to a butter yellow. Carried away with what I now thought of
as *that feeling*, I would squeeze with both palms, my forearms
plunged into the smooth grease. "No need to mix it *thet* much!"
Mama would inevitably complain. "Yuh'll git yore germs into it,
sure as the worl'!"

Although she worked at a truck stop and was married to a
tenant farmer and housepainter who "didn't have a pot to piss
in," Mama knew about things like germs. Indeed, she prided
herself on having been "raised up raht." Her grandmama had
been a circuit-riding preacher's wife who had hand-painted a
quilt-top design over her raw parlor floor; her mama had served
tea—to *whom*, I wondered—in white bone-china cups on which
she had painted wisteria and magnolia blossoms.

That was why she "lov-v-ved be-*oou*-tiful thangs," she told
Musette and me over and over. We sat watching as she painted

her nails, sheer coat after coat, a fine Cutex Plum Garden or Chinese Red. Somehow, we knew this delicacy, this artistry, was not wrought for Daddy; was it for her lost aristocracy—or the truck drivers who patronized the truck stop where she worked?

"'n you girls jes' remember," she would add with a flourish, waving her nails in the air to hasten their drying, as though this had been the point of it all, "yuh kin love a rich man jes' as easy as a pore one!"

Even Musette and I could see Mama wasn't cut out for life on the farm, for wringing the chickens' necks or dishing up grits and fried eggs at the truck stop. She arrived home from her seven-to-three shift on weekdays just after I came in from the school bus, and the first thing she liked to do was to "set down 'n re-*lax* for a spell," putting her plump feet—swollen from eight hours inside her white rubber-soled oxfords yet with each cramped toenail carefully painted to match her fingernails—on the seat of a kitchen chair. Then she would sip a cup of coffee, smoke cigarette after cigarette while telling us about her day. "You should've *seen* whut happened when ole Jim put Hank Williams on the jukebox, 'n Jolene won'id to hear Patsy Cline—she ended up spillin' coffee all ovah his ole shirt!" she would enthuse, as though we, too, could envision the exciting scene. It was the one time, aside from when she was dressing to go to work on Saturdays, that she seemed really happy. She *said* she hated working at the truck stop, but as she talked or got ready, it always seemed that she didn't.

As she dressed, I liked to sit in her and Daddy's room, pretending to fool around with the makeup and Woolworth's jewelry on her dresser but really watching as she leaned over to drop her breasts into a peach satin brassiere topped with stiff cheap peach lace stitched into erect cones, then pulled a matching peach rayon satin slip over her head and wiggled her full hips into an elastic girdle. Next she dabbed Shalimar or Evening in Paris between her breasts, behind her ears with a little glass dabber, and buttoned the blue cotton uniform—smoothly starched and creased—over her now-taut breasts and ass, and leaned over once more to tease her hair into a fat brown halo. "Y'all be good now!" she would yell gaily at Musette and me as a horn in the yard sounded her ride. Secured by elastic, her

33

breasts and buttocks were as erect, her waist as compressed, as my Blondie paper doll's. I thought she was pretty, prettier even than the ladies in the Sears catalog, or even those—wearing beehive hairdos, tight satin dresses with spaghetti straps—on the covers of the *True Love* magazines she kept hidden beneath her mattress. As she sprinted out the door in her freshly polished white oxfords, I imagined she was a Hollywood star on the way to a place as foreign, as exotic, as New Orleans, or even Atlanta, full of music and laughter and strange men in dark fedoras. Yet decades later, driving through a rural village in Costa Rica, I would see a woman all dolled up—gold front tooth flashing along with her flirtatious smile, unshaved legs ending in stiletto heels—standing beside a roadside shack and would think of Mama, her equally futile attempts at glamour.

Still, back then she left behind a glow that would last until I went into the kitchen, where Daddy, wearing a scowl and probably already drunk, would be slouched at the kitchen table. "When you gon' fix my supper, girl?" he would growl. It was my job on Saturdays to prepare corn bread and buttermilk and raw onions, or fried potatoes and onions and eggs, for him, Musette, and me. Then I would wash up the dishes, change Musette's diapers, and bathe her in the washtub in the kitchen— waiting for the moment when he would drunkenly lurch from the kitchen, gun up the pickup, and take off for town. Only then could I lie in bed tracing pictures of girls with teased hairdos, hourglass figures—Brenda Starr or Wonder Woman—from comic books with my right hand, while Musette, curled beneath my left arm sucking her fat thumb, fell damply asleep at my side.

Mama's older sister, Darlene, wasn't as pretty; but she had nicer "thangs"—a squat brick house set squarely on a treeless lot, furnished with tweed-carpeted floors, bedroom and living-room "suites," tables covered in crocheted doilies, shelves full of bric-a-brac and doodads—why, there was even an indoor bathroom, and a wringer washing machine on her back porch! Because she was married to a man who was the tool-pusher— or boss—of an oil rig, she didn't "*have* to work," and as the wife of an enlisted man, then a sergeant, in the army, had traveled to foreign places like New York, even Europe. She had given Mama a machine-embroidered satin tapestry that read NEW YORK WORLDS FAIR, 1939, which now hung over the sofa in our linoleum-floored living room. One Christmas she had presented me with a wooden doll that looked like a fat lady in painted apron and scarf, MADE IN RUSSIA painted on the soles of her fat joined feet. When I pried the seam around her middle with my thumbnail, she came apart, revealing another fat lady, then another and another and another.

"You watch thet girl," I heard her tell Mama one day. "She's developin' too fast." I knew she looked down on Mama, her own sister, because she was poor and had to work, and our daddy was "no-count." But now she had found me out, she looked down on Mama because of me as well. "Has she got 'er monthlies yet?" I heard her going on, tugging at Mama's thick hair with a brush. Thinking of the ruined pink-checked dress, its blot of red, my face turned hot again. I hated ole Darlene, I decided, hated the way she made Mama look, the way Mama yelled at us after she went home.

Yet I loved to climb on the couch, stroke the smooth satin of her tapestry; even more, to click the fat ladies together, one neatly inside the other. It was almost as satisfying as sticking my fist inside the hen in search of eggs, squeezing the sudden pink from a fat crape-myrtle bud, or tearing apart a honeysuckle blossom—leaf from petal from stamen—to see how everything fit. But no matter how slowly, carefully, I did so, I could never discover their secret. It was a sensation I would later experience—separating vulva from labia from vagina, lifting penis from testicles from perineum—as sexual curiosity, a curiosity that later evolved into my prize-winning layered canvases depicting body parts. The frustrating thing about the male body, I've often thought, is its lack of mysterious caverns, a lack symbolic of the whole structure of male uptightness, from analytical mind to rigid sphincter. When I was nine, my ugly ole Cudden Jones—ugly ole Darlene's ugly ole son—showed me his ugly ole thing with that dark hole at its end. At least *my* mama had *girls*—full of curves and cavities and promise—I told myself.

35

"Well, if you evah have a baby, how's it gonna git out?" I asked him scornfully, hating the ugly way he laughed, the way he thought he knew everything, even if he *was* fourteen years old!

Darlene had brought us a package of little shells from Daytona Beach, Florida, pale mauve and salmon and cream, like sunsets or the entrails of chickens. Holding them, looking at their curved pink flutings, I thought of the pink folds between my legs. The one thing I didn't like was the starfish, with its prickly, obvious body. "It wuz alive onct—wuz when ah caught it!" Jones squealed meanly. I shuddered, grabbing it from under my blouse, where he had brusquely thrust it. That night I dreamed the starfish upright, as tall as Daddy, rushing toward me, faster than I could run—piercing my naked body with its prickles, till my hair stood on end as though I had been plugged into a socket, and I was dried out and prickly, too. The starfish made me think of the beggar lice that stuck to my socks when I walked in the woods or pasture: I *knew* they were sticky little seeds off a sticky little plant—time after time I had broken them open between my fingernails to make sure. But still, I believed they were alive, determined—like the worms ("Hookworm," the doctor at the clinic had said) that had burrowed out of the Alabama dirt into and through the soles of Musette's fat feet— to burrow themselves through and into my very flesh, where they would ultimately take over my being and will.

Sometimes, walking through the pasture, I would run my fingers through my thin—"silky," Mama insisted—brown hair, and feel fastened to my scalp a taut, smooth mound—a shape that I knew, from pulling the ticks off Daddy's hound dogs, contained my own hot blood; that if I popped it, it would spew my own hot blood, thick and red, like the blood of Jesus in the hymns we sang at the Church of God. *Are YUH washed—in the BLUD—of the—uh—LAMB?* we half shouted, half moaned; *Are yore gar-ments SPOT-less—Are they white—as—SNOW? Are they WASHED—in the blud—of THE LAMB?* As we wailed the words, I saw the blood newly oozing between my thighs, the blood spurting from the chicken's neck, a fountain into which I envisioned—though I knew it was a sacrilege—sticking my hands. I imagined a washtub like the one Mama used to wash our clothes, filled to the brim with bright, thick red; and I was glad that Mama, fanning herself beside me with a fan decorated with a picture of "Jesus Knocking at the Door," COMPLIMENTS OF SOSEBEE'S FUNERAL HOME inscribed at the bottom, couldn't read my thoughts.

"Turn *naow* to page 497," the preacher would command. *And sin-ners plunged be-neath THET flud—lose ALL the-er GUILT-y —stains,* we obediently continued, our voices rising. *Lose ALL their GUIL-tee STAINS. . . .* As I sang, I looked up at the stained-glass Jesus above me, letting myself think another of my secret criminal thoughts—that Jesus, beneath his blue-and-cream robes, was really a woman like Mama and me, that She bled between Her legs, a faucet, a fountain, our sister in mutilation. . . .

"Well, let's at *least* go to Charlene's and dance awhile," Iris insists petulantly, indicating a queer bar on Elysian Fields. As she speaks, she persuasively presses my breast through the black silk of my Yves St. Laurent blouse. But I don't want to fuck her, this man turned woman. I want to fuck boys. I want my son back.

CHAPTER TWO

WHAT I want to tell this stranger, this *Iris*, is that the caviar she holds to my lips makes me nauseous—that tonight, to lick between her legs would only make me more so.

To confess that yes, perhaps we are alike—neuters, creatures of loss, quick to oust any offending ounces of flesh. That just as she had her maleness, her convex genitalia, carved from her, tomorrow, I enter day surgery at Touro Infirmary to have sucked from my body what might well be a son to replace the one I've lost. "Perfection is terrible," wrote poor Sylvia, already ruined, imperfect: "It cannot have children." And you and I, Iris, are above all creatures of perfection, determined to create ourselves in our chosen image.

Yet Iris—when did you first imagine that a boy could be made into a woman? At eight, I dreamed men could have babies—they had stomachs, didn't they? I drew forked, hugely swollen men, fetuses moving toward birth through elephantine penises—drawings so unspeakable that Mama crumpled them up and threw them into the fireplace without comment. When I was ten, Cudden Jones tugged me inside a sideshow at the county fair, snickering that he had "sumpin' to show yuh!" As we stood behind the grimy curtains, red paper tickets staining our sweaty palms, a creature swayed before us on a purple-carpeted dais—"uh 'morphodite!" he whispered triumphantly into my burning ear. The man-woman languidly shed a blood-colored satin robe and, staring expressionlessly over our heads, lifted a tiny penis, then, with a thumb and forefinger, scissored open the vagina beneath it. I felt a thrill: If this person could be both male and female, so could I: I didn't yet understand the inner space—the *emptiness*, if you will—that is the meaning of female.

Recently, browsing through postcards in a queer art shop, I picked up one that depicted women in long dresses, a Manet-like picnic on the grass: beneath the raised skirt of one was a head, its mouth affixed to the pubic patch. And I felt a sudden anxiety, a shame: Like a child with an empty orange rind, the man was sucking at an absence, a cavity. At *nothing*. I had long realized that that emptiness, filled only by my ballooning will, my greed for life, constitutes a deformity, makes me as much a freak as you, Iris. And that it must be kept filled—by fingers or dildo, a penis or a fetus—even if filling it often rakes my will, scrapes it like sandpaper against raw flesh, making me recall *Webster's* definition of dildo—"a spiny West Indian cactus."

Like my friend Sherry, who, at forty—five years before she ran for state senate—had her uterus carved out to stop its annoying bloodletting: At forty-two, she had the flesh over her cheekbones stretched as taut as a sixteen-year-old Chinese girl's; at forty-four, her tits and ass lifted, buttressed by silicone: With her womb gone, no prospect of a fetus, she had infinite space to be filled, a constant need to keep her hollow cunt stuffed with flesh. ". . . On the streets every night . . . hasn't won a case all year . . ." people whisper even here in a town so sex-drenched that the pleasures of the flesh are considered a constitutional right. As she gaily talks to me over the phone of her latest conquest—a Panamanian sailor, a roughneck from Browns-ville—as she talks in that way women talk to one another, re-hashing over and over and over every bit of strategy used in her efforts to keep her emptiness filled, explaining why this time—*this* time—it's different, I recall that she, too, lost a teen-age son—she to a tumor of the brain; I, to a disease of the spirit.

Yet if abortions had been legal in rural Alabama in 1952, maybe I wouldn't have been left—as we say in the South—"barefoot 'n pregnant"; Daddy wouldn't have discovered my sin, and Mama wouldn't have been maimed for life.

And maybe I wouldn't have stood last week behind a lectern at the Atlanta College of Art, talking about figurative modes in the painting of the seventies, but really—the Provera the doctor had given me to provoke my period churning my belly, a fine sweat breaking across my forehead—hoping, praying—despite my pink Givenchy pantyhose, my hundred-dollar pink silk dress—for the stickiness between my thighs, in the crotch of the fragile designer garment that would mean I was free of this unwanted fetus, free of punishment for my sins.

And this killing wouldn't be about to take place: a minor—and morally, socially, and philosophically—insignificant operation, the literature implies. "It's nothing, Mother," Lily told me over the phone last week from New York, "not near as bad as havin' my IUD put in." Listening to her blasé twenty-year-old voice, I flashed the time when, at fourteen, she sat on the side of the bathtub to gingerly open the folds of her vagina and reveal—like a maggot within the petals of a beautiful rose—a blazing white blister that could only have been caused by the herpes or gonorrhea of relentless fucking. "It hurts, Mama," she had whimpered; and coiled in her single bed, the infection raging through the fine channels of her teenage belly, she had cried like a little girl.

Just as two years later, riding to the gynecologist's office for her first abortion, she whimpered in a voice softer than her amethyst eye shadow, "I don't wanna kill this little baby, Mama. . . ." I tried to console her—this young woman, my child, hunched beside me in the front seat of my Alfa, cheeks concave with the makeup of a Kabuki dancer—with a metaphor of kittens, of how there are always too many in the world, always more waiting to be born. I could almost see her mood brighten, memories of the cats she had clutched in her bunk bed year after year, living security blankets, moving behind her made-up eyes. And while my daughter went in to see the doctor, I sat on hard curved plastic, staring alternately at low fashion in a Coke-stained, year-old copy of *Good Housekeeping* and the snot-

41

smeared face of the two-year-old who had detached herself from her hugely pregnant mother to stand at my knee, peer solemnly up into my face, but really seeing only blood and tissue sucked through a clear tube, expecting any moment to hear an enormous scraping sound, magnified through the Muzak speakers, then Lily's shriek of terror or pain.

But it never came: Lily walked back into the waiting room, her powder and blusher making it impossible for me to tell how pale she might be. I wrote out a check for $115; we spoke to a doctor who never looked up from his desk. In the lobby of the medical building, I bought her a box of Kotex maxipads, a Tab, the antibiotics he had prescribed, a fashionable magazine with a cover article on "The First Month After Your Abortion." And now Lily is tough, tougher than I am—cheerfully doing in New York the things that I undoubtedly taught her, the things about which I would rather not think. . . .

Yes, even Norman Mailer would approve of my guilt tonight. Once, I would have thought this pregnancy my chance for reparation, redemption—that by having this child, submitting to twenty years of personal slavery, I could make up for my sins. In the very middle of Dwayne's early madness, my second husband, Johnny, and I saw Pasolini's *Life of Christ* at an Atlanta art theater. As Mary lay crumpled at the foot of the cross where her son hung crucified, I wanted to bruise my face in the dirt alongside her. For a long time, Dwayne's room, his things—a tattered Davy Crockett cap; a complete paperback set of the Tarzan books; an unmailed letter, signed "with a deep hunger for friendship," to a ten-year-old girl in Vietnam; plus photographs of him pensively, always pensively, smiling, a cat in his arms, or a parakeet on an extended finger—were my own personal crucifix, my shrine. Every time I saw a sheriff's car, some poor dark head bent behind the heavy wire mesh separating the front and back seats, it was like pressing an excruciating nerve with my tongue.

But I no longer have the sensitivity of Christ's mother—if I ever did—nor do I imagine that my own petty sins matter that much. I no longer believe that what happened to Dwayne was my fault, or that what I have done, the way I have lived, has really hurt anyone—a self-indulgent notion, I learned through

42

therapy: The victim loves to be victimized; and guilt, according to my most recent therapist, is "at least ninety percent neurotic." "I've never met a woman who was not depressed," an analyst— his new wife looking depressed at his side—told me at the same Garden District cocktail party where the Faulkner scholar talked about the long-suffering role of Lena in *Light in August* and his own personal wish that "Sylvia Plath had just controlled herself." I thought of Musette down on the farm being "good"— as "good" as Faulkner would have liked. And then of Lily's, Sherry's, and my own escape into pleasure with relief.

Still, the images persist: A suicide's unborn children call out to her in purgatory, I read just last week in some crappy rag, the *National Enquirer*, I think, as I stood in line at the Schwegmann's on Annunciation Street, my basket filled—in contrast to the local blacks' collard greens, dried beans, pig ears—with one artichoke, a basket of fresh raspberries, a small jar of caviar. "In the eyes of God, you're bound to every man you've slept with," cried a Born-Again Jesus Freak lover last year, frustrated by my lack of commitment to anything, especially him.

For the past four Sunday mornings, after a night of drugs, dancing, fucking—perhaps an oil rigger or South American sailor still asleep in my rose-satin-sheeted bed—I've vomited before I even had my coffee. As I bent over the toilet, I flashed throwing up a hundred tiny men—one-night stands, lovers, husbands, Dwayne.

Will this child, too, call out to me in nightmares, become a character in my own personal purgatory, punishment for my life of pure art, pleasure, and little else? During the inevitable and banal sexual couplings of the next years, will I imagine this life, too, as another I've run through in my greed?

For whatever my nightmares, sex will go on. I may be a painter, but I haven't always been thinking of *art*, not by a long shot. As Truman Capote said of Lillian Hellman, I'm "lower-body oriented"—indeed, I've probably put as much energy during my life into getting laid as I have into work. Last month, a lover dying of cancer suggested we travel to Paris together, to snort coke, suck each other off, in the most beautiful city in the world: He had just spent Christmas at Club Med, bought a silver

BMW, a stereo with colored lights—the proposed trip the last on a list of projected indulgences, part of his plan to pleasure himself until the very end. Like many people, he has long viewed sex as something to do for fun or exotica, on the level of going to a new Hunan restaurant, or smoking some extra-fine Hawaiian gold. I've never thought that, even during one-night stands with people whose names I forgot to ask. I knew from the beginning that sucking at each other as we had our mothers' breasts, fucking or being fucked—penetrating another's very entrails, and being thus penetrated—are more than just novelties to help us through the night, keep us from the boredom that leads to suicide. Like the New Orleans D.A.—so successful in his womanizing that another man said his dick should be cut off—who told me that he had never met a woman who didn't like to have her hands tied behind her back, I realized early that the images sex taps inside us are darker, more primitive, than anything Coppola came up with in *Apocalypse Now*. I knew what sex meant—*everything*.

Yes, despite—or because of—Daddy's early brutalities, I've been as receptive as anyone I've ever known to the idea of being struck through by a prick.

By the time I was twelve, he had quit caring if Mama was watching when he touched me. By then, he was always drunk when he came through the back door at night. He would drive his rusting old pickup into the yard and go out to the shed or the outhouse—though I didn't know how he could stand the stink—to drink some more. "Yore Daddy's good-lookin'," my best friend, Galeta, whispered to me one evening when she had come home from school with me. He had given up on farming and had become a housepainter; the smells of turpentine, liquor, and sweat seemed permanently bonded to his Sears work clothes, but his biceps still moved beneath the khaki cloth, and his auburn hair lay damp and curly on his thick red neck. I was hurriedly encouraging her to leave before he came inside the house, for when he did, he would walk straight up to me, grab my ass or breasts, as though I were his wife, not Mama. He didn't seem to care what she did at the truck stop anymore, or that working there for a decade was draining her face, dehydrating it as though some vital fluid were being slowly but relentlessly leached out, or that her hair was a dry gray-brown from too many Toni home permanents, her peach satin bras limp and faded, or that she had stopped wearing the Evening in Paris altogether. He only cared about me, calling me *ho-ar* and *slut* when he caught me giggling and whispering to Galeta on the phone. It was as though he were a mind reader, and he could tell that the thing we were talking about was boys.

Once, just after I had tried on a pretty new dress Mama was making for me—one in which I felt my waist and breasts curving in some new way—he jerked the scissors out of her hand as she sat at the treadle Singer, and cut it up into a dozen pieces. "Jes' cause yuh're a ho-ar, no use in makin' the gal look lak one!" he snarled. Mama, stupid Mama, laid her head on top of the machine and cried. But I had long since learned to harden myself: I just went on sweeping, gathering up the pieces of pink cloth along with the gritty gray dirt on the picture-smeared floor as though I didn't even care.

It seems as if his meanness would have turned me off, but it didn't. Instead, it made me feel ready, open, a hole just waiting to be filled. It was as though I had become the red clay just after a summer rain—hot and wet and gooshy, crying out to be pried and penetrated. I was just waiting for that first time, though I couldn't have named *what* beyond that phrase, *doin' it*, that we whispered on the playground or in the girls' bathroom at school. We didn't call it *fucking*—nobody did in rural Alabama. I had never heard the word, or of the things human beings do—sucking, clawing, biting—that I now take for granted. All I knew was my craving for slippery things, the fire rummaging my newly furred genitals were somehow related.

I had been fourteen for just a little more than three months the August day Wayne stopped his daddy's Chevy pickup to offer me a ride. I was walking down the dirt road in my navy-blue gym shorts, my white cotton blouse sweat-stuck to my shoulder blades, watching the orange shimmer of heat in the distance, when he burned to a stop beside me, his elbow out the truck window. I knew who he was—he had dropped out of school three years before when he had been in ninth grade;

45

now he worked the shrimp boats, or hung around the ball field, cutting up with the boys, making dirty remarks to the girls. "Ah heard he done *done* thangs," Galeta had whispered, adding that we should never "give 'im the time a day," and I had agreed, already feeling guilty, some strange shiver rising up my thighs.

Now I felt him looking at the tops of my legs in a way that told me he didn't think they were as fat as I did. "Come 'ere," he said, flicking ashes from a Lucky Strike toward my bare feet: "Ah've got somethin' to show yuh." I half expected him to open the door and reveal his exposed penis. Instead, he held up a small puppy—black, white, and shivering—in his big left hand. "The mama dawg got 'erself kilt, but ah still got this 'un—ain't she sweet? Come on," he added persuasively. "Ah'll give yuh a ride, 'n you kin hold 'er."

At his unexpected gentleness, some hot thing started at the back of my eyes, and I climbed up through the door he had stretched to open for me, into the high front seat beside him. As he screeched off and made a U-turn in the direction away from my house, I sat upright, suddenly alert. The puppy seemed to shiver on my bare thighs, but I couldn't tell whether the trembling was mine or the dog's, especially when I saw where Wayne was headed. Yet when he parked beneath a patch of pines beside the rock quarry and came around to my side of the truck and opened the door, I stepped out as though it had all been planned. He shoved me up against the hood, sticking his tongue into my mouth, his hand inside the top of my gym shorts; the puppy, still in my arms, whimpered between us. "Don't hurt 'er," I cried, twisting my face to one side.

"Come 'ere, girl," he said, grabbing me by the hair and pulling it back. The gentleness I had heard in his voice was gone; his eyes looked at me like Daddy's, slitted and mean, aswim with something I was afraid to read. He pulled me down to the pine straw, pushed the puppy out of my arms, and tugged my shorts down with one motion. I noticed that the hand he raised to clamp my wrists was yellow with nicotine stains, the fingers thick and callused. As the fingers of his other hand dug inside me, the puppy licked the tears from my cheeks. When Wayne shoved what felt like a stob or a broom handle where his fingers had been, the pine straw pierced my bare back like

46

a hundred tiny needles, the late afternoon sun shone down into my eyes, splintering colors beneath my eyelids: What I saw inside my skull was red, blood red; red pounded inside my ears, keeping time with the way Wayne was pounding my body into the pine straw, the ground, the very center of rock. *This throb this sin what the preacher yells about his voice going up and down down and up Jesus on Her cross the nails pounding in and my groin once dry dust turns wet clay blood fire. . . .*

Beside my head, my hair, the puppy lapped the salt from my face with her hot red tongue. Wayne lay on top of me as though he were dead. I will never paint magnolia, wisteria, the delicate azaleas, I thought. . . .

Yet beneath Wayne's weight, I knew. I was in love. Oh, not with him. But with blood, with sex, with the pounding in my flesh. *With pain.*

First comes love/ Then comes marriage/ Next comes Easter/ with a baby carriage—during jump-rope contests in the wilds of South Alabama, I had learned the proper order of things. It was an order confirmed by Mama, Aunt Darlene, my Sunday school teacher, and the preacher at the Church of God. I might have had sex, but I couldn't tell anyone, not even my best friend Galeta; to admit to breaking that order would be to admit to being as much a freak as the "'morphodite" at the fair. The order decreed we would remain—at least publically—virgins until, at fifteen or sixteen, we married one of the boys who a few years before had put crawfish down the necks of our feedsack dresses on the playground, boys now turning into truck drivers, shrimpers, pipe fitters. If we were lucky, we would move into a new mobile home, put our hair up in pink rollers, and watch the soaps over lunches of white bread and bologna sandwiches; wearing wrappers all day, we would dress only in time to make our man's supper of fried chicken or meat loaf, maybe trying a new recipe from *Woman's Day* or *True Confessions*. Our only *real* duty, we knew, was to spread our legs in the middle of the night for the angry, blind sex generated in boys suddenly thrust into the raw world of manhood, daylong obscenities, and fatigue— that, and waiting to be filled up with the babies that would stretch our teenage bodies, fill our days, at last wearing us down as finely as our young husbands. If we were unlucky, we would live in a shack perched on bricks or concrete blocks with an outhouse out back, work in the cotton mill or the truck stop even after the babies started coming, cooking the supper each night on legs turning knobby, blue-veined, by twenty, washing up, then scrubbing the diapers by hand, hanging them on the line in the backyard after dark. As often as not, our husbands would go out with the boys, come home to beat us or fuck us, as though there were no difference in the two acts: each Sunday morning at the Church of God, we would pray for their salvation, that they get possessed by the Spirit; and sometimes, by forty—the meanness drained out of them by years of drinking, breaking our arms, careening down highways in pickups—they would.

It was at the Church of God that I realized I hadn't bled that month. Six weeks had passed since Wayne had taken me out to the rock quarry. For the first of those weeks, I had been sore between my legs, stunned by the exciting sinfulness of what I had done, had had done to me. Then pictures of that foreign hardness, Wayne's flesh shoving into mine, had begun coming to me in the middle of the night, drawing my hand—stealthily, so I wouldn't wake Musette, breathing her innocent milky breath beside me—beneath the quilt. The pictures were mixed with images of raging hellfire, the terrible screams of the damned, because I now knew for certain that what I was feeling was the very thing one burned in hell forever for. My shame had deepened because, though I had seen Wayne in the schoolyard, he never spoke and neither did I. There was not even love to justify my sin. One day, as he jostled with the boys, they looked my way, snickering; my face burned with what I knew was a hot crimson: Did they know that, despite everything, I wanted Wayne to take me out to the rock quarry again?

Now I thought of the green box of Junior Kotex Mama had bought me to replace the rags; it sat on the shelf of my chifforobe, where it must be covered—by this time—with a thin grainy dust. *He's the—Lil-lee—of the Val-lee—the bright 'n shinin' star* poured from my open mouth, and it was as though a bright white light suddenly shone through the stained-glass window above my head. *The fair-es'—of ten thousan'—to my soul,* I sang, flashing a small pink form, like a pink rose or crape-myrtle bud, as pink as the pink I already knew was inside me, embedded deep inside my belly. Though I knew in that instant that I was ruined, that I might never get a husband, might have to stay on the farm for the rest of my days, I felt as though the light from the window were streaming from my mouth. "Turn *naow* to hymn number 351," the preacher was commanding: *Lay it all on Je-sus—lay it awl on Him.* . . . Inside, I was still singing *He's the Lil-lee—of the Val-lee—the bright 'n shinin' star.* . . . The hurt of Wayne snickering in the schoolyard, along with everything Daddy had ever done, from breaking my ashtray through cutting up my new pink dress to sticking his ole nicotine-stained finger up me, ran out of me in a swish. I felt good, the way I did every time I made something out of clay, or painted a picture I liked. Now I would have someone who would love me, someone I had created; my baby would be a part of my secret criminal self, and I knew that wanting him was part of that, too. Suddenly, it was as though I had walked down that dirt road, as though Wayne had met me there, for a reason; there had been a plan for the sex and the pain. "Whut you grinnin' 'bout, girl?" Mama scowled, pointing to the page in the hymnal.

Would Wayne suggest we get married, get a regular job at the shrimp-processing plant, and buy a mobile home on credit? I wondered idly, inside me knowing the answer already. "Wall, whut you want *me* to do about it?" he sulled. I had waited on the road at a time I knew he might pass. Looking down at me, he gunned the motor of the pickup; the black-and-white puppy, now a quarter-grown hound dog, sat on the seat beside him, her tongue wagging, not recognizing me at all. "Fur as ah know, it coulda been anybody." I tried to explain about the pink bud, but he didn't seem to understand. In a minute, he screeched off, leaving me standing in the road covered in red dust.

There was nothing left to do but tell Mama. She screamed the scream of a sow with her throat being cut and slapped me upside the face. Then Daddy took me out to the barn and whipped me across the backs of my legs with a chain, yelling about how he'd always known what I was. I held on to the ladder to the hayloft and thought about the pink thing curled inside me, protecting it with my body, refusing to scream. A few hours later, he had another notion: "Ah'll *blow* thet thang outta yuh!" he yelled drunkenly. In a few minutes, he came back into the kitchen from the pickup, carrying his shotgun. Mama hadn't cared when he beat me, but now she screamed, "Patrick! *Whut* 'er you *doin'*?"

"Whut uh you thank? Ah'm gonna stick this thang up this slut!" He grabbed me by the back of the neck with his free hand and shoved me from the chair where I had been bent over the kitchen table, shoving me facedown toward the smiling *Ladies' Home Journal* faces, smeared across the kitchen floor. Mama came up behind him, pulling him by *his* neck, near thick as a bull's, with both her small hands. He turned, roaring at her with a roar that mixed with the sound of the shotgun going off.

Mama lay on the floor, a funny look on her face, a thin trickle of red running from beneath her back. As we waited for the ambulance, Daddy sobbed hysterically, his head between his knees; I dabbed Mama's forehead with a damp dishrag. Daddy was crying about how he blamed himself, but I knew it was my fault—just another incidence of my will hurting someone I loved, like the time Musette had cut her feet on the jelly glass.

When Mama came home from the hospital, she was in a wheelchair. She never said any more about my being pregnant, nor did she seem to notice when Daddy reached out to feel my belly through my dress when he passed me in the kitchen—just as though it were his, and he was proud. I had started showing and had had to quit school, but I didn't care; except for home ec—the mixing and baking and sewing—I had never liked it much anyway. As soon as my status as fallen woman was certain, the kids had stopped calling, except for the one time Galeta visited. We made grilled-cheese sandwiches fried in bacon drippings, and she pried me for the details of what "doin' it" had felt like, then told me that she had heard Wayne had got Saved and joined the army. I could tell she had just been waiting to tell me, and that I had disappointed her by not getting upset.

But I had other, more important things to think about. I did all the cooking and washing; fed the chickens scraps from the supper table and wrung their necks. I helped Mama onto the bedpan, emptying the wastes in the outhouse, and washed the pan and boiled it on the cookstove, or set it in the sun to dry. Each night, I gave her a sponge bath and helped her into her gown and her bed, where she now slept alone, sucking at her fist as though she had become a baby again, whiter and skinnier than she had ever been. She didn't even seem to notice that Daddy had taken to sleeping on the couch, snoring drunkenly.

I talked to the visiting nurse each week when she came; and though Aunt Darlene's mouth now turned permanently down when she came from Mobile and saw me, Mama's paralysis kept her words—"see, Mon-a-que, ah tole yuh"—unspoken, bubbling against her tight lips. Saturday afternoons I set Mama's hair—now as dry and wiry as a Brillo pad—on curling papers, and made Musette iron Mama's church dress as well as her own and mine. Once, I looked in Mama's dresser drawer for her Cutex nail polish, thinking to cheer her up by painting her nails; but it had all turned viscous, near solid in the little glass bottles, and Mama didn't seem to care anyway.

After supper each evening, I lolled on the front porch in the swing with a glass of iced tea, drawing or just thinking. I thought about the fat painted dolls, of the way the parts of flowers fit together, of how the perfect ovals of eggs grew inside chickens, and of the baby growing inside me, kicking against my very walls, pink, heavy, perfect—*my own creation.*

When he finally lay on my belly, his little sex tickled at my slack stomach. Red smeared his black hair, as peaked and jet as a Seminole's, or a small pony's mane. He kicked his feet like a little horse and, with eyes still clamped shut, sucked his thumb so hard that a dimple deepened in one tiny cheek.

"Wall, see whut yuh done now," Mama moaned from her wheelchair, rolled in beside my bed, "'n yuh gotta live with it the rest of yore life." She added that Wayne was in the waiting room, wanting to see his son. "If yuh play yore cards right, maybe you kin still git 'em to marry yuh."

I didn't care—I was already more wedded than I ever would be to any man. My son's soft pink lips were attached to my teenage nipple, sucking harder than he had sucked at his own thumb. I was already imagining us walking in the pasture, he at my breast through the unbuttoned front of my cotton dress, absorbing through my very flesh the smell of grass, the morning sunlight. . . .

Mama was still carrying on: "You better git while the gittin's good, girl. . . ." She stopped abruptly as Wayne came into the room in his ugly khaki army uniform, burying his crew-cut head against my chest, scratching at my breasts as though he wanted to push the baby out of the way. "Kin yuh ever forgive me, Easter?" he sobbed. The nurse came into the room, waving the birth certificate. "Will yuh name 'im after me?" Wayne lifted his head, brightening. I had wanted to name him David, after some beloved son in the Bible; I loved the full round vowel on my tongue. "Wall, whut about a mix—Wayne and David?" Wayne said; "Dwayne—that's purty, ain't it?" I wanted him to leave so I could be alone with my baby. "Dwayne, okay, Dwayne," I said. The nurse carefully inscribed the letters, D-W-A-Y-N-E. "Ah'll come back tuh-morrer, we'll git mar-rid 'fore ah go back to the base," Wayne went on. But as he kissed me on the forehead, I turned my face away.

When Dwayne and I came home from the hospital, Mama was cross. With his birth, she had gotten her voice back, and now all she did was screech. If I had acted nicer that day in the hospital, she said, Wayne would have come back. It was even worse a month later, when we heard Wayne had gotten killed way over in Korea, though it didn't mean any more to me than a smushed dog on the road—in fact, my first thought was, what had happened to that black-and-white puppy of his? No, Mama was the one who was upset about it: "See?" she sobbed afresh; "You cudda marrid 'im, gotten thet army insurance 'n all— maybe *then* you cudda had somethin', 'n thet boy a yores had a chance. . . ." Aunt Darlene said Wayne's mama, Homerdessa, had been calling her, "wailin' about wontin' to see 'er gran'baby, now thet her own baby wuz gone." I was just mean enough not to want to let him be taken over there; I didn't want my son influenced by such a low-class woman—especially one with a husband in the state prison for armed robbery and a son like Wayne.

"Now yuh've got them tracks on yore belly 'n a bastard, 'n yuh'll *never* git a man!" Mama went on. I looked in the mirror at the cerise worms engraved across my pale stomach. I had just turned fifteen, but I thought they were pretty; after all, they had gotten me Dwayne. "I'll do exercises, Mama, I read about 'em in a magazine." Her crossness was becoming my cross to bear. She was tired of sitting in the wheelchair, and she knew she would have to sit there for the rest of her life. She nagged that I didn't mop the picture-smeared floor enough, that my gravy was lumpy, the biscuits were flat. And she didn't even have Daddy to hate—while I was in the hospital, he had run off to a woman from the next county.

Besides, as far as Daddy was concerned, she had decided to forgive him—and blame me instead. "It sez hyah, 'Charity suffer-eth long,' " she would point out to me from the Bible she had taken to reading for hours every day. But her forgiveness didn't extend to me—we all knew women were supposed to be better than men were. Her life was ruined, it was my fault, and there was nothing she could do but scream.

Though I knew I was guilty, that Mama wouldn't be sitting in that wheelchair, her once-plump thighs turning white and flabby, but for me, I didn't care. I was happier than I ever had been. The welfare sent a check each week that just covered our dried beans and sugar and flour, with a little left over for piece goods or a drawing tablet from Woolworth's; because Mama couldn't shop anymore, I had control of it all. The county nurse came once a month. Aunt Darlene, her lips tighter than ever, drove in from Mobile to take me to town, or all of us to the Church of God. Musette hummed while she did her homework, and every night we fought over who would change Dwayne and who would bathe Mama.

We had learned that Mama's whining would subside if we ignored it, like the words to a country song over the radio. Then she would lapse into her old silence. Once a man from the truck stop came by to see her, but he seemed embarrassed by the white streaks in her hair, the way her legs lay still beneath the quilt on her lap, not showing her once-plump little feet at all. He didn't even sit down, but stood shuffling his feet, his Red Rose feed cap in his hands. "Wall, guess ah'll go on, Mon-a-que—yuh take keer naow," he said, bending to kiss her on the forehead. He looked at the fading blue roses in the wallpaper over her head. Mama didn't look at him, or say anything at all. In a couple of minutes, we heard his Chevy screeching off in the yard. Mama turned her wheelchair around and stared at the roses. I got her a copy of *True Confessions* and went back to boiling Dwayne's diapers.

Every day, I boiled them on the black potbellied kitchen stove. It was what the visiting nurse had said I should do, and I followed her directions for infant care as carefully as later, a suburban housewife, I would follow the most complicated recipes from Julia Child. I held out spoonfuls of mashed yellow summer squash, or biscuit dipped in gravy, and watched his mouth gape, all cerise tonsils, reminding me of the baby birds in the side yard, their throats the color of Pepto-Bismol. Sometimes I fed him from little glass jars, Gerber's green beans or mashed bananas, extravagances I secretly put away when I came in with the grocery bags, so Mama wouldn't see them and complain. Every afternoon, I bathed him in a white enameled pan set out on the oilcloth-covered kitchen table. As I slid the soapy rag over his fine-pored skin, his flailing arms and legs, the sweet pink snail of his tiny sex, he crooned, crowed, and reached out to me like a lover. Sometimes I let him take a second bath with me; I didn't care when he laughed and peed in the water, a tiny yellow swirl like the coloring I had mixed in the margarine. I liked changing his hot wet diapers, even when they were filled with steaming yellow baby shit. It was as though I had been one body but now was two—a Siamese twin, a hermaphrodite; that just as my pictures, the things I made, were artifacts of what whirled inside my head, Dwayne was simply my maleness, manifest in the world—my teratoma; my embedded twin; that forbidden part of myself made flesh. *Symbiosis*, the psychiatrist would call it later: *an excessive closeness, a neurosis*, something that felt good but was bad—a condition in need of radical surgery.

But I didn't know about all that then. All I knew was that out of my fifteen-year-old womb had come someone I loved in a way I had never loved anyone; it was as though I had known him all my life, even before my own birth. As I had dreamed when he lay bloody on my belly in the hospital, I walked in the pasture with my dress half-open, Dwayne clamped to my breast. Never mind that he was hotter, heavier, bonier, and wetter than I had imagined. "Be still, wiggle worm!" I would whisper, kissing the wisps of his hair, the throb of his soft skull. I would point out the quick slither of a rose-colored salamander, a tiny frog, shimmering like a drop of green oil paint in the grass; or I'd hold out a worm, which he quickly squashed, yellow and gummy, in his fist. Together, we visited the little red horse that danced up to the fence and pressed his nose between the boards—Dwayne squealed and lurched toward the velvety face. Sometimes, walking with him sucking at a breast, I would come upon a mother cat, or one of the sows, suckling her young as well. In the drawings I did after supper, I drew teats, animal and human, clamped by small mouths. Dwayne suckling my nipple was as natural as breathing, as everything animal in the countryside around me.

Twenty-five years later, I would read a novel—by Joy Williams, I think—about a woman who runs away to Florida with her two-month-old infant. In the opening scene, she sits on a barstool, the damp baby on her lap. I wanted the book to stick with that scene forever: I could imagine nothing finer than sitting in an air-conditioned bar at a Holiday Inn, drinking gin-and-tonics, a baby son on one's lap. The woman and her son. Me and my son. Us against the world, as though we were truly one person. *He's the—Lil-lee—of the Val-lee—the bright 'n shinin' star—He's the fair-est—of ten thousan'—to my soul.* . . . The words reverberated through my sleep at night, entwined with images of Dwayne's dimpled smile, his fat knees, his tiny sex. I would have named him Jesus if I could. Later, when I traveled in Mexico and Central America and heard Indian women calling "Hay-su! Hay-su!" after small, dusty boys, I felt a queer thrill: these ignorant women in remote villages had had the courage to name their sons after the very son of God. It couldn't be a sin that *this* child had been born. I nursed him at the Church of God proudly, his small mouth gustily suctioning my flesh in time to the hymns—or was it that, just as decades later male flesh would thrust itself into my willing mouth, mine now thrust itself into his? All I knew was that when he cried, my milk spilled in response, as though we were still bound by that throbbing cord of skin. "Outlaws love ladies like ladies love babies," goes a Waylon Jennings song; well, I was a girl who was an outlaw who also loved babies, and *would*, despite the dirty looks given me by Aunt Darlene and all the matrons at the Church of God.

Another girl pregnant out of wedlock had dropped out of high school a few months before I did. She didn't go to church, but I remembered her from ninth grade, her dark stringy hair and wobbly hips, the sly look on her bumpy face. Once I had opened the door to the stall where she sat in the girls' bathroom, her graying underpants around her knees, dragging at a Camel. Now, since we were both ruined, I walked the mile—Dwayne at my hip—down the road to the weathered shack where I knew she lived. I had heard she had had twins, and I could hear them screaming jaggedly as I approached. A fat boy I recognized from the next county came out onto the porch, tucking his dirty shirt into his Levi's. In a few minutes, Louise slammed the screen door and joined us; we all sat silently on the porch, gazing down the heat-baked dirt road. She didn't seem to hear her babies' screaming. "Wall, come on in, y'all," she finally said. We went into the kitchen and sat down around an oilcloth-covered table layered with fat black flies that buzzed around our heads as well. She set three warm Pabst Blue Ribbons on the table, then went out of the room, coming back in a moment with a pale, fat infant squalling on each hip. A fly wiggled on one baby's eyelid, like a bird pecking at the ground. Louise looked as though invisible wires were pulling her body—now wobblier than before—toward the floor. The babies' faces were greasy, their diapers gray, droopy, wet-looking. I took a sip of the beer. It tasted like what it looked like. Louise slapped one of the babies, which made it scream even louder, then wiped the back of her hand beneath her nose. "These thangs are a' drivin' me crazy," she said. She took two nippled Coca-Cola bottles from beside the sink, stuck one in each baby's mouth, and laid them on their backs on the grimy linoleum floor. "Do yuh think yuh kin go down to go to thet club down on Highway 90 with us this evenin'?" she asked. I smoothed Dwayne's freshly laundered shirt over his belly; he smiled up at me. "No, I don't think so," I said primly. I knew that even though I was ruined, I wasn't like Louise—that, even back then, I had class, though

I couldn't have said what class was, or why I, of all people, should have it.

It was something that just came to me, like the voice in my head that had spoken one day as I suddenly caught my reflection, my own serious jet-brown gaze, in the dull glass above Mama's dressing table: *AS LONG AS YOU HAVE YOUR EYES AND CAN SEE THINGS, NOTHING BAD CAN EVER HAPPEN TO YOU*, the voice boomed. It sounded to me like the word of God.

Since she could no longer pump the treadle machine with her feet, Aunt Darlene loaned Mama her electric Singer; when Dwayne was eleven months old, Mama made me a pink cotton-piqué dress, with ruffles at its scoop neck and hem, plus a matching polished cotton petticoat, to wear to church on Easter Sunday. I was almost sixteen now, I should have high heels, maybe even some shell-pink nail polish—maybe I could still even get a man—she and Darlene concurred. When Darlene took Musette and me into Mobile on Saturday, I picked out white plastic patent-leather sandals with tiny straps that crossed my instep and wound around my toes; in Woolworth's, I bought a garter belt decorated with pink satin rosettes to match my new dress, and creamy nylons that would let my soon-to-be painted toenails show through. It was as though I was getting ready for something, though I couldn't have said what.

Sunday morning, I left Dwayne in the church nursery for the first time, and walked down the aisle feeling naked, yet curiously free, without him at my breast. From the corner of my eye, I glimpsed a boy I had never seen before: he had on a pin-striped shirt and a tie, a coat, and horn-rimmed glasses, and didn't look like anybody from around here. Looking demurely at the wooden floor, I swayed my hips, swishing my petticoat, the ruffled bottom of my skirt, as I walked past him. Flipping the long cocoa-colored pageboy I had carefully set on Musette's old socks the night before, I slid onto the bench beside Musette and Mama, who was always helped in first by a deacon.

As we rode home, Mama and Darlene talked excitedly. "Thet nice young man come to visit Leler for Easter—her nephew from New Or-leens, she says—ast whut yore name wuz after church. Lela told 'im yore story, but he warn't put off. 'Aint Leler,' he said to 'er, 'I wonna meet thet girl.' . . ." Dwayne was gnawing my knuckles with his new teeth, then began tugging at the neckline of my new dress, struggling to reach my breasts. "Now, don't go lettin' 'im mess up yo' dress—whut if thet boy comes over, 'n you don' have nuthin' to wear. He's a *college* boy 'n all thet," Mama elaborated reverently. "Goin' to Too-lane, Leler says, then into his daddy's car business. Prob'ly ust to girls with store-bought dresses. . . ."

"The *main* thang," Darlene inserted, in probably the first time she had spoken directly to me in a year and a half, "is not to let 'im 'round the baby too much, so he won't git scart off." Mama nodded vigorously; it was the first time since the accident that she had seemed pleased about anything. "'n *don'* let 'im git 'is way with yuh," Darlene went on. "*You* have to be extra keerful about *thet*. . . .'

And that was how I got married, became a respectable matron despite my sins. Oh, not in the way Mama and my aunt dictated—I wasn't about to start following the rules, coloring inside the lines, now. Indeed, I let Bobby "have his way" with me that very afternoon. Mama and Darlene were anxious for me to get him away from Dwayne, his eleven-month-old drooling, his tugs at my breasts. "Goin' for a ride," we told them, and they waved gaily from the porch as we drove away in Bobby's bright blue Chevy with the silver fins, straight out to the woods. They would have died if they had known that what Bobby liked was sucking the warm milk from my nipples just like Dwayne, that as he licked between my legs, he ran his fingers reverently through the silver fish at the base of my now-concave belly. He may have been a college boy with his own car—the first I had ever known—but he seemed to me pathetic, as vulnerable as Dwayne in his need for my skinny body. His eyes, without his horn-rims, were a sad, watery blue; I knew that I had more power than he, just because of that pink hidden between my thighs. And that because, not in spite, of it, he would marry me, with Galeta and all the girls who wouldn't speak to me after Dwayne staring on enviously.

From the Sears Roebuck in Mobile, Aunt Darlene bought

me a magnolia-colored sheer nylon dress—"Near to white, but not really white, so nobody kin say anythang"—with a little Peter Pan collar, tiny tucks across the bodice, the same tucks repeated near the bottom of the gathered skirt. The dress had its own cream-colored rayon slip, and a rose-colored velveteen belt with a shaped fabric rose, almost like the rose I had shaped on Daddy's ashtray, right slap in the middle of it—it was that rose I liked more than anything. "Now you be sure he uses a rubber, you make 'im stop at the drugstore if he don't have one," she said with distaste as I pulled the dress over my head. But even she couldn't spoil my pleasure. I had a cream nylon nightgown with tiny satin straps, pink rosebuds embroidered at the V that came down between my breasts, and a set of seven pairs of panties embroidered with *Sunday* through *Saturday*— more store-bought panties than I had ever had at once in my life. "After all, you're marryin' into a good fam'ly," Darlene said, explaining her sacrifice on my behalf. "We cain't have 'em thankin' you're white trash, even if yuh *did* go bad. But maybe you kin make all thet up to yore pore mama now."

As was the custom, the whole congregation of the Church of God was invited to the wedding. All except Daddy—Darlene told Mama it wouldn't be right, and Mama tearfully agreed. During the ceremony, Mama held Dwayne on her lap and sobbed in rhythm to the preacher's solemn voice. Afterward, we all moved to the Sunday school room, where Aunt Darlene shook hands with people and read aloud—as though she had had some major personal triumph—from a thin yellow piece of paper that turned out to be a telegram from Bobby's daddy, Big Bobby, and his stepmother, Miss Lisa, in New Orleans. In a new pink dress of her own, Musette pensively served white cake with white icing and pink flowers on plastic-coated paper plates bordered in pink flowers; and making sure that a fat red cherry floated on the top of each serving, she ladled ginger ale mixed with maraschino syrup into matching pink-rimmed paper cups.

When Bobby, Dwayne, and I climbed into the shiny blue Chevy to drive away to New Orleans, Darlene and the rest of the congregation stood throwing rice from an Uncle Ben's box. Mama had always told Musette and me that before she had married Daddy and had us, her one dream had been to go to New Orleans. Now Musette stood with a sad look on her plump face, and Mama sat in her wheelchair in the churchyard, sobbing loudly. I flapped Dwayne's arm over and over, saying "Bye-bye! Bye-bye" until he crowed in imitation.

I had long suspected that anyone who moved beyond his or her family, rural Alabama, and the Church of God, was evil, guilty of some nameless sin. I knew, too, that to do so required a detachment, a cold, un-Christian strength, a hardening of the kind I had learned the day Daddy had thrown the ashtray against the wall.

Now, Dwayne's little clothes, my own, and my drawing tablet and paints were packed in new plastic suit-and-overnight cases in the backseat. Yet how could I drive away to Louisiana, taking Mama's only grandbaby, leaving her with Musette, her hateful sister, and nothing else?

It was easy. I knew that in families like ours, there were the casualties and the survivors. I was determined that Dwayne and I would be among the latter.

What I didn't know was that blood sacrifices to the god of survival must be made afresh year after year, generation after generation—that, yes, the sacrifices continue unto this day.

Like this baby to die tomorrow. Like Iris's cock, Lily's innocence ("Don't you mean *stupidity*, Mother?"). Yes, like Dwayne, my beloved son.

That sacrifice after sacrifice leaves one burnt out, an empty case.

That after some sacrifices, none ever count again.

CHAPTER THREE

"I JUST CAN'T see you behind a grocery cart," a man said to me recently at a party, his eyes grazing me from cleavage to crotch, just as Iris was still doing. I had been telling an amusing story about my life as a suburban housewife. But what he and Iris and others of my critics couldn't imagine was what a conscientious little homemaker I had once been.

For I had fully intended to be a good wife, I really had. No, not just a good wife—a perfect one. It would be "as easy as buttered greasy" as Mama would have said before her accident. But I should have known even back then—coloring inside the lines was definitely not something I was good at.

Still, as soon as we crossed the Alabama line on Highway 90 into Mississippi, I took out my tablet, and with Dwayne sitting on my lap, laughing and trying to grab my pencil, began planning a week's menus: *Monday: Black-eyed peas, corn bread, slaw, and strawberry shortcake.* My biscuits always puffed up nice and fat, like little chef's hats. And if I wanted to make a shortcake, I just added a little white sugar, patted them out extra big, then split them and filled them while hot with margarine, a dollop of canned peaches, just as Mama had. But this time I would make it extra special, topping the shortcakes with partly thawed strawberries from one of those blue-and-white Birds Eye boxes—that might be something I could afford now. And I wondered if Bobby would let me order a cast-iron pan for corn sticks—the kind that made them really nice and crisp—from Sears? I had seen them in the catalog for $3.95.

Tuesday: Squash casserole, sliced tomatoes, and collard greens, I wrote, pausing for a moment to caress the curve of Dwayne's dimpled elbow—I could serve that with the leftover corn bread. *Wednesday: Hoppin' John*—made from the leftover black-eyes and rice. *Thursday: Fried pork liver with onions, mashed potatoes, and field peas.* Sometimes Mama had scrambled pork brains and eggs together—I always liked the pale gray-pink clumps, the strange texture on my tongue. But would Bobby like them?

My secret—and this was something Bobby didn't know yet—was that I knew how to make a "French" pastry called chocolate éclairs. I had pored over the recipe in a *Seventeen* magazine at the counter at Butts's Drugs so long that Mr. Butts, the pharmacist, kept looking up at me to see if I was getting it greasy. I stared at the line drawings, the step-by-step instructions, until I had memorized them. Then I walked the three miles home as fast as I could—I was seven months pregnant then—and duplicated the entire page in my drawing tablet. One of the things I liked about the recipe was the fact that after you first cooked the flour and butter together, *stirring constantly,* then beat in the raw eggs—*one at a time,* as illustrated, *until batter is glossy when dropped from a spoon onto a baking sheet,* the dough was supposed to puff up in the hot oven like magic, leaving a big hollow space in the middle of each round pastry, the pure opposite of my pregnant belly. The other thing I liked was that but for the Hershey's cocoa and confectioner's sugar for the icing, the ingredients called for were simple ones, things we needed each week anyway. So Mama wouldn't put up a big fuss when I brought them home. And sure enough, the next week after the shopping, I set out the picture and the ingredients and spent the rest of the afternoon making the chocolate éclairs to perfection—crunchy and egg-flavored and hollow, filled with a sweet vanilla custard, then topped with the shiny chocolate icing. Even Mama had liked them—she had long since stopped watching her figure, her once-rounded thighs already falling to flab against the sides of her wheelchair—picking at several before going back to staring at the rose-printed wallpaper. And Musette had gobbled down so many that I was afraid she was going to make herself sick. Now I imagined setting a plateful of them, uniform and shiny with chocolate, in the center of my own gleaming Formica dinette table.

I was trying to think of something else fancy for Friday night—meat loaf with Campbell's tomato soup on top of it?—when Bobby glanced over at my tablet to see what I was writing. "But I don't like liver, honey," he said shyly, disrupting my thoughts. I immediately erased the words *Fried pork liver with onions* and changed them to *Country-fried steak*, already dreaming of my hands on the moist meat, flopping it around in the seasoned flour, then plopping it into the skillet full of hot bacon grease. "Darlin', we'll eat out sometimes, too, you know," he went on as though to reassure me, though I never would have expected such a thing in my life. Mama had sometimes brought food home from the truck stop where she worked—hamburger meat mixed with seasoning and bread crumbs about to go bad, or cold grits or fried potatoes for us to fry up again. But we had never ourselves gone "out to eat"—though I had heard Aunt Darlene bragging about eating something called "Wiener schnitzel" in Germany—was it made out of those little dogs called wiener dogs? I wondered when she first said it—going on and on about it while Mama just sat there looking more and more depressed. In fact, often there had only been grits and cabbage and, if we were lucky, some crusty fatback.

"'n this Saturday night Miss Lisa 'n Big Bobby 'er havin' us ovah for a crawfish boil, to introduce you to all their friends 'n my fraternity brothahs 'n all."

"Ugh!" I couldn't help laughing. "You mean those ugly things that was always in the creek out back? I sure never heard of anybody eatin' em!" And it was true, I had never even heard of such a thing—just as I had never heard of anyone who called his stepmama and daddy by their first names.

Now, for what seemed like the first time, I realized what a rich family I had married into—a family where people ate weird foods just because they wanted to and had people over to eat just for the fun of it. As I hugged Dwayne close to me, unknown luxuries floated around in my brain, sparkling bubbles like a picture I had once seen of the stars in the galaxy, each one spinning inside its own pastel light, like the lights that swam behind my eyelids when I first closed them at night. I realized Bobby was glancing over at me with that sappy look he got, as though he was almost crying behind his thick glasses. Sometimes he seemed so dopey to me that I almost felt sorry for him, and I wondered if that meant that I was "in love." "You mean I could even have me a dress that cost seventeen ninety-five?" I asked, teasing and taking advantage a little bit, coming up with the wildest dream I could think of. "Well, sure, darlin'—when we can afford it. But we do have to stay on our budget." I still felt a little shock when he used that word *darling*: I had never heard anyone actually say it before, and every time he did, I felt like a movie-star bride—Elizabeth Taylor with Nicky Hilton, or Janet Leigh with that cute Tony Curtis—even if Bobby did drop the *g*, which I was sure Robert Wagner or Tony Curtis would never do.

My excitement felt as though it would bubble right through the top of my head—not because I was married or because of Bobby, but because for the first time in my life—other than having control of our little household after Mama's accident and Dwayne's birth—I had power. What I had that Bobby wanted—though I still couldn't imagine why he wanted it so bad—would make him buy me the Birds Eye frozen strawberries, the corn-stick pan, even the dress—and other things I hadn't even thought up yet. But I would hold up my end of the bargain, I told myself. I would study and learn to be a perfect wife. I would never be sloppy or whiny the way Mama had been; I would never become ironing board–stiff, wearing long-line bras and ugly old boned corsets, or get deep, ugly lines by my mouth like Aunt Darlene. And more than anything, I would never let the still-neat cleft between my legs, now briefly seamed at its base toward the opening behind it by something the doctor had called an *episiotomy*, turn to the damp, dirty rose Mama's had been. Somehow I already knew what was most important about me to Bobby, and it had everything to do with my body, my small, rose-tipped breasts, the hipbones that created angles at the edges of my lap, the rosy folds, covered in thick brown curls, at the base of my belly, that whole skinny housing that had already given me Dwayne. It had become, it seemed, the source of everything good I had ever had—my son, and now a husband and home.

When we stopped at a drugstore for cherry Cokes, Bobby even let me buy two magazines. For the next twenty miles, occasionally wiping Dwayne's drool from the slick pages, I read the *Good Housekeeping*, then the *Ladies' Home Journal*, as though I were studying for a test, by far more interested than I ever had been in anything in school. Jeanne Crain, I learned, kept her complexion smooth by scrubbing her face daily with cornmeal, then smoothing on baby oil. As I perused the pages featuring "Ten Unusual Ways to Cook Chicken," I added the recipes for "Hawaiian Delight" (made with celery, raisins, and Dole pineapple chunks), "Far Eastern Treat" (cooked with peanut butter, mashed banana, and something called *chutney*) to my meal plans. I pondered seriously the dilemma of the wife with the angry husband in "Can This Marriage Be Saved?"— the counselor suggested his wife could make his life easier, and thus hers, by having his slippers, his paper, and his favorite foods ready when he came in from work each day, by keeping the children out of his way, and remembering that "a soft word turneth away wrath." As I read, I couldn't quite imagine how this could have helped Mama with Daddy; but then, he hadn't had slippers, in fact, hadn't worn any underwear at all, and when he was raging, had often stomped into the kitchen as naked—but for the red hair of his thick chest and groin, the red of his sunburned neck, which had made him look as though he were wearing some kind of perpetual bandanna—as the day he was born. But now I was married to a boy who wore boxer shorts printed with cocker spaniels or golf clubs, and I was certain that such a man could be dealt with. Indeed, I now felt as though every page, every picture, every article—such as the one on "How to Understand Your Husband's Most Intimate Needs," even though after reading it I didn't feel that I knew much more about what those "intimate needs" were than I had before—had special meaning for me, as though I had suddenly

65

been inducted into some secret society, the one that had caused those conspiratorial looks between Mama and Aunt Darlene, among the Sunday school teachers at the Church of God, and all those condescending remarks I had heard for my whole life about "men." It was like a female version of the Shriners or Masons, and had nothing to do with real sex; instead, it was a special vocation, like living in a convent or a harem. I was sixteen years old and a mother and a wife, and though I had only briefly been each, I had total confidence in my talent for my new calling; all I had to do was follow the rules, and the rules, I was certain, would be revealed to me in these and similar full-color printed pages.

As Bobby whizzed us along the highway, I felt I was on a magical carpet, my and Dwayne's destiny as certain and secure as the outcome of a perfect recipe. In Gulf Shores, Alabama—"the scenic route," Bobby had called it—he had stopped so we could step inside a doorway made to look like a huge shark's mouth, complete with scary-looking teeth. It was almost as though the very names of the towns we were passing through—Bayou La Batre, Pascagoula, Fontainebleau—were making me dizzy.

As we neared Biloxi, Bobby parked the car alongside the road so we could look at an alligator held captive in a chicken-wire cage. The thing was ugly, and more a muddy gray than green, but Dwayne laughed and waved his arms, his jet eyes sparkling, as it ran faster almost than we could see to snap up a piece of bony meat thrown into the cage by a thick-necked man in overalls. He kept on laughing back in the car while I quoted over and over from the Arbuthnot's *Time for Poetry* I had never returned to the South Alabama library: " 'How doth the little crocodile, Improve his shining tail, And pour the waters of the Nile, on every golden scale! How cheerfully he seems to grin, How neatly spreads his claws, *And welcomes little fishes in, With gently smiling jaws!*' " As I reached the last line of the verse, my mouth clamping down on his sweet belly button, he giggled as though in ecstasy, and glancing over at us, Bobby smiled, too.

Then Bobby took us to a beach where it seemed as if we could see the whole ocean. I just stood there holding Dwayne and couldn't say anything. It was huge, a dull gray-blue, worse than the sky just before a storm or in tornado season, a no-color I knew was deep and full of secrets. I shuddered, remembering Cudden Jones and his ugly prickly starfish; thinking that that murky color, that wetness, was a brine chock-full of them, that beneath that moving surface, they might be writhing by the hundreds and trillions, crowded like sardines into a giant tin, right up the waving edge, awaiting only the turn of a key by a huge hand to release them. I felt a kind of chill and hugged Dwayne, who, picking up on my mood, had turned pensive, too, clinging to me more tightly. His diapers were damp, and I could feel his tiny penis poking into my chest, his little balls squashed against my rib cage.

But by the time we got to Gulfport and Bobby pulled into a motel beneath a bright neon sign that read, in colors like candy Easter eggs, SEASIDE VILLA, my brain was bubbling again. I watched as Bobby took out his wallet, then a sheaf of bills that looked like more money than I had ever seen in my life. His hands were skinny and white like the rest of him, with dark hairs on his knuckles; the heavy gold band he now wore on his left hand seemed to weigh it down. He leaned over and kissed me on the mouth and went inside a screened door marked OFFICE. When he came back out, he drove a short distance to what looked like a little house with the number 15 on it, and got our stuff out of the trunk.

When we went inside, the room was like nothing I had ever seen: There was a big double bed of wood the color of a girl's dishwater-blond hair, with matching tables and lamps on each side, and a cot to one side for Dwayne; a chenille bedspread the color of a rusty tin can, or the bottom of a cast-iron pan when it had been put up without drying; and an orange-plastic-covered chair with wooden arms and no dents. Over the head of the bed hung a framed picture of what I imagined an English garden must look like—full of sweet peas and pansies and lilacs. The floor was covered in a thick baby-blue carpet—my white high-heeled sling-backs sank right down into it.

But the bathroom was the best thing—everything was "modernistic," just as I had seen in pictures in magazines. There was a sparkling white sink marked only by a creamy concave space where a new, baby-sized bar of Ivory soap lay; a big, shiny bathtub, with silver-colored fixtures, set right down onto the floor; a shower curtain with an orange and sky-blue design hung inside it, its pattern echoed in the bathroom curtains. Thick, thick towels, so white that they must have either been new or else soaked all day in Clorox, hung on little silver-colored racks; and on the floor was a bright orange plush rug. It was both the ugliest and most beautiful place I had ever seen in my life. It was ugly—I knew that as certainly as I had ever known anything, though I didn't know how I knew—but the shock of it also made it beautiful, excited me: It was ugly, and it was alive.

I had heard of TV, but had never seen it. Now Bobby turned on the news, the gray-and-white designs flickering across the orange-and-blue room like a peopled fog while I nursed Dwayne, then changed him into double diapers, plastic pants, a clean white undershirt. It would be the first time my son and I would sleep in separate beds, and I lay down beside him on the cot, rubbing his hot little back, each tiny bone down its center, until he fell asleep, his thumb in his mouth, the dimple showing deeply in his cheek.

After a while I got up, went into the bathroom to change into the nightgown with the spaghetti straps, to brush out my shoulder-length curls, and to put on fresh Tangee pink lipstick. As I came back into the room barefoot, I wished for a moment that the orange of the bedspread were more complementary to my nightgown, but then I saw how the color jarred, even enhanced, the soft pink of its shadowy batiste folds. And as my feet sank into the blue carpet, I glanced down, loving the way my arches shone, blue-white, my Cutex Plum Garden toenails gleamed, rubylike, amid the fibers. As I lay down on the double bed in the dark beside Bobby, a faint white light was coming in through the blue curtains, like a living force. I held up my left hand, admiring the perfect single diamond in its "Tiffany" setting, a design I had known without question to be prettier than any of the ornate bands, carvings obscuring diamond chips, that the jeweler had held out on his velveteen tray a few weeks before. "Eastah, Eastah," Bobby murmured, hovering over me, staring down at me, his eyes looking, without his glasses, even more watery and defenseless than usual. It was

the first time we had ever lain down full-length on a bed together, and one skinny black-furred leg hooked over both of
mine as though in total possession, one hand grasped a breast
still tender from nursing Dwayne. He leaned over, licked away
the drop of flavor lingering damply on its tip; then, with the
fingers of his other hand, he traced the silvery stretch marks
downward, then awkwardly separated the tangled curls at my
vulva. Almost before he was finished, I was asleep, dreaming of
alligators and chocolate éclairs—Dwayne and I, exactly the
same size, were gaily digging them out of the ground, like
buried treasure.

The next morning, I put on my other trousseau dress—a
navy cotton with a straight skirt and a big white sailor collar.
Before we left the motel room for breakfast at the café across
the road, Bobby cupped his hands possessively around my bottom, pushing his tongue deeply into my mouth while Dwayne
crowed and clawed at the black forelock that hung awkwardly
atop Bobby's thin, bespectacled face.

"It won't be long now," Bobby said after an hour back out
on the road, and I shivered, the goose bumps suddenly popping
up on my white forearms. I had heard the preacher at the
Church of God, yelling many a Sunday about "N'aw Aw-*leens*,
thet *uh* city 'a hellfire and damnation, thet—*uh*—*Sodom* scooped
right outta thuh—*uh*—*sea* by *Satan* 'n his—*uh*—*de*-mons. . . .
Surely, thuh *den* uf *e-nick-quitee*! Thet wile jungle fur Satan's
own! . . ." And truly, as we drove into the outskirts of the city,
it was like nothing I had ever seen or heard of. Short and tall
buildings were everywhere, with houses stuck in between. We
passed a huge neon Bible, rising high over the highway—did
they need that because there was so much sin?—and an enormous cow painted brown and white, beneath a sign that read
SEALTEST. Then there were the billboards, with pictures of everything, from a huge loaf of Sunbeam bread to an oversized
woman in a one-piece sarong-style swimming suit. "What is
that?" I cried as we passed what looked like an endless, closely
trimmed lawn covered in small white marble buildings that
looked like little houses and beautiful statues of angels and
children and flowers. It was a place as beautiful as a dream, or
heaven—"The dead are buried above ground," Bobby said, "so

when the waters rise, the bodies won't float away." He went on to explain how some families, the poorer ones, buried their loved ones in the same graves, on top of one another, until finally the ones on the bottom floated on out to sea.

Our new house in Airline Park in Metairie was one in a row on a street of similar, but to me miraculously well-kept, tract dwellings, rented for us—"cheap," Bobby said—by Miss Lisa and Big Bobby. It was, unbelievably, even more "perfect" than the motel had been, with more of that dishwater-colored furniture, and an automatic—not even a wringer!—washing machine, plus another machine that Bobby said would dry the clothes. That first night, I dreamed of my and Dwayne's bodies—him facedown on my stomach, his fat arms clutching me tightly—as I lay on my back, rocking helplessly atop the ocean, floating out to frightening, endless sea.

Yet in the morning, everything seemed clean, white, bright. I glanced through the window at the neat, small yard; I was ready to jump out of bed, to clean and to unpack and to cook, to tend to Dwayne and to wash clothes in the new washing machine. But when I tried to get up, Bobby pulled me back down into our bed, to "make love," as he called it, again. I was still sore from the night before, but I obediently peeled the condom and began to unfurl it around his erect penis. "Did you come?" he later murmured thickly, almost sleepily, as though it were night again instead of morning. "Uh-huh, I think so," I answered quickly, only wanting to get up, start another exciting day. Oh, sometimes when I was nursing Dwayne—his small, hot body close to mine, his Seminole-dark eyes staring up into my own almost as though he were reluctant to even blink, I felt a satisfying grab, a rhythmic contraction like what I imagined African music to be like, begin deep inside my vagina. But I wasn't about to tell Bobby that—any more than I was about to tell him that this was getting boring, even irritating, the way Daddy's caresses had been.

For I knew which side my bread was buttered on. I was a wife now, and there was something called wifely duty, something—sitting in the Church or God, or at Mama's and Aunt Darlene's feet, listening to their conversation—I had heard about all my life, something had to do with those "intimate needs" hinted at yet not spelled out in the magazine article I had studied the day before. And that duty—which had nothing at all to do with the pounding in my flesh, the breaking of barriers, the red behind my eyelids on that afternoon in the piney woods when Dwayne had been conceived—was a small price to pay for the home Dwayne and I would now have. Though I wouldn't have wanted to admit it, some of Aunt Darlene's practicality had rubbed off even on me. And besides, I knew how to create my own release, to make the colors sparkle in my thighs, but I also somehow knew that that was something I shouldn't share with Bobby.

Back then, I was into survival, and survival was enough. For a long time—more than a decade—I would continue to believe that I could repress my natural outlaw self in its favor. I had—successfully, I thought—escaped Mama, Daddy, Aunt Darlene, and South Alabama. What I didn't yet know was that most reprieves are only temporary, that they exact a price, and that the answers I had thought I had seen so neatly laid out on the magazine pages were only to be the first of the many sets of rules that would tumble like Dwayne's brightly colored blocks, fall like my heaviest soufflé.

The house was bigger and finer than I could have imagined. Instead of worn linoleum, the floor of the front—or "living"—room, was covered in a gold-colored carpet, as was the "dining alcove," an L-shaped space—with the Formica dinette table of my dreams already right there—opening into the kitchen through the "breakfast bar." Looking around the house with me, Bobby said the names of these spaces naturally, as though he had grown up with them. And the kitchen, oh, the kitchen! I felt like I'd died and gone to heaven: The "appliances"—an electric "range," the washer and dryer, even a dishwasher—were all built in, and the color of a sunny morning—ingenuously stacked atop each other in a way I had only seen in those magazines. There were rows of empty "knotty pine" cabinets, just waiting to be filled—Bobby said we would go to the supermarket that very first morning—and the floor was a glossy pebbly cream.

Then there were three boxlike bedrooms—one even had

71

a long closet with sliding doors covered in mirrors across it, and Bobby whispered into my ear that he wanted us to keep that room for ourselves because we could see ourselves in bed in the mirror. Looking out the window beside the bed, I saw a small pine tree, with what looked like wisteria winding around its base. In the next room, which was painted blue, I held Dwayne up, pointing and smiling: "This is yours, honey, your own room now—blue." "Blooo-oh," he mimicked, pursing his lips; and as I kissed him, I did feel a slight twinge, remembering his hot little body beside me, his warm wet double diapers each morning as we had woken together on the farm. Each of the one and one-half baths was as lustrous as the one in the motel room—if only Mama and Musette could see them (though not Aunt Darlene, for I knew she would find some way to diminish my pleasure). And best of all, I would be able to use the third bedroom for the Singer sewing machine and the easel Bobby had promised to buy me; I was already dreaming the dress—seventeen gores in the skirt, with contrasting piping between each one—I wanted to make for myself from a Vogue designer pattern.

I thought with a flush how pathetic—how embarrassing, really—Mama's attempts to beautify her linoleum by pasting on the magazine pictures, then shellacking them, had been. What had Bobby thought of us, our ramshackle little house? But even as I realized this, I felt anxious, as though something was wrong here, too. Dwayne over my arm, I wandered about the new house in shock. The whole place was filled with some furniture Bobby called "Danish Modern," the seats and cushions covered in an ugly tan tweed, left over from Big Bobby and Miss Lisa's old house when they had moved into their new one. In fact, I knew that despite my delight in the place, its roach-free corners, the closets with the hangers, the shining floors, something was wrong, and then I realized what it was: Except for the kitchen, it was ugly—just as the motel room had been ugly. It was neat, it was clean, but it was squat, arranged in a box shape with low ceilings that felt as if they might suddenly come down and squash me. But how could I know this when the only place I had ever been was on the farm? As I pulled back the nubby beige rayon drapes in the living room, looked through the "picture" window, I saw that the yard was a perfect square, too, that there was a squat, neatly pared hedge just beneath the windowsill, and nothing else beyond but the tiny dull green trimmed lawn, a black-painted mailbox, and a street full of houses, with pale gray driveways leading up to "carports," just like ours. When I returned to the kitchen, parted the ruffled cotton curtains, and looked out the window there, I saw only the gray inside of the carport, the side of Bobby's car. But the window from the dining area did look out onto the backyard— another slightly larger trimmed rectangle beyond which I could see a gray mesh fence, an aluminum doghouse. As I glanced at the room's tightly sealed corners, its floorboards, I remembered the slugs that would come in through the cracks each night back home in Alabama and crawl across the linoleum, leaving the silvery trails Musette and I carefully crept around when we wanted another hunk of Mama's corn bread or scratch cake. Yes, the farm had been ugly, but in a different way. And then there had been that whole world beyond—the yard where the chickens wandered, constantly clucking, and Daddy turned his old truck around, the raggedy barn and the fields and dirt roads. Here, everything was so silent, and for a moment I felt as though I couldn't breathe.

But as I held Dwayne close, I heard a sound from the "family room"—Bobby had turned on the Magnavox television set Big Bobby and Miss Lisa had given us as a wedding gift. This had to be better, didn't it? And today, I would fill those knotty-pine cabinets with brightly colored cans, put the Birds Eye frozen strawberries in the freezer at the top of the yellow refrigerator—yes, I reminded myself, I had a freezer now! I would prepare the first of my menus, ask Bobby for the corn-stick pan, maybe even surprise him with the chocolate éclairs. And then, if I had any time left, I would get out my paints, my pencils, and my drawing tablet, and set them up in a special place where I could sit and draw anytime I pleased. . . .

"Well, how do you like it?" Bobby said proudly, coming up and putting his arms around me, pressing up against me from behind. I didn't want to hurt his feelings; besides, how could a girl from a tenant farm, used to an outhouse and tin washtub, complain about a house like this? My spirits fell further as I felt the hardness in his pants pressing the cleft of my bottom. As he turned me to kiss him, not noticing my restlessness at all, I could feel Dwayne struggling between us, making the sounds he made when he shit in his diapers. "Let's hurry 'n go to the store, so we can come back 'n do it again," Bobby said thickly, in that voice I was beginning to associate with the rising of his desire.

"Just let me change Dwayne first," I said. The smell of shit was filling the air, causing Bobby to push away with an irritated "Whew!" I was getting the definite feeling that my son didn't want to share my body either.

"Ah jes' don't know how this lily-livered boy got a good-lookin' gal lak you!" Big Bobby said admiringly just after we had been introduced on the afternoon of the crawfish boil. He was patting my ass and winking even though Bobby, looking pained, was standing right there. He was stout, thick-necked, wore a butter-yellow polyester jumpsuit, and held a sweating Dixie bottle in one nicotine-stained, short-fingered fist. On one fat finger shone a ruby-colored ring. Small red veins covered his big nose; a thick cigar hung from his lower lip. In fact, most of the men there—the ATO "brothers" and Big Bobby's associates at the used-car dealership where Bobby now worked, too, all looked a lot like Wayne, though they were better, that is, more expensively, dressed. "Thet boy did reel well at studyin' over thar at Toolane—but, hell, not at football. 'N he shore don't have sales in 'is blood!" Dwayne hung on my arm, sucking his thumb, but Big Bobby never mentioned him at all. Instead, he looked around him and winked again—not at me but at the circle of men. "But mebbe 'is luck 'll change with a purty gal like you at home!"

Inside the house, through the sliding glass door from the patio, Miss Lisa was stirring a pot of red beans 'n rice while bossing a uniformed Negro maid who was smearing butter strongly smelling of garlic on huge loaves of what I would learn was "French" bread. Her bright, taffy-colored hair was arranged in a beehive on top of her head—it looked almost like a froth of yellow cotton candy, and she wore an azalea-colored linen dress that I knew from the Simplicity pattern books was "princess style": Two parallel seams ran up the fitted front over her broad hips, wide waist, protruding stomach, and big bosom.

Her linen pumps matched the dress exactly; I realized she must have had them "dyed to match," though I had only seen such shoes in pictures in magazines. "Why, you're such a skinny li'l thang!" she said when Bobby introduced us. It was something I would hear her say time after time through the years, especially when she would catch Big Bobby squeezing my waist or patting my ass, and I never would know whether it meant she found me pretty or ugly. "How 'bout a Seven 'n Seven, honey?" she asked as I came inside. She held up her glass, shaking it so that the ice tinkled. "No, thank you," I said demurely, feeling somehow superior, as I had way back with Louise. Miss Lisa might have had on a princess dress with shoes dyed to match, might have lived in a big house and had a maid—the first maid I had ever seen—but she had puffs around her eyes and was twenty pounds overweight and was married to Big Bobby. I was struggling with Dwayne, who was writhing with his desire to get down on the slick floor. "Do you thank you can keep 'im off the doodads on the coffee table, honey?" she said, indicating the "family room," thickly carpeted with what looked like a fuzzy marshmallow creme, only a bit more platinum than her hair, on the other side of the breakfast bar. In fact, everything seemed light, bright, and frothy like her beehive. She and Big Bobby had recently "redecorated" their house, Bobby had told me, "with Danish Modern," and it was bigger—the biggest house I had ever seen!—and more luxurious, and even uglier than the house Bobby and I lived in. It was also even farther out in the suburbs. "Lake Pontchartrain," Bobby had said, as though it was a special place. To come here, we had driven away from, rather than closer to, the city as I had hoped. But I didn't see a bit of water, and this place didn't seem to have one thing to do with the evil and exciting New Orleans of my dreams.

"Come on, honey," Bobby said anxiously, taking my elbow and guiding me back outside. "I want you to meet my very best friend from Tulane." He led me over to a slender man, dressed in a shirt and tie as Bobby was. He was standing over by the fence, looking at the sky beyond it as though watching for a message. "This is Jimmy—he wuz mah brothah in the frat house. He works downtown as an architec'." Jimmy's eyes were fine-lashed, sandy; he looked as out-of-place as Bobby did. I saw something I would later recognize as male interest flicker in his eyes. "Nice to meet you, ma'm," he said shyly.

But I was distracted. Looking down, Dwayne had discovered the barrel of blindly writhing crawfish—there must have been thousands—and was wiggling, stretching out his arms, and calling to them as though they were potential pets. I could see the steaming washpot on the grassy area beside the patio, and now Big Bobby and another man came over and poured hundreds of the thrashing things into a wire-mesh basket. "Come on ovah here, darlin'," Bobby said, pulling me toward the washpot as though watching the doomed creatures boil were something I would surely want to see. I was remembering the crawfish swimming in the creek behind the house back home, that shameful day when—out of some mean impulse, to show off to Musette, to horrify her and make her cry—I had caught one, and had torn it apart, claw by claw, head from torso, as she screamed. Now, as I reluctantly glanced down, carefully holding Dwayne back from the heat, the steam, the terrible vision of death, I saw that, even as the things were writhing in the bubbling water, they were turning first a sunset pink, then a brilliant tomato red, and it was that color, that transformation, that kept me from looking away, that helped me rip them apart as avidly as everyone else at the long redwood picnic table just a little bit later.

Bobby proudly demonstrated how to tear the shell off the body, draw out the sweet bit of highly seasoned meat, then at the last, to "suck the heads." As he explained that, all the men at the table guffawed, looking at me, then back at Bobby, whose color rose pinkly. I had to admit they were good, and I gave one bit of meat to Dwayne, seated beside me in his new plastic seat, for every piece I ate myself. Bobby was drinking Seven 'n Seven now, and his face was getting flushed. "You'd be so goo-oo-d at suckin' head, honey!" he whispered into my reddening ear. That night, still fevered from the beer and Seven 'n Seven, he told me exactly what that meant and, pushing my head with his hand, had me go down on him for the first time.

Every weekday morning at eight, Bobby left in the bright blue Chevrolet to drive to Big Bobby's Used Cars on Airline

Highway. Listening to the radio in my shining new kitchen, I would hear my father-in-law's business advertised between the Hank Williams or Patsy Cline songs, even his burly voice saying "Yaw'l come, now. You cain't git a better deal then with Big Bobby" over the airwaves. When Bobby took me by the lot with him, Big Bobby called me "bebe doll," or "sugah bebe," and pinched my cheek in a way I don't think he would have if Miss Lisa had been there. The other salesmen, all older, looked a lot like Big Bobby—paunches overhanging their belts, fat cigars in the corners of their perpetually grinning mouths, and I knew by now that when Bobby was around his father, he tended to say "yes suh, yes suh" a lot, all the while looking at the ground. I knew he was nicer, more sensitive, than they were, but when he was there, it was as if he had to prove himself. I still couldn't imagine my husband, with his horn-rimmed glasses, his skinny shoulders, his tweed jackets, successfully talking anyone into buying one of the big Coupe de Villes or Grand Prix on his daddy's lot, but sometimes he did. And when he did, he came home and drank to celebrate.

But when he didn't—when Bubba or Earl "got to thet suckah first"—he came home and drank because he felt bad. He would sit and whine about how he hated Big Bobby and the other men at the lot. Sometimes he would begin to tell me about his terrible childhood, of being teased and called a sissy by Big Bobby, of how Big Bobby and his real mama, Celanese, had argued longer and longer every night. There was something about Bobby's real mama being no good, something nobody in his family ever talked about: about her drinking and driving her big Pontiac up onto a sidewalk and killing a little child, then going to the state prison at Jackson, and dying there. He would only talk about that when he sat drinking for a long time. Then the tears would stand in the corner of his watery eyes, magnified by his glasses; I would feel as if he were dumping a bucket of chicken guts over my head. But all I could do was make myself numb and plan menus in my head, or think about what I would draw the next day.

I knew there were husbands like Daddy, who when they wanted to drink didn't come in until late, and sometimes I wished Bobby were one of them. For whether he was in a bad mood or a good one, he wanted me to come over and sit on his lap in the family room, even if I was in the middle of stirring a sauce or flouring a chicken. "Don't yuh wanna sip, honey?" he would tease, holding up his glass, already knowing what my answer would be: "Ugh! That stuff must taste like what it smells like!" Then he would laugh and put his hand right up my skirt as Daddy had done, as if he owned me, and I guess in his view, he did.

Each Saturday, he drove me to Schwegmann's Giant Super Market. Then he would often take me to the Sears on Baronne Street, where he would sit patiently as—Dwayne at my feet, playing with whatever we had bought to occupy him—I tried on dress after dress. Then he would tell me which one he liked best, and buy it for me, even if it cost $17.95. "Yuh're mah wife now, 'n I want yuh to look nice," he would say. And the clothes he had bought me—more than I had ever even imagined having—were beginning to fill the mirrored sliding-door closet: I had three pairs of high-heeled sandals; five dresses; Capri pants, pedal pushers, and black velvet toreador pants; and a felt circle skirt with a fuzzy poodle on it that Dwayne kept trying to pull off and pet. I had a dresser drawer full of sweater sets and blouses; two others full of stockings, garter belts, and waist cinchers; bras with push-up pads shaped like little butterflies (these came from Sears Roebuck); and baby-doll pajamas—I had a set of baby dolls for every night of the week now, almost enough to fill a shop—frilly, crotch-length tops with little panties, in pink, blue, yellow, and black (I could tell the black set was Bobby's favorite, though it made me feel washed out to wear it). I also had shortie gowns in some of the same colors, like little baby dresses that just came to the tops of my thighs.

To go along with the nightgowns and baby dolls, I had gone to a doctor who asked me to lie on a table while he looked up inside me, then he showed me, as I reached down awkwardly to follow his instructions, how to insert the diaphragm, which meant that Bobby never had to wear the condoms anymore. Every night after putting on my gown or PJs—sometimes Bobby would tell me which one he wanted me to wear—I would fill the rubber disk with the clear jelly that reminded me of the gunk that had surrounded the tadpole eggs in the creek each spring on the farm; then I would slip it inside me, already dreading sticking my finger back inside myself the next morning, the semen and melted jelly making the disk slide around like a wet fish—though it was better than the wilted condom, filled with white sticky stuff, left cold and clammy on the floor or the bedside table for me to dispose of. Then I would obediently enter the bedroom for my nightly performance—a performance during which I was honing my skills—conducted for my husband's pleasure; at times, I felt a bit of scorn at how easy it was to please him. Yet if I ever, for a moment, felt resistant, I reminded myself of my wifely duty, of what I had left behind. With Big Bobby and the other salesmen—sometimes even with his ATO brothers—Bobby might seem shy, even pained. But at home, I was his domain.

What had surprised me most was what he had given me on my seventeenth birthday. He had brought home the big dress box with MAISON BLANCHE printed on top of it and plopped it proudly on the dinette table before me. "I wanted to get somethin' special for my bebe doll," he said. When I opened the box and pulled out what at first looked like a fat, sleeping animal, I could feel my mouth open, but nothing came out. My first thought was of Daddy skinning a rabbit, peeling its coat off. "Mouton," Bobby said proudly. "Miss Lisa said you'd like it. Go on, try it on," he said when I hesitated. I did, and felt bulky and strange, wearing some other animal's skin. Looking up at me from the floor where he had been playing, Dwayne began to scream, as he had when he had seen my new hairdo. "Um-um-m," Bobby said, holding me at arm's length, then arching me back in a kiss. "Miss Marilyn Monroe!" My hair was now blonde and short, and I had had a short cut shaped like a bubble, and a permanent wave at a shop recommended by Miss Lisa. I didn't like the style, but I had been amazed that chemicals applied to my fine brown hair had had the power to turn it crinkly and blonde. Bobby looked disappointed when I took the jacket off to pick up Dwayne and comfort him. He would have been shocked if he had known that I had finally gotten Dwayne used to the coat by letting him nap on it or cuddle it in his playpen, crooning to it as though it were a cat.

Once, I tried to explain to Bobby that I didn't really like the way Miss Lisa looked, but I could tell he didn't know what I meant. He was beginning to be a bit critical—in the same way I was critical of the drawings I was making each day of Dwayne—as though I were his work of art, and he wanted me to fit some idea he had: "Your freckles are cute, doll bebe, but isn't there somethin' girls put over 'em, pancake 'er somethin'?" He would look through my *Good Housekeeping* and *Redbook* magazines, picking out the hairdos, the clothes, he thought would look good on me. Twice a week, I spread the MiraCol he had bought me at Merle Norman over my face, peeling it off like a thin pink skin; on two other days, I scrubbed with Helena Rubenstein Beauty Grains, which left my complexion glowing. Now he wanted me to wear Maybelline cake mascara and black lines around my eyes. "But wouldn't that look cheap?" I asked. "Naw, honey, you'd jes' look like a doll bebe." He liked straight skirts and the tight Capri pants to the point that I felt too self-conscious to put on the comfortable flowered cottons I had worn on the farm. But sometimes, zipping up the side of the polyester pedal pushers I now wore during the day with pull-overs called "turtlenecks" or sweaters that buttoned up the back, I missed the soft feel of the washed-out cotton, the faded flowers, beneath my fingertips.

I kept those clothes folded in a drawer now, intending to cut them up for dustcloths, but instead I just opened the dresser sometimes to touch them. And when I did, the whole thing— the farm, the red dirt at my bare feet, the gentle cluck of the chickens, the feel of holding a warm, shit-smeared egg fresh from the nest in my palm, the heaven of walking with Dwayne at my breast in the fields, the view from the porch at twilight as I sat with a glass of iced tea, drawing—all came back to me, like a movie with the bad parts cut out.

And then I would remember that I was in the midst of bed-making or dusting, that Dwayne was bouncing, bouncing, in his plastic chair, waiting to go out into the backyard where Bobby had put up a swing set for him. Or I would put my hand up to the back of my neck, thinking to feel my long, silky brown hair, my fingers instead meeting my new permanented coif, the stiff bristles at my nape.

The part of the day I liked best was the time just after Bobby left at eight in the morning. I would sit with my coffee, the eggy plates still on the dinette table, Dwayne perched in his glossy new metal high chair, banging his spoon or making designs with his Pablum. I would look out the plate-glass window, and while the yard was as drab as ever, the redbirds that flew up to the sill, looking in at me through small beaded eyes, were like winged flame, quick and passionate. I would try as quickly as I could to capture them in the tablet I kept in a nearby drawer, then would sketch in their color with chalky pastels—blue-red, vermilion, a purple-brown shadow at the wing, then the sharp yellow beak. Each day they would come, and I would sketch them over and over, each drawing becoming closer to my dream of the birds. It was then that I was the most myself, and Dwayne was a part of it. "Burd-d-d, Mama!" he would laugh, looking down at my picture, then out the window, and I felt in his recognition the growing rightness of my drawings. Soon the shape of birdwing, the glittering, blinking eye, the dash of yellow at the breast, were embossed in my brain. As I lay beneath Bobby that night, I would dream of the birds—of the birds all over my body, of their feathery touches, of the shiver I would feel as a bird pecked lightly at my crotch. As Bobby pounded and pounded, I would dream of them scratching, brushing all over me, of being pecked to death. But as he finished, the birds would suddenly fly off, leaving me bereft. I was beginning to realize that no matter how often or how long Bobby "did it" to me, something inside me always remained untouched.

Every weekend I called Mama and my baby sister, Musette, in South Alabama. Musette and I would chitchat for a while—about what she was doing in school, the gossip about all the kids we both knew, and all the cute things Dwayne had been doing—I could tell that she missed him—even about whether she had gotten her period yet. We didn't talk about all the things she had to do now that I was gone, things that I knew were harder for her, at thirteen, than they had been for me—washing the clothes and cooking the meals while listening to Mama's whining, or else feeling the weight of her silence; giving her her sponge bath each night; and emptying the bedpan into the outhouse, then scrubbing it. But before, we had had each other, and my guilt was in knowing that now she was having to do all alone, because of me, my drive to escape. So I would downplay the luxury I lived in—I just couldn't go on about it as I had first dreamed of doing.

The worst part was when she would put Mama on the line. Mama always started crying, saying, "Ah cain't even see mah own gran'chile, ah jes' set here in this chair all day. 'n yore pore sister, ah don't know what's goin' to become of 'er, she'll never meet a college boy lak you did. . . ." As she whined and cried, I could feel the red dirt of the farm scratching inside my veins and beneath my nails as I clutched the receiver with sweaty palms. But instead of hanging up, I put Dwayne up to the mouthpiece: "Say 'hey' to Grandmama now," I crooned, as though this were a normal conversation. And after I did hang up, I could feel myself hardening, hardening, the way I had had to do to live this new life.

Still, for a day or two afterward, I would have this uncomfortable, grainy feeling beneath my eyelids, as though I had done something wrong. Some days I sat rocking and rocking, holding my son on my lap, tears rolling down my face, then his as well. He couldn't really talk much yet, but he would stretch his small arms up to my neck, gazing worriedly into my face, murmuring "Mama, mama . . ."

On other days, going inside the closet so I wouldn't scare him, I had crying jags, feeling as though my insides were coming up my throat, making me heave and gasp with a pain I couldn't have described and didn't understand—after all, hadn't I successfully escaped, didn't my son and I have the home I had dreamed of—the house with built-in appliances, the (still, to me) rich husband who went off to work each day, coming home every fourteenth night with a paycheck I could never even have imagined back in Alabama, more than Mama and Daddy together—Daddy painting houses, Mama at the truck stop—had made in three months? And didn't I now have a separate room with the easel and sticks of charcoal and a whole box of watercolors in fat, satisfying tubes, colors like yellow ochre, vermilion, burnt sienna, cobalt blue—an indulgence Bobby didn't understand, but bought for me anyway? And the black velvet toreador pants I had dreamed of wearing ever since I had first seen them in *Seventeen* magazine, and all the other women's magazines I ever wanted—I even read *Mademoiselle* and *Glamour* now—plus the ingredients for any recipe I might come up with?

All I knew was that sometimes this dark feeling, this oppressive cloud, would come on me, like a tornado I had seen in the distance once on the farm, bending the very pine trees backward against a charcoal sky. If Bobby was there, I would muffle my sobs in the mouton jacket, my snot matting the soft hairs that somehow seemed to me in that moment like the fur of an animal actively responding to my pain. Or I'd go into the shower, locking the bathroom door behind me, until finally Bobby would call out, "Honey! What a yuh *doin'* in there?" I had read in one of the magazines that a man didn't like to see a woman cry—it was amazing how good I had become at following the rules, when I had been so "hardheaded"—as Mama had said time after time—on the farm. So I would rinse my eyes over and over, dry off, put on another of the pretty nightgowns, and dab some White Shoulders behind my ears, ready to go back to bed or to his lap.

"Whut's wrong with you, darlin'?" he asked once, his watery eyes worried behind his thick glasses, and I tried to explain how in seventh grade I had been sent out off the stage during the school play because of my expression: "It's just the way my mouth is made, I guess."

So I tried to remember to smile even when I didn't feel like it. I knew that while it was okay for Bobby to dump his bad feelings on me, it was *not* okay for me to tell him mine—as the magazines instructed me that it was my duty to protect his fragile male ego, and any indication that I was less than happy would make him feel like less of a man. Even though Bobby seemed interested—obsessively interested—in my body, my appearance, he didn't listen for very long if I talked. And when he *did* listen—impatiently, for just a minute or two—he would quickly come up with a solution to what he considered my small problems; after all, he provided everything I really needed, didn't he?

"Thet li'l hobby a' yours is been takin' up a lot of your time, darlin'—don't you thank you'd be bettah off if you made frien's with some a the girls 'round hyah, or went back to the Garden Club?" he asked. I had been to the Garden Club once, and a woman who from across the room had looked about forty in her purple matron's dress and broad hat had turned out, close up, to be about my age; she had talked to me seriously about the best ways to clean toilets. And as for my neighbors—those women older than myself whose kids ran about their yards with faces smeared with peanut butter and jelly and snot, fighting or making noises like machine guns, somehow reminding me of Louise's babies with the flies on their eyelids—well, they just stood hour after hour at the aluminum-mesh backyard fences, Bermuda shorts exposing their white, varicose-veined knees, as they discussed their favorite radio soaps and the best buys at Schwegmann's. Later, when I first saw the photographs of Diane Arbus, I recognized my early neighbors immediately. They all seemed content with ugly, and at the very least were totally unlike the ideal, controlled women who moved coolly across the pages of the magazines I read, or even my best fleeting visions of myself.

Just before our second Christmas together, Big Bobby gave all the salesmen at the car lot a half-gallon of Wild Turkey, and Bobby came home lugging the big bottle inside, plopping it onto the kitchen counter. Up until recently, I had never touched whiskey: The only alcohol I had ever tasted was a sip of warm beer that had tasted to me like the piss that it looked like, first pushed on me by Louise back in South Alabama, then by Big Bobby that day of the crawfish boil. Drinking was a sin: along with lewd thoughts, or worse, actual sex, which was *the* sin, according to the preacher at the Church of God, and I had seen the proof in Daddy. Why, Mama might not be in that wheelchair right now had it not been for "Satan's brew." But even before then, Mama had sometimes come home from the truck stop with an exciting story of a fistfight or a crashed pickup: "He'd been drankin', sure as day!" she added ominously. Whiskey made Daddy crazy, and everybody in our church, our little town—except for the drunks like Daddy—were teetotalers for

the Lord—*CHAST-id in throat 'n CHAST-id in THOUGHT*—*oh,
YESSUH*—*BLESS-id are the CHAST-id!* was how the preacher
put it.

But Bobby felt differently: "Hell, honey, at Too-lane, we
got drunk ev'ry Friday night 'n stayed thet way till Monday
moanin'!" Now he drank Dixie every night, sometimes a whole
six-pack, but I knew that was just men's ways. And when he
came in with the Wild Turkey, he said, "I'm savin' this for you
'n me, darlin', for New Year's Eve—jes' you 'n me 'n nobody
else."

Bobby had finally gotten me to try a drink with him, and
Seven 'n Seven had become our Saturday night ritual. At first
I gagged, thinking it tasted like medicine, but soon I began to
notice the faint distortion in the world around me, a vague, at
first almost unnoticeable, change in perception: It was like
seeing a picture by Picasso or Modigliani, like those in the art
books I had started getting from the Jefferson Parish Library;
or spinning round and round with Musette in the farmyard,
until we both fell down laughing onto the crabgrass.

Just as the world was spinning round and round Bobby
and me. I watched the news along with him, and I knew that
things were going on, crazy, exciting things, everywhere but
here in Airline Park in Metairie. It was 1955, and I had even
seen an interview with a man who a few years back had had his
body changed to a woman's and had renamed himself Christine.
"Ugh!" Bobby said in disgust, getting up for another Dixie.
"Who'd wanna do a thing like that?" I hear that nowadays,
she's a boring housewife in Anaheim, but even back then I was
intrigued by people who transformed themselves.

And before long, there would be more changes to amaze
me. A cute southern boy named Elvis would be driving people
crazy every time he sang and played his guitar on TV, just
because of the way he moved his hips. Some people in New
York would begin calling themselves beatniks; they would wear
black turtlenecks and black fishnet stockings, and the men
would play the bongo drums. One of them, a cute guy with
curly black hair and some foreign name, would write a book
about hitchhiking all over the country.

But even then, I knew that closer, all around us in New

Orleans, there were people who spoke dialects called Cajun, Creole, or even pure French; that Catholics—as exotic to me as foreigners—were everywhere; that plain old counties were called "parishes"; and that the French Quarter was only ten miles away. But I could have just as well been on the moon, or back in South Alabama. I had married into a plain Scotch-Irish Baptist family in some ways similar to, even if richer than, my own—Miss Lisa, I had come to realize, was not that unlike Aunt Darlene. But every time I begged Bobby to take me to the French Quarter, he would say, "Aw, bebe doll, yuh don't wanna go down thyah! I ust to party thyah all the time, 'n it's jes' sleaze—too sleazy for my sweet l'il ole wife. . . ."

I felt a coldness descend around my heart. But I associated the feeling with the Wild Turkey or the Seven 'n Seven. For I had noticed that after that initial pleasant dizziness, drinking also made it harder for me to conceal what I thought of as my gray storm cloud. Back then, I didn't even know to call it depression—only that, periodically, a feeling of chilly lethargy, of sadness, permeated my whole body, as though cold sorghum syrup were flowing through my veins instead of blood. For hours, I would lose interest in everything—in waxing the white-pebbled floor, vacuuming the gold-colored carpet, even preparing the new recipes—or at least, in everything but holding Dwayne or sitting at the dinette window, drawing. But when Bobby was drinking, I saw a side of him that was less shy, even intuitive, and one Saturday after we had watched Milton Berle, he pulled me right down onto the living-room carpet: "I know whut yuh need, honey," he said, nibbling my earlobe while pulling down my baby dolls, without even giving me the chance to go back to the bathroom to put the diaphragm inside me.

And that turned out to be the one thing Bobby was right about. For that was how I got Rose, and then, the year after that, Lily. "Look at that little girl who's pregnant," people would say wherever I went. And if I had thought I could love only Dwayne, I was wrong. With her white, white skin, jet hair, indigo eyes, eight-pound Rose looked like an infant Snow White; born on Sunday, she was a mystery from her first placid moment, and, in her self-contained separateness, would remain one. But

Lily, auburn-haired, anxious Lily, was the hollowed-out female to my female, an echo of my own emptiness, a small creature who held out her arms, whimpering, in need from the very beginning of comfort and of love.

Now I was one body times three, my once-small breasts perpetually milk-filled, my hand constantly behind a wobbly neck, one shoulder usually the resting place for a small, satisfyingly dependent body, distractingly sweet despite its scent of sour milk. Since their passages through it, my vagina, which Bobby claimed as well, was less mine than ever. Yet somehow this division of self multiplied my pleasure, giving me the same satisfying grab I had felt in my lower belly the day the red had first appeared on my dress in the cow field, the same deep joy I had felt, all good sense to the contrary, that moment back in Alabama when—*The Blood of the Lamb* pouring from my mouth—I had first realized Dwayne was inside me. I would sit on my and Bobby's bed, nursing Lily or Rose, Dwayne playing at my feet, inhaling their sweet odors while the wisteria bloomed outside the window. All three—big-eyed and appealing—clung to my body as though to one tree trunk, at the same time looking out toward the world, like the newsprint picture I had seen of a baby lemur. " 'Lucy the Lemur weighs four ounces and purrs like a kitten,' " I read to Dwayne from the caption, hoping to create a feeling of big brotherhood. " 'She can expect to grow to twelve pounds and live twenty to twenty-five years. . . .' " "But Rose n' Lily won't live that long, will they?" he asked hopefully.

By the time we got Lily, Mama, over the phone from Alabama, was horrified: "Now you're really stuck, girl. Ah jes' hope you're keepin' thet man a yores happy, 'cause you sure are agoin' need 'im for the rest a yo' life!" But despite the mounds of diapers to be soaked free of shit or urine, the jar after jar of Gerber's to be spooned into the mouths that opened and closed like a trio of small birds, raising blind eyes, open beaks to me— I was certain that I could keep everyone around me happy, and that I could do so with far more success than Mama had ever had, or even dreamed of. She had permitted bad things to happen, things I would never allow to exist in my world. For the other difference between us was that I had standards.

"Bananas Foster!" Jimmy, Bobby's architect ATO brother, said with delight as I brought out the dessert. Carefully following the recipe in a cookbook, I had served beef Wellington for the main course, and I could tell that Bobby was proud. But I didn't know that the bananas baked with brown sugar, butter, and lemon juice, then topped with Sealtest vanilla ice cream, had a special name. In fact, I had made the dish up, but I didn't say anything. It was the first time I had seen Jimmy since the crawfish boil, and as soon as he had come into the house, despite the baby on my hip, I had seen that look in his eyes again. I had blushed then. But after dinner—made bold by the Seven 'n Seven, and despite what I could see was Bobby's embarrassment—I brought out my pastels of the redbirds to show to Jimmy; then, at his encouragement, even the drawings of the babies. I could tell that he liked them, and I blushed again; for once, Bobby looked almost as proud of my drawing as he was of my looks or my cooking.

Two nights later, when Bobby came home from work, he called me into the carport with an excited voice. Wiping my floury hands on my apron, I pushed the screen door open and saw the red 1957 Bel Air Chevrolet convertible, as bright and as red as blood. As my mouth fell open, he innocently grinned, the crocodile welcoming little fishes in: For my twentieth birthday, my husband had unknowingly given me the gift that would become the literal vehicle of my betrayal—of him, of Dwayne and Rose and Lily—the car that would carry me toward my destiny of crime, if not redemption.

A destiny in which I would know many like Iris—Iris, who is still leaning toward me, looking a bit pensive. "Everybody has a hungry heart . . ." sings Bruce Springsteen from the living-room stereo. I remember the small brown mole just above my first woman lover's light-brown pubic hair, how she said to me almost wistfully—she, a woman of experience and no small cruelty—"I always just wanted someone to love that mole, to love me. . . ."

Now, disengaging Iris's muscular arm from the refrigerator above my head, I say almost kindly, "Have you ever heard what the rock poet Patti Smith said? 'To be *any* gender is a drag!'" And despite that she's getting the picture that I won't be licking her cunt this night, she laughs. And as I walk toward the kitchen sink for more ice, I think what I have thought time and time again through the years:

As long as people want to be loved—as long as they care what happens—they are as good as slaves.

CHAPTER FOUR

THE FRENCH QUARTER—what can I say about it? It was beyond what I had imagined, my unconscious desires made manifest.

I knew the moment Bobby turned the convertible off Canal into the Quarter that it echoed something inside me, some design that had never been matched before: the tight streets, the flat, paint-peeling, pastel wooden doors, like blind eyes turned inward, a foot above the sidewalks; the gardens hidden, barely glimpsed, behind lacy iron gates; the balconies where people sat half-dressed, the women in wrappers, or the men without shirts, sipping drinks or calling down toward the people milling in the streets below—it was the most secret and provocative place I had ever seen or dreamed of. And the names of the streets, foreign and weird, after saints: St. Anne, St. Peter, St. Philip; Bobby told me that *Burgundy* wasn't pronounced like the wine, but with the middle syllable stressed. Perhaps because I was from South Alabama, Baptist territory, even the names of the places we passed—the Villa Convento, the Ursulines Convent, the Napoleon House, Maspero's—had that strange foreign sound to me.

And then there was Jackson Square: As we walked up, an

old—very old—Negro woman in a plaid cotton blouse, frayed chartreuse rayon slacks danced slowly, sensuously, to a jazz band—a rickety-looking player piano, a trombone, a flute, played by an equally elderly and lined group of Negro men—set up just outside St. Louis Cathedral. She was smiling, swaying, her eyes closed, as though she didn't even know or care whether the crowd watched. Looking back, I realize she was possibly stoned on the reefer of the fifties. But I didn't know about reefer then, only that in the sidewalk cafés beneath the Pontalba apartments (in one of which I now drink, banter with Iris) people were drinking exotic-looking beverages from tall, curvaceous glasses, and laughing and yelping, and spilling out into the square, where a few tattered painters were hunched over easels, painting bad portraits of people who posed on folding chairs. Well-dressed women and men, some in tuxedos and cocktail dresses, milled around us, holding cocktail cups aloft, as though trying to avoid the groups clad in Bermuda shorts, shirtdresses, and short-sleeved white shirts and slacks, cameras slung around their necks, many of whom sat in an open café—"the Café du Monde," Bobby said—sipping coffee from thick white cups, eating doughnuts that looked like small white pillows. A full-grown boy dressed in what looked like a ballerina's tutu, frilly pink tulle, and pink ballet slippers, pink ribbons winding up his muscular calves, brushed by us as though in a hurry. Nearby, a worried-looking man in a clown suit juggled crumbly-looking red rubber balls. I could see the Mississippi River, huge and endless, just beyond the levee. "Why cain't we live here, honey?" I begged as we walked. It was a question I would ask again and again, and his answer was always the same: "It's not safe, darlin', you know thet!" He would add patiently, "'n besides, it's so ugly 'n dirty!"

By now, I knew that what meant ugly or beautiful to me was not what it meant to most people. I had seen pictures in an encyclopedia of the poison-dart frogs that lived in South America, all knobby elbows, wet yellow, or orange striped with moist black; then there had been another photo of a transparent frog, its insides gleaming through its thin skin like the workings of a watch, and I had thought it, too, was beautiful, so beautiful that for moments I had wished I could be right there in the jungle, holding one in my hand despite the danger, the poison. And Dwayne, sitting in my lap, had seemed to agree, gurgling and reaching out his fat hand to caress the creatures. But still, I was puzzled at what, for some people, constituted "ugly": They seemed to be able to tolerate low ceilings, Danish modern furniture, lawns mowed to shorn blankness, shoes with a strap flat across the arch of the instep, but didn't like—or at least didn't like enough to live with—such things as this place with its boy rushing by in a pink tutu; its bricked sidewalks and secret openings; its doors peeling paint to show delicate ghosts of color, layers I could almost taste—faded mauve or teal or rose.

And the dirt: Sometimes in my pristine house, I even craved it—that grainy feeling between my toes, the vista of a winding red-clay road. When I later went to New York for the first time with my second husband, Johnny, I visited a woman friend who told me before I arrived, "I live in the most beautiful place in the world, a castle beside the Hudson." And once there, I saw in her tiny eleventh-floor apartment overlooking the river, yes, the tapestries from all over the world, the paintings, the sculpture, the books—but also, puzzled, I saw the dirt—coating a windowsill, outlining the tiles. During my stay in the city, I washed my hands many times each day; but my friend had lived all over the world—in Hong Kong, Berlin, Rome, Paris—and she didn't seem to notice at all. Later, I would read Santayana's statement, that true beauty is too intense for the average person to bear; and Mary Douglas's view that "Dirt is only matter out of place." And I would come to chalk that initial response up to the last remnants of my original ambition, my desire for safety, for a secure life—way back when I had still imagined such bourgeois comfort to be compatible with my art.

But I'm sure that at the time, Bobby thought he was doing everything he could to keep me satisfied, "to give the wife a li'l night out," as his buddies or Big Bobby would have put it— something on a par with paying for my beauty-parlor appointments or buying me the new dresses, just what a man had to do to keep himself in nooky, not to speak of meat loaf and lemon-meringue pie (which I had discovered was his favorite and had learned to make to perfection—just as I had perfected all his favorite sexual positions). Now we had a baby-sitter most Saturday nights, and Bobby would usually agree—provided I dressed up in a dress, hose, high heels—to take me to the French Quarter; in fact, he seemed to enjoy it. The permanent wave had grown out, and I wore my hair in a French twist like Princess Grace; Bobby had bought me a rhinestone pin to paste directly onto my skin, which came with its own little tube of glue, and sometimes I wore that, too, thinking it added glamour to my skinny collarbone.

We were wandering down Bourbon Street, Bobby's arm possessively around my shoulders, when I looked up with a small shock to see, at a second-floor window curtained in red velvet, what looked like a near-naked girl on a swing, sexy high-heeled legs pointing outward as she swayed back and forth above the street. "She's a *doll*, jes' like you, darlin'," Bobby laughed, enjoying my expression. I glanced furtively past the neon-lit signs into the dark "topless and bottomless" bars, listening to the hawkers yell, "Buoys *and* gulls, topless *and* bottomless, come raht in, folks, come raht in. . . ." Their voices reminded me of the suck-back preachers at the Church of God in South Alabama; the sounds from inside recalled the hymns I had sung beneath the stained-glass windows.

"Please," I begged one night, "please, honey, let's go in." "It's borin', sweet thang, I tell yuh. . . ." he protested, just as he had once protested taking me to the French Quarter at all. I could tell he didn't really like it that I, a woman, not to speak of his wife, would want to see such a thing. But he reached inside his pocket and pulled out the two dollars. Inside the dim room, we took seats at the edge of a small, low stage. Glancing surreptitiously around the room, I saw that I was one of the few women there, and the only one dressed like a wife. But soon, sipping the Seven 'n Seven Bobby had ordered for me, I had forgotten my shyness. For a few feet away, a woman—the most seductive woman I had ever seen—was beginning to dance across the small stage with gestures that made me think of the black snake back on the farm—graceful yet quick, darting, like fast and slow mixed together—and as she moved, she ran her hands up the insides of her thighs, between her breasts, then behind her head, as though she were caressing a fur stole or holding some live thing. I sat breathless as she removed, in a

94

slow progression of increasingly sinuous movements, first her white chiffon skirt, then her silver-sequined bra. I noticed that the fat, balding man beside me was staring up at her with the same look Bobby sometimes wore as he watched me undress. And it was then that I saw that there was something wrong with the woman's breasts: They were small, stringy, malformed, like a girl of ten or eleven before she has filled out; the metallic blue pasties at each tip seemed precariously perched there, with little to cling to. Next, with what appeared to be one motion, and with a smile that looked almost like a snarl, she jerked off both a bouffant blonde wig and the final flounce of chiffon, holding them above her head like a boxer while revealing a bulging metallic-blue G-string. The person who stood before us was a skinny, blond, acne-pitted man, grinning down maliciously, triumphantly, at the fat man and at me. As he left the stage, dragging behind him what I now saw was a rather bedraggled piece of dingy net, he walked haughtily, like a queen. The man beside me had turned red-faced, sweaty, but the music had already started back up, and this time real "buoys 'n gulls," yes, naked but for narrow G-strings, danced by us to a jungle beat, staring blankly off into space.

I sat stunned, while Bobby laughed. "See—whut did ah tell yuh, bebe doll?" He thought I was upset, but that wasn't what I was feeling at all. For one thing, I had just had my first taste of real perversity. Later, when I involuntarily researched drug addiction, I learned how addicts, from the first moment of contact with their drug of choice, were hooked; and I was like that. By then, I would have done the paintings of figures like the dancer, from the live sex shows of Costa Rica—many of them. But in that moment I knew that, however properly dressed I was in little linen dress and pumps, Tiffany-style engagement ring gleaming on my left hand, I was somehow like the man-woman I just had seen on the stage. I didn't know what "drag" was, or that, in my role as perfect little housewife, I was constantly in it. I only knew I had been looking at someone who in some way matched me, and the likeness seemed to have to do with the wild boy inside me, the one who would choose, time after time, the forbidden over the familiar. Waiting for my excitement to subside, I sat very still, my hands folded in my lap; yet I could almost feel my criminal self, shifting, surging—beating at my edges, struggling to be born.

When Bobby solicitously took my arm, guiding me back out onto Bourbon Street, I didn't protest. I let him walk me across Royal, then to the Napoleon House on Chartres, where people sat drinking cool-looking pale amber drinks with cucumber slices floating in them—"Pimm's Cup," Bobby explained—and I ordered one. "Are you okay, darlin'?" he asked anxiously as I sipped it. "Ah hope goin' in thet dirty ole place didn't upset you." "Yes, fine, thank you," I murmured. I looked down at the watch he had given me for our third anniversary: It was beautiful, a slender gold band covered in tiny carved gold blossoms, more of the delicate flowers encrusting the cover over the watch's face; of all the gifts Bobby had given me, it was the one I liked best. "But don't you think we should go on home? The sitter will want to leave soon. And I do need to nurse Lily."

Bobby had finally tired of the drip, the flavor of milk on my nipples. Despite his nagging, reluctant to give up that pleasure, I had put off weaning Lily. But now I determined that I would. Then I would be free—but free to do what? Bobby was giving me driving lessons each Sunday in the new red convertible. I had delayed getting my license, thinking that putting all the babies into the car to go anywhere while Bobby was at work was too much trouble anyway. Yet during our drive back to Metairie, I found myself silently memorizing each turn and street name. And then, unbidden, as though by magic, a name popped into my mind—MRS. BLOODWORTH'S DAY NURSERY read the large brightly colored blocks stacked to form a sign only a mile from our house.

Despite my slight shiver of foreboding, that I would drive here alone in the red convertible was now foreordained, unarguable. For me, fantasy—however vague, amorphous, miasmic—was already as good as reality. ("Miasma," I would later read in a book by Susan Sontag on AIDS, "that condition thought to cause disease . . .") Little did I know what following those fantasies would cost me—not only me, but those I loved most. As time went on, I came to realize that, for me, curiosity was a force stronger than sex, stronger even than the desire to protect my young (not to speak of myself, though what others

96

called safety I would later have called prison). And once that curiosity had been aroused, there could be no going back. Yet had I known, could I have done things any differently? I think not. All I knew—as purely, as clearly, as I had once known that I would steal the Artist's Colors—was that coming here— exploring that wild boy inside myself—was something that I had to do, as imperative as labor pains or my desire to escape South Alabama. For in some way I couldn't have explained, what I had seen that night tapped an unnamed desire inside me, the very thing for which I cried in the closet, into the mouton jacket, something that promised a transformation as vivid, as magical, as that I had experienced mixing red dirt with water for the first time to make clay. I thought of the book Aunt Darlene had given me at eight: When I painted inside the lines of the black-and-white drawings with clear water, color had suddenly blossomed, like magic. And though the color had been thin, unsatisfying—nothing like the colors of my dreams—*not* to daub the pages with water, *not* to see what would happen— would have been impossible.

Though it would take a long time, a decade, for me to realize it, my perfect family life began to go downhill from the first moment I saw the French Quarter. But first there was what I would come to think of as "the happy period"—the time before I knew that bad things—*really* bad things—could and would happen. True, with three babies, things were more complicated than they had been. When I went to the hospital to have Rose, Dwayne had stayed with Miss Lisa and Big Bobby. But I knew that he hadn't been happy. Once, when I talked to him over the phone, Miss Lisa reported that big tears were rolling down his cheeks. "But he got over his constipation after he ate a whole big bowl a stewed prunes," she said as though that were what was ailing him. When I came home, he looked up at me, his eyes lighting, his whole little face brightening, then rushed to embrace my knees. Bobby had taken Rose into our room; and while we were eating the lunch prepared by Desiree, the nursemaid hired for us by Miss Lisa, Dwayne slid off my lap and wandered down the hallway; seeing Rose sleeping in his old crib, he had let out a scream. And after Lily had been born, he had started urinating in the front yard, straight toward the street. "Cain't you stop 'im from doin' that, honey bebe?" Bobby asked, looking pained. In fact, my first duty each morning, after being wakened by their large and small cries, was changing diapers and stripping the urine-soaked sheets from the beds: Dwayne had begun wetting his again, regularly soaking the sheets printed with cowboys and twirling lariats. As I nursed Lily, he would stand in front of my chair wearing the Davy Crockett cap that he refused to take off even when he bathed, his fat little hand on the silver-coated plastic gun at his hip, dimples deepening in his cheek as he mimicked her sucking motion. Rose would be playing beneath the table, patiently stacking her blocks or making cooing sounds to the yarn-haired doll she had gotten for her first birthday. And I would be torn between answering Dwayne's questions or glancing out the window for a glimpse of the redbirds I had once spent this time of day drawing. I wanted my manila tablet, my crayons, but by then Rose would be crawling up my knee, smiling, and the milk would still be stirring in my breasts, suctioned by Lily's strong little mouth.

The little third bedroom—once my "studio"—was now crammed with a crib and a slatted baby bed, a plastic changing table, a pink-and-white painted chest of drawers, the rocking chair, and stacks of the diapers brought each Monday and Thursday by the Tidee Didee man. And the toys were every-where: The ones with small parts had to be kept separate from the larger ones so that Rose and Lily wouldn't swallow them. Still, I knew that later, if the weather was good, or if I had stuffed them into snowsuits—an irony in a land where it never snowed—I could put them outside in the fenced backyard to play in the sandbox, or on the swing set—though still I had to watch them carefully; that watching had almost become second nature for me. (Once, when I saw Lily carefully picking small objects from the crabgrass, then popping them into her mouth and chewing them, I ran into the yard to see what she was eating. It turned out to be the tiny green frogs, as bright and shining as drops of viridian-green oil paint, that sometimes fell after a rain. I swooped her up, laughing at the same time I was prying her mouth open, poking my finger down her throat, remembering how Mama had said I, too, had tried to taste those vibrant colors. And that my darling Lily had done the same thing was just another sign to me of our shared souls.)

Then maybe—just maybe—I would have a few minutes to dream and to draw, even to get out my pastels. I had quickly learned not to use the watercolors: If I turned my back to put clothes into the dryer, or to answer the phone—"I wuz jes' thankin' 'bout whut I'm gonna do to yuh tonight, sweet thang," Bobby would say into my ear from the car lot as I stood taut, irritated, the receiver pressed hard against my head. Then I would go back to find the moist colors smeared everywhere, the picture I had begun a blob of tiny finger-size streaks.

Now that I didn't have time to draw anymore, there was nowhere to put the images racing through my brain. One night soon after Lily's birth, I had dreamed of Dwayne's head limply rolling to one side, red gushing from his open mouth, past his lolling tongue, his jet eyes staring mutely up into mine. As I woke sobbing, Bobby pulled me to him, and planting himself atop my still-shorn pubic hair, stuck his penis into my vagina above the half-healed stitches, and the pain almost banished that other pain.

Nowadays, since I was so busy, Bobby caught hold of me whenever he could: in the hall as I carried a stack of clean diapers or sheets, rubbing up against me like a dog; or else by the nape of my neck, my long hair, as I had seen the tomcats do on the farm; and despite my protests I could feel his erection between my legs. "Aw, come on, bebe doll," he would say, guiding me into our bedroom, shutting the door behind him, pushing me down to the bed, while I anxiously strained to hear what was going on in the rest of the house. Between their births, the nursing, and Bobby, my body felt like a house with frail walls, people tromping in and out. I pushed back thoughts of the simplicity of my life, the control I had had back in Alabama— with Daddy gone, Mama harmless, if whining, in her wheel- chair—during the time between Dwayne's birth and my and Bobby's marriage. But now I had three precious children, I told myself; and sometimes, in order to advance in control one had to lose it. These were the mantras I came up with, lying beneath him during those moments, rigid with my desire to get back to my duties.

A few years later, watching Peter O'Toole walk across an endless Sahara in *Lawrence of Arabia*, I was reminded of my life around then. Each morning as I lifted my legs from the bed, I felt as though I were about to trudge across a desert, the heavy sands tugging me backward with each step—a repetitive journey that never got me anywhere other than into the midst of more: more laundry, more cleaning, more mouths to feed. I would hurry to the bathroom to retrieve the slimy diaphragm, already hearing the babies crying from their soggy beds. And my belly would grab, often sending me back into the bathroom with diarrhea.

There was the changing of diapers, the ever-present diaper pail, with its pungent scent; then the beds and the laundry— load after load of it—and the small mouths to be fed and re- fed from the jars of Gerber's. Dwayne had gone back to eating the strained bananas, and wanted me to feed him, too. Now that he ate at the dinette table, rather than in a high chair, he banged his spoon on the Formica, dumped bowls of strained spinach over his head, tilted glasses of milk that dripped through the cracks between the leaves of the table onto the ugly tweed carpet. "Cain't you stop 'im doin' thet, bebe doll?" Bobby asked with increasing irritation. I knew he was used to Big Bobby's calm house, with its modernistic furniture, the bar stocked with Seagram's Seven and Wild Turkey, his stepmother sitting coolly, stout calves crossed, on the long beige couch in a beige linen princess dress. The two convenient things were *Captain Kangaroo*, which kept Dwayne occupied for an hour each morning, and *The Mickey Mouse Club*, which held him enthralled before the television set for another hour late in the afternoon. I could put Lily in the playpen, leaving Rose free to crawl around at my feet, banging out a cacophonous music on the bottom of a pan while I started dinner.

Every day I began cooking at three, and there was no recipe too ambitious for me: I made Mama's 1-2-3 cake (one cup sugar, two eggs, three cups flour), topping it with Sealtest vanilla ice cream, a fudge sauce made from Hershey's cocoa and Pet milk.

I learned to stuff mirlitons, a strange vegetable I had never seen before moving to Louisiana, with shrimp and bread crumbs in the way Bobby liked. I baked his favorite lemon-meringue pies, topped with perfect beige swirls, meat loaves centered by boiled eggs that formed perfect ovals when sliced, even puff pastries filled with minced and creamed oysters, circled in caviar. The manipulation of materials—inspired by the bright visions from the magazine pages, the fanciful inventions from the *New York Times Cookbook* I had checked out at the Jefferson Parish Library—gave me some of the same feeling I had had in shaping the red clay or sketching the redbirds. At the same time, cooking satisfied my desire for adventure: Bobby, Dwayne, Rose, Lily, and I were eating what people ate in foreign countries, or even in New York. There were so many ingredients I had never heard of, and I used the yellow kitchen as my laboratory. The chickens I bought at Schwegmann's were already cut up, as though they had never had any blood at all, much less had had their necks wrung. I had stacks of them, already dismembered, in the freezer, along with diagonally scored flank steaks and butterflied legs of lamb and thick pork chops cut like little pocketbooks. In a rack over the stove stood jar after jar of spices in flavors I had only recently learned of—tarragon, rosemary, filé, dill, thyme, oregano, cumin, basil—their scents evoking amorphous, exotic places. I even had a little machine to press garlic out in small white worms. "Darlin', cain't we ever have the same thang twice?" Bobby complained after a while. "Whutevah *this* is, it looks more like prison food than anythang else!" I laughed, for I had to admit that the creamed mushrooms I had just set before him in their sculpted puff-pastry ramekins had turned an unappetizing gray during the cooking. But the next day, when I searched my cookbooks and discovered that the properties of lemon juice prevented discoloration, I felt as exhilarated as I later would by a perfect line, a perfect brush stroke.

Even back then, Dwayne shared my taste for the unusual: One morning, when he should have still been in bed, I heard him gagging and, thinking *poison*, rushed into the kitchen: Wearing the Davy Crockett cap, he stood on the chair he had tugged up to the counter, choking on a dusty mouthful of

101

Durkee's cinnamon, the can still tipped to his mouth, his thoughts written on his surprised face: If a little was good on cinnamon toast, then a lot should taste wonderful, shouldn't it? At other times, I found him choking on rotting Limburger cheese, or crunchy bits of leftover fried soft-shell crab. "Exciting things—like blue cheese and crawfish!" he would reply at nine when asked his favorite foods.

On an afternoon years later in the French Quarter, I would rise from my bed and ask the offshore oilman who was lying there, muscular limbs still entangled in my satin coverlet, what he wanted for a snack. "Bebe, go to Popeye's, get me some a' thet *excitin'* chicken," he said, meaning the spicy, Louisiana-style recipe. And before I could push it back, I felt a little gut wrench, a longing for my disappeared son.

One weekend I talked Bobby into taking us on a picnic to that beautiful cemetery I had seen. I marinated chicken, then broiled it, made a macaroni salad with green peas and bell-pepper pieces and stuffed olives, baked an apple-walnut cake with caramel frosting, and packed the whole meal in my new Tupperware. When we finally arrived at two in the afternoon, the sky was overcast, the Metairie cemetary was quiet but for the insects, and even Dwayne, Rose, and Lily were strangely silent, sitting on their haunches examining the dusty ground for bugs and rocks. "I guess it's past their nap time," I said to Bobby, but I felt an ominousness as I spread the tablecloth, then laid out the food. The graves, built on pedestals to keep them from the fate of the sea, rose all around us like small gray buildings. Above us hovered marble angels, larger than life, and the mausoleum, up close, looked slick, forbidding. As we walked through it—me holding Dwayne's and Rose's hands, Bobby carrying Lily—I thought of the bodies, stacked in those chilly drawers like the meats in my yellow freezer. All Saints' Day had been the week before, and the flowers were purple and orange and cerise, with brown curling edges, bending from thick green stalks as though they had broken necks. Personal messages were everywhere: *Daddy, I know you are really alive somewhere,* I read on a piece of lined Blue Horse paper scrawled with orange crayon; *Lucia, my darling Lucia, whether in Hell or in*

102

Heaven, I hope to be with you soon, an elegant hand had inscribed on a tear-marked linen-weave page.

"Isn't this interesting, children?" I said brightly. "So beautiful—and it's history." I explained what Bobby had explained to me during our first trip into Metairie—about the ocean and why the graves were built upright, but I made it sound like a wonderful story. "You mean there are dead people in there, Mama?" Dwayne whispered, squeezing my palm. "You don't have to talk that way, honey—they can't hear you!" I laughed, reaching down to hug his small hunched shoulder. But I shivered, thinking of the sea, shifting, surging, beneath our very feet, our bodies as fragile specks that barely hung in place on the earth's surface: It was a thought I had more and more often since Rose and Lily had been born and I realized I had only two arms with which to save them from whatever evil fate, whatever tidal wave, might come. During the Cuban Missile Crisis, I rushed out to buy canned water, and planned how I would hover with them in the crawl space beneath our little house in case of attack. I didn't know that by the time Hurricane Camille happened in 1969, literally ripping the coast near us from its moorings, washing whole families out to sea, two of the children whose sweaty hands I gripped would be drowning in a different kind of ocean.

But back then, I still thought I could control things. As Bobby drove us home, I told Dwayne, Rose, and Lily the story of Marie Laveau, the voodoo queen, about how the ground around her grave in St. Louis Cemetery was still considered lucky ground, that people still marked her grave with an *X*. But I was careful to describe the story as a myth, subscribed to by ignorant people. Back home in Alabama, we had never had any books in the house except the Bible, Daddy's *Farmer's Almanac*, and Mama's *True Confessions* or *True Romances* magazines. But my children had a full set of Compton's encyclopedias, *Mother Goose*, the complete Hans Christian Andersen, *A Child's Garden of Verses*, and the Dr. Seuss books; and records designed to teach them conversational French and Spanish and the names of all the instruments in a symphony orchestra. Dwayne had a freckled Dennis-the-Menace doll (which he would hold up to make Lily scream when I had my back turned), and three birds who lived in a cage in his room—Asia, Sunshine, and Guacamole, all named for their colors, azure, yellow and chartreuse, with wings tinged in cobalt and black; plus with two fat red fish in a round glass bowl and a little painted turtle that he insisted on removing from its Woolworth's rock garden to carry with him into the bathtub, where it paddled frantically between the blue porcelain cliffs. And then there were the two male cats, Marmalade and Edward; Marmalade, named for his orange coat, had magically turned to licking the leftover orange marmalade, the apricots stewed with lemon rind—anything that matched his color, as though he were color-coded as to what he ate—from our leftover breakfast plates. Each Sunday, I created special brunches, serving things like homemade popovers and "Puffy Apple" (whipped like a meringue, dusted with powdered sugar) or "Nantua Shrimp" (with a delicate sauce made from the liquid from the boiled shrimp shells) omelets. I had a special cast-iron pan for the popovers, and Dwayne and Rose loved puncturing them with a finger before slathering on the melting butter and jam.

Nor would I allow them to sit in Sunday school and church as I had in South Alabama, listening week after week to stories of missionary children who had been buried alive rather than deny Jesus. At moments, I may have missed the stained-glass windows, the bloody hymns. But for Dwayne, Rose, and Lily, I wanted something different. I hadn't yet heard of the philosopher Rousseau, but like him, I believed that children—*my* children—were innately good. I wanted everything to be perfect, for them to feel as though they held the world in their fat little hands—that every good thing was possible—and I determined to carve away anything that claimed otherwise. For hadn't the *Ladies' Home Journal* taught me that setting the tone for family life was the woman's responsibility? And all I had to do to know what I didn't want for them was to think back on my own life with Mama and Daddy. "You are the best things I ever made," I would say, hugging them to me, covering them with kisses. Above all, I didn't want them to suffer pain—not yet knowing that the very thing one feared most was that which was most likely to happen, or that my own early instruction in poverty, compulsion, and violence was already carved into their very

genes. Instead, making it up as I went along, I force-fed them—
like baby geese destined for pâté or little athletes pumped up
on emotional and intellectual steroids—on what I thought I
would have wanted as a child, not realizing it was what I still
longed for; or that I was giving it out of a deficit, and emptiness,
thinking I was fulfilling their needs while really trying to fulfill
my own. "You may have been a mother, an 'adult,' but you were
also still a child yourself," one of my less accusatory therapists
pointed out years later, recommending that I read Alice Miller's
The Drama of the Gifted Child.

And as our little family became more of a unit, Mama,
Daddy, and the farm did seem to fade further and further into
the distance. On Friday nights, Bobby cooked out on the gas
grill on the patio and I made the salad and dessert, smearing
the French bread with garlic butter, putting it into the oven to
warm. He would drink a six-pack—Jax or Dixie—and turn the
hamburgers or steaks or ribs I had marinated that afternoon
while I pushed Dwayne and Rose on the swing set and kept an
eye on Lily in the sandbox. On some Saturday nights, he took
me downtown to Chez Hélène in a black section outside the
French Quarter, where we ate a combination of soul food—
collard greens and fried chicken, and Creole dishes—oysters
Bienville or Rockefeller. On special occasions, we'd go to An-
toine's or Galatoire's, where we would eat strange things like
turtle soup and crawfish étouffée. We'd usually end the evening
over chicory coffee and beignets at the Café du Monde, where,
like a lover whose affair must be kept secret, I'd take care not
to show too much interest in what went on around me in the
French Quarter.

But on other Saturday nights, we drank red whiskey—
Black Jack or Wild Turkey, Bobby brought home the more
expensive stuff now—and sometimes I felt depressed, even
starting to cry, especially if Musette and Mama had called.
Bobby, still staring at the TV set, might not even notice the fat
tears rolling down my cheeks, but Dwayne would look up at
me, solemn-faced, his hand on the silver-colored gun in his
holster, ready to take on anyone who might harm me. "Don't
yuh thank it's his bedtime, Miss Bebe?" Bobby would say without

looking up. It was what he liked to call me now, the same name I had heard Big Bobby call Miss Lisa. On weekend evenings at home, he liked for me to dress up in a peignoir and the black satin mules he had bought me. And even though Dwayne was older—five—now, Bobby wanted him to be in bed, like Rose and Lily, before we had dinner, which meant that if I was having a hard time getting Dwayne settled, the drinking time went on longer.

Whenever I look at photographs of those years, they appear to be happy times: a smiling Dwayne, wearing the Davy Crockett cap, holding the newborn Lily in his arms, or else sitting in his small chair, talking on the telephone to Mama or Musette down in South Alabama; Rose, staring solemnly toward the camera, serious, contained, as she will turn out to be about almost everything—while Dwayne, again, grinning broadly, pushes her on the swing set; Lily at a plump two, one of the parakeets perched atop her head; wearing only my harlequin-shaped sunglasses, two small pink nipples, and the sweet cleft between her legs—both her unselfconsciousness and her nudity harbingers of things to come. Then, during their one visit to New Orleans, Musette, standing behind Mama in her wheel-chair, who even manages to smile as Lily sits on her lap and Rose and Dwayne lean against her dead legs. And me, cutting birthday cakes, leaning over to help someone onto a tricycle or to open gifts beneath the Christmas tree—me pregnant or not pregnant, but always with a child in my arms or on my lap.

Or the five of us lined up—me with my hair in the French twist, in a dress much like the one Miss Lisa had worn on our first meeting; Bobby, wearing a dark polyester jacket and tie, his curly forelock hanging awkwardly down toward his glasses; Dwayne grinning in his striped polo shirt, his perpetual Davy Crockett cap, gun, and holster; and Rose and Lily in matching puff-sleeved dresses from Sears, little legs rising like stalks from thin, lace-edged socks, clunky-looking saddle oxfords.

Yes, in the pictures, we look like a normal family, the ideal of the fifties, living out the American Dream.

"It'll be fun—you'll see!"

The first time I strapped Rose and Lily into the car seat

inside the red convertible to take them to Mrs. Bloodworth's, I felt my insides clench. But I set my mouth in a Revloned smile and told them how great it would be—with the other kids there, new toys, maybe even a jungle gym. "Like Dwayne—going to kindergarten," I added, and Rose brightened expectantly, though Lily, her thumb in her mouth, looked glum. Since I had learned to drive and had gotten my license, I had been taking Dwayne each morning to the preschool adjacent to the Old Metairie Grammar School. Rose, seeing him jump out of the car, join a waiting group of five-year-olds at the edge of the playground each morning, had been jealous, wanting to do what her big brother did. Other than to Schwegmann's Giant Super Market, where Lily, riding in the cart, reached out to snatch things from the shelves, and Rose and Dwayne trailed along behind arguing, I hadn't yet driven them anywhere. But this morning, looking out the window beside my bed, seeing the mauve wisteria blooming in its winding trail around the pine tree, I suddenly knew that today was the day when I would go to the French Quarter. I hurried to wash the breakfast dishes, to strip the beds—Dwayne was still wetting his—then dressed the babies as fast as I could, poking their plump legs into overalls, their little arms through shirtsleeves, pushing the brush over their soft fine hair, smoothing it over their pink scalps. I pinned my own hair up in the French twist, then dressed in hose, pumps, and a sheath dress, as though I were going to a luncheon or a Garden Club meeting. Dressing that way gave me a feeling of security—if I felt uneasy once I got there, I could just pretend I was in the wrong place.

Now, as I handed Rose and Lily over to Mrs. Bloodworth, who stood tall, stout, and blue-haired, smiling grimly through blood-red lipstick, Rose looked scared, and Lily whimpered; but her cries only blended with those from the rooms behind her. Yet I hardened my resolve: "Bye-bye! Have fun now!" I called gaily, waving and backing my way to the car. Driving off, I could still hear Lily's screams and felt a tug of pain somewhere in my center, a strand of flesh being tugged from inside me through my navel. But I had to concentrate on the street names, the turns, and my tension at going into the Quarter alone on a weekday morning. I steeled myself, making a plan: I would go to the Café du Monde and have coffee and beignets—in fact, that might be all I would do.

And that first morning that was what I did: I sat at an outdoor table, sipping cup after cup of the thick chicoried coffee, tearing apart beignets and licking the powdered sugar from my fingertips. At first I gazed only out over the Mississippi, but gradually I began to look around me, and what I saw was that no one was looking at me at all—not the waiter tossing crumbs to the pigeons, nor the winos who sat eating what others had left, nor the drag queens, their makeup smudged from the night before. As I glanced toward Jackson Square, I saw several people slouched on benches; others had set up easels; a peddler was arranging his wares; and I realized that I was alone, truly alone, for the first time since I had wandered in the pasture behind the barn. The very idea of it gave me a rush, a weak feeling—especially when I realized that no one knew where I was: I suddenly felt the tug in my gut again, the strands that felt like living flesh, connecting me to my young, and I shivered with fear at the notion of anything happening without me there to save them. But I was also excited, almost as excited as when I had discovered the Artist's Colors. And though I didn't know it yet, it was a feeling to which I was to become addicted—a feeling that would later lead me to love the disconnected moments spent in airport waiting rooms, inside jets flying coast to coast, or wandering the twisted streets of a foreign town alone after dark—feeling, somehow, despite the small thrill of fear, more secure in my insecurity than I ever did in my own life, with others' needs pulling me away from myself.

Certain of my anonymity now—easily ignoring the black who murmured "Hey, Mama," as I passed—I wandered down a narrow street, glancing into bars where seedy-looking people already sat drinking. Then I turned into a small jewelry shop where I looked into the dusty glass case, peering around a middle-aged businessman and a stout woman in cropped hair and slacks. "But I want it set in *twenty-four*-karat, Joseph," the woman was saying. When I glanced over at her, I saw the dark beard on her lower jaw, the bright blue eye shadow on her fat lids. "I want this thang set in gold—I don't care about the cost. And be sure it has those little thangs on the side, just like in the original," Joseph was telling the clerk. He signed the ticket with a flourish, as his companion, in bright blue plaid cotton sport shirt, clung girlishly to his arm with her own well-muscled limb: "Oh, I'll just love it, Joseph. . . ."

Behind the glass I could make out earrings shaped like small full-blown roses, pink or gardenia cream. "Gen-u-wine iv'ry," the man behind the counter said aside to me. As I looked at them, the ivory seemed to quiver like tender living membrane. I felt that I had to have them, in celebration of my first day of escape.

Wearing the small roses in my ears, I joined a group that was following a tour guide into St. Louis Cathedral. Along with the others, I gazed into a glass case in the lobby gift shop at the busts of plaster-of-Paris virgins, their faces painted a clear salmon pink, shoulders robed in a violent royal blue, hung with pendants of glued-on gold-colored glitter. I touched medals with the same woman enameled in bright blues and pinks. There were plastic crucifixes on which Christ hung resignedly but bled vividly, seeming to vibrate, and postcards of "the Crucifix Fish" ("Of all the fishes in the sea/our Lord chose the lowly sailcat/to remind us of his misery. . . ."). Inside the sanctuary, four or five people were kneeling in the pews, and I trailed with a few others behind our guide, a fat man in short-sleeved white shirt, black rayon pants. The interior was dim and cool, but the sunlight piercing the stained-glass turned Jesus' robe a rich plum; I manipulated the color in my mind, mixing it lightly with cerise, then turning it to fuchsia. "Our Laird—holdin' the pore lamb, the one lost from the flock . . ." I looked down at the floor, which was hard and marble, feeling dizzy with my new freedom, then focused on the crucifix to the side of the altar. "This famous antique crucifix wuz dedicated in 1792," the fat man was intoning. "The first church wuz destroyed durin' the d'astrous fire of 1788. Don An-dray Almonster ee Rock-as offered to rebuild the present church at his own ex-pense. The foundations were laid in 1792, 'n the church wuz dedicated in D'cembah, 1794. . . ." My eyes wanted to suck the garish colors from the life-size statues around me.

The guide turned to lead us down the center aisle and indicated with a fat raised finger the ceiling above us: "This

hyah is the masterpieces painted on the ceiling in 1850 by Ca-
nova, a Sil-yan artist—this one, as yuh see, is our Laird, handin'
the staff to Saint Petah. . . ." We bent our heads back obediently,
and I had to hold on to the arm of a pew to control my dizziness:
the reds, the royal blues, the metallic golds, were radiant. "Our
Lady of Prompt Sucker . . ."

Now we moved back toward the entrance where bright
sunlight poured in through the dim doorway. "And this hyah
is our statchew of Joan duh Ark. . . ." He gestured toward a
figure dressed in painted-on silver armor, blue sleeves, sword
in raised hand, cropped blond hair, and I felt stunned—instead
of a woman with the genitals of a man, here was a boy with the
genitals of a woman, a woman who was as strong, as courageous,
even as foolhardy, as any man. As the guide, his voice droning
on, led the others back outside, I remained staring up at Joan,
drawn by the notion of her transformation, her refusal to do
what she was supposed to do. Could a woman be a man inside,
just like the man in the bar had been a woman?

I noticed a girl about my age, standing nearby looking up
at Joan, too, then sketching on a pad. She wore pants made of
heavy indigo cotton, a black turtleneck; her long ash hair was
twisted up like mine, though less perfectly, and she wore no
makeup at all. Though she was pretty, she had a boyish look
that gave me a funny, though not unpleasant, feeling. And she
looked purposeful, as though she had real work. When I
glanced down at the gold-carved watch, I felt overdressed and
was almost relieved to see that I would have to hurry to get to
Dwayne's preschool on time.

From then on, when I went to the Quarter alone, I wore
my face scrubbed, my hair pulled up in a ponytail, a sheath
skirt and oxford-cloth shirt, or else pedal pushers and a Lady-
bug blouse; since Bobby didn't think they looked feminine, I
didn't have any of the new pants called blue jeans yet. In that
uniform I would sit in Jackson Square and draw, or wander
through the narrow streets, often still and quiet during the
morning, the people who lived behind the secret doors still
sleeping off whatever the night before had meant. The things
I liked best were the silence—no fighting kids or roar of the
washing machine—and knowing that no one—no one at all—

knew where I was. Small lemon-yellow birds pecked at my feet, and the bright white dogwood, with petals like blood tips, echoing Christ's crucifixion on the cross, were blooming. Some flowers I had never seen before—speckled red ones complete with fangs, protruding from their centers, looked like open-mouthed snakes, As I stared at them, glancing back and forth to my drawing tablet, I realized that, on my page, they had become the open vulvas of decaying dolls.

Once I passed the man I had seen undress at the topless-and-bottomless bar—he was in pants and low-heeled women's pumps, his small breasts pressing against a too-tight woman's cotton blouse. He looked exhausted, frail as he hurried into the A&P at the corner of Royal and St. Philip streets. I followed him from a distance. As he rushed up and down the cramped aisles, he jerked up a half-gallon of milk from the dairy counter and moved on to toiletries, where, from between the rubber gloves, the hair color, he picked up first a bottle of hydrogen peroxide, then a narrow cardboard box—*KY Jelly*, I read from my vantage—his hand seeming to know exactly where to go for each. He went to the checkout counter, and I followed; but by the time I got there with my basket holding a packet of cheese crackers and a Coke, he was gone, and the man in front of me was setting out twenty whole heads of garlic, making me wonder what he planned to cook.

I would meander into the gift shops, where I would shuffle through the postcards—pictures of enormous red lobsters, or even a house dripping Spanish moss, being hoisted through mobs of people; or floats on which costumed men and women stood, throwing down what looked like bead necklaces to the crowds. Sometimes I nibbled a pecan praline, or perused a rack of dusty paperbacks. One book, a history of New Orleans, mentioned Kate Chopin and her novel *The Awakening*, and I determined that the next time I went to the public library I would find it. I walked past the Voodoo Museum several times before I finally went inside: There, among the faded prints of Marie Laveau, a blond boy of about eighteen yawned as I looked at, and away from, things that at first seemed strange—dusty cellophane packets of something called gris-gris, flat stones with huge glaring eyes painted on them, stuffed black cloth dolls with gigantic penises, and the fanged, smiling heads of real alligators, stuffed and priced by size.

I also discovered the small galleries, where much of the work was watercolors of the French Quarter buildings with their black lacework balconies, or of Negro mammies in white turbans, long red-checked dresses, and white aprons. But there were also paintings of a kind I had never seen before: In one I glimpsed strange figures—neither male nor female, vaguely malevolent yet floaty—moving across the canvas amid uncertain lines, a thin wash of pastel color. In another, a muscular yet sensuous-looking dwarf was painted in a way that made his deformity seem almost beautiful. The first was signed by a woman, the second by a man; both names sounded French. And then there were the pictures in vivid primary colors, as simple as the kind I had colored in second grade but more complex, almost like stories that my eyes wanted to eat. *Sister Gertrude Morgan, Artist and Street Preacher*, read the caption beneath a photograph of a plump Negro woman dressed in white like a nurse. Across the white backgrounds of some of her paintings, tiny Negroes in white marched and danced, and small houses jumped about like bright white blocks. In others, some of the buildings were aflame while happy-looking white-clad people rose toward the sky, and the huge head of a white, brown-bearded Jesus looked down from a corner.

One day, as I walked down Bourbon Street, I heard the sounds of live music in the distance, and I stood with the crowds on the sidewalk, watching a jazz funeral procession approach—first, the Negro men in white shirts, black suits, playing the musical instruments; then the Negro women, dressed in dazzling white or brightly colored print dresses, broad, flowered picture hats, holding umbrellas and prancing and zigzagging and gyrating backward and forward and sideways among the musicians, singing and sobbing and moaning and dancing—"second-lining," it was called, I would learn later. It was so beautiful that tears were stinging the backs of my eyelids.

As the procession passed, I let myself walk along with the crowd, then wandered into a place called Felix's. Though it was only eleven in the morning, I sat right down at the bar, as though it were something I had done before, and to cover my

112

embarrassment ordered a half-dozen oysters on the half-shell. In the meantime, I sipped a Dixie, feeling that slight conscious-ness-changing dizziness I had only experienced at home with Bobby. When the oysters were set before me, I marveled at their wet sleekness, their silvery grayness—inside their irides-cent shells they seemed to quiver like small seals. I had never tasted an oyster raw before, but I squeezed on the lemon juice, tugged one free of the little muscle, the tiny fist with which it seemed to be holding itself in place, and popped it gingerly onto my tongue. The colors burst inside my mouth—pink, rose, magenta, plus a sweet, slimy saltiness that could have contained the whole ocean. The oyster tasted like something familiar, and suddenly I recalled that sunny day in the pasture when I had been nine, when I had put my finger inside my vagina, then tasted it, and the colors had burst behind my eyelids, inside my body, for the first time—it was a rainbow I had almost forgot-ten as a properly married woman of twenty. Later, my second husband, Johnny—who considered himself a connoisseur of both food and women—would like to say, whenever the sub-ject of shellfish arose, that a man who didn't like raw oysters was a man who couldn't deal with female sexuality (or woman, he could have noted as easily, for it was a texture, a flavor—a total sense memory—that immediately flooded me, during my first night with a woman lover). He was also the one who told me that the oysters were still alive until severed from their shell—something I'm glad I didn't know back then. For uncon-sciously I would have identified with them, quivering on their beds of ice, clinging to their shells for their very life. "Bound-aries—you lack boundaries," my final therapist told me. And it was true: I identified with everything and everyone. Indeed, it would be this very closeness, this desire for merging, that finally caused me to have to rip my beloved children from me like Velcroed paper dolls—so that we could all live, or at least hope to live.

But back then, I would sometimes find myself forgetting about all of them: the house in Airline Park; Bobby; even Dwayne, Rose, and Lily. It was as though some other person— that girl who had stolen the Artist's Colors, played in the cow droppings, lain in the pasture, making the colors rush into her legs—rose again untouched inside me. Then I would check the gold watch, rush back to them in the red convertible, and all afternoon, I'd feel guilty—letting them watch TV as long as they wanted, cooking a dinner even more elaborate than usual.

"What did you do today, darlin'?" Bobby asked each evening, as he came into the kitchen from the carport, kissing the side of my neck before I answered. "Oh, I took the kids to Mrs. Bloodworth's, then drove over to the library"—or "to the shopping center 'n wandered around awhile," I would murmur, pretending to be distracted by the meringue I was beating, or the apple-walnut stuffing I was poking inside the pork-chop pocketbooks. I suspected that Bobby had long since congratulated himself, feeling that he had dealt with the source of my angst with the gift of the red convertible, with his willingness now and then to take me into town, even to the French Quarter for dinner—and, in a sense, he had, though not in the way he suspected.

Later that night I would behave so responsively in bed that a smile of surprise would accompany his groans, his endearments, an enthusiasm he probably attributed to my new "happiness." But the next morning I would be exhausted, the involuntary gray filling my brain again. It was the first time I had ever lied to anyone about anything—though I told myself it was not really lying, just not telling. "What's wrong, Mama?" Dwayne would ask anxiously, coming up to the dinette chair where I sat looking out the window into the rectangle of crabgrass, and putting his arm around my shoulder like a grown man. And feeling even guiltier, I'd turn and smile, put my hands around his face, and kiss it all over, making the kissing noises that always made him giggle.

In some way I didn't understand, my secret trips to the French Quarter saddened me. Yet once I had begun them, I had no choice. I was in the grips of my compulsion, just as I had been when I had made the rose ashtray for Daddy—I had had the fantasy, and then I had had to execute it. It was something I would later feel about sexual desire—that once I had had the notion, had visualized the acting out of lust, even for a split second, it was as good as done—regardless of what havoc that acting out might play with my life. For I had to know secrets, whatever that knowing cost.

One morning, a group of white children herded by light-skinned Negro women invaded Jackson Square, carrying something that looked like papier-mâché alligator heads on long sticks, with which they pretended to bite each other, laughing and jabbering as they opened and closed the long green mouths with a latch at the bottom; and I felt a twinge, thinking of Dwayne, Rose, and Lily. ("Oh, I got them at Woolworth's," I replied casually when I returned home, after searching the souvenir shops, with one for each of them.) On another day, I watched a red-haired woman about my age—hair flaming, plump white thighs crossed—gaze petulantly out across the square. Chewing gum broadly, she seemed to look nowhere. But in a few minutes a black man sitting nearby swaggered over to her, whispered something in her ear, and she didn't look at him, or even change expression. Two shirtless, rough-looking long-haired men were lolling on a blanket nearby, laughing and passing around what looked like roll-your-own cigarettes. The snake flowers were quivering slightly in the warm breeze, their black tongues waving from their speckled heads like little erections.

And in that moment, I knew that I was somewhere I shouldn't be, somewhere I didn't belong. For who was I really but a housewife? A housewife with three babies and a husband who worked at a used-car lot on Airline Highway. A housewife who on occasion took out her drawing tablet, her charcoals, her pastels, and sketched what a woman would sketch—a redbird at the windowsill, Marmalade and Edward entwined on an afghan, or Lily on all fours, her round little ass jutting into the air. A woman who wanted everything to be perfect and pretty and feminine, who kept sealed off what was bubbling inside her, everything that was bloody and indelicate and carnivorous.

A woman who sobbed as she read Kate Chopin's story of her heroine Edna's choice to drown herself rather than give in to her improper desires and thus ruin the lives of her children; a woman whose paintings would later draw the same charges of notoriety Chopin had received for that rather innocent book.

115

But all I knew then was that having escaped South Alabama to live in a house with built-in appliances was no longer enough. For I had seen my first person like Iris. And a milieu that came closer than anything I had known to matching the strange pictures inside my head.

CHAPTER FIVE

THESE DAYS, to be at cocktail parties with people like Iris is hardly a novelty to me. We outsiders tend to cluster, and while others may imagine that we glory in our difference, it's really that we just accept it—as others accept going each day to their law offices or Junior League meetings.

I'm also used to the kind of gathering where people like Iris and me stand out as though illuminated, where indeed, we've been invited to do just that, to add a piquant, even thrilling flavor, something only slightly above the level of a special caviar, a peppery vodka, for those who usually lead lives of oatmeal; yes, to give them a chance to rub up to those who live on the edge, to be able to say they've met their own southern-variety Diane Arbus or Robert Mapplethorpe, a commodity of feeling, an offering—not a sex surrogate (though at times that, too) but a blotter, a sponge, a sacrifice surrogate. Indeed, we can't suffer too much for them.

But there was a time during the early part of my marriage to Bobby, when I was a young mother with no inkling of what was to come, when I barely knew what a cocktail party was, much less attended them as someone emblematic.

117

* * *

At a bash held by Bobby's ATO brothers, I saw Jimmy looking at me across the room. I was wearing a new two-piece peach wool jersey dress—the back swooped down like swan's wings, contrasting with the sheath skirt—and black suede slingbacks with gold-lamé heels. I had felt glamorous, wrapping the mouton jacket around my shoulders before driving off to pick up Bobby in the red convertible. It was the first real cocktail party—other than Big Bobby's raucous gatherings—I had ever been to, and standing among well-dressed others, sipping a bourbon and Coke, nibbling cold green beans that had been marinated—in what? oregano, garlic, vinegar?—I felt, at twenty-one, both sophisticated and dizzy with drink. "They're even *good* for you," the woman who had brought the green beans was slurring, waving one an inch from my face. Though a lot of the people around New Orleans had a strange Yankee accent, using words like *dem* and *dose*, all Bobby's friends talked like good ole boys. I could see him across the room, glass in hand, looking depressed, as a blond man who might have been a football player told a long story—I heard the words *stocks . . . bonds . . . profits.*

Now I felt Jimmy standing beside me. When I turned, I noticed for the first time the black specks floating within the pale liquid green of his sandy-lashed eyes; I followed the specks dizzily, feeling I might drown. "Did ah evah tell you—you are the *most* beautiful gull ah've evah seen?" he breathed, and I could tell he was drunk. I stepped back, uncomfortable; I was used to Bobby thinking I was pretty, but I was only beginning to realize that other men thought I was, too. Besides, his desire—I didn't know enough then to realize it was partly my own—was like a force field, a demand I was used to only sensing from Bobby, who at that moment stepped up, putting his arm around my waist, pulling me toward him.

"Ah wuz jes' tellin' your wife how gorgeous she is," Jimmy said, sloshing his drink onto the carpet as he raised it in salute. *Gorgeous*—the very word gave me another rush, and I moved closer within Bobby's embrace, for once experiencing it as protection rather than a prison. Bobby was whispering something in my ear, and despite the bourbon, I flushed, feeling like the tiny hummingbird I had seen that morning, trapped between the two panes of glass of a partly closed window. I knew that Bobby liked and admired Jimmy, who was different from Big Bobby and the men at the car lot, but now something bristled between them.

As we stood in the parking lot, getting into the convertible, Bobby clutched my hand, pulled me over for a sloppy kiss, forcing his tongue deep inside my mouth. "Yuh love me, don't yuh?" he said. "Yuh wouldn't like Jimmy better'n me, would yuh?" It was as though he could read my mind, knew of the weird rush I had had, looking into Jimmy's eyes. During the drive home, he repeated the question three times, rephrasing it to a mean-sounding "wudden *fuck* Jimmy" by the third, and by the time we arrived in Metairie, I felt as if I had done something wrong, even had already had sex with Jimmy. For it was I who had caused—just by being—Jimmy's desire and Bobby's anxiety. Hadn't Daddy told me time after time that it was my badness that had caused him to touch me? "Yuh jes' remembah—yuh're mah wife. 'N nobody else kin have yuh but me—*evah*!" Bobby mumbled as we went into the house through the carport, his hand firmly on my ass. As he paid the baby-sitter, I felt the cold grayness forming around my heart. I didn't want to have sex that night—I really wanted to lie in bed and ponder the marvel of the black flecks floating in Jimmy's green eyes—but I knew I would have to; in fact, Bobby would proba-bly want something extra: my hair in his hand, as he pushed my head down over his penis—I had never told him how I hated that—or my back arched or legs parted in some way that seared my muscles, making me long for an end to the burning. I was beginning to understand the rules: He wanted me to look beautiful—"sexy," he called it—wanted other men to look at me, but not for me to look back, my sexuality all his, a little bird caught permanently under the glass. But then, that was just part of my job as a wife, wasn't it?

Still, that night, my duty turned out a little differently. For I discovered that while Bobby was pounding away, I could still think of those moving black flecks, of Jimmy's face close to mine, and in that way I could almost feel the rainbows inside my legs again.

119

* * *

"Are they good?" Jimmy whispered into my neck. I turned
with a start. I was sitting at Felix's again, sipping an iced tea,
enjoying the tug of an oyster from its silvery shell, and I flushed.
He was the first person I had met here from my other life, and
I could tell in a moment that he felt that his seeing me here
gave him some kind of power over me. "I just like to come down
here some days, get away from the kids," I said guiltily. He had
on a suit with a vest; his sandy hair was slicked down. I felt self-
conscious in my cotton blouse and pedal pushers. In fact, shame
was flooding my whole body. I couldn't tell whether I was more
embarrassed by his catching me in my secret life or in my everyday clothes. Or was it the fantasies I had had that night after
the cocktail party? "Whadda you doin' here?" I mumbled, my
pleasure in the oysters gone. "I come for lunch sometimes—
they have great gumbo," he said, nodding in the direction of a
table full of similarly clad men. He stuck his hand in his pocket,
pressed a small piece of cardboard into my palm; without looking at it, I stuck it into my purse. "Mah business card—call me.
We could have lunch," he was saying, more sure of himself
than I had ever seen him, and from the look in his now-hazel
eyes, I knew only too well what he meant. "Please don't tell
Bobby," I pled, not wanting to say it but feeling I had to. "Don't
worry 'bout it, gull," he said, winking and touching my shoulder.
How had I ever thought he was handsome or sensitive? As he
walked away to join his group, I felt a kind of dread. I could
see him accepting a cigar from one of the men. Head down, I
paid my bill as quickly as I could and walked out into sunlight,
back toward Jackson Square, where I sat on a bench, the warm
but not hot sunshine lulling me into an uneasy peace.

Then I noticed the man—a boy, really, about my age—
sitting nearby, wearing a scuffed black leather jacket, a black
T-shirt, and a pair of the blue jeans that were just becoming
popular—though his already looked weathered, as did his cowboy boots. He was throwing peanuts to the pigeons in a lazy
sort of way—on the back of one hand was a tattoo of some
kind—and was looking off into space. His hair was black, a
straight lock slanting down over his forehead; his lashes were
long, casting shadows over high cheekbones: that cute actor,

James Dean—that was who he reminded me of, the one who had died in the car crash after his heart had been broken by Pier Angeli when she married Vic Damone. When he turned slightly toward me, his arm resting on the top of the bench, I could see that his chest was slender, and at the side of his throat was a bit of printed red cotton, like the flash of a bird's wing. A cigarette hung casually, sexily, from the corner of his mouth, and suddenly I wanted more than anything for him to look directly at me, to see through my disguise, to see how like him I was—even to look at me as Jimmy had, as Bobby did, as James Dean had looked at Pier Angeli. But when he did glance my way, it was to look past me toward a girl with orange hair—flaming, the noonday sun behind it—who was passing along the levee. As he rose to wander in that direction, I saw the coiled tiger, hand-painted on the back of his jacket, and he seemed to me in that moment, as the sunshine now formed an aura around him, to be the most gorgeous creature I had ever seen. As he passed, I felt a wave of helpless lust, a desire to press that thin, almost concave chest to mine, as intense as my nausea had been in Felix's. And with a fresh rush of shame, I realized what he would have seen had he looked at me: a housewife in Tangee pink lipstick, circle pin on her prim cotton shirt, her brown hair tied up in a chaste ponytail. I sat there until I had to leave to pick up Dwayne. Driving back toward Metairie, I realized—just as I had realized I would come alone to the French Quarter—what I would do to break my disguise, this impasse: I would take out the card Jimmy had given me, and I would call him and meet him.

I was still in the shock of these new thoughts as Dwayne, looking eagerly up into my face, jumped into the passenger side of the convertible. "Look, Mama, look," he said excitedly, bouncing up and down. In his palm was a sheet of poster paper on which that same little hand was imprinted in bright red tempera. "Oh, it's nice, honey," I said, too stunned by my decision to commit adultery to do anything but reach over, give him a perfunctory kiss. I was still stunned when the convertible swerved, crashing into a dogwood tree in full bloom, and I looked down to see my son, still and bloody on the seat beside me:

121

. . . as bloody, as bloody as the blood tips of flowers, and I was the crucified, the serpents of guilt crushing my skull as in a vise as I screamed, screamed in a voice that seemed to belong to someone else. The scream went on for a very long time; the whole time I was inside it, the guilt was crushing, crushing my skull. Then the scream turned to sirens, and I was being helped, stumbling, held by elbows, as some crazy woman somewhere cried, "My baby! My baby! My baby!" over and over and over, into the ambulance beside my still son to ride through the streets, the sirens screaming for me, in what seemed like a chariot of hell. And after a while, I was in the emergency waiting room, where Bobby tried to hold me as I pummeled his chest, and for the rest of the day I sat in numbness. "A bruise on his brain," someone called a neurosurgeon was saying.

At nine the next morning, after Bobby had convinced me to go home, to eat something and bathe, I was again seated beside my silent sleeping son, each needle in the arch of his tiny foot, the bend of his little elbow, piercing me afresh. I had tied my long ponytail with a ribbon, applied fresh mascara and lipstick, put on the navy dress with the sailor collar, the sheath skirt from my honeymoon. "My, don't you look pretty," the nun said brightly as she came into the room. And my heart plunged even further: How could any woman look pretty—take the time to comb her hair or apply lipstick, much less slip on a fresh dress, when her beloved son lay in a coma, moaning and writhing from side to side, possibly dying? But I already knew the answer: A bad woman could look pretty anytime. That my own injuries were merely small cuts, covered by Band-Aids shaped like butterflies or beauty marks, only made my shame worse. New snakes twisted my skull, making my ponytail feel like a helmet of steel. By then, I knew that the guilt was all mine— and that it would be and would be and would be. I bent over and kissed Dwayne, holding his olive hand tightly in mine—the same hand that he had dipped into finger paint to preserve for me the morning before—and vowed that if God would let him live, I would never again think of art, of the French Quarter, of my own perverse desires.

I vowed that and I meant it. I vowed that and I meant it and I lied.

* * *

Thus began my life of being good. Of contrition, even.

Oh, only partly through the dark dogma of Bible Belt sin and retribution, but via my belief—instilled as much by Aunt Darlene and the *Ladies' Home Journal* as the Bible—that by being a good woman, a good mother, I might possibly save my precious son's life.

And he did survive. But not without weeks of fear, and the hacking through of his skull—the very thought gave me nightmares, of someone reaching inside his head, opening it right near what had been the pulsing soft spot I had shielded with my hand just after his birth. And a thick seam left to crawl up one side of his scalp that would remind me, each time I brushed his soft brown hair, or ran my fingers through it, of my sin.

I was at his bedside almost every moment of the coma, was still there as, after a couple of weeks, his lids faintly blinking, he opened his jet eyes and began to whimper "Mama, Mama . . ." His gaze held mine like a newborn's, and I kissed him and kissed him, feeling almost as if he were one, that getting him back was as miraculous as his birth had been. I was there to hold him when the nurses came in with a new needle, an enema bag. Instead of twitching and moaning as he had when he had been unconscious, he buried his face in my breasts, crying piteously. But when the neurosurgeon came into the room to swing his gold watch before Dwayne's eyes, to look into them with little lights, to tap his knee with the rubber hammer, he began to giggle. He laughed again, listening to the stories of the cat who wore a hat and the elephant who used the telephone. He got brightly colored cards from Mama, Musette, Aunt Darlene; and from Wayne's mama, Homerdessa, he got lots of notes and a plush bear that I let him keep, though I never wrote her back.

The nurses had put a cot for me in his room, and Bobby came by with my clothes each day. "Eastah, Eastah, I miss you so much," he would murmur, bending me back in a kiss when the nurse wasn't in the room, putting his hand, his hard-on, between my thighs, despite Dwayne watching us from his bed. But once I had heard the news of Rose and Lily, I could barely conceal my impatience for him to leave so I could turn back to

123

Dwayne. Rose and Lily, who were with Desiree, would cry and fight when I talked with them on the telephone, and I would feel that strand of living flesh, now forked, attached at the farther ends to my two little girls, stretching over the miles, tugging painfully at my insides.

On my first night home, Rose and Lily ran to me, grabbing me around my knees and looking up into my face, inconsolably in love; crying and wrestling like little chimpanzees, both struggled to sit on my lap at once. That their brother had been carried in, unable to walk, his skull half-shaved and stitched, seemed less important to them than their fears: "You're not going to leave us at nurs'ry anymore, are you, Mama?" Lily asked anxiously, and I hugged her to me, reassuring her that I wouldn't. I had told Bobby that even if it could be fixed, I never wanted to see the red convertible again, and when I got home, a new blue Plymouth station wagon stood in the carport. We would use it, I told them, to go together to the shopping center. Relieved, Rose turned to analyze Dwayne's incision. "He got sewed, didn't he, Mama? Did they dood it with a sew machine?" she asked in wonder, and we all laughed, even Dwayne, who put his fingertips proudly to the purple welt. After I had dismissed Desiree and had finally gotten them all settled with fresh assurances that I would still be there in the morning, I got into bed in the modest granny gown I had worn in Dwayne's room in the hospital. "Whut about *me*, darlin'?" Bobby asked, pressing his face into my thin breasts as though he wanted to nurse again, and I thought how like Mr. Mole he looked without his glasses, with his watery eyes, his thick black eyebrows. I had one more duty to perform that night; was it the fact that I hadn't done it in a while that made it seem extra unpleasant, even distasteful?

"Ah'm worried about yo' mama—she's gittin' worse 'n worse," Aunt Darlene said when she called, barely concerned about Dwayne at all. But what was I supposed to do, with three babies, one of them crippled?

Because of his injury, Dwayne had temporarily relapsed to diapers, and I would reassure him, as I changed him, about what a big boy he was, that I just knew he would beat Lily, who

124

was still in diapers, in being potty-trained. Except for the scar on his head, his little body, wiry and muscular, with rosy balls and penis, was still perfect. Twice a week, we went to the hospital for physiotherapy, where he giggled as he was massaged and exercised, charming me and the young women therapists, who were laughing and falling in love with him, too. He graduated from the playpen to a walker in what the neurosurgeon called record time, with only a little weakness on the right side—"That might be with him always," the doctor said dismissively. Back home, I brought him his favorite foods on a tray as he sat like a child king amid pillows and new toys, watching Mr. Green Jeans or *The Mickey Mouse Club* while I watched him, my heart overflowing with fresh passion.

I kept my face scrubbed, left my toenails unpainted, and didn't care at all about the veins that had crawled onto my thighs like tiny red spiders. "What are those silver things, Mama?" Rose asked, touching my belly with a fingertip as we shared a shower. "They're stretch marks from when you were in my tummy, waiting to get out," I told her, remembering her weight inside me, heavy cream that refused to rise. "So pretty, so pretty—I hope I have those things, those stretch broads, when I grow up," she murmured tremulously, and I hugged her slick little body to mine. Her own skin was white as pink-tinged snow, her hair jet, her black-lashed eyes a deep indigo—Bobby's coloring deepened and fine-tuned. My scars, the giving up of my evil, frivolous self, seemed a small price to pay for her, Lily, and Dwayne's survival. I couldn't even recall what had driven me to the French Quarter; all I wanted was to be safe, a matron. I wore my long brown hair in a pageboy, held up at one side by a brown plastic barrette, and my daily outfits were almost like a uniform—a plain round-necked Orlon sweater with a white piqué Peter Pan collar, a chunky pleated plaid skirt, and penny loafers. I was vaguely aware that Bobby was not as happy with the new good me, the one who was Amish-plain, serious, who rarely had a drink with him or sat in his lap anymore but who went straight to the kitchen to wash the dishes after supper, then on to bathe Dwayne and Rose and Lily, and to read to them in their little beds. But I associated my new gravity with Dwayne's recovery. I was needed, necessary—the accident had

125

made that clear. And if sex was over for me, so be it. For now, in my heart, I knew: It was my children and me, and would be and would be—not me and any man.

Every few months at first, then every six months, then each year, I took Dwayne for electroencephalograms, the wires glued to his scalp amid his soft dark brown hair as I patiently waited, reading the magazines. "Looks good, all clear," the neurosurgeon would say. And I would know then that I had been good, that I had been able, by the sheer force of my will, to drive out the evil, to control the Satan within me: *'n sinners plunged— beneath THET flood lose ALL their guilt-tee stains . . . lose ALL their GUILT-tee STAINS*, crescendoed the choir singing in my brain. Dwayne's weakness, his awkwardness on one side, was gradually disappearing—oh, he was left with a vague limp, there was a slight tension in the way he held his pencil, and later, he would lack the motor skills to hit the ball in Little League. But by then I considered my son too good for such bourgeois activities. Just as I wanted my children to have special foods, special books, special knowledge, I wanted them to have *aspirations*, dreams having to do with art and higher things. My snobbery, once based on wearing White Shoulders when Mama had worn Evening in Paris, in baking puff pastries rather than poor man's cobbler (made with white bread rather than a real crust)—which had been about all we could afford back on the farm where the blackberries grew wild—was now of a different sort. The insurance company had paid us a settlement, and I insisted that we put it away for camp and art and music lessons. And though Bobby complained that I spoiled him, Dwayne seemed sweet, sweeter than ever to me—flesh of my flesh, my male part made manifest.

But all I knew then was that I was twenty-one years old, and that once again, my curiosity, my perverse desires, had hurt someone I loved. To the list of my victims—Musette, Mama— I added my beloved son, Dwayne. And all I had to do to remind myself was run my fingers through his soft brown hair, feel the thick seam on the left side of his head.

And foolishly, I imagined that I had conquered those desires forever—that the worst that could happen already had.

* * *

Some days, I took the children to the Isaac Delgado Museum of Art, where they ran up and down the corridors as I tried to shush them and show them the Impressionist paintings of Edgar Degas. ("He visited here in 1871–72," I said, trying futilely to interest them.) I pointed out the big pictures that looked more like musty representations of the English countryside than anything similar to the Cajun lushness of New Orleans. (As teenagers, they would rebel against museum-going just as other kids rebelled against church.) Dwayne hadn't been calmed by his accident; he seemed more energetic than ever, spurring his sisters on to new wildnesses, hanging out over the balcony rails as I sucked in my breath in terror, or picking cigarette butts out of containers of sand, pretending to smoke them. They had made up their own curse word—*bott*—and they would yell it at passersby from the backseat of the Plymouth as I drove, and I couldn't help but laugh, too. Around them, I felt more like a child than I ever had back on the farm. When a policeman held up his hand for me to stop in a line of Metairie Avenue traffic, I stuck out my tongue at him, and Dwayne, Rose, and Lily did the same.

We went regularly to the New Orleans Public Library on Loyola Avenue, where I settled them into the children's department before picking out books for myself. I shivered, reading *Madame Bovary* and *Anna Karenina*, thinking how close I had come to their fates. Faulkner's Temple, in *Sanctuary*, was almost—in her Memphis whorehouse—as sin-filled as I felt myself to be; while the rest of his dark vision was so familiar that it seemed to have been imprinted in my cells since birth. On the other hand, Thomas Wolfe's *Look Homeward, Angel* struck me as naively hopeful; while Conrad's *Heart of Darkness*, Camus's *The Stranger*, and Gide's *The Immoralist* matched my nunnish moods. And when I read *The Outsider* by Colin Wilson, I felt immediately that I had discovered a heart as alienated as my own. I sought answers to my restlessness in *Modern Man in Search of a Soul* by Carl Jung, *The Sense of Beauty* by Santayana, and *On Love* by Ortega y Gasset, but after reading them I felt further stirred: as excited as I had been by going to the French

Quarter, but in a way that seemed safe, contained as it was inside my mind. How I learned of these books, I can't recall: No one around me—certainly not Mama, Daddy, Bobby, or Big Bobby and Miss Lisa—read such books, and they were certainly never mentioned in the *Ladies' Home Journal* or the *Times-Picayune*. It was just that they were there, at the New Orleans Public Library, as though awaiting me, my curiosity.

But best were the art books. That the library would actually allow me to check them out, carry them home, made me feel richer than I ever had dreamed. The back issues of *Art in America* were filled with images that shocked yet thrilled me, in the ugly-beautiful way the motel room had on my and Bobby's honeymoon. Using the bibliography of *The Artist's Handbook*, I systematically searched out each of the works that told how other artists had done things. I flipped slowly through heavy tomes, their huge pages filled with color plates. Their texts used a language I had never heard or read before, a speech that described an artist's or a critic's way of looking at paintings. Read apart from the pictures, the text didn't seem to make sense; but reading it side by side with the pictures, I felt as though a door had been opened: I understood everything without really understanding the words. The shapes, the forms, the brush strokes, the colors (so luscious I could eat them), communicated as directly as Dwayne, Rose, or Lily had, tugging at my nipple with aggressive pink mouths to start up the flow of milk.

Modigliani, with his distorted faces, their mongoloid features, scared me, gave me the same weird feeling that I had had thinking of the bodies layered beneath the earth, in danger of detaching, drifting out to sea. Picasso's blue period was gentle—I especially like a painting, "The Mother," that the book said he had painted when he was even younger than I was; but I didn't like the cubed edges, the distortions of his later periods— there seemed to be an ugly arrogance in them. I couldn't look long at Edvard Munch's "The Scream," reminding me as it did of Dwayne's accident. Van Gogh's paintings were like screeches of joy or pain—I couldn't quite tell which; shrieks that I wanted to stare at until I could hear them more clearly, and when I did, his great gobs of paint made me almost dizzy: what would they look like close up, from an inch away? Matisse's goldfish, swimming amid flowers and pieces of furniture, were like the feeling I had with the kids when we were laughing, having fun. Gauguin's curved brown women were as peaceful as phlegm. Because I was uneducated, I could feel anything about the paintings I wished, and feeling was how I first experienced them. And when the feeling was good, I would look more closely, trying to see how the artist had done it.

And as I looked, a door opened inside my mind, the *paintings*, my *own* paintings, were there—kicking against the walls of my brain, churning and writhing, little beings waiting to be born. I was undeterred when I read in Jung that "the artist's life cannot be otherwise than full of conflicts, [that] the creative force can drain the human impulses to such a degree that the personal ego must develop all sorts of bad qualities—ruthlessness, selfishness and vanity. . . ." For I knew I already had those traits, and I envisioned the romance of the artist's life as being worth the price, headier than any existence I had dreamed, but especially that of a Metairie housewife. *Art and ideas*—could anything be more exciting?

One afternoon, still exhilarated by the art books, I stopped at an art-supply store on the way home, even though I knew that the kids would run around like wild Indians while I tried to browse through the delicious implements. But I bought them each colored pencils, compasses, and tablets; and they sat on the floor, turning circles into fat people, fighting only mildly. As I drove back toward Airline Park, we sang a song we had made up about the Plymouth, which we called the "Great Big Bouncing Blue Ball." Besides my three beautiful children, I had a stack of delectable art books from the library, big flat paperbacks—*How to Watercolor, How to Paint with Oils*, and *A Beginner's Approach to Perspective*—a pristine white canvas, stretched in a frame of pine, and a box of acrylics, colors as pure, as luscious, as the azalea blossoms in March, the lemon-yellow wings of the birds I had seen in the French Quarter. Now I would prepare a perfect dinner, bathe my sweet children, and go to bed with dreams of swirling color.

But as I turned into our driveway, my heart fell: Bobby came out into the carport with a plastic tumbler of whiskey, not even looking at our piles of books or packages of art supplies. "Whyah yuh been, Miss Bebe? Yuh know I like yuh to be hyah when I get home, that I like my din-din by seven," he whined, putting a hand to my breast and squeezing it just as Dwayne looked up from where he was struggling with my books and packages. As Bobby followed me inside, his warm breath on my neck, I felt as blank as the canvas. My mood, the colors in my head, dissolving like cotton candy, I hurried to stick a chicken beneath the running faucet, put the water on for rice.

I had devoured Erich Fromm, Viktor Frankl, and Carl Jung. But I didn't have to have read psychology to know that after a time my restlessness, my criminal self, was beginning to bleed through again, like the color in a madras plaid blouse. For one thing, I had tried, unsuccessfully, to convince Bobby to move us closer in, out of the ugly little house in Metairie, maybe into a bigger one in, say, the Garden District? "Then the children could grow up watching the streetcar named Desire go by," I said, delighted by my own literary reference, not yet knowing that the streetcar had not gone that way. But Bobby hadn't noticed my cleverness at all: According to him, our option to buy at a low rate of interest was too good to give up, and besides, he had *always* lived on that side of town.

Worse, I was no longer content with what I could do on my own with the pastels, the paints. When I copied the drawings in the ads for the Famous Artists School and sent them off with the filled-in coupon, I always received a glowing, if printed, letter, offering to teach me more by mail for the huge sum of $430. But now I heard of something even better: ADULT EDUCATION: TULANE AND SOPHIE NEWCOMB COLLEGE read the ad; miraculously, among the courses listed was "Basic Drawing and Painting"—that wouldn't be deserting them, would it?

It was harder to get Bobby's attention, for he now drank red whiskey every night. Reading from the brochure, I sat on his lap, wearing my new pink shortie gown. I had even painted my toenails, and I secretly told myself I would go down on him ten times if I had to.

"Darlin', you know I don't like you to drive by yuhself at night," he protested, uninterested in the piece of paper I waved before him. I could feel his hard-on rising, and I was excited, too, thinking of going to an art class on an actual college campus. It was like imagining flying in an airplane to New York City, or—as I had dreamed not long before—lying naked with ten boys in a row like the one I had seen in Jackson Square that day!

And it did turn out to be that wonderful.

As I drove to the first painting class, I told myself—pushing back the thought of how nothing could have stopped me—how lucky I was to have a husband like Bobby, who would let me go out alone at night and take art classes.

When I walked into that classroom filled with easels, I felt as if I had come home. Most of the students were people in their late twenties or early thirties, plus a few odd-looking older people. A scrawny-looking naked woman, her dark hair twisted in a coil at her neck, sat on the edge of a platform at the front of the room, smoking a cigarette. The instructor, a thirtyish, sensitive-looking man with curly dark red hair and beard, assigned me an easel and explained what we would do. I felt that I had stood in this very place before, and when we began drawing, the charcoal lines flowed deliciously from beneath my fingertips, as if they had been dictated by someone else. The instructor came over and stood silently beside me, a strange look on his face. During the break, some of the other students stood around, looking at my drawing without speaking. "Please call me Martin—I'm glad you're in this class," the instructor said as I left. I drove home, floating in a bubble of elation that didn't burst until I pulled into the driveway.

Inside the house, Bobby was watching TV. "Come on ovah hyah, Miss Bebe," he said without looking away. When I did, he pulled me into his lap. As he sipped his drink, his free hand went between my legs. And I was a blank canvas again. Later that night, he would be a familiar weight, slipping in and out; the creaminess inside me was beginning to match the creaminess of my days now. And occasionally, in some mindless way, my body even desired him, craving the loosening he offered.

Every other Saturday, Bobby was off from the car lot. He had taken to working in our overtrimmed yard, manicuring it beyond perfection. At my request, he had built a little pond in the sterile backyard. I would sit beside it and draw—the fish, the pine trees, the hedges—on paper, even those hedges looked interesting.

"Look, Mama, look—the red fish in the pond look like the redbirds in the pine trees," Lily said, pointing at their reflection. Squatting on her fat thighs, she was making her own drawings— of the birds, of the cats, Edward and Marmalade, walking away, oversized balls swaying. But more than drawing, she liked making poems: *The little birds have eyes/ that burn through their skulls,* she block-printed tediously as I helped her with each letter. And: *The red fish fly through the air/ flapping their red wings/ that are really fins./ They sit in the pine trees/ trying to breathe. But they can't/—they're fish, aren't they?*

"Is it hurt, Mama?" Lily asked anxiously as we walked through Schwegmann's, looking at the fish behind glass, its one eye gazing at us from its icy bed. "He doesn't feel anything, honey," I assured her. I had begun writing little poems with her in a composition book: *Spread open on that ice, your eye glares at me, and I feel guilty,* I wrote that night, and then helped her write another one: *To a Fish in a Seafood Counter: Your eye looks like glass/ with tinfoil under it, and a big black dot./ You look at me with it/ and I want to ask: Does lying there like that hurt?* She looked puzzled as I explained about colons, but said it over to herself, liking the effect.

"Remember the man we saw, coming out of the back of the store?" I asked, thinking of the butcher we had seen, wiping his hand on his bloodied whites as he walked toward the Coke machine. "Well, here's my poem about him: *Wearing bloody aprons/ the butchers have coffee and cake.*" "Mommy! that's good!" she squealed, grabbing up the pencil again.

As she would again and again: *Divide the bush into four parts/ plant them where you will:/ Bushes cannot scream,* she would declare almost twenty years later, in her incarnation as Lillee, Jazz Poet—in memory, she would explain to her East Village audience in preface to her reading, of her father chopping away at the wisteria vine in our little yard in the horrid suburbs of New Orleans.

132

* * *

"Why in the world do yuh buy 'em this stuff, Easter?" Bobby complained as he walked into the kitchen one evening. Dwayne, Rose, Lily, and I were shaping clay into fat cats in various poses to bake in the oven for one hour, as the instructions on the box read; we planned to paint them the next day with tempera. I was already envisioning two orange ones with Edward and Marmalade's subtle stripes, then a tortoise one, and a calico. Dwayne's dimpled face was smeared with the gray clay; the sleeves of his cowboy shirt, rolled to the elbows, were crusted with it—he was the best and most enthusiastic of the three.

Rose and Lily, fighting over which cat was to be Marmalade, which to be Edward, wore gray streaks up their cotton dress fronts. I wanted them to feel they could do creative things anytime. In a big mixing bowl on the kitchen counter, I saved every broken eggshell; when the bowl was full, Lily and I put them between a dish towel and rolled them flat with a rolling pin—Lily squealing at the satisfying crunch—and we used them to make mosaics. Spreading the cardboards from Bobby's shirts with Elmer's glue, we would sprinkle on the shiny shards of eggshell; wait for them to dry; then paint them with tempera from the huge jars I now had everywhere.

"Honey, they *need* to have creative experiences," I would say, placating Bobby with a kiss. I could tell that he didn't like my new uniform of long, loose hair, turtleneck, and blue jeans any more than he had liked my costume of scrubbed face, plain sweater or turtleneck, pleated skirt, and bobby socks. "Yo' wife's turnin' into a reg'lar li'l beatnik, ain't she?" I heard Big Bobby sneer when I stopped by the car lot one day. By the look on Bobby's face, I could see that he didn't have to add, Cain't you *control* 'er, Son?

Along with learning that Bobby didn't like messes, I also knew that he basically liked straight lines and things that made sense; that he didn't really understand the voluptuous curves I favored in my drawings and paintings, the twists and turns that looked—but didn't *really* look—like people and things. "Now what the hell's *that* s'posed to be?!" he would snort, looking at my pictures. He seemed to think I was trying to pull something

133

over on him. In fact, the only curved thing he seemed to like was my body. Lily was auburn-haired, dark eyed, rose-colored, and curved, and he tolerated her. Rose, snow white and jet-haired, was straighter, more slender, almost as boyish looking as Dwayne. He ignored her, but Dwayne he didn't seem to like at all these days. "Mother, not Mama," he would correct him from behind the *Times-Picayune* when Dwayne came running in, excited, with a spider or a bird's eggshell. "Can't you do something about his manners?" he would complain as Dwayne gobbled his dinner, wanting to hurry back outside before dark. It was almost as if Bobby was jealous of him.

One morning, thinning tempera with water, I did a picture on manila paper: Dwayne and I, walking naked in a green field, the sun before us, dark clouds at our backs. One of his small shoulders is hunched; I painted his nipples a deep rose, emphasizing the hollow of his chest, the dark circles of his Seminole blood coloring the flesh beneath his eyes. His fine brown hair, my long brown hair, are blowing in the same direction: the two of us against the world. It was the way I had always thought of us, since I had first dreamed him: "The Lil-lee of—the Val-lee—the bright 'n shining star . . ." I hummed as I worked.

"Like the woodcuts of Dürer," Martin said gravely when I took the painting into class. The rest of the students stood around to look. A woman from New York was visiting, and after the class she introduced herself, asking if we could have lunch. "If I can get a sitter," I said absently, wondering who Dürer was, resolving to look him up the next day.

The woman was Oriental, so I suggested a Chinese restaurant near Metairie. I couldn't tell whether she liked the food, or me: As she spoke, she was formal, almost ceremonious. Drinking cup after cup of tea from the little cups without handles, she talked mostly about New York, the painters whose works she sold at her gallery there; it was like a foreign world to me. Her hair was a thick jet, sliced bluntly at the bottom in a way I had never seen before; her dress was a plain oatmeal sheath with little nubs all over it. She wasn't the kind of woman Bobby or Big Bobby would have considered attractive. But I had a feeling that in her world, she probably was, in the same odd way that *Vogue* models, as skinny as rails, were. Sitting beside her, I felt messy, unfinished, too voluptuous. But as she spoke in her measured way, I also felt a growing excitement stirring inside me like sex, and glimpsed a vague vision of vertical imagery, swirling color—taxicab yellow and fire-engine red—that seemed to be New York. As she pulled her sleek leg inside the rental car, she pressed a card into my hand: PAULA LING, THE LING GALLERY "Call me when you come East," she said, as though my traveling there was foreordained.

Dwayne was still wetting the bed, although it had been three years since his accident. They all had the chicken pox and the measles at once, and for weeks their rooms stank of urine. Then Dwayne had little white worms that crawled out of his anus at night; on the pediatrician's instruction, I pulled the cheeks of his buttocks apart as he slept, looking for the pearllike white eggs, applying the larvae-killing salve. A bulge popped out at the base of Lily's plump belly, and when she went to the hospital for the hernia operation, I just took my drawing tablet with me, and, sitting beside her bed, sketched and ate Fudgsicles. When Rose came home from school one day with a fever of 104, a cough that turned out to be pneumonia when we got to the emergency room, I knew she would be all right: Our future was like a bright, if incomplete, painting, the colors of azaleas and wisteria blossoms.

I should have known that something bad would happen to me for the joy I had found. And it did.

Strange things were taking place in the world around me; the news on my kitchen TV made my insides churn. Girls my age were marching with the Negroes (whom I would soon learn to call blacks) and getting arrested over in Mississippi and Alabama—I wondered what Mama, Aunt Darlene, and the preacher at the Church of God thought about *that*? People talked more and more about a place called Vietnam—already, some Americans called "advisers" had been killed there. And not long before, college students had rioted in San Francisco, angry when their teachers were fired by something named the Committee on Un-American Activities.

I had the strange feeling of living on the brink of something—something that would soon turn out to be a war in which boys my age and younger lay dying in jungles on the other side of the world. It would also become a time when women my age, dressed in a way Aunt Darlene definitely wouldn't have approved, would be parading with banners, angrily protesting the very life I had dreamed, back in South Alabama, of living. And by then, I would be wondering why I had wanted it either.

Too, it would become a period when many—apparently unaffected by the teachings of the Church of God or anything similar—would be wearing flowers in their hair; and draped in what looked like tableclothes, would be smoking something called marijuana while sleeping twelve to a room in a slum called Haight-Ashbury (I would wonder then if the boy in the black leather jacket was one of them). And after a while, more students—openly exhibiting a rage that thrilled me—would be demonstrating at a place called Columbia, burning up flags and even themselves.

From the beginning, the people in my art class seemed more connected to that world than I was. My teacher, Martin, with his long-lashed eyes, his serious demeanor—the way he would stand looking gravely at what I had done, his hands in his corduroy pockets before speaking—was unlike any man I had ever known. Every other man—from Daddy to Bobby— had focused on my breasts, belly, legs, and what was between them. My talent seemed to be what interested Martin, not the way I looked or whether I had on a tight skirt. I now wore my hair long, slightly teased and center-parted, and my new blue jeans to class, and while he didn't seem actively to notice my appearance, I could tell I was pleasing to him. "Would you like to go to the Maple Leaf, have a beer?" he asked one night as class was ending. "I can't do that!" I said, my face flushing. But the next week, I felt differently: "How 'bout that beer?" I asked, trying to sound casual.

And that was how I, who had vowed to be good forever, began my life of art, of adultery.

Martin said my tears were like crystal and talked to me about light and color and the tints—red, aubergine, nutria—in my brown hair, about the delicate shell pink of my nipples, and the color of my cunt. He wanted me to come live with him in his house in the woods, the house he had built himself—to eat peaches and drink wine and raise rabbits and ride horses and read poetry aloud in bed, to bake bread and have a garden and fuck and suck each other. He wanted me to leave Bobby and do all this with him.

But he didn't want Lily, Rose, and Dwayne.

One day I drove the children to Martin's house, where they stood around looking puzzled, then bored, playing at the edge of the woods while Martin and I went inside.

"Your tears are like crystal," Martin said again on that last day, holding me lightly to him but already letting go a bit. That he was gentle made me cry even harder. And in truth, I couldn't tell whether I was crying for the loss of him or of my life as it could have been.

"Why did we go there, Mama?" Rose asked, puzzled on the way home. "Because he's an art teacher and has a lot of pretty art at his house," I said. "Oh, yeah—he did! 'N he let us have those kinda chocolate cookies you won't give us!" Lily agreed. I noticed that Dwayne looked sullen, even angry. "But it's better we don't tell Daddy," I went on, encouraging them in their first lies.

Unfortunately, I drew too well. Out of my longing, I had made sketches of Martin and me, a tablet full of them, me in bed with a man who was obviously not Bobby, a man with a beard, hooked nose, thick biceps, short torso. As I came in the door with the groceries one Saturday, I saw the book spread open on the dinette table: "I can't stand it! I can't stand it!" Bobby was sobbing, his face in his hands. "I can't stand it, thankin' of some othah man's dick inside you!"

Dwayne, across the room in front of the TV set, turned toward us, looking anxious; my eyes reached desperately out to his, wanting to ease his pain as much as Bobby's. But now Bobby was on me, shaking me by the shoulders. "I can't stand it, do you hear me, I can't stand it!" he cried loudly.

For three nights, he cried and ranted, Dwayne, Rose, and Lily standing around solemnly, afraid of what might happen next. On the third night, I ran into the bathroom, locked the

door, grabbed up my Diamond metal nail file and scratched
NEVER on my forearm.

"Here!" I screamed at him back in the bedroom, holding
up the message, blood beading at the jagged edges of the letters.
"Here. I'll never do it again. *Never!*"

He pushed me backward across the bed, not paying any
attention to the blood. I didn't either, just to the hard bone of
my body, the circular O that at first refused to give, then opened
as he tore aside the crotch of my panties, my shorts, forcing
himself inside me. From the other side of the slammed bedroom
door, I could hear Lily crying "Mama? Mama?" and Rose shush-
ing her. But they had scurried away before I could extricate
myself and go to them.

The next Saturday when I came in from grocery shopping,
Bobby had chopped down the pine tree beside our bedroom
window, and along with it the wisteria vine, which had been in
full bloom. "It was gonna die anyway," he said when I began
crying, thinking of how I loved the frilly lavender blossoms
pressed against the glass, the only respite in the dull yard.

The next week, Marmalade was hit by a car; his tail, severed
at its base, was replaced by a row of black cross-stitches. Dwayne
would rush out, looking sick, when the cat slunk into a room,
ears back as though he had been castrated. But when Edward
began fucking Marmalade atop the stump in the backyard,
Dwayne and Rose snickered, as Lily looked on, puzzled: "Aren't
they both *boys*, Mama?" Soon Marmalade went into the basement and quietly died; Dwayne dragged him out stiff and matted a week later. At the Humane Society, Rose and Lily chose
a new yellow kitten, one with the yellow eyes of a mongoloid.
"I want *him*, Mama—he's pitiful-looking!" Lily cried, pointing
him out among the healthier ones. "Yeah, maybe we can heal
him up," Rose, who was currently into doctor sets, concurred.
"What will we name him, Mama?" they mused in the car on
the way home. "Pathos," I pronounced absently. Within weeks,
despite Rose's ministrations, Pathos had died, too.

Every night, Bobby came home, poured a tumbler of Wild
Turkey, and talked about my adultery. He talked about it at the
dinner table, and on the way to visit Big Bobby and Miss Lisa.
Then he began to talk about Wayne, and how had I gotten

Dwayne—he wanted to know all the details. I felt as if I were in the grips of a white-hot vise—he wouldn't stop until I told him, and then when I told him, he wanted me to tell him again. He wanted to know everything Martin had ever said or done to me, wanted to know why he was not the man Martin was.

He would put his face into his hands and cry about how I could do such a thing to him, how he wasn't man enough for me, until I would wish he would leave me, though I had no idea how I would take care of myself and the children. In fact, I had had a flash flood of relief at the thought that *yes, now he would leave, it would be over,* that day when I had come into the house to find him holding my sketches. But that was not to be.

One night, as he lurched at the sink, about to refill his glass, it slipped from his grasp, breaking; a jagged edge slashed the tender part of his palm. "*See?* See whut yuh've done now, Eastah?" he cried as I wrapped the gushing wound in a towel, and I knew he was right.

"You're not meant for each other, Mother," Lily said with sad, watchful eyes, her lips prim. She stuck a rock in the back-yard and said it was a gravestone: "My body lies over the ocean, my body lies over the sea . . ." she hummed, drawing on it a picture of my and Bobby's heads, kissing, trying to keep us as we were when we still loved each other—or at least when Bobby loved me.

One day I was so upset that I drove out to Martin's, even knowing he didn't want me anymore. And as Bobby came in from the carport that night, I could tell right off that he had checked the mileage on the Plymouth again. I was standing there innocently beating a bowl of egg whites, and he came straight up to me, reached beneath my skirt, and jabbed two fingers inside me. "God. Anothah man's cum drippin' down your filthy legs!" he cried, then shoved me over, forcing me to grab my ankles to keep from falling. "You bitch, you bitch, you bitch!" he sobbed over and over as he fucked me. As my face hung between my legs, Dwayne's anguished eyes met mine from across the room.

At other times, Dwayne, Rose, and Lily—ages ten, eight, and seven—seemed happy. Rose and Lily shared a room with bunk beds; they had jungle sheets, full of animals, and our new

139

cats, Chaos and Pathos Two, slept there with them. They played recorders, and then real flutes, and drew pictures of underground purgatories and torture chambers, full of spiked pits, pools of flame, writhing bodies. Rose did scientific experiments, operating on her G.I. Joes, her Kens and Barbies, painting Mercurochrome on their wounds, their crotches, then layering them with Band-Aids. Every afternoon, they sat enthralled before *Dark Shadows*; every Saturday night, they religiously watched *Outer Limits*, which, because they believed in UFOs and aliens, they viewed as literally as a newscast. One day, as Lily and Rose followed me through the supermarket, Rose unfurled a horoscope from a gum machine: "You will have an argument with your mate," she read aloud. "Who's my mate? Oh, yeah—Lily!"

For Lily, cats were the metaphor for our family life: "Mama, don't you think cats are like people?" she asked, delighted at her own ingenuity. "Marmalade was like Daddy, Pathos is like me, Chaos is like Dwayne. . . . And you're *be-oou-ti-ful*, like Lulu," she said, referring to our new calico, "and I guess Edward—Edward is like Rose!" she went on. "Bossy!"

Dwayne, wearing cowboy boots, took acting and guitar lessons, but he seemed to want something different: "Mom, I've got this great album—" he said excitedly, coming into the kitchen. "Mothah, not Mom," Bobby corrected from the dinette table, where he sat reading the *Times-Picayune*. Dwayne held up the cardboard cover, printed with a picture of a group of young men whose hair looked as if it had been trimmed with the aid of a soup bowl. "And now that I've got my paper route, I'm gonna make so much money that I can have all the albums I want!" He pulled out a notepad from his pocket and began excitedly multiplying and dividing. His fifth-grade teacher had said he was near-genius level in math, that with his personality, he should be a great entrepreneur.

All the way down to South Alabama for our annual visit to Mama and Musette, Bobby talked about my adultery. In Gulfport, we sat looking at the water, watching the kids run in and out of the faint breakers, and he grilled me over and over for details, extracting promises. It was hot, steamy hot. The palmettos were quivering against the sky; the Spanish moss hung motionless, like a dead woman's hair. The air had a shiny yellow glaze. As Bobby talked, I tried to sketch; Rose and Lily chased each other in and out of the frothy tide; and Dwayne sat sullenly at a distance, his arms around his knees, staring off at the sky. I was wearing the first bikini I had ever had, a dark blue one with white trim that I had ordered from Sears Roebuck—since I had become more involved with my painting, I had become, to Bobby's irritation, less interested in shopping, in searching out the kind of clothes he liked. I was conscious of the slick white curls of stretch marks carved into the skin of my belly, which, after my three pregnancies, was white, soft, puffy. With my long brown hair, my dimpled baby face, I could have been a teenager, walking with my brothers and sisters, but my belly belied everything. As we walked along the beach, I caught Dwayne looking at it. At eleven, he still had the slight limp, and baby fat padded his breasts in a way that I could tell embarrassed him; but he was as tall as I was, and suddenly, disproportion- ately—overnight, it seemed—had become thick, muscular, in other parts of his body.

At first, sitting on the sand, I sketched and Bobby and I argued. Then Bobby took some pictures of us, standing at the edge of the water. "Do yuh wanna go up to the room while they're down hyah playin'?" he asked meaningfully, pulling the towel closer around his neck, down over his still-skinny white chest covered in fine black curls. When I mutely shook my head, he stalked off angrily, back toward the motel.

I put down my sketchbook and stretched out on the sand, closing my eyes; I could feel the cold grayness descending. "What's the matter, Mama?" Dwayne suddenly said from above me; when I opened my eyes, he was like a grown man standing over me. Then, kneeling, averting his gaze, he began to cover my body—feet, ankles, calves, thighs—with the damp heavy sand, beating it down with his fists. When he reached my groin, my belly, he jumped up, throwing a fistful of the sand down near my face, and ran toward the ocean. But not before I had seen his look, black with misery. He could have been a glass, standing between me and the sun, magnifying my pain until it burst into a flame that was dangerous to both of us.

* * *

Back at the same motel we had visited for our honeymoon, the children had a room adjoining ours. That evening after supper, Bobby pulled me into bed with him despite my protests that the children were still up, that the door between the two rooms was warped—that I could still see the light from the TV flickering through the crack and could hear them laughing and jostling.

The next day, as I repacked their clothes, Rose's little notebook, the one in which she kept her secret code, her scientific experiments, fell open among the T-shirts and socks. *Daddy pulls mother's top off. Then he pushes her legs apart,* she had written in her careful hand. *He sticks his finger into her front botem, then into her back botem. Mother is crying, she puts her hands over her face. Now Daddy puts his thing into her back botem. Mother is crying that it hurts. . . .*

"You look funny, Mama," Dwayne said, looking over at me from beside the cot the management had put into the room for him. He was pulling his striped polo shirt over his head, and his eyes, emerging, looked like a turtle's. I tried to smile, but instead felt something give way inside my body. I fell to the blue acrylic carpet, unable to move.

It wasn't the way I wanted to go back to South Alabama, leaning on the cane the local chiropractor had sold us after his "adjustment" for what he called "a back virus." Feeling very old and tired, I held on to Bobby for support—I was too tired even to hate him anymore. But at least the tears, which had run down my cheeks continuously for the past two days, had stopped.

Musette looked at me with worried eyes, but Mama, thin and mean-mouthed in her wheelchair, didn't even seem to notice. And would I have wanted to confess that despite my earlier feelings of omnipotence, I had ended up recreating her life— that the scenes that went on between Bobby and me were not that different from those I had watched between her and Daddy, that at twenty-six, I was a crippled woman and as much a prisoner as she had ever been? Instead I focused on showing off, bragging on the children, my house, how much money Bobby was making.

I was so weakened that I even let Dwayne visit Homerdessa. She looked large and homey in her oversized print housedress, reaching out her fat arms to suck Dwayne up inside them, but her eyes were little and mean, as Wayne's had been. And I remembered what had happened the last time I had let him go: He had come back with what looked like a white Oriental food container full of more goldfish. When I told Homerdessa he already had five of them, the blood suffused her fat face, and she dashed the container toward the ground, where the red fish writhed and gasped among the pebbles while Dwayne looked at me as if it were my fault, and Rose and Lily screamed.

This time, after a few hours, Dwayne came back to Mama's house with an air rifle, a new pocketknife, and a photo of Wayne in his ill-fitting army uniform—it was a dark face I had never wanted to see again. And I certainly didn't want Dwayne to have weapons. But as he ran around shooting BBs at Musette's chickens, I was too drained to protest.

"Ah hope he don't take after his gran'daddy on thet side," Aunt Darlene said, watching him from the window, referring to the common knowledge that Wayne's father had spent most of his life, until he was stabbed to death by another prisoner, in the state prison over at Atmore on an armed-robbery charge. All that time, Homerdessa had been a single mother with just Wayne—some said she had still been sleeping with him when he was twelve—working as a clerk at the county courthouse, and now she even had a pension. And my grief was that, having lost Wayne, she wanted my son. And I could feel myself weakening, losing my grip on him.

When Mama did talk, she regaled me with how Musette was out running around with boys, and that she didn't have any control, that my sin had ruined her life and probably my sister's, too. Musette was tall and gawky, but she had breasts like little melons, sticking right off her chest; I had secretly worried that she was old maidish. But as Mama spoke, she flushed, grinning behind her hand, and I knew that what Mama was saying was true; but how could I—who had become pregnant at fourteen—fault her, a twenty-year-old woman? I could feel that guilt, the red dirt of the farm, scratching inside my veins again.

Now Mama was telling me that Daddy had called her, begging to come home: "'N Ah guess Ah will—he's got cancer of the lung now, so Ah don' guess he's up to much meanness." For a moment, I felt somebody walking over my grave, wondering whether the cancer would keep Daddy from doing to Musette what he had done to me.

When I was there on the farm, it was as if all the knowledge, the worldliness, I had tried to find in New Orleans hadn't happened at all.

"Listen to this, Mama: *Chickens are like old maids/ And they are so dumb they sit on doorknobs . . .*" Lily read from the backseat of the Plymouth. She was writing a poem about what Musette had told her, that to teach the chickens to lay, she put white porcelain doorknobs in their nests. Lily and Rose laughed hysterically, then Dwayne hit Lily on the arm, saying, "*That's dumb!*" and she began to cry. "Mama, he hit me! . . ."

On the way back to Louisiana, we rented rooms at the top of a hot old house in Pass Christian. That afternoon, the temperature over 100, we dipped a wire crab trap beneath the pier, and after a while carried two dozen writhing blue crabs back to the house. The temperature in the kitchen must have been 120 as I dumped the creatures into the enameled pot of boiling water, and Rose and Lily jumped up and down. "It's cruel, Mama, it's *cru-el-l-l!*" they screeched in protest. Dwayne was standing by silently, wearing that new look of his. "They'll turn a pretty pink—just like canned salmon or a sunset," I murmured weakly, trying to soothe them. As I tediously picked the white meat from the sharp shells, carefully removing the gray-green liver so we wouldn't be poisoned, they rushed back into the room with a jar full of smaller creatures: "They're fiddler crabs, the lady downstairs said, Mama, they can walk backwards and forwards—can we take them home, can we?"

I ruffled Rose's hair, then Lily's, with the back of my wrist: "You can—but they may not live, honey."

For supper we ate the small mounds of white meat drenched in lemon butter with soda crackers and some corn I had shucked, then the children went out to the sun porch to watch TV. "Come on," Bobby said drunkenly, grabbing me by the wrist, tugging me toward our room off a main hallway. I took off my shorts and shirt, and resignedly lay down on the thin white chenille spread, thinking how every door in this place was warped, too, with cracks big enough to see through. As Bobby pulled off his belt, I was still thinking of the crabs, writhing in the boiling water. "Git yo' mouth down hyah, woman," Bobby was saying, swaying above me. I closed my eyes, but not before I had seen Dwayne walk down the hall, glancing, as he passed, through the cracked door into my and Bobby's room.

After Bobby was finished and snoring, I went down the steps to the beach. The tide was coming in, beating against the seawall; the black water could have been a thousand feet deep. I sat down beside Dwayne, running my fingers through his brown hair, stroking the seam of his scar. Angrily, silently, he was tearing the legs from the fiddler crabs—one after the other, then tossing the bodies into the night-black water. As soon as he had ripped the legs from one, he would grab up another of the frantic creatures, as though he could never dismember enough of them.

"Dwayne, don't do that!" I cried. But not looking at me, he kept on, picking up a rock and smashing another legless body, turning it till the crab had become a smear of shell and flesh, its black popeyes on either side of the stone. Where was the happy home I had dreamed of as a teenager back in South Alabama? The black ocean opened before us, as cavernous, as monster-filled, as my nightmares. As the tide broke against our bare legs, I propped my elbows on my knees, put my head in my hands, and sobbed.

That summer, I watched the man across the street toss balls to his two sons after supper every night. One son, Gary, was Dwayne's age; the other, slightly older, was severely retarded and would stumble around the yard after his father and younger brother, squealing with delight. Sometimes they rested, and the man held both boys on his knees. The scene seemed strange, foreign, to me, and I realized it was the first time I had seen a father's gentleness.

When I had still been "good," Bobby had said he would adopt Dwayne. But now I knew he wouldn't, and I wouldn't have wanted him to. For it had dawned on me that his little

145

cruelties to Dwayne had started long before my affair with Martin: He had been angry when Dwayne had dabbled, babbling and smiling, in his food as we ate in greasy spoons during our honeymoon. Bobby would slap him, openhanded, when he leaned against a wall in the house in Airline Park, leaving a small grimy handprint on the paint; or when he disturbed the order of the "thangs"—the chain of keys, the heavy Tulane class ring, the mechanical pencils Bobby wore in a shirt pocket— that Bobby left out on his dresser top each night.

Bobby had always been willing to bathe Rose and Lily, soaping them thoroughly, caressing every tiny crevice ("I wish Daddy wouldn't bathe me, Mama," Lily said back then, giving me a message I didn't yet understand). But when he bathed Dwayne, he would scrub, and scrub hard, the terry washcloth reddening Dwayne's natural tan, his Seminole swarth, trying, maybe, to rub away the evidence of my earlier sexual sin with Wayne, or even to rub his stepson out of existence. Sometimes Dwayne would cry out, and I would rush into the bathroom. That I would comfort Dwayne would seem to anger Bobby more. Was it because he suspected that I loved Dwayne more than I could ever love him, or any man? And now that I had committed adultery, insulted his manhood, Bobby had reason to hate me, and to take it out on my son.

Yet Dwayne, with his satiny olive skin, his sparkling black eyes, his constant excitement—the very mood that seemed to set Bobby's own mood on edge—was more alive to me than Bobby, with his watery blue eyes, his barely contained melancholy, had ever been. "He's so cute, we just fought over him— all the teachers wanted him in their class!" his sixth-grade teacher told me when I ran into her at the shopping center.

"Your son just doesn't seem . . . considerate," the same teacher called to tell me only months later, when he was asked to leave the acting class because he had "disrupted the group." I tried to chalk the young woman's complaint up to Dwayne's excess energy; playing a soldier in *Joan of Arc*, he had looked sad, dispirited, in his black tights. "Mama, I just want to live on a farm all alone, have animals, and paint pictures like you do when I grow up," he told me earnestly.

"Did you know yo' boy sits out in the yard a lot, not playin',

146

jes' starin' out into space?" asked a motherly neighbor. Of *course*, he's more introspective than *your* son, I thought. But later, I would think back on her remark.

One morning back home in Metairie, there was blood in my diaphragm, and I thought I was dying. A doctor stuck what looked like a knitting needle through my cervix, and a giant hand grabbed my insides and squeezed, scraping at the insides of my uterus with its fingernails. Soon, I began bleeding from my urethra, flames enveloping my lower body as I pissed. "Cystitis—the 'honeymoon disease,' " the doctor said, smirking. But that didn't stop Bobby from fucking me any time of day or night, whether the children were within hearing or not—in the ass till I cried out from the red pain, or grabbing me by the hair, shoving his swollen penis into my mouth. Since discovering my adultery, he seemed determined that I should swallow semen, despite—because of?—my gagging, my rush to the bathroom, where, leaning over the basin, I would look down at my forearm and see the faint scar from the NEVER I had engraved there. One night, lying in bed beneath him, I saw myself smashing my own groin, breaking the very bones of my pelvis with the heavy black cast-iron skillet I used for making the roux for gumbo or baking corn bread. At other times, sewing on a button for Rose or Lily, or cutting up carrot sticks for their after-school snack, I would flash myself swallowing the needle, or slicing through the blue vein at my wrist.

My only hope was something I had read: that the creative personality disintegrates and reorganizes itself every seven years. But when would the reorganization begin? I was taking little white pills four times a day—"A lot of young mothers feel that way," the doctor had said, writing out the prescription, not knowing of my evil heart. For as though I couldn't help myself, I was thinking of myself, my own desires, again.

Ironically, when I told him how much it was worth, Bobby hung the painting Martin ("shell pinks and aubergine, like your beautiful body") had given me over our couch. It was almost as though he liked lacerating himself on the edges of my unfaithfulness. "There you go," he said sarcastically. "There's your crazy boyfrien's crazy paintin', jes' where yuh wanted it." As he tap-tap-tapped the nail into the wall, I saw Dwayne looking up from the TV, watching silently from the family room. Was he recalling the day I had taken him, Rose, and Lily to Martin's house?

Martin had married another art student and left with her for Rome, Italy. It was only because of that that I was able to convince Bobby, after nights of pleading and crying, to let me continue art classes—that and the fact that my new instructor was a woman, one of the ones whose paintings I had seen that first day in the French Quarter. She told me that I was doing well, that I was "really coming from the color," and that color was, increasingly, red: Dwayne's blood spattered over the seat of the red convertible, Bobby's hand gushing blood, then soaking a towel over the kitchen sink, the blood in my diaphragm and urine, my blood when he tore into my body with rage: the red red red of blind pain.

I had always dreamed of moist things, dripping, extruding, pouring from my body—pale mauve grapelike forms, quivering on a forearm, a glistening rose glaze covering my sex. Now they turned to abortions from my mouth, extrusions of flesh. Mutilated Dwaynes, stitched as Marmalade had been, hundreds of them. Dwayne's sex cut off, blood flowing from a wound that became my vagina. Later, I would hear of a woman with cancer of the breasts who waited until she had begun bleeding from the nipples before she saw a doctor. Was I like that? I wondered. Was time the way it was in paintings, in dreams, everything really happening at once? It was a question I would ask myself over and over, wondering why I, an artist, didn't see the patterns.

But back then, all I knew was that something bad was happening, would happen, to punish me for my sexual sin, even for the joy I found in painting. And it did.

In fact, the world as I knew it was about to end.

PART TWO

On Incest and Iguanas in the Deep South

you fit into me
like a hook into an eye

a fish hook
an open eye
—Margaret Atwood, *Power Politics*

CHAPTER SIX

DRUGS—MARIJUANA. LSD. Speed. Angel Dust. Coke. PCP. *Those* were among the first.

And probably Iris, and others at this party tonight, could tell similar stories. For it was a time of epidemic, of a plague still going on (in newer and more refined forms) to this very day.

We had recently moved to Algiers, across the river from the Quarter, which was as close as I could convince Bobby to go, in a section that sounded exotic but wasn't. I let the children choose their own room colors: Dwayne chose purple with blood-red ceiling and trim; Lily wanted a bubble-gum pink, but Rose prevailed, and they decided on a sunny yellow with a sky-blue ceiling painted with white clouds.

I had heard of drugs, just barely, on TV, and then suddenly they were on us, infesting our new house, like a nest of snakes that had been breeding in the basement, just waiting to cut loose, to destroy two of those most precious to me.

They rose up, it seemed, in the cerise fluorescence of Dwayne's room, amid his softball bat, his stamp collection, his pictures of horses; his sketchbooks and his crumbling pastels, his Davy Crockett cap hanging on the wall, his dirty socks, his stinking guinea-pig cage, his record albums and his guitar. Creeping up through some opening unknown to me, writhing and hissing, venomous and truculent—just as Dwayne would soon be.

And I would soon be that crazy woman again, the snakes of a different sort wrapping her skull, a helmet as secure as the straps on an electric chair, but without the hope of the jolts that would put a quick end to her pain. For this wouldn't be something that could be fixed by a surgeon's scalpel, a mere seam up the side of her son's head.

It was hot that spring of 1965, like walking through hot water. During April, Rose and Lily sketched whole classrooms of children, sitting at their desks inside huge Mason jars, boiling atop giant stove burners. "That's the way it feels, Mama," Lily said, spreading the drawings on the kitchen table. She had added a few ballerinas, leaping desperately in their attempts to flee the flame.

By May, my once-sweet little boy, just twelve years old, was hiding the tubes of glue, the brown paper bags, beneath the pillowcases printed with the cowboy hats and lariats. "It only hurts you if you do it sixty times; so fifty-nine times is okay," he explained patiently when I found them. ("Us'lly the ones that're doin' thet margee-juana, do thet between," the first policemen would tell me.)

By June, Dwayne's feelings of persecution were spreading like fungus. He was taking Sominex to sleep, the empty bottles strewing his desk, atop a poem entitled "On My Death" (*Why do some people treat other people like cockroaches? Why not just step on them?*).

July felt like a pressure cooker, with the five of us inside it. By August, the backyard was slick with rotting tiger lilies. In the grips of the monster that sprang to life when the fumes of glue first entered his brain, Dwayne was going crazy. And our little family was living in hell.

Rose came into the kitchen with a rare flush of indignation, holding aloft a Barbie, a Ken, each dismembered, a swastika

152

carved onto Ken's pale chest, then scored in red ink. "Look what he did, Mama!" she cried. "I hate him!"

"Don't yew sull up at me like thet, buoy!"

As Bobby raged, he and Dwayne stood eye-to-eye; Dwayne weighed almost what Bobby weighed—160 pounds—and was his exact height.

"I can't find my flute, Mama!" Lily cried anxiously, coming into the kitchen, referring to the shiny new instrument we had just bought her. "I've *got* to practice for band, 'n I *know* I left it on my bed!" "I can't find mine, either," Rose muttered as she came into the room, her fair face flushed. "'n my jar of pennies is gone, too!"

"You should have *heard* the language he used!" an elderly woman on his paper route complained. "I jes' couldn't possibly repeat it!" The newspaper "counselor" had called to say that Dwayne wasn't always meeting his bills for papers. Often now, I heard him placing collect calls to Homerdessa in South Alabama. A few days later, he would receive a fat envelope—I would see him counting out the dollar bills. He would come in from his paper route looking dazed in a way I'd never seen before, go straight to his room, lock the door, and stay for a long time. Once when I knocked—made timid by the sweet smell coming from beneath the door, the violent clash of the music from his stereo—he came out of the room, wildly waving the air rifle Homerdessa had given him, and I flashed the metal shot embedded fast in my iris, cutting off my view of color forever.

"Every day, we prayed that you would still be alive when we got home from school," Rose and Lily said later of that time. At the school bus stop, they would see the silent blond teenager whose brother had murdered her mother. The girl now lived alone with her father, trapped in what seemed the impermeable bubble of her loneliness, and they feared her fate for themselves.

153

But it would be a long time—decades—before they would be able to talk about that.

It seemed to start with a haircut.

One morning, the children at school, I answered the door-bell wearing sudsy rubber gloves. Two crew-cut men in ugly black suits held out plastic-coated I.D.'s. It was as though I had been waiting for them all my life. "We're frum the fire department," one said, seating himself in the living room without an invitation. The other one sat down, too. "We've jes' been ovah to the parish grammar school to question yore son. A buildin' burned down las' Sunday mornin' a block away, near whyah yore boy picks up 'is Sunday papers." *A hut*, I had heard Dwayne saying over the phone to his sidekick, Leroy. *If you help me with the papers, we'll build a hut down there.* "Thyah wuz evidence of a campfire, some matchbooks 'n so on. 'N the shopkeep at the store across the street says he come in, ast for a bunch a matches."

"I know Dwayne couldn't have been involved in such a thing," I said indignantly, a stone sinking in my belly; the suds off my red rubber gloves were dripping into my lap, onto my jeans. "Wall, we watched 'im when we went to the school," the man went on sharply. "The princ'pal don' lak the length of his hair—did you know thet, Miz Bowers?" I thought of Dwayne's hair, newly grown out Beatle length, soft and brown over the scar. "Did yore son tell you that's he's gonna be expelled if he don't cut it, if he don't behave—did 'e tell yuh thet?" I was silent. I saw the other man looking around the room with distaste at the paintings, the books, the stacks of *Art in America*—seeing clues all around him as to why Dwayne was the way he was.

"Do yuh thank it's raht fur yore son to disrupt a whole classroom with 'is hair, Miz Bowers?" He stood, the other man rising simultaneously, then started to hand me a card but, looking at my sudsy rubberized fingers with distaste, placed it on the coffee table instead. "It's to yore boy's advantage if yuh call us, let us know anythang you find out about this." He paused before closing the door behind him. "If it wuz *mah* boy, ah'd be worried. Ah thank thet boy's sick!"

I remembered my prayers after the accident, Dwayne's

injury, how I hadn't lived out the vows I had made. After sitting there for a while, my brain spinning in frenzy, I tore off the Playtex gloves, rushed to the telephone, where I looked up "Psychologists" in the Yellow Pages. I didn't yet know that there was nothing I could do—no attitude I could take, nothing that anyone else could tell me—that would keep that crazy woman I had been after the accident from taking over again.

"Miz Bowers, may I put Miz Brice on the line?" the school secretary said before transferring me to the principal. The older woman's voice cut in briskly. "Do you think you can see to it that your son has a proper haircut? The length of his hair is simply unacceptable. Otherwise, we must expel him." As I hung up, I felt this new hatred surge through my brain. I hated her and the fire inspectors.

"Yew look hyah, buoy! we've had just about *enough* outta you!" Bobby shouted, bashing his fist on the wall above Dwayne's head. Dwayne didn't speak or move. "Yew *hyah* me, buoy?" he repeated. Lily sat still, building a hill out of her rice. Rose looked up from the science book she was reading at the table. "You git on that bike 'n git thet hair cut by tomorra or else!" he continued. I looked down, knowing what he would like to add—that if Dwayne didn't have this weird mother, he wouldn't be acting this way. Dwayne looked straight ahead, out the picture window, unblinking, then threw his plate, red beans and rice and all, onto the carpet. He jumped up, knocking over his chair, muttering something about killing himself; then, slamming the door behind him, he ran into his room. I hated Mrs. Brice and the fire inspectors. But I hated Bobby even more.

"I'll pick you all up after school today," I said gaily to Dwayne the next morning. "I might need you to help carry some groceries 'n stuff." That afternoon, everything seemed normal; the three of them struggled and shoved as they climbed into the Plymouth from the sidewalk outside the grammar school, ending up with Dwayne in the front seat beside me. When we pulled into the shopping center, I cut off the motor and turned to him, fixing his reproachful jet eyes with mine. "Please—let's go in the barber shop, have your hair trimmed just a *little* bit," I pleaded. He looked away from me, fighting back tears. I went around to his side of the car, opened the door, and he stumbled out, Rose and Lily following. I marched toward the barber shop, trying not to look behind me. "Wall, hallow, young man," the barber said. "You've been the laughin'stock 'round hyah with thet hair, boy. Why didn' yo' daddy brang you down hyah afore naow?" the man went on, tying a white cloth at Dwayne's neck. Dwayne wouldn't look at either of us. I gave the man a fierce glance but walked to where he stood. "Just give him a light trim," I said lightly, then whispered, "cut it a little shorter—just don't say anything." When he winked at me, I felt a surge of pure hatred, the same hatred I had felt for the fire inspectors. He had greasy black hair, a greasy, pockmarked face, and sideburns like Elvis. I sat down between Rose and Lily; while Rose worked on her secret code, her science homework, Lily and I looked through a *Good Housekeeping* we had brought with us. "Look at this recipe, Lily," I said pointing out a pork loin draped with mandarin oranges. "Maybe we can make this for supper tonight." But Lily was staring at her brother, who, I saw in the mirror, was holding his eyes closed as though in pain. "Mama, he's cuttin' *too* much!" Rose was punching her on the arm: "Shut up, Lil-ee!" "Thar yuh are, young man—one hunnert percent better!" the barber was saying, whisking off the cloth thick with Dwayne's fine jet hair as Dwayne raised his eyes to the mirror for the first time. The look on Dwayne's face made me feel sick. The man had cut his hair so short, the scar showed. "Dwayne, don't you understand, honey—I just couldn't let you be expelled," I tried to explain, putting my arm around his stiff shoulders. But then he was running from the shop, down the sidewalk. "Don't worry 'bout 'im, lady—he'll git ovah it," the barber laughed, sweeping Dwayne's soft hair up from the floor. I wanted to tear the broom from his hands, beat him down to the floor with it. Instead, I handed him the three dollar bills and walked out, Lily and Rose behind me.

"Where are we goin', Mama? Where did Dwayne go?" Lily and Rose kept asking from the backseat. I drove slowly, my heart pounding, through the shopping center, then behind it. "There he is, Mama!" Lily shouted, pointing to the viaduct over a wooded area. Dwayne was standing on the tracks; when he saw the Plymouth pull up, he bolted, running in zigzags toward the woods. I drove mindlessly around and around the shopping center, then parked, and we went into Baskin-Robbins, where Rose ordered a bubble-gum cone, Lily a licorice one.

That night, Dwayne had still not come home. Lily came into the bedroom where I lay trying to calm myself with a glass of Bobby's red whiskey, to read me the poem she had written: *Hairs./ Hairs are something/ that people say don't hurt/ when you cut them./ But for my brother Dwayne/ it does.*

I hated the barber, Mrs. Brice, Bobby, and the fire inspectors. Years later, I heard that Dwayne's seventh-grade teacher, who loved him, had cried when he was expelled. I heard, too, that Mrs. Brice had been run over by her husband, in a car in her own driveway. And I didn't even care.

"Glue—for one thing, he's been sniffing glue, ordinary airplane glue," the first counselor began. "Research has shown that this can result in serious brain damage." Bobby looked impatient; he'd had to leave the car lot in the middle of the morning. It was a good thing we had the settlement from the accident: He certainly wouldn't have liked to pay for this. "Your son also told me—in a braggadocio tone, by the way—that he's been ingesting lysergic acid—what they call LSD; that an eighteen-year-old girl who is on his paper route, who has a broken leg in a cast and is home every day, has been very 'nice' to him, sharing the substance with him. We don't yet know the results of the use of lysergic acid, but we suspect it, too, can cause brain damage. And certainly it's contraindicated for adolescents, whose ego boundaries are barely formed. And then, there's something that's growing in common usage—cannabis. The leaf of the marijuana plant. It distorts reality, can cause paranoia. And the common forms of speed—Benedrine, Dexedrine—which are both mood elevators. He brags that he's used all these drugs. Also, that he leaves home, hitchhiking downtown or to the Quarter, after you two have gone to sleep." He paused and looked up from the cat's cradle of his fingers, fixing me, rather than Bobby, in his gaze: "Do you think that is possible, Mrs. Bowers?"

I sat inside the numbness, unable to speak. All I knew was that Dwayne, not yet thirteen, was going crazy.

And that I had this innocuous-looking, balding man, mechanical pencils in his polyester shirt pocket, to hate too.

"I wuz in town with my Garden Club, 'n saw Dwayne in the Quarter on a school day, eatin' at Brennan's with a crowd of long-haired kids," one of our new, equally nosy neighbors told me, catching me off guard.

I had just noticed the first checks missing from my checkbook. Before, it had been mostly a ten from my pocketbook, a five from Bobby's dresser top. Dwayne had hidden the remaining checks in the garbage can outside the carport, along with a butcher knife. A possum eating from the cats' dish scurried away as I clattered the lid. "Two hundred twenty-five dollars," the bank said when I called.

When I asked Dwayne about the checks, his sidekick Leroy—a bit less sullen-looking, a foot shorter, than he—was with him. They had just come in from the carport, and I was standing at the kitchen sink, washing greens.

Dwayne picked a butcher knife up from the counter and came toward me. For a moment, I stood looking at him in disbelief. Then I ran out the kitchen door, slamming it behind me.

He came out that door, still grasping the knife. I ran around to the front door, went inside, locked it behind me, and raced back to the kitchen door, locking it, too.

He loomed at the open window over the sink, slashed at the screen with the blade; then, tearing the mesh with his hands, he climbed through it, his cowboy-booted feet landing atop the counter.

"Dwayne! *What are you doing?*" I screamed.

His face crumpled, and he threw down the knife—which quivered upright in the pebbly floor—then leapt down from the counter, ran to his room, and slammed the door.

"Wall, ah guess ah'll go on home now, Miz Bowers," Leroy said sheepishly. He had stood in the kitchen the whole while, and it was the first time he had spoken. I noticed that his hair was growing slightly longer, the way Dwayne's had been before his haircut.

"No—no way kin Ah come home right now!" Bobby exploded over the phone when I called him. "I'm right in the middle of a deal!"

For a moment, I had hated Leroy, just because he wasn't crazy the way Dwayne was. But I still hated Bobby more.

When I found the first suicide note, I remembered the bearded man I had waked at a crash pad in Faubourg Marigny while out searching for Dwayne. "Oh, yeah—Dwayne. I know 'im. The guy who's been talkin' suicide, thanks his girlfriend wants to kill 'erself, too."

"If Dreama wanted to die, it would only be because of her sinus headaches," Dreama's mother laughed when I called her. "She's in bed with one right now." But the mother *had* seen Dwayne an hour before, walking past her house toward the wooded area at the dead end of her street. I thought of the Tulane boy, recently found O.D. 'ed in a woods—he had been covered in ants, ants running in and out his nostrils, trailing like chains over his wrists. I rushed out to the Plymouth, drove to the dead end, then walked through the pine trees, calling out hysterically. Back home, I walked inside the house, and as I entered my room, I saw him, lying on my bed. When he reached up to hug me, I was so happy to see him that I hugged him back. He looked so handsome, lying there in the ray of late afternoon sunlight.

"Your freckles are so pretty, Mama," he said, smiling up at me. "I love you so much, I feel like I should just kill you. Because then I wouldn't *have* to come back. . . ."

He followed me around the house, talking his horrible death talk. He felt like killing a *lot* of people, he told me. At other times, he talked about killing himself. It was as though we were roped together, as though he were tied to my waist. The more shocked, sickened, and frightened I became, the more extreme were the things he said.

Then, perhaps suddenly realizing he had gone too far, he

would write me a two-page letter, reengaging my love through his charm.

Naturally, while he was out of the house, I went through his things, as frenzied as a woman who suspects her lover of cheating.

To Dreama in Her Cosmic Beauty, he wrote.

But he also wrote other things:

> *Dear Maureen, or Constant Agent of the Horrors of the Minority: Other people don't understand like we do that, that death is not a bad thing, and we may want it. The Other People think that Death is the worst thing, but nobody knows whether it is or not because they haven't been dead. My idea is to start a Death Club of all the people our age who might want to study it and learn all about it, and even experience it. We could wear black clothes and have a skull ring and things. There are already a couple of the Death Clubs in other parts of the United States, and more in Switzerland. I have been told about them by some of the people I now hang out with. I know it will be a great success, and we might even make a profit. . . .*

> *Peggy, Hi! What do you think of people treating people like cockroaches? Cockroaches have little rights, they are usually stomped out on sight because some people think they are dangerous. Are people dangerous? Why people are the most dangerous creatures of the living, or the dead, or the invented, in my opinion. Have you ever seen a smushed armadillo on the road? Or a beautiful silver snake that got smushed thin as a piece of dirty aluminum foil? Think of the spider in Kipling's story—'she knifed me one night because she wished she was white.' Or the cockroach's point of view in that story by Kafka—nobody loved him because he was a bug. . . .*

Then there were the letters to the president, talk of communism, Naziism, and the advent of World War III. His Blue Horse notebook was covered in swastikas and was filled—along with his barely begun math homework—with elaborate drawings, geometric madnesses in gorgeous primary Magic Marker colors. At first glance, I was carried away by their vibrancy, recalling how he had once told me that he wanted to be an artist who lived on a farm. But that brief moment of visual joy burst as I studied them: The theme was always two worlds—a scene of order, peace and beauty, such as a blue stream beside a grassy green space, a grazing horse, next to wild scribbles of flying bodies, dismembered animals, exploding buildings: a chaos liberally accented with more of the swastikas. And in every drawing, the two worlds were clearly separated, with the destructive portion dominating the page.

Paula was visiting from New York again (courting me, I would realize years later). As we sat in the backyard drinking white wine, the phone rang inside the house. "Has anyone at this number tried to put a call through to the White House?" the operator asked when I answered. As I hung up, I saw Dwayne lumbering out of his room, looking angry. Back in the yard, I started to babble, telling Paula a subdued version of what was happening. "Don't worry about it," she said dismissively. "All my clients in New York who have kids are going through this sort of thing right now—you'll be a better painter for it." And the notion that some good could come out of this, for my painting, if not for Dwayne, just added to my guilt.

When Dwayne discovered I had been in his room, he piled his Beatles and Monkees albums, his copies of Jack London, Dickens, Kipling, and Tarzan, plus stacks and stacks of his papers and drawings—even some of his clothes—in a huge mound in the backyard and set them afire. Later that day, I found my new penis-shaped vibrator, the one Bobby had bought to try to make me come, on my bedtable, bloodied, shit-smeared.

The next afternoon, Dwayne pointed Bobby's rifle at me, threatening to shoot me if I didn't give him my checkbook. The week after that, he held a knife to the side of my throat as he reached for my purse. The third week, he chased me into the backyard with a small hatchet just as Bobby was pulling up into the carport. When Bobby rushed over and twisted his arm behind him, wresting away the weapon, Dwayne burst into tears and ran back into the house, slamming the screened door behind him. Bobby followed but went straight to the sink and poured himself a tumbler full of Wild Turkey. As I sagged into a lawn chair, I saw Rose and Lily, white faces pressed against the family-room window.

But the worst was that the cold gray numbness I had always known was now coming on because of Dwayne. I thought of the painting I had done of the two of us—Dwayne and me against the world. That was why I had married Bobby, why we had come together to New Orleans—he, a miniature man sitting on my teenage lap—didn't he understand that? I remembered how, when Bobby had once been droning on and on about Martin, his voice rising in increasing anger, Dwayne had hovered outside our bedroom door, holding his air rifle at the ready, my little protector.

But now I was his persecutor and his victim. How could I be his rescuer as well?

Scissors, kitchen knives, shish-kebob skewers; Bobby's rifle and shotgun—I kept them all locked in the trunk of the Plymouth, or any other new place I could find as Dwayne discovered the old. I had to go out to get the paring knife from the car trunk before I could peel the celery for a salad or trim the stalks off collard greens. One day when I went out for the blade, one of the tires was flat, slash marks on its side, a clear message to me that he now had a knife of his own.

Yes, Dwayne *was* sodomized by three black youths while in custody, the officer at the detention center where Bobby had taken him after the hatchet incident was saying defensively, "But then, boys of his caliber aren't us'ally placed here. I'm sure he has no problems you and your husband can't solve at home with a little firmness. . . ."

"I can't help it," I would cry, exhausted by my day with Dwayne. My vagina felt like an ivory O, a circle of bone, impenetrable. That my son was going insane seemed to fuel Bobby's lust for me. "I bet you could open up with *him!*" he would hiss, referring to Martin.

What Bobby didn't know was that though I was still living there with him, Bobby wasn't even a part of my life anymore—any more than a dead dog on the road.

The six o'clock news, once so thrilling to me, was now the conduit of my terror. The black-and-white screen on the kitchen TV was filled with stoned kids and crash pads and crisis centers and hustlers and dealers. A fourteen-year-old girl held by bikers and tortured to death. Middle-aged men picking up boys Dwayne's age and paying them. Kids on acid dropping from hotel windows. Girls found dead in back alleys. All only miles away in the Quarter and the nearby city.

I lay in bed beside Bobby, the cold gray fear descending like a blanket, reading the *Times-Picayune*: TEENAGE GIRL, HER MOTHER, LEFT BUTCHERED BESIDE INTERSTATE 10. *The pair was said to have picked up a young male hitchhiker in New Orleans two days earlier.* This time, Dwayne had been gone for a week.

The police wanted us to come down to Jackson Square right away, I told Bobby in the middle of the night, hanging up the phone. Bobby cursed, looking long-suffering as he pulled on his pants. It was 3:00 A.M., and he was still drunk from the night before. I thought of the park, what I had seen on the news—that runaways were prostituting themselves there, boys as well as girls. I thought of what Dwayne had done with my vibrator.

The patrol car was parked on the Pontalba side; the patrolman stepped out, pushing Dwayne in front of him. "This boy says he's thir-teen. Thet true?" I nodded, but the man looked at Bobby. "We found this hyah knife on 'im—it's ovah six inches long. Now doncha thank you kin keep a kid lak this home?" Bobby, his brow furrowed, looked down at the ground through his thick glasses. This man was seeing he was not a man: He couldn't control his stepson; he couldn't control his wife. I looked away, ashamed because I knew it was all my fault.

* * *

I had always known it was my fault. But now other people knew it, too.

"It's 'cuz you ain't axcepted Jesus Christ as yore savior," moaned Willadene, our fat white sitter, the one who had had "female" cancer, and who had confided to me that on doctor's orders she periodically used "a candle to keep mahself opened up," raising visions of her gummy vagina.

Then there were the New Orleans City policemen, leaning against doorjambs, picking their teeth, looking down at me with languid curiosity when I went into the station to file yet another missing-persons report, big, burly men whom I could see thinking, Gull, you must've been fuckin' at thirteen. They would look me up and down, while I looked at the floor, remembering lying on the pine needles beneath Wayne. "Yeah, we seen 'im around," they would leer, perhaps spitting out a chaw of tobacco. "Whut's 'er mattah, gull—cain't yuh keep 'im home?"

And part of my guilt was that I knew I was the one who had first introduced him to drugs. That had I not been a housewife, and mother to Dwayne, Rose, and Lily, I would probably be one of those people called hippies, too. When Dwayne was eleven, I had picked him, Rose, and Lily up after school and had taken them to Faubourg Marigny to visit the attic apartment of a painter from my art classes. Sean was a dark bearded man who didn't seem to have any bones. "Come for a cup of tea, my dear," he had said almost girlishly. He had set his easel at one end of the gable, overlooking Esplanade. The place was one huge room, with windows looking out into the trees, a mattress on the floor over a worn Oriental rug, two aging lounges covered in wine velvet. His paintings—huge jungle beasts, lions, tigers, monkeys—were everywhere, yellow eyes glaring at us from the walls; one was of a red-brown orangutan, a baby at her human-looking breasts. Lily put her finger in the viridian on his palette and smeared it, unthinking, on her skirt. "It's just like a zoo, Mama!" she squealed.

Rose sat silently on a couch, looking around, but I could tell that she liked it, too. Dwayne hadn't wanted to come—"I get *tired* of art, Mother," he had protested, but I had persuaded him, and now he looked around in wonder. My friend lay back languidly on one of the couches, a funny little pipe in his hand, and I noticed the sweet smell in the air. "Have you ever smoked this?" he asked, patting the seat beside him but looking at Dwayne. I shook my head. "Well, maybe you'd like to try it sometime," he said, still smiling at Dwayne. A strange, tinkling music played from a turntable.

"He was neato, wasn't he, Mom? 'N that place—it's a real *pad!*" Dwayne enthused as we got back into the car. "Yeah! 'N I liked all those pictures of animals!" agreed Lily. "If I was an artist, that's what *I* would paint!" I drove home, happy: I was jealous of my friend's freedom, his studio—his "pad," as Dwayne called it—but at least my children were interested in art, in new ideas: I had been able to give them that.

In fact, when I was honest, I had to admit that what Dwayne was doing now was just an extension of what I had wanted for him in the past. I had wanted him to feel free to piss in the front yard when he was four, to have the clay, the crushed eggshells, the pets. And even now, like a glimpse of white light, a hole between charcoal clouds, I sometimes admired him: He wasn't afraid to wander the French Quarter alone at night, to try those strange substances, drugs, to live among strange people, to go strange places with them, to go against the authority of parents (to defy Bobby!) and school principals—to color much farther outside the lines than I ever had.

Nowadays I was dazed, punch-drunk, even exhilarated. I had read that men in battle rarely suffered migraines or depression, and I was like that. My tension was so high that it didn't allow any other form of suffering. In the midst of days that began and ended in tears, I would suddenly feel an incredible rush of happiness; the colors around me would become sharp, heightened. In Schwegmann's, the yellow summer squash, the blue-black eggplants, the orange-red tomatoes, the sleek viridian peppers, would blaze, quiver, beneath my fingertips, living extensions of my forearm, my hand. "Peak experiences," I would read later in Maslow. "Those moments when the universe seems to flow together." When Lily spilled Welch's grape juice on our new cream-colored carpet, she looked anxious, waiting for me to yell, but I only stared at the spreading spot, mesmerized by its shape, its rich purple, then ran for my pad and felt tips so I could capture it.

It was during this time—just when I was about to leave Bobby—that I first began having orgasms with him. The little colors would sparkle inside my legs, my arms down to my fingertips, the tips of my toes, making them arch, and I would try to lie very still. I didn't want Bobby to know how happy I was— he might think I loved him. It was just that I had reached such a state of tension that my body could do nothing else but break open. Dwayne, my beloved son, was crazy, and everything else was out of control.

"Carry what you're doing as far as you can without crossing the line into the ludicrous," my painting instructor advised of my work. And now my life was doing that, too. I was beginning to understand that every moment, every event, was the same, and each had its own beauty, like those poison-dart frogs in South America. One hour, I might be worried that Dwayne would murder someone and have to spend the rest of his life in the state prison; that I would be doomed to live the rest of my life visiting him there, bearing the unbearable. Then, the next hour, things would seem hilariously funny—Lily's guinea pig, squealing for grass, the way Rose was arranging her G.I. Joes, her Barbies, in inhuman poses for her science project on human sexuality. If Dwayne was there, he might think it was funny, too, and the two of us would start laughing and laughing, almost at nothing. And for moments, it was just Dwayne and me, caught in that bubble of craziness.

"Mama, Dwayne asked me to sleep with him in his bed," Lily confided. "He said he would give me ten cents." She was spreading the cream-cheese frosting on top of a banana loaf cake. "He said *please*, he gets lonesome. Do I *have* to do it?"

"No, doodlebug," I said, kissing her forehead to smooth away the worry lines. She was ten years old, three years younger than her brother. "I feel sorry for him, Mama—I don't know why." She looked as though she might cry, and I felt that way too, but I had to be strong. "Have you ever heard of mental illness—well, it's something like a tummy ache in your mind." "Will I get it, Mama?" she asked, sounding anxious. "No, dar-

ling, I won't let you." "Do you promise, Mama?" she persisted.
"I'm sure you won't," I reassured her in another of those promises I would later look back on, marveling at how carelessly I
had made them. But something was tearing inside me, like the
lettuce I was tearing into bits; the chicken pieces sautéeing in
the skillet sounded as if they were screaming, as they had back
on the farm when I was a child.

"Well, I hope not," Lily went on. "All the kids at school are
always saying 'Lil-lee has a cra-zee bro-ther, Lil-lee has a cra-zee
bro-ther'—I hate them!" she said vehemently, then squealed,
"Mama! You're squeezin' me too tight!"

One of the therapists who were now invading our lives
thought it would be good if Bobby and I attended something
called a "marathon group therapy." "Now call us if anything
comes up, any emergency," I told Willadene over and over. I
couldn't imagine a whole weekend without a crisis with Dwayne.

"Was everything okay?" I asked breathlessly, arriving home
on Sunday night after forty-eight hours spent listening to other
couples argue and "get into" their pain, then trying to get into
my own. "Oh jes' fine," she said, her fat arms crossing her huge
breasts, her print rayon dress. "But Dwayne got marrid over
the weekend 'n brought the girl home. They spent the whole
weekend in 'is bedroom, 'cept for stayin' out all night on Saturday." "Yeah, Dwayne got *married*—'n him 'n this girl was actin'
crazy!" Rose and Lily chorused beside her. Despite Jesus—or
was it just believing in the sanctity of holy matrimony?—Willadene had sat and rocked and ate and watched TV while my
thirteen-year-old son had fucked and drugged the weekend
away.

Now, at thirteen, Dwayne was taller and heavier than I
was, if still a bit lumpy, out of proportion. But the breasts had
disappeared, replaced by a man's hardening chest. Though his
dimples didn't deepen much these days, he was handsome with
his satiny olive skin, jet eyes, dark silken hair, dark-downed
face.

Once I thought he was Bobby, coming home early. I was
lying on the bed with the bedroom door closed, wearing one of

the black push-up bras, the black see-through slips Bobby liked me to wear, when I heard the door open and saw Dwayne standing there. I jerked the coverlet to my chin, but not before I saw the look in his eyes.

After that, when he came in from school, he went straight to my and Bobby's room, throwing his books and coat on our bed, as though he were my husband, coming home from work—retrieving them only when he heard Bobby's car in the driveway.

Sometimes, I would dance in the living room to his weird new music. First there had been the Beatles, the Monkees, and Country Joe and the Fish; now there was Cream, the Grateful Dead, and Jimi Hendrix. I was only being my age, I told myself. But as I moved hips and shoulders, trying not to feel self-conscious before my son, lying grim-faced, man-sized, on the couch, I would become aware of my breasts, my buttocks, of the black lingerie worn like mourning beneath my jeans, my turtleneck. For those moments, Dwayne and I were enveloped together in the music, in a cocoon of the forbidden. And even as I burst the mood by leaving the room to start dinner, reverting to my role as housewife, I would feel the moment's guilty residue. Had he heard Bobby and me the night before, arguing and fucking and arguing?

One morning, when Dwayne should have been getting ready for school, I went into his room in my pink chenille robe. He was still in bed and wanted to talk about whether God existed. For a moment, the sulk dissolved from his face, and I felt the rush of what seemed like an ancient happiness. But as I leaned over to kiss him on the cheek, I saw him staring at the breasts he had nursed for so long.

"What do you think a man should be like?" he asked the next week, mentioning one of the therapists. "Like Dr. H.?" I noticed he never asked about his real daddy, Wayne. He lay back on his bed looking depressed, fully clad in khaki pants and plaid shirt. I had bought the *Playboy* for him myself and was tacking the centerfold on his wall in hopes of encouraging him in more "normal" behavior. But instead, he was pulling me down onto the bed toward him. "*Please* lie down with me, Mama," he pled softly: "*Please*." "That wouldn't be a good idea,"

I said gently, tugging away, but not before my heart was wrenched by how sad he looked.

"You're trying to make a lover out of him," the first therapist said as I sat, mute, in what I had come to think of as the torture seat. I was thinking of the play *Oedipus Rex*, which Bobby and I and Jimmy and his new wife had recently seen at a downtown theater; of the young actor's exaggerated anguish upon learning he had slept with his own mother. "Your father molested you, you married a man you didn't love, you've been an unfaithful wife, and on top of that, you further emasculate your husband before your son by selfishly insisting on following your own wishes. For example, how many wives and mothers do you know who spend half their days on *art*?"

I knew he was right, but something inside me protested that I had married Bobby as much for Dwayne as for myself. That I *had* given Martin up, hadn't I? Indeed, that Dwayne, Rose, Lily, and my painting were the only things that made "everything else"—my captivity, my life as a wife—bearable. And beyond that, that I didn't *know* how not to be me in order to save my son—though I would be happy to do so if only this wise man would instruct me.

"You're not a good mother," the next doctor said bluntly. I sat silent as visions—Dwayne suctioning my teenage breast, the dimples in his cheek deepening as his eyes stared up into mine; Dwayne sitting on the couch before he could walk, his bald head bent, cooing over our gray-striped cat; Dwayne in yellow velour feet pajamas, grinning, holding an infant Rose or Lily in his lap—swam in my brain.

"Did you see the movie *Darling*?" asked the third. By now, I had given up trying to tell about the rape, or the drugs, or Bobby's mistreatment of Dwayne. They all seemed more interested in me than in the son whose life I was desperate to save. Yes, I had watched Julie Christie flee her ego, her narcissism, and yes, I admitted, I was probably trying to do the same. "Also, you're very proud." Yes, I was willing to admit to anything if only he would give me the key to saving my son. "The boy does those things because they're what *you* want to do yourself—for example, why do you wear that miniskirt if you don't want *him* hanging around with hippies?" he went on, looking pointedly at my bare knees.

And the last therapist would tell me, "Your son was sexually agitated by hearing about your adultery, your husband's constant references to it—by the lack of boundaries in your home." Even twenty years later, I would cringe.

"There's a doctor who has a school for disturbed boys up in Northwest Louisana," one of the therapists, Dr. H., said. "He keeps them there for a year minimum, no visits from the parents; they have to want to go. Since Dwayne's been expelled from school again, I see no use in his roaming the streets. And we have no way of knowing whether or not he's really dangerous—he may kill you, or himself, or someone else. . . ."

"I'll take him right away," I said gratefully.

Bobby told me crossly that he wasn't sure his insurance would cover the four hundred dollars a month tuition: The very thought made me feel weak, even more exhausted. I would just have to get some kind of job somewhere. And in truth, just before this nightmare began, I had been dreaming of escape again—escape from Bobby, escape from the suburbs. I scoured the ads and had secretly gone for interviews for jobs for which I never seemed suited—or was it that the interviewers smelled my despair? After each, I went into the closet and sobbed, smearing more snot onto the mouton jacket.

When I timidly talked with Bobby about divorce, he scoffed that I didn't even know how to balance a checkbook, much less hold a job. "'N thyah's *no* way you gonna make any money off thet stuff you do!"

Looking out the bedroom window, I thought of how cleanly Bobby had chopped the wisteria vine in two back in Airline Park, severing its very life; I wondered whether he had done the same thing to me. Was I trapped forever, with no way to make the money it would take to support Dwayne, Rose, Lily, and me, and at the same time go on with my painting?

Ironically, despite the chaos of the years since my adultery, my painting was getting better and better and I knew it. Just as I had learned, sitting at Dwayne's bedside after his injury, that

170

a bad woman could look good anytime, I was learning that art had its own life, and a bad woman could paint despite anything. I painted in the family room, and my work dominated the house, our lives. It was almost like having another child, no—was *more* than another child, because it was still a part of me, inside me, like a constant pregnancy; indeed, a part that—and this was my most awful secret knowledge—I would put even *before* my flesh children.

Until the summer of Dwayne's craziness, my feeling for my children and for my painting had been one entity—visceral, ever-present, satisfying. But suddenly, there was a division, a splitting off, a conflict. I had a new, secret name for my painting—I called it My Oblivion.

It was a stormy blue-gray late afternoon when I got Dwayne, Rose, and Lily into the Plymouth to drive across town to the office of the doctor who ran the private school for boys. In the waiting room, Lily watched the fish in the aquarium, and Rose drew pictures and worked on her code. Dwayne played his transistor radio, sticking the transistor's earplug, emanating the cacophony of Cream, into his ear, then sat smoking a Camel. Soon he was called into an inner room; within minutes, I was called in, too. Dwayne stood before the doctor's desk, still sullenly smoking.

"He's incorrigible," the doctor said curtly, not looking up from his papers. As he spoke, Dwayne spat angrily on the floor. "You might as well go ahead, take him to Mandeville."

Outside the rain was pouring; the sky was dark. I laid my head on the steering wheel and sobbed, the racking sounds coming from deep inside me. Rose sat silently, but Lily, beside her in the backseat, began to cry in unison. "Don't worry, Mama," Dwayne murmured like a lover into the side of my neck. Somehow my sobs seemed to please him; he settled down in the front seat beside me, lighting up another Camel almost contentedly.

"Goin' to the state hospital, to Mandeville"—it was the joke everyone used about going crazy, and my worst nightmare come true.

171

* * *

The crew-cut, no-nonsense off-duty orderly Dr. H. had recommended handcuffed Dwayne, then frisked him, finding the razor blade in his jacket lining, the knife inside his boot. He and Bobby had finally located Dwayne after several hours searching the Quarter. Now my son and I sat together in the backseat as the two men took the front. It was 2:00 A.M., and everyone was silent but Dwayne, who intermittently hissed to me during the drive, "You'll never see me alive again."

The night was dark, moonless, and we rode for what seemed an endless time over a narrow two-lane bridge over Lake Pontchartrain. As we rode, I looked down at the black water below, its black depths. Outside Mandeville, we drove through the tall gates of the hospital, and I felt Dwayne stiffen. We had directions to the looming intake building, and after parking, Bobby and the orderly took Dwayne by the arms as I stumbled alongside them, watching him anxiously. The orderly pushed the buzzer, and we were let into a huge gray chamber— the light in here is terrible, I thought irrelevantly—where Dwayne and I sat on a couch with a torn plastic cover while he and Bobby took care of the paper work. There were no other sounds, and Dwayne occasionally glanced at me with loathing. Eventually, a huge black man in a white hospital coat strode across the vast space and took Dwayne by the elbow. I pressed his Davy Crockett cap into his hand, and he took it without looking at me. But halfway across the room, he turned to hiss once more, "Remember—you'll never see me alive again." He spit at the floor at my feet. But the muscular black kept tugging, carrying Dwayne along with him. *Oh, Lily of the Valley, my bright 'n shinin' star, where are you now?* And the heavy metal door clanged shut. The baby I had ecstatically held in my skinny teenage arms thirteen years before had walked through the barred doors of the crazy house, the Louisiana State Hospital for the Insane.

Hysterical at the news of Dwayne's hospitalization, Homerdessa had driven up from Alabama to visit him the following Saturday. We both arrived at the visiting hour.

The huge black man escorted us through the same clanking door, then up a barred elevator, along a urine-scented, concrete-floored corridor. The inmates who milled around us looked demented—old men with grizzled gray shaven heads who had just had shock treatments, paunchy younger men wearing crew cuts and V-necked white T-shirts, middle-aged men who sat on wooden benches, drooling, crying, hands trembling, or walking aimlessly.

The orderly led us out onto a porch where a rusting window screen covered the bars. In a few minutes, Dwayne appeared, dressed in a wrinkled, ill-fitting tan khaki uniform that made me think of the last time I had seen his father, Wayne. His silky hair had now been cut to a bad crew cut, the seam up the side of his head showing through clearly. He wouldn't look at me, and he wouldn't speak. "My pore gran'baby," Homerdessa cried, hugging his wooden body while glancing at me malevolently.

That night over the phone, Mama reassured me. "Ah know you done the raht thang, Easter—thet boy wuz interferin' with you 'n yore husban'. I could feel it when you wuz hyah last sprang." "Now you jes' tell Dwayne ev'rythang's gonna be fine, long as he does whut they tell 'im to," Aunt Darlene said, getting on the line. "'N 'sides thet, we wuddn't wont 'im visitin' down hyah with thet long hair anyway. . . ."

Every Saturday for a year, I went back there, sometimes taking Lily or Rose, but mostly alone. And every Saturday, Dwayne was under glass. Sometimes he came out with a boy of about nine who told me he had been living in the hospital since he was six. The boy would talk and talk, entertaining me like a little monkey, all the while trying to steal things from my purse when I wasn't looking. But Dwayne wouldn't say a word.

After three months, I was given permission to take Dwayne into Mandeville, where we ate hamburgers and drank Orange Crushes at Badeaux's, then went on to the picture show. The only thing playing was *The Boston Strangler*. "That was a good movie, wasn't it, Mama?" he said as we left. It was the first time he had spoken. "It *was* interesting. Do you want another ice cream before we drive back?" I asked, uneasily recalling the naked legs spread across the screen, the broom handles, the Coke bottles with which Tony Curtis had raped his female victims, then the last scene, where he had been in a hospital much like—yet much whiter, more sparkling than—the one to which I was just about to return my son.

Dear Mom, How are you and what have you been doing? How are Edward, Chaos, and Pathos Two? How are my birds? Goldfish? Frogs? Grandmama? Aunt Musette. . . ?
P.S. I hope Dad's okay, too.

Dear Mother, I'm in a new ward. I like the way they do things here! You get tokens for everything you do. You have to pay for meals and everything. But to buy stamps and Cokes or candy, you need money. I would like you to send some. . . .
P.S. I lost Dreama's address. Please get it and send it.

Dear Rose, Thanks for the letter. I hope you are getting along well. I know you are studying hard. I couldn't quite understand your code, though. So let's use the one I figured out: A-z, B-y, C-s, D-w, E-v, F-u. . .
And tell Lily thanks for the poem—it was neato!

Dear Mother, I want you to get that album by Jimi Hendrix called **Electric Ladyland.** *It's supposed to be pretty good. It's two albums and it cost about five dollars. . . .*

Dear Mom, Just dropping you a few lines to say "Hello!"
I got my report card today. I made C in Conduct, B in Social Studies, and B in Math. . . .
Yesterday, the high school went to see a trial at court. A colored man about 23 years of age was found guilty of voluntary manslaughter with a life sentence. He shot a man with a .22 caliber pistol threw the man's eyeball all the way threw his brain. The trial lasted about 5 1/2 hours. It was quite enjoyable. . . .
I'm getting to know how you feel about hippyism, and

174

*I've made up my mind to cut all that stuff out—at least until
I'm two or three years older. . . .*

*Mother—Dr. Rodriguez will be here Saturday, and he
wants to talk to you about letting me go home. . . .
So come on down!*

"Adolescent adjustment problems," said the doctor, who
spoke with such a thick Spanish accent that I could barely understand him, giving me the only diagnosis I would receive for
twenty years.

"You've got gray hairs on your head, Mama," Lily said,
sifting my lank locks with her plump fingers from the backseat
of the Chevy as I drove, but I didn't even care. I knew there
were dark circles beneath my eyes—circles that showed up more
on me than on Dwayne, since I was so fair. I was still skinny,
but my belly was bloated; the only way the Crazy Woman could
sleep was by drinking tumbler after tumbler of the red whiskey,
the narcotic booze. Then, in the morning, after she had cried
herself to sleep, a night of nightmares, her head would throb,
her eyes burn, and her waking hell began all over again. That
woman wanted nothing but blacks, grays, shadows—though
when I stood before a canvas, some rage would break through,
and I would see visions of slashed flesh, mutilated breasts, peri-
neums, penises, scrotums, the images that would later populate
my most "aberrant" paintings.
I wanted to wear black, a veil, no makeup, and go everywhere alone. I wanted to be a widow, grieving the one man I
had ever loved.
The ways I betrayed Dwayne, let me count the ways:
*When I chose Wayne as his father. When I married Bobby, when
I slept with him. When I nursed Rose and Lily at the breasts that had
been his. When I even thought of sleeping with another man—hadn't
the mere thought led to the wreck in the red convertible, his crippling—
possibly for life?*
*And then the minutiae of it: When I let Bobby bathe him, or
discipline him. When I stood silently by as the pediatrician lanced the
boils on his belly when he was nine.*

175

And later: When I lied to him in the barber shop. When I let Bobby take him to the detention center. When I signed him into the state hospital, amid crazy people and electroshocked old men.

When I put my own life, my painting, first. When I didn't set him free—when I held and held him in the thrall of my love.

CHAPTER SEVEN

AND THEN he was out.

And thus came the period of accepting the unacceptable.
Or, at least, accepting more of it. In order to keep seeing and
loving my son, I had to wrench everything around, twist, contort
my earlier ideals—ideals that now seemed as unrealistic, as un-
related to my real life, as the pastoral English landscapes in the
New Orleans Museum of Art. I was no longer that girl with
dreams of love and beauty, or that young woman who had only
wanted—not realizing the incongruity of her desires—to paint
and to be a perfect wife and mother. Instead, I had learned
to drink, had committed adultery, and had hurt, through my
wildness, my beloved son.

None of these things could I have imagined back in South
Alabama. Then, collecting the eggs or walking in the pasture,
carrying Dwayne inside me or at my breast, I didn't even
know—despite Daddy's meanness, his crazy jealousy of
Mama, which I chalked up to his drinking—that a married
woman could drink or even want to sleep with a man other than
her husband. Or worse, that a beloved child could grow up to
go mad.

Now what had happened had given me my first sure clue that the world was not as I had dreamed it. And for a long period, each time this awareness stabbed me afresh, I was pierced by a thousand small shards, glittering glass stuck all over my exposed body, an image that became the best known of my early paintings as I tried to put the pain outside myself, onto canvas. In that picture, blood beads at the point where each jagged piece of mirror, reflecting a tiny miniature of my own agonized face, penetrates my soft flesh; the outer lips of my vagina are sewn lengthwise with a particularly malevolent-looking sliver; the stretch marks on my convex belly have turned to writhing maggots. The painting—which I called realism, but which the critics would call surrealism—took me three months to complete, and when Paula saw it, I could tell it pleased her, a faint smile forcing itself through her Asian mien. It became the first picture I sold, the beginnings of what I would think of as my "career"—a career built, ironically enough, not on the ecstatic pastoral images of my girlhood, but on the agony of what I was going through with Dwayne.

And *that*, I realized with chagrin, was what Paula had meant when she said I would be a better painter for it.

Though not everyone would agree—not by a long shot: "Masochistic . . . self-destructive . . ." some critics would write of my images. Some seemed to feel my pictures should be suppressed—and this long before the days of Jesse Helms, the Mapplethorpe hoopla. To the interviewers, I would say, "I believe in going into the pain. . . ." But I couldn't quite explain to my detractors how my paintings lessened, balanced, even satisfied, the hurt—that all-consuming monster—inside me. And I wondered: Did they really think their small barbs would deter a woman who dreamed the kind of images I dreamed, who was as driven to their expression as I was? And did they really imagine that these images, their execution, were a conscious choice?

Years later, in a friend's Santa Fe living room, I would thoughtlessly—in my desire to touch—put my whole hand around a small fuzzy cactus, then quickly pull away a stinging palm full of shards. But removing those small needles had been easy—rubber cement painted over my life, my love line, had

turned to a gummy opaque coating with which I had peeled
them away all at once, as my friend laughed at both my stupidity
and my cleverness. If only that pain back then—the "inspira-
tion" for that first truly characteristic painting, the one that
critics would call my turning point—could have been peeled
away as easily.

"Say 'hey' to Dwayne," chided the sad-faced fat woman in
a flowered rayon dress. "Naow say 'hey' to yore li'l frien'. . . ."

As soon as he had gotten home, Dwayne had wanted to go
to Charity Hospital to visit Sean. Strung out on drugs, Sean had
tried to kill himself by placing a .38 inside his mouth, pulling
the trigger, but had only succeeded in inflicting brain damage.
And now the beautiful Sean—until recently, a French Quarter
icon, Pied Piper to kids like Dwayne, and my son's pre-Mande-
ville idol—lay hollow-eyed and mute, a tube into an incision in
his throat. And as we sat there, I knew that however dissimilar
Sean's mother and I might seem—she in her rural shape-
lessness; I, hollow-cheeked, skinny, in my mini and high heels—
we were somehow alike: each in utter despair, yet relieved to
have her son back on any terms.

"Please—let's do some of the things *he* likes," I begged
Bobby. Finally, I talked him into taking Dwayne and me to a
"concert," while Rose and Lily stayed behind with Willadene.
We rode into the country, where Bobby parked the Chevy a mile
from a pasture, then spent the afternoon stumbling through the
mud over sprawled seminude bodies—Bobby grumbling, me
smiling brightly, Dwayne looking as though he'd like nothing
more than to lose us. The whole hot time, a screeching sound
came from a barely visible bandstand. "Janis," I heard some of
the half-dead figures murmur reverently as a wild-haired figure
flailed in the distance.

"Aren't yuh Dwayne's mama?" a man of about thirty, dirty
long blond hair matted, bare belly hanging over the edge of
grimy jeans, tattoos on biceps and forearms, greeted me as I
stood at the bottom of the broken wooden steps, holding out
his hand. "Dwayne tole us you paint pitchers—fact, he brung a

couple ovah hyah to purty up the place." I had wondered what had happened to the mauve nude. "Fact is, I draw some, too. Yuh wanna see some a' mah stuff?" "Mainly, I came to find Dwayne," I said from the sidewalk, trying to hold myself aloof, maintain my dignity. "He's back in the kitchen wid Miz Dwarf," the man said, leading me through several rooms furnished only with mattresses covered in dingy, tangled sheets and cardboard cartons full of what looked like garbage—except for my missing acrylic, which quivered against one wall like a chunk of my own flesh.

In the kitchen, Dwayne turned from the table where he sat drinking a Coca-Cola; before him, flies buzzed around some bread crusts spread with peanut butter and jelly, and cookie crumbs and crumpled paper napkins littered the dirty oilcloth. Mrs. Dwarf was sitting there, too, and as I entered, she stood, rising her full three feet to greet me. "So plu-*eezed* to meet yuh," she said, smiling a crazy grin—like my former neighbors, she was a Diane Arbus photograph.

"I came to take you home—let's go," I said to Dwayne.

Mrs. Dwarf looked offended. "But he promised to stay hyah wid me fur the *res'* a' his life," she protested. "Ah take *good* keer of mah boys hyah—they kin do a li'l drugs, bring in their gulls—'n ah see to it thet they eat right." Dwayne, still seated, was grinning more broadly. "'Sides," Mrs. Dwarf went on firmly; "It's the Laird's will. The Laird done showed me in a dream, Dwayne's s'posed to stay hyah wit me the *res'* a' his life." The man with bare belly stood behind her, smiling, nodding in agreement: "Yes'm, she's right, she shore is." Dwayne put his hand tenderly over mine; it was sweaty from the heat and the Coke bottle. "I wanna stay here, Mama—it's great!" "But he's only fourteen," I gasped, then plopped down in one of the dirty folding chairs, put my arms down onto the oilcloth, my head on top of them, and, before I could stop myself, began weeping. "Don't cry, Mama," Dwayne said softly, stroking my long hair. "Yes'm, ever'thang gonna be all *right*, jes' lak it *always* is wid de *Laird*," Miz Dwarf was saying in a singsong tone; then she hummed a hard-shell hymn I hadn't heard since leaving South Alabama. *Ah was sink-in' deep in sin—far from the peace-ful shore,* the words reverberated through my brain, *when He came—'n took me in—AND LOVE LIFT-ed ME—YES—LOVE LIFT-ed ME. . . .*"

"You could stay, too, Mama—that would be fun. I *know* she would let you . . ." I heard Dwayne saying through the noise in my head. As he spoke, he lifted my chin and smiled guilelessly into my eyes.

"They all look like *you,* Mama," Lily said of the girls who came to our house, sleeping in Dwayne's room with him, watching him shoot up, having sex with him—loudly, just as Bobby had done with me. They were thirteen, nineteen, fourteen, twenty. One wore purple suede boots and a fringed vest; another wore what looked like an Indian print tablecloth tied around her breasts sarong-style; yet another worked some nights as a topless dancer—I would hear her and Dwayne come in at 4:00 A.M, their drugged laughter. They all had long hair, whether Clairol blonde, stringy brown, or hennaed a rusty orange. Some believed in witchcraft, some had tattoos on their swelling breasts or earrings through a nostril.

One, running a fever of 104, lay writhing on a cot in the family room while Rose and Lily looked on curiously. When I took her to Charity to the emergency room, she refused to tell the doctors who her parents were. "They hate me and I hate them!" she hissed after admitting to being fourteen. I paid the bill for the treatment for the infection of her Fallopian tubes and took her home, and in three days she was gone. All of them looked to me like girls who were already old women. I would think of them again later in New York, seeing the prematurely aging young women, depleted faces lined, long hair stringy, squatting on a street corner with their scraggly-haired men, selling tarnishing beads and earrings, perhaps pressing a pasty-looking toddler to breasts already sagging, stretch-marked by twenty, as tattered and scarred-looking as the walleyed cats mewling harshly around the city garbage cans.

But the girls were better than the muscular, tattooed men, the crazy-eyed ones with shaggy hair, the ones who wore black metal-studded leather bands and vests, who frightened Rose and Lily, who did strange things with Dwayne in his room just beneath the sounds of heavy metal, of Jimi Hendrix, the Grateful Dead, Cream, making me try not to think of the bloody dildo; who raided the refrigerator and stole the stereo and the TV, disappearances of which Dwayne would confess no knowledge. . . .

"You his girlfriend?" the doctor at the public-health clinic asked sternly.

I swallowed. I hated to make the familiar admission. "No, his mother."

He paused, staring. Dwayne and I each wore jeans, work shirts, moccasins; in addition, I had on faint pink Revlon; he was fifteen, I was thirty, but we both looked eighteen. "This boy's had gonorrhea five times this year—more than anybody else in this parish. . . ." He coughed into his fist, looking tiredly down at a chart. "How old did you say he is? Fifteen? Now we're havin' to give him this special medicine—he's already resistant to the penicillin. Do you think you can make sure he takes it?" He cleared his throat again, then went on rotely, "And—oh yes—it would be *good* if we could get the names and addresses of some of his sex partners." He paused once more, looking at me dubiously. "And by the way, have *you* been tested . . . ?"

The next month, Dwayne almost died, a gorgeous yellow ochre blazing his Seminole swarth. "Hepatitis," the doctor at Charity said, looking unconcerned as Dwayne writhed, golden against the hospital whites. His hot yellow skin, a lick of flame, burned me. As he tossed, I glimpsed the purple of needle marks. "Give him plenty of liquids, no alcohol, complete bed rest. . . ."

That night, a radiant wraith, he took to the streets again.

In South Alabama, there was a long-standing tradition, a halfway acceptable something called being "no good," as in "He jes' turned out no good." It was an indulgence, a dispensation given some men—men like Daddy, Wayne, Wayne's daddy. Such men were exempt from making a living, from abstaining from drink or adultery. I had heard them whispered of often enough by the church ladies: "He lives off his pore mama, goin' out at naht to them honky-tonks, then lyin' abed all day," or "I don' know how she lives with it, him slinkin' aroun' them graveyards, drankin' brown whiskey frum a paper bag the way he does. . . ." ("No, I don't talk to 'im about it, 'cause it would just come between us," Miz Lillian would later say on national TV of her son Billy's drinking, and I would know just what she meant.) And had Dwayne grown up back in South Alabama, he could have been like that: secretly envied by the more upstanding men of the community, and feared (yet secretly desired) by the churchgoing girls. Perhaps he could have lived that way, "gittin' Saved"—married, a job, and so on—in his late thirties or forties, accepted, like the Prodigal Son, back into the loving, if rigid, arms of the community.

But now, everybody except Musette—who had loved Dwayne when he was little almost as much as I did—thought I should just give up on him, cut him out like the defective kitten in a litter.

"Jes' bad blood, Ah guess," Aunt Darlene said dismissively. *Bad blood*—it was a phrase I had come to hate. It meant Daddy's blood, Wayne's blood, Wayne's daddy's blood, rushing, bubbling, surging, through Dwayne's veins, circling and circling its way through his whole body, and there was no way of stopping it. I had heard of people who had had their whole blood supply changed—but how did they do it?

And genes—what did they look like? I saw them as small, clawing creatures, tenaciously burrowing via legs like tiny wire filaments, into Dwayne's brain, the very soft tissues of his body.

"You jes' tell thet boy to come on home," Homerdessa said when Bobby kicked him out for the last time.

When Mama had lain in her back room dying, we had all gone to visit. Dwayne, let off on furlough from the hospital to see her, had taken off with Homerdessa in her big Oldsmobile. I knew that when he came back, he would have an armful of packages, a pocketful of money. It was always like that.

And now—perhaps because he suspected that with Homerdessa he could up the ante—to cars, to credit cards, and total unaccountability—he went.

And I had lost him.

The only things that seemed left to me were Rose and Lily and my painting.

Big Bobby had long since stopped patting my ass when I saw him. He and Miss Lisa had become disgusted by our problems—by the upstart woman Bobby had married, and her defective son.

Even Bobby's fraternity brother Jimmy—once so interested in my body and my art—had turned against me. "Your wife gone hippie?" he asked Bobby after an ATO alumni party to which I had worn long, straight hair, painted African beads, and a cotton shift (sans bra) that said MADE IN INDIA. I could tell that Bobby's buddies considered me the cause of whatever problems he had. Their wives still kept house, served little dinners, and wore eyelids thickly lined with Revlon; like me, they wore miniskirts, but the lace edges of the elastic panty girdles they still wore showed beneath them. "Can't you at least put on some *makeup*?" Bobby said, aggrieved.

One dawn, when I thought Bobby was in Shreveport on a car-buying trip, the doorbell rang, and Jimmy, holding Bobby by the elbow, stood at the front door. Dried blood outlined a gash across Bobby's forehead; his good seersucker jacket was ripped at the armhole. He groaned, his now-balding crown bent, his forelock down over his bushy eyebrows. He stumbled about blindly, pale and molelike; his glasses had been smashed, Jimmy mumbled, not looking at me, then helped Bobby inside and onto the couch.

After Jimmy left, Bobby sobbed out the story—how he had left a mid-city bar with a black woman—"a ho-ar"—had gone with her to a house on Desire Street where two black men sat ominously on the stoop, how he had gone upstairs with her anyway—"She was so pretty, so pretty, so smooth, like brown silk"—he moaned here, almost as though he expected me to empathize—and as he had come back out, the two men had jumped him, shoving him to the sidewalk, stomping his glasses, ripping his wallet from a pocket.

I led him, still weeping weakly, back to the bedroom. That he told me this made me know that he knew there was nothing he could do anymore to turn the tide of my contempt, to stop me from leaving him. And though it would be two more years before our divorce, he was right. Dwayne may have been gone, but the damage had been done, with as much ravage to our little family as Hurricane Camille had just done in South Louisiana. Even Rose and Lily, now twelve and thirteen, knew it: "I just wish you'd get a divorce 'n get it *over* with, Mother!" they would complain as the dinner hour got later and later, and Bobby and I drank Wild Turkey and raged at each other, wrangling over the carcass of a marriage that was already as dead as a dead dog on the street.

So now I add Bobby—*poor* Bobby, as I had come to think of him—to my list of victims. After all, he had saved me from the tenant farm, had given me the mouton jacket, the toreador pants, the red convertible—not to speak of Rose and Lily. He had taught me to drink and had "let" me take art lessons. He lived through my craziness with a son who wasn't his.

I was thirty-one years old, my wretchedness etched beneath my eyes. When a sculptor friend did a study of me, I saw that crazy woman bloom on the page, and had to look away from what I saw engraved there.

"I wonder how things would have turned out if you had just stayed with Bobby?" Musette asked years later. "That wasn't even a *choice!*" I answered instantly, shocked by her question.

She also talked about the time of Dwayne's injury, how his prognosis had been possible brain damage, perhaps the inability ever to walk again—of all the long months he had spent first in a wheelchair, then cheerfully stumbling through the rooms in his metal walker. She told me because I could now remember none of it—only that moment of the accident, of my guilt sitting beside his bed the next morning.

Things had been hard for Musette, but in a different way. She had nursed both Daddy and Mama, and a year after first Daddy, then Mama, had died, she had married a boy whom she had considered a nerd back in high school. But he had inherited his own farm and had bought the tenant farm we had grown up on, too. They lived in a big, roomy farmhouse with wide porches filled with rocking chairs around three sides—the kind of house we had only dreamed of living in as girls. Musette's own three stair-step children seemed about as wholesome, as ordinary, as cow pies, though she did have a girl who would get that hurt look in her eyes as Musette always had.

And when I came down to the farm to visit—which I did more often once Dwayne was nearby—Musette, rangy but still dressed by Sears Roebuck, was often in her kitchen baking a cake or pie, and she would look up at Rose, Lily, and me in astonishment. Lily, thirteen, her plumpness magically transformed to small breasts, jutting hipbones, might be walking beside me wearing one of my new Twiggy-style dresses, looking better in it than I ever had ("See that freckle, Mother?" she would say looking down at my hand. "It's an age spot, and it's goin' to get *worse and worse!*"). Carrying her usual load of books, Rose, fourteen, straighter and a few inches taller, would sullenly stomp along beside us, wearing the bib overalls, the hiking boots, she now affected, her jet hair falling like a silky nun's coif around her angelic yet stern and unmade-up face.

I wore hair under my arms, leather miniskirts, and white vinyl boots. On occasion, I drank martinis straight up, and smoked little imported cigars from special tins. I had sold paintings, found out that I could teach art and even balance a checkbook, and had shed Bobby, I told Musette, almost as easily as the snake must have shed one of those snakeskins we used to find out in the pasture.

As my baby sister sat shelling butter beans, a metal collander between her knees, I enthused to her about the flood of new books by and about women—*The Second Sex, The Feminine Mystique, Sexual Politics, The Female Eunuch*—and instructed her in how foolish, self-sabotaging the ideas we had garnered from Mama, Aunt Darlene, the Church of God, and *The Ladies' Home Journal* had been. I described to her the mixed-media presentation I had just done in which I had had a sister feminist run inside the open double doors of a Frigidaire, as though they were her lover's arms—representative of how chillingly subservient married women have been to their roles as housewives.

As Musette wiped her hands, her unpolished nails, on her flowered cotton apron—she still wore aprons!—and made more coffee, I talked about my new consciousness-raising group, and the fact that women all over the country were leaving their husbands, so what I had done was not unusual at all—that marriage, if not motherhood, was death anyway. I espoused the benefits of open marriage, of how I thought that if one *had* to be married, it might be a good idea—after all, we had the Pill, freeing us once and for all from those gunky condoms and diaphragms. I discussed the Myth of Vaginal Orgasm and told her about a woman named Betty Dodson who had shaved her head, and who had just published a book on how to masturbate, illustrated with drawings women had made of their own vaginas. I enjoyed the slight shock on her face as I mentioned self-help groups during which women looked into mirrors at their own and other women's cervixes. I talked about Thomas Altizer and *The Death of God* and about how passé fundamentalism was these days, and worse, repressive of women. I described the new therapists who did Gestalt and bioenergetics and primal-scream therapy. I told her about R. D. Laing and Thomas Szasz, and a publication called *The Radical Therapist*, and how reading them had helped me realize that everything that had happened with Dwayne was probably just an illusion. Too, I had heard of a lot of people who were having similar problems—it was just a part of the revolution, of the Greening of America.

As I talked about these things, she would listen, pouring me a fresh cup of coffee or wiping off the Formica tabletop while watching me sadly, taking in my thin hair, the bluish hollows beneath my eyes. Then, leaving Rose poring over her science homework, Lily listlessly wandering around the farm or trying to pick out "The Age of Aquarius" on Musette's kids' upright piano, I would leave to visit Dwayne, hoping to see him for the few minutes I could get him away from Homerdessa's, his late risings and roaring around the countryside in her car.

"He's jes' gittin' up," Homerdessa would say, gloating, as I knocked on her door after noon. In a few minutes, Dwayne, a dark and malevolent-looking, if sleepy-eyed, young man, would come into the room, zipping up his jeans, pulling a T-shirt over his head. While we ate at the local Huddle House, he shoveled down the ham and eggs and grits without looking at me; then, inevitably, angrily, he would ask me for money.

"Why couldn't you just have been like other mothers— stayin' home 'n makin' pies 'n things?" he said once, his jet eyes looking at me accusingly. And for a moment, guilt would pierce my soul again, pierce it enough to make me place the folded bills in his palm as I kissed him good-bye, and he would look off in the distance almost as angrily as he had when we had first taken him to the hospital.

As I gradually realized that nothing was going to change for the better anytime soon with Dwayne—that he really did prefer what Homerdessa was giving him—my visits to South Alabama tapered off.

After all, I had options now, didn't I? I didn't *have* to have anything to do with that kind of mentality anymore. I was getting better and better in my work, and I was slipping further and further away from the self that had to do with the farm, with giving birth to Dwayne, with the very red dirt of Alabama.

All my baby sister ever said later about that time was, "I sure was glad when you started shavin' under yore arms again."

My new lover, Johnny, liked the soft hair beneath my arms—in fact, insisted on it—and he didn't think what had happened with Dwayne was all that serious. "The boy is just going through a stage," he said dismissively, stroking his dark beard, his eyes going as gray as mirrors.

French, handsome, and artistic, Johnny was as exotic as I pleased, and was the opposite of everything I had ever known. His family spoke French at home; he had gone to the Sorbonne and had come back to New Orleans to start a little gallery— "With your help, my darling, I will make it a success." Unlike Bobby, when Johnny said "darling," he didn't drop the *g*. Too, he was handsome in the same ascetic way Martin had been, but more so. Instead of cords or denims, Johnny wore shirts shaped to his body, open at the throat, often boldly imprinted with blossoms, and tight, pocketless pants fitted to his well-formed buttocks—"Continental style," he told me, asking me to carry his Gauloises, his money clip in my purse. And though he was by far too worldly to be a believer, he—a French Jew—would soon be jokingly wearing amid the thick curls at his chest the religious medals I had bought for him in the gift shop at St. Louis Cathedral, giving me my first real experience of kitsch.

The week before we met, something had happened that had triggered the bubbles of happiness again: The *Times-Pica-yune* had run a story on my first show, and in my photo, I had seen another person—a beautiful, if gaunt, young woman who looked removed, sure of herself. Yet at the opening that first night, I still couldn't believe that a man like Johnny was pursuing me. He had stalked me around the room, padding on his European shoes, inserting himself amid the perspiring, noisy groups who surrounded me. I felt the same way I had when I had seen Bobby looking at my legs that Sunday way back in South Alabama: that I was lucky, that I didn't deserve it, and that this was a way out. But despite his sexual joking, the innu-endos, Johnny didn't focus on my body the way Bobby had. Instead, he approached me by speaking of my art, my mind, and then by saying a great deal—a great, great deal—about himself, his New Orleans lineage, the fact that his mother was from Philadelphia "society," his experiences abroad, and the poetry he had lately been reading and writing—not even seem-ing to notice the crepe dress that barely covered my breasts, the gold chain at my curve of skinny hipbone. He had studied the French symbolist poets, adding that, of course, they had to be read in the French for any comprehension at all. He was impressed, I could tell, that I knew Paula, and wanted to help "direct" my career; he felt that I was naive, might make mis-takes. Even though he was five years younger than I was—twenty-six to my thirty-one—he talked as though he were older, more knowledgeable—as though I might need his expertise if I was to have any kind of life or success at all. He had a boldness, even a sardonic arrogance, that Bobby had never had. And who was I to question him? He had been to Harvard, and then to the University of Paris, hadn't he?

His only detractors were Rose and Musette. "Mother, he's just snowing you!" Rose said, not even taking her nose from her book.

"When Johnny smiles, it's like somebody else frownin'," Musette said tentatively after meeting him. "Those gray eyes a' his feel jes' like ice cubes." But I chalked her remark up to her own lack of worldliness, her dis-ease around someone more "sophisticated." It would take me a while to learn that those who were not useful—much less the suffering, the disenfranchised—had little place in Johnny's life; that he wouldn't like hearing about my pain any more than Bobby had—though he wouldn't mind the excruciating images in my paintings; they were, after all, what was making me semifamous, and that was more important to Johnny than anything.

Soon Johnny had moved in with Rose and Lily and me in Algiers, and the household was under his control. Johnny could cook as well as I could, and at first it was disconcerting to come home from my new job teaching at the John McCrady School of Art on Bourbon Street to find him in an apron, the Simone Beck at his elbow, concocting a dish he had obviously prepared before. "Don't you have any truffles?" he would complain, looking crossly through the cabinets. We had to have just the right beans for the espresso machine. And the wines had to be perfect: "I can't believe you drink this stuff," he said, holding up the jug of Gallo I had taken, pre-Johnny, to drinking by the glassful while cooking dinner for Rose, Lily, and me. French wines were the best, he insisted, and we had a cabinetful of everything from Pouilly-Fuissé to Lillet vermouth, which he checked regularly to see that I had kept up-to-date; when he served the Lillet, Johnny insisted on making a ceremony of flaming the twist of orange peel. "My little primitive," he would say fondly when I asked what arugula was, or questioned his serving pasta as a first course: "But that's the way it's always served in Italy," he would explain patiently. If I had felt superior to Bobby in matters of taste, there was no way I could feel superior with Johnny. And since he didn't focus on my body the way Bobby had, I was at a loss—I couldn't control him that way, either.

On the other hand, my life was more exciting, more bohemian—and thus closer to my dreams—than it had ever been. Aside from painting at home in the family-room-turned-studio, I actually worked in the French Quarter, teaching at a school across from a gay bar with the romantic name Lafitte in Exile. On many nights, Johnny would meet me after my last class at Lafitte's Blacksmith; then we would go on to Lucky Pierre's, the nearby after-hours club, to hear jazz.

Johnny seemed intent on saving me from my provincial

ways. He wanted me to take a second mortgage on the house in Algiers, which I had been awarded in the divorce settlement from Bobby, to help him open the little gallery where he would feature my works, and I agreed. "Money is to be shared, don't you think?" he remarked, implying that feeling otherwise would mean I was hopelessly bourgeois, even nonfeminist. Now, rather than the fraternity brother–car dealer gatherings I had known with Bobby, Johnny and I gave parties for other artists, psychologists, or the well-off bohemians who lived in the Quarter, often organized around some special dish Johnny had created. "It's bad enough that you have to live in Algiers," he mused, looking around the house for ways to rearrange it— though I did have some things that he seemed to approve of. "It looks like it's sucking itself off," he commented in that slight accent I found so exotic, looking at the basket in which I kept my brushes; it was made of an armadillo shell; its tail was held in its mouth to form a handle. He liked Martin's piece but consigned it to my studio, then hung the living room with my new paintings, the dining area with pictures from his own erotica. He and the painter Jacques Dupree had become fast friends, and now Jacques's dwarfs and malformed male figures looked down on us as we ate.

Aside from the erotica, Johnny had a collection of pornography—photographs of women jamming large, even huge, double dildos inside other women, who were often chained or held down by other, more muscular females; or dwarfs, black and white, riding openmouthed blondes twice their size. He kept these books and magazines out on a shelf in the family room, insisting that it was healthy for Rose and Lily to look at them. ("But the one I *really* hated," Lily would tell me later, "was that one you had that showed the two girls on that commune in Oregon havin' babies, with the heads coming out 'n all the blood. Then them making a stew out of the afterbirth!") In Europe, he told me, the pornography had been far more extreme, though I couldn't imagine how. But who was I, who had never been anywhere or done anything, to doubt him?

Next to what Johnny showed and described to me, the Mi-O-Mi Club and the drag shows of Bourbon Street were harmless costume shows. His best friend was a psychologist who special-

191

ized in treating prostitutes, and who believed that viewing a
certain amount of hard-core pornography was periodically imperative "to clear the cobwebs from the brain." Thus, Johnny
regularly led me into theaters where we watched double features such as *Deep Throat*, and *The Devil and Miss Jones* ("Don't
be so literal, Easter," he said when I protested mildly that "no
woman *really* has a clitoris inside her throat"), and I was one of
a few women among men barely concealing their erections,
their masturbation. I sat through the movies at first willingly,
then bored and uncomfortably, as I clenched my thighs, trying
not to have to go to the rest room. Some nights, we wandered
into neon-lit shops where wall-to-wall vaginas spread open to
pink mucus membranes, magazines with titles like *Emily and the
Enemas* and *Women Who Like to Be Whipped* stared down at us,
the images burning themselves into my brain, later to find their
way into my paintings. In one shop, Johnny insisted we buy a
tiny vibrator—"But why? It's so little!" I blurted, as the man
behind the counter smiled knowingly, and suddenly flashing its
intent, I blushed. That night, Johnny showed me how he liked
it inserted in his anus as we fucked. If he was not as obsessed
by my body as Bobby had been, he was more imaginative.

" 'The history of the world in one word—repression,' " he
would say, quoting Freud. "The repressive tool of the bourgeois," he would comment with a sneer in regard to the idea of
sexual exclusivity. And after a time, he suggested open marriage
and group sex—forces he could control, or believed he could
control. *Jealousy . . . masks a fear of losing control*, Johnny had
underlined in one of my new feminist handbooks, poring over
it for passages to which he wanted me to pay special attention.
Lying in bed together at night, I felt slightly queasy as he read
aloud to me from a book called *John and Mary*, the true account
of a New York married couple who had had themselves video-
taped having sex, then had shown it at a "happening"; in subse-
quent chapters, the couple alternated in graphically describing
their extramarital affairs. But finally, my wildness would turn
out to want more than such tame, suburban alternatives. And
years later—when Johnny had long since pronounced me "too
kinky, too insatiable" for him—I would be the unshockable
one, watching live sex shows in a sleazy bar in San José or the

Reeperbahn of Hamburg. But by then, after all, I would have done, as they say, "everything." And it wouldn't have been the healthy "everything" aspired to back then by the Esalen Institute and the new therapists.

Rose and Lily were supposed to visit Bobby every weekend in the apartment complex in Metairie where he now lived, but they didn't want to go because Bobby was moping around so much and dumping his depression on them (or at least, on Lily, whose tenderness made her blotterlike), and because he always tried to get Lily to cook. Also, they didn't want to go because— with the dope and the pornography and the art—things were so interesting at home now. At thirteen and fourteen, they were reading Henry Miller, Jean Genet, and *The Story of O*, and when we had the cocktail parties, they served the drinks, then sat up late, smoking dope with the guests. Drugs no longer seemed the way they had seemed—like malevolent snakes—with Dwayne, but like part of a way of life, like the right wines and gourmet cooking. Rose worked with me on a mixed-media presentation featuring her Barbies and G.I. Joes, and Lily had a new poem or set of song lyrics to read to us at dinner almost every night. They attended a progressive high school where the students went at their own rate of speed, and attendance at class was not compulsory. Rose, single-minded Rose—what the new social scientists called "inner-directed" (fueled, I would later realize, by her desire to leave) let nothing interfere with her studies, her "research." But Lily—other-directed Lily—smoked dope with the boys in the woods near the campus rather than going to class, and spent her time at home trying on exotic getups and applying the makeup that looked, to Johnny's amusement, like a Kabuki dancer's.

I knew from Lily's journals that she fell in love with almost every boy she met—*They're so cute, so adorable, with those muscles in their brown arms, and those tiny golden hairs on them, and with the cute little hairs on their faces. . . .* Now every poem disintegrated into a paean of longing for one of these lumpy adolescents, the prologue to a lifetime of trouble with men. Musette suspected already that Lily had already "gotten too thick" with "a wild boy from the next town over" back in South Alabama during her last visit ("They went off in 'is pickup, 'n were gone a long time. And when Lily came back, she looked like she'd been cryin'. . . .") But she had *really* been "in love" with Johnny— Johnny, with his iciness, his gray eyes, was merely the first of the men we would share over the years—she insisted a decade later. And hadn't that been only logical, considering how trained she already was in inextricably braiding love and pain?

In the meantime, I was seeing one of the new therapists, and Lily had written about it in the journal left open on her desk: *Mother told me about her childhood. It was awful. Her father was an alcoholic and her mother was a matchokist. (Did I spell that right, I wonder?) He would do terrible things to her. And in this therapy she's in, she resaw her trauma and was able to kill both her parents. . . .*

Encouraged by Johnny, we were all into therapy and journals; they lay around the house like dropped handkerchiefs, messages from the psyche. Every week, we had family meetings. Johnny, legs crossed (I had never before known a man who crossed his legs), his hands folded, or holding his pipe, served as guru; the purpose was to talk about feelings, but usually the subjects were allowances and housework. Everybody in this family is equal, Johnny would say from his privileged position, and it was true that Lily, if not Rose, who scorned such things, brought out her own stash at our parties and sat, perhaps smoking it, with the fortyish psychologist friend of Johnny's who believed in prostitution and pornography. And I pushed down my bourgeois discomfort at the lust I saw in his middle-aged eyes as he looked at her.

CHAPTER EIGHT

AFTER I got the offer to teach at the Atlanta College of Art, Johnny decided that I should sell the house in Algiers, that we would go to Georgia, where I would enter the Ida Cason Callaway Gardens Show, and that he'd look for sites for his gallery there. But that before we did any of that, we would go to New York for a few months to be there for my opening.

When I visited South Alabama to tell Dwayne that I was marrying Johnny—who was nine years older than he was, five years younger than I—rage suffused his dark face. "He'll just have to get over it, won't he?" Johnny said abruptly when I told him about it, going back to his reading of *The Denial of Death* by Emil Cioran, from which he occasionally raised his head to share some particularly nihilistic—and thus, wonderful—quote about how, in the face of death, nothing really matters anyway.

Johnny reserved a suite for the two of us in the Chelsea Hotel on West Twenty-third Street, where, he told me, a lot of artists had stayed. There was a fireplace and a little kitchenette and a lumpy mattress and plastic window shades and grimy windowsills covered in cigarette burns and a phone book with the middle cut out as though it had been used to hold somebody's stash. He reserved another room down the hall for Rose and Lily, which thrilled them. Plump maids chattered in Spanish, and the lobby was filled with paintings and men who looked like rock stars and women in black tights and black leather miniskirts, often tugging an exotic dog on a leash, or pushing a dress rack full of sequined dresses onto an elevator. People I had only read about, like Janis Joplin and Dylan Thomas, had stayed there; I saw the newly notorious Daniel Berrigan checking in, and the Beat poet Gregory Corso, his teeth gone, wearing a floury white apron, asking for someone at the desk; he worked at a bakery now, Johnny said.

Johnny's brother, a jeweler in New Orleans, had recommended that we visit Van Cleef & Arpels on Fifth Avenue. The crown jewels of some tiny European country were on display in the window, he said. But when we got there—Lily in a tight mini, Rose in bib overalls, Johnny and I in jeans—the space behind the glass was empty. As we walked inside, two uniformed guards opened the door for us; two more stood beside us as Johnny asked to see the crown jewels. We gazed seriously at the tiara, the pendants, as the stiff matron behind the counter gravely presented them, offering them like a platter of sparkling candies. "Oops, I must have forgotten my checkbook," Johnny said, reaching into his back pocket. Out on the sidewalk again, the four of us burst into laughter. Sometimes my new husband was like that: we were a family.

Every night, we ate at a different restaurant, its selection the day's major decision. There were fine wines and simple foods—a huge dripping lobster, a hunk of calves' liver so perfectly broiled that it could have been filet mignon. Walking into Balducci's, seeing the colored pastas, the tall rum cakes, thick with whipped cream; past the Greek cafés, with their huge juicy rotisseries of beef and lamb, the scent wafting out onto the sidewalk; or even into Ray's Famous Pizza, where the pies lay heavy with broccoli, escarole, meatballs—was like being in a dream. The quality of everything was beyond my most sensuous imaginings. Taxis—until Johnny complained of how much I was spending on them—were like magic carpets to take me anywhere, instantly. The city's vertical aspect, the banners of fire-engine red and taxicab yellow in my first flash fantasies of

the city, sitting with Paula in that "Chinese" place back in Metairie, were turning out to have been prescient if understated.
(And now I also knew just how bad that restaurant, and how
patient Paula, had been!) I was flooded by a sense of recognition
similar to, but not quite as indelible as, the one I had felt during
my first trip to the French Quarter. And then there was the
noise and the dirt: Walking down Seventh Avenue near the
Chelsea, we could hear a constant humming, staccato voices all
around us, speaking a special New York language, and other
languages, too, its relentlessness making me yearn at times for
the soft patois of home. That summer, the garbage set out by
the curbs smelled rank, a greasy stench that was different
from the fresh, clean dirt of Alabama or Louisiana, or even the
aging grime of the French Quarter. Johnny didn't notice these
things; indeed, he seemed to think everything in New York was
better, even though we didn't do the fun things here that we
had done in New Orleans, like hanging out at Lafitte's Blacksmith. Every Saturday night that we weren't in the country,
weekending with friends of his, he drummed his fingertips on
the tabletop of whatever restaurant we were in, waiting for the
Sunday *Times* to come out, then he would rush out to the nearest
newsstand to pick it up, just as everyone else in the world seemed
to be doing. Sometimes, I longed to get away from it all—the
noise and smells and the people, to get back to birdsong and
azaleas and the moss between the cracks of cobbled sidewalks,
even to the slugs out around the garbage can and the opossums
eating at the cat food. And I wondered at such moments why
everyone there seemed to think the city was so wonderful. But at
other times, I felt—as Mama had often said on a good day before
she had had her accident, perhaps when the biscuits for shortcake
had risen perfectly, or her pin curls had turned out just like
Claudette Colbert's—that "I had died and gone to heaven."

We usually dined with school friends of Johnny's—people
who all, it seemed to me, had had exactly seven years of psycho-
analysis. Was that a requirement for living here? I asked him.
His school friend Madeleine was wealthy—"old money—she'll
never have to work for a day in her life," Johnny told me
enviously on our way to meet her. She had a tumble of long
blonde curls, and that night she wore a sweater tied at her

throat—"the one Robert Redford wore in *The Way We Were*," she said casually; she had bid for it at an auction. Then there were Harold and Kissy, a darkly handsome literary couple; she was British, and she enthused in her elegant accent about what the enemas their physiotherapist had recommended had done for them. Hannah had an equine look, accentuated by longer and redder fingernails than I had ever seen, and at a recent party had seduced Harold's analyst. She reported to Harold with malicious delight that the man hadn't been able to get it up, thus effectively ruining his analysis.

"I wasted seven years and probably fifteen grand on that guy, and he's not even sexually functional!" he groaned as we trudged up Ninth Avenue toward yet another gourmand meal—this time in a little Italian hole-in-the-wall Harold had heard about that had only four tables and homemade everything. The one thing I didn't like about all the walking was that I couldn't wear high heels, which I knew made my legs look longer and better, but Johnny didn't seem to care about such things anyway.

Many of the artists Johnny knew lived in places that would have been considered slums back home, places where we stepped over urine-scented bodies before entering grimy metal doorways fitted with several locks. But the artists themselves seemed proud, even arrogant in the same way Johnny was. And I knew that most of them, when Johnny first took me around, didn't take me seriously, that they considered me a cracker, an innocent, especially when they heard my accent. "Listen to that!" I heard a long-haired woman in a diaphanous shirt that clearly showed her sagging tits giggle behind her hand to another woman wearing what looked like a long embroidered feedsack. But if the two women thought I felt intimidated, they were wrong: Actually, I was mentally running a hand over my own smooth curves, looking admiringly down at my own small breasts jutting just so, and was wondering why the first woman, if she was so smart, wore such a garment—didn't she know better than to reveal that less-than-perfect part of her body? No self-respecting southern woman would do such a thing if she could help it. It was a feeling much like the one I had at fifteen, out on that porch, holding my baby Dwayne in my arms, walking

away from Louise and her sticky twins and the flies—that without knowing how or why, I was somehow superior. Then, looking smug, Johnny would pull out my slides; and when they
heard that Paula was representing me, they became silent. And
later, when they saw my paintings for the first time, I could see
the envy and confusion battling within their faces. What they
didn't know was that there were other things in my life that
were far more of a problem for me than my work. For me,
painting was my pleasure and, at times, My Oblivion, as natural
as having sex or nursing a baby; and it was that ease—so different from their strivings—that offended them most. According
to the new women's movement, we were all supposed to be
sisters. And perhaps if I had stayed in my place as supplicant,
as primitive, they might have accepted me. But it seemed that
the sisterhood stopped when it came to competition.

Later, as I became more aware of the art world, its obsequi-
ous postures, its politics and machinations, I realized how easily
my early recognition had come, and how frustrated some of
those women must have been. After a while, more used to the
idea of my early success, I sought to diffuse their envy, and if
that was not possible, to protect myself from what I by then
called "negative vibrations." In the meantime, I was guarded by
a shield of innocence: "How did you get from there to here?"
interviewers would ask, as though being born in South Alabama
would surely have left me with nothing short of brain damage.
On the other hand, they tended to see my background as an
asset—as my "primitive roots," as though I were from darkest
Africa. "Everybody has to be from somewhere," I would demur,
simply not knowing what else to say—a response they then
assigned to what they assumed to be part of some deliberate
plan or pose as ingenue.

Johnny's friend Madeleine had given me a temporary studio in her own huge space, which was called a loft. Because she
was rich, she could afford the loft and everything that went
with it. Through Johnny and Madeleine, I met other women
who had grown up on the Upper East Side, in Connecticut,
Boston, or Philadelphia—women who wondered (I could tell)
that I could do what I did without having been nurtured by the

School of Visual Arts, the Rhode Island School of Design, or even the Art Students League; who wondered at how I had gotten along without a daddy's money or the requisite seven years of analysis. Occasionally, I met expatriated southern women, but they seemed to be spending more of their energies on not being southern, on erasing the very roots that I felt held me safely in place, than on making paintings.

Most of the painters seemed to be men, and the women— their wives—were as wifely as any wives back in South Alabama. Even if they had children, most had jobs as waitresses or typists to support their demanding men, the insatiable need for paint and canvas, for hours and hours of talk without them at the White Horse or the Cedar.

Back then, I didn't know about those bars or about the East Village. Or the way painters were *supposed* to be, à la Jackson Pollock—male, alcoholic, broke, broken, as pugilistic, as punch-drunk, as prizefighters. But I *had* intuited that a woman who didn't follow the rules would be punished. At first my male peers were titillated by the imagery in my paintings. "Wanna fuck, bebe?" they would say to me out of Johnny's hearing, smirking, not commenting on my work at all. But later, as my paintings became more extreme, and as I began to sell more than they did, they became angry, calling me a bitch, a ball-buster, and later, whenever they could, they would sit on juries, cutting me out of shows or awards, even—especially—the ones I had slept with. After all, I, a mere woman, had not only not been reduced by the power of the cock, but had even bested them.

Yet I felt comfortable, even at home, when Paula took me to meet older, more established women artists. She arranged a visit with Alice Neel, a grandmotherly-looking woman, in her studio full of muscleless yet sensuously detailed nudes of angry young men, and sitting in her studio, I felt as natural as I had back on the farm. Paula introduced me to Charmion Von Wiegand—"one of the first American abstractionists," who personally knew the Dalai Lama and who used tantric symbols in her work—and to Gerald Van Syke—"the father of existentialism"—and his wife, Buffie Johnson, who lived with him in a beautiful hotel suite, full of her sinuous paintings of snakes. Paula's best friend was another elegant Asian-American, Ce Roser, whose watercolors were as ephemeral, as vibrant as fireworks. Ursule Molinaro was a glamorous Frenchwoman who painted open-eyed animals, and had once lived with the editor of a chic literary review called *Chelsea*. Her teeth had been knocked out by the Gestapo when she had been a part of the Resistance, Ce and Paula told me.

Several years later, Paula would introduce me to women closer to my age who seemed as unthreatened, and as certain of themselves and their work, as I did. Anita Steckel, for example, had recently been featured in a *New York* magazine piece on women who painted erotic pictures.

I was also beginning to hear of the women on the West Coast, painting in a Disneyland I couldn't imagine—women like Judy Chicago, who, by 1975, would publish a book, *Through the Flower*, about her struggles as a woman artist, and a woman named Audrey Flack, who was painting pictures of feminine artifacts, ribbons and beads and laces, in a way that I liked.

And already, there was Gloria Steinem's new magazine, *Ms.*, and Germaine Greer, author of *The Female Eunuch*, arguing on TV with that chauvinist Norman Mailer.

Johnny enjoyed the contrast of my naïveté and what he called my "redneck outrageousness." We went to the Guggenheim, a museum shaped inside like a huge snail, where we looked at Francis Bacon's pictures of the pope screaming—or was he laughing? Bacon had also painted hanging sides of meat that were both beautiful and malevolent—it was that ambiguity that I liked; just as I liked the Fauvists with their crazy, flat-out use of color. Pictures, it seemed to me, said what words couldn't. But at the same time, I preferred the figurative. And I had begun to put lines from poems into my paintings: "I am the magician's girl who does not flinch," I inscribed, quoting my new favorite, if dead, poet, Sylvia Plath, on a streamer that flowed from the swollen mauve vulva of a woman upright on a marble slab to which she was nailed through the palms by iron stobs. Abstract expressionism held little appeal for me. For a long time, viewers labeled my work "primitive," but only later when someone said "surrealism," as they would also say of Frida Kahlo, would the designation seem right.

The four of us visited a narrow triangular building, round cutouts fringing its edges like a doily, at Columbus Circle in mid-Manhattan. Starting at the top floor, we looked at the nude as done by many artists, ending on the lowest level, where a naked figure in one corner looked so real, her skin so perfectly mottled and dimpled and discolored, that she was like a live woman standing there, motionless. "Look, Mother!" Lily, amazed, rushed over to inspect her at close range. Even Rose was staring at the figure, looking impressed.

Lily was amazed by everything in New York; it was as though she was, in fact, already staking it out as her territory. She and Rose liked to walk down to Greenwich Village and hang out in Washington Square. One day, a segment of a TV series, a cop show, was being filmed there, and the director walked over to Lily, curvaceous, full-lipped, and fourteen, and asked if she'd like to play a bit part. At that moment, she said, she fell in love with the public arena.

And Rose felt that way, too, but for a different reason. "Mother, I'm going to go to school here," she told me when she discovered Barnard and New York University. She was so smart in the progressive high school back in Louisiana that the head-master had readily agreed to recommend her for early admission to college, which meant that she would be leaving home forever at sixteen. Whatever Rose decided, she just *did*, barely asking our opinions at all.

At my opening at Paula's gallery, people I had never met before seemed suddenly to love me, and others to hate me, as though they thought I had somehow contrived for all this to come about. They couldn't know that I was as amazed as they were—that I didn't feel I could control the way the world received my art any more than I could have controlled Daddy, keeping him from throwing the rose ashtray I had made for him against the wall. It was just that I was driven to make it, and I did, and this was what had happened—indeed, at this point, I felt that my being here was due more to Johnny's efforts than to my own. I was wearing a floor-length flowered crepe dress with my breasts showing in the front, bikini panties, and nothing else. Since I was skinny, I had decided that my small, still-jutting breasts were my strong point. "I just can't wait to get you back to the hotel!" Johnny said into my ear, turned on by my success, cupping my ass with his hand. He was wearing a white linen suit—"my plantation suit," he laughingly told his friends to let them know he realized that things southern were "tacky," that the suit, however handsome he looked in it, was his version of kitsch. When a creamily coffee-skinned man, well dressed and unlike any black I had ever met in Louisiana, leaned forward, reeking of scotch, to praise me, Johnny pushed me toward him—"He's important!" he whispered; but I leaned away, my southern upbringing rearing up like a snake, momentarily overpowering my new liberalism. Then a rough-looking man in work shirt and jeans, whom I recognized as a famous painter because of the black patch over one eye, came up to me and placed a callused hand directly over one of my near-nude breasts, cupping it: "You're a good wo-man," he pronounced in a booming voice, as though it were his role and prerogative to make such a judgment—a judgment that had more to do with my sexuality than my work. Or was it that if I was also properly sexy, it was maybe okay for me to paint?

The funny thing was, that with all the craziness of New York, even gallery-goers and reviewers there seemed shocked by my imagery—the images that had just come out whole, as though by magic, from my South Alabama brain, the brain of a woman who still, underneath it all, walked in a pasture, wearing a homemade skirt—who was, yes, I had to admit it, a primitive. It was then that I first glimpsed the fact of what New York was about—it was a place where people wanted and bought a surrogate unconsciousness, and if the country was a body, the Deep South, where I lived, was the genitals; and no matter how shocked they were, they loved it. In one way, they were jaded and had seen everything, but it was also as though their own unconsciousness, their own genitals, had been erased, leaving them as harmless, as neutered, as Rose's G.I. Joes and Barbies, and they needed for us—the artists—to do it for them. I was beginning to understand that we, the artists, were surrogates,

203

surrogate sufferers, the ones who "did their living for them." And the thing I did because I had to do it had a value in that world, a value that could bring me a bit of money, even fame.

So now I had a handsome, worldly husband, two beautiful daughters, and recognition for my work. I had been to New York and had been accepted there. But I wasn't taking into account the tenacious claws of my history. Despite therapy, my recent successes, I was just what they accused me of being—a psychological savage, my soul still filled with images from the past, the primal urges to destroy, if only myself. It was almost as though I was lonely for my pain, longing for it just as I sometimes longed for the dirt and soft sounds of home. Obviously, too much civilization disagreed with me—my craving for sleaze, for chaos, was once again worming its way to the surface. And as usual, New Orleans would seem the best place to find it. I might have gone to New York. I might have become semifamous. But I was still in the Deep South in my brain.

If it hadn't been for the nagging pain of Dwayne waiting inside me like a lime-hole sink, I might have enjoyed my life at that time. But he was like a scab that was constantly picked at; that pain was destined to be torn open over and over again. While Johnny and I were in New York, and then back in Atlanta, I would get phone calls from Alabama that left me distraught—Dwayne was in jail again, Homerdessa had gotten him yet another lawyer, there was no one who understood "thet pore boy." Johnny and I had seen Pasolini's *Life of Christ*, and as Mary watched her son crucified, I had begun, to Johnny's disgust, to sob, so loudly that I had to leave the theater, feeling again that longing to take my son, my first love, back inside my very body, to protect him.

When we returned to Atlanta, we rented a three-bedroom condo, and, uninvited, Dwayne had Homerdessa drive him there from Alabama. But we weren't home, and he and Homerdessa had an argument in the parking lot, a fight witnessed by the property manager, who had stepped out of her office to see what was going on. During their screaming match, Dwayne threw his grandmother's glasses to the pavement and stomped them, then jerked the beehive wig from her head. Walking over to the manager, he said, "My grandmother's having an attack—call an ambulance!" In the meantime, Homerdessa had jumped back into her Oldsmobile and sped off. Dwayne left the wig hanging on our doorknob, then talked the woman into driving him to the nearest bar.

When I heard the story from the still-stunned manager, and found the fluffy bouffant Dynel scalp hanging from our doorknob, I went inside the apartment and rolled on the bed, laughing until I sobbed.

The next time, Dwayne hitchhiked to Atlanta, and Johnny accused him of stealing cash from a dresser top. We were having dinner—trying to keep things normal, I was passing the platter of tongue with mustard sauce—and Dwayne rose from his seat and overturned the table. Then he and Johnny wrestled and fell to the floor, Dwayne pulling the Bowie knife he wore at his hip. Rose, Lily, and I ran from the apartment in panic; I was trembling as I dialed the police from a neighbor's, already imagining going back to find either my son or my husband dead. As we rushed back toward our front door, we saw Dwayne running toward us like a dervish, swinging what looked like a hatchet but turned out to be his belt, its heavy metal buckle twirling in the air. Now I knew that Johnny was already dead, and that we were about to die, too. Then I saw the police car pulling up behind him.

"Those crazy kids of yours," Johnny said, dusting off his L. L. Bean plaid shirt and camel flannel pants while they took Dwayne, still raging, away in handcuffs. Johnny had successfully wrestled him to the floor, and was now disgusted. He was tired of Dwayne's threats to set our condo afire, of seeing me in tears, my face puffy; he had changed his mind about this being a phase and wanted me to forget I had ever had a son.

That night, Lily tearfully confessed that she was the one who had taken the money. The day stood out in my mind as the night of the Terror of the Twirling Belt, and for a time spinning knives and other weapons whirled, Chagall-like, through the space of my canvases.

ROSEMARY DANIELL

* * *

By then, it didn't matter anyway. Johnny had gotten his gallery and I had won the big prize in Georgia. And I already had a new lover back in New Orleans—not somebody who fit Johnny's chichi ideas about upward mobility via open marriage, but a boy much like the one with the black leather jacket with the tiger painted on the back—the one I had seen so long ago in Jackson Square. "This is what I get for involving myself with someone so déclassé," Johnny said with a smirk when he discovered the affair. During a trip back to Louisiana, he had happened on the boy and me, stepping drunkenly arm-in-arm into the sunlight out of Johnny Matassis, a sleazy bar on St. Philip where we had spent the afternoon drinking fifty-cent martinis. There, the boy touching my thigh, the sides of my breasts, I could forget my new success, could slide back into being the girl who had lain in the pine straw with Wayne, who still craved dirt and lust. "Mother warned me against this alliance all along," Johnny went on, referring to his clan's barely concealed tolerance of me and my wounded little family.

Johnny was having affairs, too—with a wealthy Jewish woman in New York who was sending him clients for his gallery, as well as with a wispy, anemic-looking "old-line" blonde who had been a queen at one of the Mardi Gras krewes' balls. Despite my sixties ideals and the boy in New Orleans, I wasn't able to be cool about them. Yet Johnny didn't seem to be jealous—it was merely my choice of lover, of setting, that he disapproved of, not to speak of my own reactionary attitude toward his adulteries. In any case, the marriage was over, and my attachment to Dwayne and my new, niggling fears about Lily were just a part of it.

Thus, during our next trip to New York, I found myself hurtling up Eighth Avenue in a taxi that seemed to have no shocks at all. At Johnny's request, I had just signed the divorce papers at a notary office near the Chelsea. Seated beside me was fifteen-year-old Lily, looking like a gorgeous Italian boy with her new haircut from Vidal Sassoon. Yet her long-lashed eyes were teary, her heart-shaped face morose. Rose was doing research at the New York University library, and Lily had spent the morning calling the Elite, Ford, and other agencies, who

206

THE HURRICANE SEASON

had all told her adamantly that at five foot five, she was an inch too short for photography modeling. Too depleted by my arguments with Johnny to deal with her sobs, I had suggested that the two of us go to the Plaza for tea. Now we two women sped uptown, each encapsulated inside her own grief—a grief that went deeper (though I didn't know it yet) for each of us than a mere divorce or job rejection.

At the Plaza, everything I said brought on fresh tears or a venom that poured from her full lips like the ravings of a madwoman, despite the waiter's hovering and my embarrassment. Often, nowadays, Lily seemed to have a crazy woman inside her very similar to my own. "It's because she's a *Pisces*, Mother," Rose, now into astrology and as a Virgo relentlessly in control of her own life, would say impatiently, explaining away her sister's new mood swings. I had been trying to attribute them to adolescence, to her poetic temperament. But all I really knew was that my sweet Lily, once my partisan, my sister in art—so sunny, so eager to share verses and feelings—was becoming more and more often an angry stranger.

But how could I know that day that she had already found her own form of oblivion? When one of the handsome bisexual boys who always seemed to hang around her appeared at our table at the Palm Court—making me suspect she had called, asked him to meet us—she rose from her chair and jerked up her purse. "Let *Trevor* have tea with you, Mother—I'm going off on my own!" And then she stomped out, her high heels moving rapidly across the thick Oriental carpet, leaving me wondering what I had done wrong. But I sat there with Trevor, sipping tea and chatting, and then went off to the Museum of Modern Art with him, where he proved, as Lily would have predicted, to be the perfect companion—then, as Lily would also have predicted, to be an amusing diversion during an afternoon in bed.

At Mama's funeral, I had seen how Lily had stared down into the casket at Mama's wasted body, her thickly powdered face with its garish slash of red, the nails painted with her favorite Wild Rose polish, looking almost like claws on her poor gaunt hands. But all Lily had said then was "They sure did do her makeup ugly!" Yet later, as I walked through the cool rooms of Musette's house, I found her poring over the album into which Musette, as the keeper of our mutual history, had glued pictures of Mama as a young girl—one in which, wearing a flowered cotton dress, she leaned against a big pine tree, smiling dreamily, expectantly; another in which she looked flirtatiously up toward a grinning, dimpled Patrick, whose muscular arm clad in World War II khakis was around her small shoulders.

"Mama, she was beautiful—like me!" Lily blurted, looking at me with a mixture of wonder and horror, tears quivering in the corners of her huge eyes. And yes, I had to admit it—it was Mama who had given Lily her heart-shaped face, those golden-brown eyes. And the reason I didn't want to admit it was that I didn't want Lily's life to have anything to do with Mama's life or with South Alabama. That's why, when she asked for the first time how her grandmother had become paralyzed, I didn't want to answer. But of course I did, watching her face become more and more stricken. And I felt again that guilt I had felt about Mama, about how she had gotten that way because of me, but how I had gone on and left her anyway—and how, despite my sacrifice of Mama, Dwayne had turned out wrong after all. And now it felt as though some of that guilt was rubbing off in some way on Lily—that against my will, and without even knowing it, I had infected her with the Crazy Woman, had cloned the genes of that hated part of myself inside my younger daughter's body.

Once Lily's baby fat had melted, zapped from her flesh by diets of bananas or tofu milkshakes, her brown eyes perpetually outlined with as much kohl as an Egyptian's, she had turned into one of the most beautiful women I had ever seen. Rose was pretty, too, but Lily made use of her lusciousness. She had begun using my art brushes to make up her face, and took as much time to do it as I would with a section of canvas. Nobody knew about anorexia or bulimia yet, and though I teased her about her strange diets, about looking like a long-legged spider in a black jumpsuit that barely tied between her almost nonexistent breasts, showing white flesh to the concave navel set between her wide hips, I also admired her the way I would a beautifully painted canvas. I still couldn't believe I had made her—that my plump little Lily had turned into this woman of bones and eyes. Indeed, her visual aspect was something I slurped up, usurped both with my eyes and as a model for my work.

I was never more in love with her than when, in one of her moments of exuberance, she would press me *hard* to her small breasts, making me a part of her mood. "You're so manipulative you even manipulate yourself," one of the many psychiatrists who would later treat her—and, yes, fall under her spell— teased with exasperated affection. Being her mother didn't protect me at all; I was as taken in, as infatuated, as everyone else.

In addition, her beauty distracted me—if she had that, what more, in the real world, could she need? Because of the confidence it seemed to give her, I couldn't quite believe in her pain. There was no way her problems could be as unmanageable as Dwayne's. Yet without even knowing it, I also had taught her that she, like every woman I had ever known but Rose (and Rose was born an anomaly), was destined to sacrifice and sacrifice, to distort herself in favor of the men in her life.

I also had taught Lily that she could become an artist, and that to be sexually active was her right. I knew that both she and Rose had experimented, with girls as well as with boys. Yet things weren't working out as I had hoped. For one thing, Lily was already having bad problems with men, going back to that first time on Musette's farm: Now there were tearful calls to a boy she had met hitchhiking just after he'd been kicked out of boarding school for drug possession, and to a twenty-five-year-old who came around between trips to Amsterdam. Later, there would be the one who beat her, the one who wanted her to hook for him, and the one whom she just sat around with all day, smoking dope. "Mother, you worry too much," she would say smiling, sticking her heartbreakingly beautiful sixteen-year-old face through the car window for a good-bye kiss.

Then the next week I would receive the distraught call from whichever boy she was living with, telling me how she had disappeared with "three guys in a white Camaro"—men they had met in a bar in the Quarter—and how he hadn't heard from her in three days. Next, to my relief, would come the call from Lily herself—from Coconut Grove or Corpus Christi, describing some crisis situation, asking for airfare back home. And having already lost one child, I would send it.

Finally, the day came when, a broken strap on her high heel, two hundred dollars in her pocketbook, she was off to New York to live with a jazz musician. "Don't look so sad, Mother," she said as I dropped her off at the airport. "I always told you I was going to live there." She was seventeen, and I wondered whether I'd ever see her again.

Shame: There must be nothing—no matter what her successes—that can induce it more in a woman than problems with her children. Well, you might respond (especially if you're one of my never-wed lesbian friends), that's an old-fashioned, even shockingly nonfeminist, thing to say. But it's true. The sense of self that had survived Daddy, Mama's paralysis, and my giving birth to a baby out of wedlock, not to speak of my failed marriages to Bobby and to Johnny, had given way, caved in like a lime-hole sink, at my inability to protect my young.

And the shame is somehow worse when it has to do with a daughter: *He brought me a little shame flower/ opening purple at the heart/ left it for me, blooming/ but when it closed down/ the shame was mine*. . . . Lily wrote in one of the many poems in which she tried to deal with her feelings about her brother, her father, her stepfather. And I knew what she meant. Like every southern mother I had known, black or white, I had doted on my son while expecting my daughters to be as strong as I was.

For Dwayne's sickness had just been the beginning. What started when he was eleven began a period that would bleed over into years. As though a door had been opened that couldn't be closed, Lily would take up the slack whenever Dwayne dropped—temporarily, ever temporarily—out of the picture.

And Rose—how had all this affected her? For one thing, she had developed a steel, or at the very least, polyurethane, coating, shielding herself in the numbness I thought I had so successfully developed on that night Daddy had thrown my ashtray against the wall. She had learned early to make her mind float off elsewhere, and fortunately, she even had a talent for it, filling her brain with a myriad of things, languages and facts and rationales. She also had a talent for overlooking things.

210

"I don't like losing propositions, Mother," she said later, when I tried to engage her in my own battle to save Lily's life. And despite my anger at that moment, I experienced a flash of admiration for her. She was capable of doing something I had never been able to do—to turn from someone she was tied to by blood.

I open the heart-shaped white plastic Halston cylinder Lily gave me last Christmas, along with the matching heart-shaped box of blush in two shades, mulberry and mauve. Shoplifted from Saks? I wonder idly. For I know how Lily comes by some of her most lovingly bestowed gifts. "This is just perfect for you, Mother!" she says tenderly, handing over a small box with a kiss to my cheek—and even suspecting the gift's origins, I will flush with pleasure, the quick rush of my love for her.

As I look at myself in the mirror of this bathroom in the Pontalba where I've come to escape Iris and to put on fresh lipstick, my mouth is awash with the acid of sudden nausea. There are people at this party—Iris, for one—who don't know I have even had children, who will certainly never know about this fetus to die tomorrow: people—"friends"—for whom the first thirty-five years of my life don't exist. To them, I am the Artist, the *wild* woman, a symbol of the outrageousness they don't dare live out for themselves. And isn't this what I wanted all those years when I craved the Quarter, a free life?

Yet what Iris doesn't understand is that tonight, tomorrow morning, I don't want her pseudo-breasts pressed to mine. I want my Lily's small soft ones against me, her strong young woman's arms around me, against what will be my grief. And as far as sex is concerned, I want to fuck boys, not a man turned into a woman. For even if only symbolically, I want my son back.

I lean over the basin and hold to the mauve porcelain till the sickness passes. Then look up into this mirror, at this still beautiful thirty-nine-year-old face.

Thinking, imagining—despite all that has happened—that the woman looking back at me is still in control of her life.

211

CHAPTER NINE

"KOHUT SAYS there are two crises," Paul, Catholic priest-turned-lay-analyst told me at a cocktail party in Atlanta. "The first occurs during the first couple of months of life, when the mother gives an empathetic—*not* a hysterical—response to the child; she doesn't get uptight, but she *perceives* his need if he cries and so on. . . ." He pulled his petite blonde bride, a graduate student, closer to him. I'd heard he buys her gifts—fur pieces, perfect little dresses, like the one she's wearing right now.

"The second," Paul continued, giving his new wife a peck on the forehead, "occurs when the child is eighteen months of age or so—when, through the father, the child perceives that others exist outside himself."

"Can the second crisis be met by the mother as well?" I asked.

"No, *no*," Paul said emphatically. "The *father*—society, law and order, patriarchy . . ."

"And what if one fails one or both crises?" I asked casually.

This was the kind of party I went to, once I'd become a media, if not a financial, success. My breasts, always small— an advantage now that I'm near forty—rose almost as perfectly as Iris's. I had on a black crepe dress with a low-carved throat, a sweetheart neckline, tulip skirt, little shoulder pads, a watermelon satin shaped belt from Gus Mayer for two hundred dollars. I didn't have to have a *man* to go with me to these parties —I was semifamous, an entity unto myself.

Paul was giving up; he saw that I was not properly respectful of patriarchal authority, his credentials. But then, I never had been.

However, he did call me the next day, wondering casually if we could have lunch before I flew back to New Orleans. What about the little blonde wife? I asked. Oh, well, you have such an interesting mind, he said.

Doesn't he know that I've long since given up the American Dream—of long-stemmed roses, fur jacket, and coiffed hair; of minor adulteries and men like him?

In fact, the only dreams I haven't yet given up on are those for art and for eros.

Thus began what I would think of as the time of the Glittering—the time that led to my being pressed against a refrigerator in the Pontalba apartments by Iris that night, to my trip to the abortion clinic the next morning. The time when pure pleasure still seemed harmless enough.

"I should have considered my daughter more," I would hear foreign correspondent Barbara Newman tell Geraldo ten years later, during that period when I was watching a lot of television in yet another attempt to heal myself. She was speaking of how she risked her own life in Lebanon, where she, a Jewish woman, had penetrated the Hezbollah to interview the terrorists, and in Beirut had had an affair with the country's Christian Phalangist leader, almost forgetting that she had a ten-year-old daughter at home. "But it was the way I was made. . . . I don't know anything but reporting. . . ."

And that was the way I was made: All *I* knew, despite years of trying, time after time, to fit myself into "normal," to elevate myself through art and literature, was the flat-out, undisguised violence and sensuality—the milk and blood and shit—that had been a part of my life from the very beginning, back on the farm so many years before in South Alabama.

So when I returned to New Orleans, I became fully and easily aware of what that city (especially the French Quarter) means: the unconscious made manifest, where anything can, and does, happen; where people come, hoping—perhaps not even knowing it themselves—for anything to happen that might change their dulled-out lives, if only for a night. Where, as commentator Maury Povich would later say on a pseudo-news show, *A Current Affair*, "They sin, they sip, they don't know when to stop. . . ."

And almost overnight, it seemed, I was as thoughtless, as pleasuring, as all the rest, as innocent as perhaps only the sensual are innocent—living out the dream for which I seemed to have been destined, a dream that those who do not pursue it must, of necessity, block from their consciousness, else they would go mad with desire and grief: a dream of sexual impulses followed and fulfilled in the moment, of continuous music and dreamlike imagery, of consciousness-changing substances constantly available and availed of, of people living at the very edge of the edge, with no thought of the next day or the next.

On the Friday before Ash Wednesday, the palm branches were burned to create the ashes to be pressed to our foreheads on the day after Mardi Gras, sign of grief for our sins.

And, for a long time, this would seem penance enough.

I had less money than I had had since I had been growing up in South Alabama. But my new life didn't require much, and for the first time, I was minimally self-supporting. I had gone back to teaching part time at the John McCrady School of Art, and occasionally I did a residency in a new national program, Artists in the Schools (after which I would sometimes be eligible for unemployment payments), or would be asked to give a lecture somewhere. When Paula did sell a painting, the lump sum I would receive (minus her 40 percent) would be more than I would have made in the previous three months.

This random life suited me: I felt released, as though I had just stepped out of a dress that was too tight. The dreams of security, of comfort, I had had on the farm while flipping through the pages of *Ladies' Home Journal* or *Good Housekeeping*, the fantasies of having my own washer and dryer, of living in a house like the one I had had in Metairie, seemed the dreams of a prisoner for her prison cell. Alone, I was able to act out my divided self—my criminality and my creativity—without fear of my sinfulness, my secret desires, rubbing off on those I loved. Dwayne was living out his chosen destiny of no-good good ole boy, safe, I told myself, in the cocoon of South Alabama. Rose had gotten early admission to Louisiana State University in Baton Rouge, where she would excel before going on to NYU. And ironically, Lily's stay in New York with the Jazz Musician seemed to be taking—though later, she would tell me of the rooms in the transient hotels with the milk on the windowsill, the dirty bathroom down the filthy hallway, the insane man beating drumsticks day and night on the other side of the wall, the one meal of pizza a day: "But I didn't want to tell you then, because I loved it—I was in love with New York the same way you were with New Orleans."

For $275 a month, I rented the rambling, crumbling apartment I had dreamed of. To enter it, I unlocked a grilled wrought-iron door, peeling dark green paint, on Royal Street. Then I walked up a staircase half-hidden by a cool green courtyard garden, made dim by palmetto fronds, huge, satiny elephant ears. The actual (and only) door into the apartment, which opened off the U-shaped interior balcony, was really a tall window that raised or slammed down like a guillotine. I had bought the first furniture I had ever purchased for myself—a tall used armoire, a tufted and slightly stained rose satin divan, and a four-poster bed, its tall posts carved with lilies and a woman's long hair, a pale pink embroidered silk shawl draping the lamp on the rickety table beside it. The large, high-ceilinged rooms were of indeterminate shape and function, except for the kitchen, which was distinguishable only because of the large old-fashioned mint-green range, a refrigerator raised on curved feet, as was the pink-lipped bathtub in the huge bathroom. The wooden floors sloped in a way that gave me a delicious sense of dreamlike unreality, of *déjà vu* for something I couldn't recall, particularly when I woke in the night, walked through the rooms still half-drunk, letting out one lover or another. Then I would slam the guillotine door down, safe again, luxuriating in my own solitude, a vague sense of unreality combined with heightened sensuality. Back in my four-poster bed, I would stretch my legs, my toes, their nails painted fuchsia, with delicious pleasure beneath the faded pink satin sheets, inhaling the scent of the man (or woman) who had just left.

The room I chose for my studio was at the front, sunlight flooding in through French windows. All I had to do when I came to a stop in my painting was to raise a second guillotine door and step out onto the other balcony, which hung almost precariously over Royal Street, with a delicious slope that gave me an easy change of consciousness, a disconcerting jar. Thus, I could walk away from my work for a few minutes, then go back to the canvas excited again.

Each noon, before I began painting, I sat on this disreputable perch, sipping thick chicoried coffee, reading the literature of the the disaffected: Capote and Durrell; Camus, Gide, and Genet; Djuna Barnes; and the Bowleses, Jane and Paul, whose lack of pleasure in the pleasure they took matched in some way my own amorality. I read Colette, who, in contrast, seemed almost innocent, flowery. Despite the forbidden nature of his works, I found Henry Miller too exuberantly bad boy, the Huck Finn of fucking; while Anaïs Nin's lifestyle, as portrayed through her self-censored diaries, were, to my taste, too pretentiously artsy, her novels too self-consciously lyrical. But I read them all, buying these books from Beckham's, a musty used bookstore on Decatur Street, where I would stand in the narrow corridors among aging queens and transsexuals, searching out the literature to match my new life.

Sometimes I would run down the stairs, out onto the streets, where, as often as not, a literal parade was taking place, celebrating one of the many pagan or religious holidays. Or there would be just the usual procession of people who had come specifically to leave limits behind, to pleasure themselves in every human way possible.

It amazed me now to think that walking the French Quarter alone had once frightened me. I meandered along Decatur

Street after dark, or had coffee, along with the late-night tourists and the remnants of French Quarter society, at the Café du Monde at 3:00 A.M. The first time I walked Bourbon Street alone after midnight—the street where Bobby had reluctantly taken me in to see my first strip show, where prostitutes lingered, waiting for johns—I felt a small thrill at living out what I had long wanted for myself—the sexual license, the boyish wildness. I became friends with some of the women, never dreaming that I later would come to dread walking that street, afraid I might see my own daughter there.

There's a picture of me back then, sitting cross-legged on my four-poster bed in a crepe wrapper, my long hair draped around my face, my breasts hanging out, my stomach relaxed and rounded (Was I bloated? Or had I gained a bit of weight?) drinking Pernod straight from a pint bottle, my nose crinkled at its licorice pungency.

My hair in the photo is a Mercurochrome red, for I regularly hennaed it. Mixing a raw egg with a quarter-cup auburn, a half-cup brown from two boxes with Egyptian symbols, and sometimes even a bit of beet juice, I stirred the goo with a wooden spoon in a glass cup, smearing it into the roots. Using a tiny white plastic spatula, some white powder mixed into a paste with ammonia, I bleached my eyebrows to a near-invisible blond, after Mona Lisa. I put on long, dangling earrings that were made from graying silver, or things that were old and frayed—bits of cloth or feathers. I often stuck a flower into my hair—an azalea or a camellia blossom. I wore a tarnished ankle bracelet with two silver-plated hearts entwined, high-heeled mules called Candies, and scoop-necked blouses without a bra, affecting, despite my growing stature in the art world, the slightly sleazy, frayed appearance of a French Quarter hooker, where everything was slightly sleazy, frayed, anyway.

I had a tattoo of my own design—a replica of a vagina, a beating, bleeding heart emerging from between its curled, curved lips—placed just over my pubis. The fat, sweating man shook his head in amazement at the drawing I handed him; then, at my insistence, let me look over his inks, select the exact shades of red, rose, mauve. Still shaking his huge head, slinging

218

sweat onto my thigh, he had engraved it at my wincing direction. I was an artist, I didn't have to follow the rules, and if this was the small price of it, so be it.

For the body, even in pain, was now the seat of my satisfaction. In New York, even in Atlanta, life had been heady. But in New Orleans, I fell with relief back into my animal life, my own genitals and the genitals of the country, feeling as natural as I had when I was giving birth, nursing babies, cleaning and creaming their curves, their crevices.

Holding an artist friend's baby, I wanted to French kiss the four-week-old, to let the infant suck on my tongue. Such thoughts were like barely restrained animals at the base of my brain. Testing out the strength of my criminality, I shoplifted a pair of cheap earrings on Magazine Street, just as I had stolen the Artist's Colors back in South Alabama.

Every month, the thick blood between my legs gratified me. My tortoise cat, Moana, was a curvaceous sensualist, rubbing around my calves, kneading the pillow at my head, echoing my own inclinations. Every pleasure was present tense—a drink, a dress, a man, a book, a new tube of paint, a fresh sheet of canvas, my nighttime life as gratifying as the days thick with acrylics, juicy oils. "Easter is a woman of the night," a man friend said, introducing me.

My new tattoo was merely an echo of the invisible one, pounding between my legs. For with no husband to hate, desire had come on me full-fledged. A need had taken over, become etched onto my very flesh, something for which my body screamed. In the middle of a night, as I lay alone in the four-poster bed, images would come to me—a scab, a congestion, a clot, pooled blood, a missed period, driving me slightly crazy, like a constant speck in my eye; yet an irritant that was actually an absence. I had once imagined sex as giving birth, something thick and satisfying emerging from my body rather than entering it. It was an image I used in a painting, a thick rosy stamen of a phallus, emerging like something born, from within a flowery, full-blown vagina. In my desire, there was also something dark, grotesque—an animal shame that needed to be routed. But now I no longer questioned my compulsions, I just lived them.

219

It was hard even to recall that other self, the young house-wife of the well-balanced meals—of the carrots grated, the cab-bage steamed, the soybeans mashed for garlicky yet tasteless patties. Instead, I tossed pasta in a pan with shucked oysters or crayfish tails, or ate cold gumbo, the spicy oysters floating like shriveled cool gray testicles, the pink crab claws adrift like pastel art forms, from a stained cardboard carton in the refrigerator. I, too, would live on oysters on the half-shell and champagne, I decided when I read of Isak Dinesen, saw her syphilitic yet elegant face in a magazine.

Once I ran into Bobby on Chartres Street. Other than our periodic fights over the child support or Rose's school fees, we had been able to avoid contact—though I did hear his voice, a thin parody of his dead daddy's, over the radio, announcing himself as "Big Bobby—of Big Bobby's Used Cars." He looked just the same to me—as pitiful, as inept-looking, as sexless, as ever: his Ichabod Crane frame a bit skinnier, his glasses a bit thicker, his hair grayer and thinning. His pastel tie was slightly awry over a wilted, buttoned-down white collar; it was hot—near 100—and he was carrying his jacket over a shoulder. The anxious-looking woman on his arm looked a bit like Miss Lisa, or an older version of the housewife I had been. Her hair was coiffed and strawlike; she wore a straight skirt, girdle, high-heeled pumps, her plump body a straight, thick column. How would he feel if he knew I was now freely doing the things he had once begged me to do—but this time on my terms, not his?

"Yuh've let yo'self go a bit, Eastah," Bobby said with a self-conscious smirk, surreptitiously taking in my dress, my whole body, from hennaed hair to low-necked blouse to drooping handkerchieflike skirt and wedgies. I could tell that I had lost my sexual power over him, but I didn't care. Nor did I regret that he would probably be the last man I would ever be able to get to take care of me.

"This is what it's like to let yourself go, my dear," I said, paraphrasing Hardy. For a moment, the puzzled-looking woman almost smiled, her thin lips automatically rising in that stiff parentheses that southern women use when they feel that good manners demand that they respond.

* * *

That year, a National Institutes of Health psychiatrist at Tulane to do research on pain tried to pick me up on St. Philip Street during a parade for Saint Anthony. When I told him I was hurrying to an opening of my work, a panel discussion, he asked if he could come along. But once we were there, I saw him visibly recoil at the content of my paintings, a look of censure replacing the one of desire.

He wasn't my type anyway, I told myself—too high a forehead, not enough animal beauty. And why didn't he, a man educated in the unconscious, understand that the pain was now outside me and on the canvases? Besides, I cared nothing for such men, or their so-called "insights": like marriage, their patriarchal views were a device to keep women from expressing themselves.

I was discovering that being outside society was easier than being inside it, that being disaffected was easier than feeling had ever been. If anyone had asked me, I would have said I was happy: as I walked into Johnny Matassis or Lafitte's Blacksmith, greeting my pals in another night's dissipation, "I'm so happy I could die" would flash across the billboard of my mind, a bubble bursting at the back of my brain. I no longer had the crying jags I had had as a young housewife, or during the onslaught of Dwayne's madness. Just as I had mentally removed myself when Daddy had thrown my gift of an ashtray against a wall, stuck Mama's clothes into the wallpaper with the butcher knife, I now tamped my feelings with sex and booze—the sixties had given me all the permission I needed, as did "the pleasure principle" if I needed more. The Crazy Woman was a part of the past, I told myself, forgetting how completely unable she had been to control herself in the face of Dwayne's downfall. My only question was why had it taken me so long to find this cure for my pain.

I was an artist and a slut, and as far as I was concerned, it was the perfect life. I kept Häagen-Dazs and Russian vodka in the freezer, crab claws and cheap champagne in the refrigerator. And I was learning how to pick up men for sex.

If I no longer yearned after doctors and car dealers—a lifestyle of little dinner parties and department-store shopping—then my artistic peers seemed the logical choice. After all, hadn't Martin (whom I had long outstripped in artistic recognition) been the most tender of my lovers?

Yet consorting with painters didn't work, either. No matter how much we had "in common," no matter how good things were in bed, that little competitive edge would creep in. "I can't paint when I know you're painting just a block away, when I can almost hear you humming to yourself because you're coming from the color, it's *flowing* for you. When I can't even get it up for the canvas—and there you are, *coming* and *coming*. . . ."

Again, it was somehow my fault for making art so easily; this even when the man was more successful than I was, such as the one who, despite the gigantic snake tattooed around his once-muscled torso, its head stopping just at the crack of his ass as though it might enter it, turned out to be more conventional than I was. "You ball-busters are all just alike," he said, grumbling, gathering up his slides after looking over mine. "Losin' your womanhood, paintin' this weird stuff . . ." And ultimately, it would be men like him, rather than the Bobbys and the Johnnys of the world, who would make sure that I would never receive a Guggenheim, or have my work hung in the Museum of Modern Art.

There was also the idea the world—especially men—had of women artists: loose, wild, out of control. And of course they were right. There's nothing wilder than a wild woman: Just as a mother will fight to the death for her young, a sexually free woman is more out of control, more outrageous, than any man, ever.

So who was left to me but the foreign sailors, the oil riggers, the drug dealers—all those men whom I had suddenly found existed for pleasure and for the moment, who cared for nothing *but* that moment, the ones who were as sensation-oriented as I was, the ones most like that first boy I had lusted after, that morning long before in Jackson Square?

Often, while I was working at my easel, I found myself humming the songs from *Hair*, especially the ones about white boys being like Chinese silk, black boys being like chocolate candy. And it was true: I wanted them all. No matter how

222

involved I was with the women's movement, men—and now boys—were still foremost among my obsessions.

Some of these boys—they all run together now—said I was the only one who ever understood them—the young outlaws, the addicts, the lost, drawn to New Orleans as though to Mecca. I listened with what psychologists back in the sixties called "passive receptivity." I accepted, and I absorbed them—a near-infinite earth mother—into my psyche and inside my body. "Sex with strangers is an alternative to language, the code that replaces speech," I read in an essay by someone named Edmund White in an issue of *Christopher Street* that lay beside a gay friend's bed. And that was what I believed then.

Each, by his habits, soon gave away his boyishness. One ate foot-and-a-half-long boxes of Debbie Kreme Cakes as we lay in bed; another was addicted to a cereal called Froot Loops. Some watched fascinated as I put in a tampon; several pored over what they called "fuck books." One liked to play an album cut by Queen as we lay in bed together; "Tie your mother down" was its title and sometimes he would, using the extension cord to the clamp light at the top of my four-poster bed. When I visited his room on Esplanade, I saw on the mantelpiece a photo of me that had gone missing, upright in a cheap gold-tinted tin frame. And there was the one who called me "Mother," describing a fantasy trip with me to Hungry Mother State Park in Virginia, where he had camped out after running away from a Charlottesville detention center. As he talked, he would lay his head on my chest, staring unblinkingly up at me much as Dwayne had done while nursing. However tough, whatever his history—felonies, hard drugs, assaults—I mentally ascribed to each a childlike tenderness, a neediness that only I could fill.

And sometimes, I tried to turn them into girls, girls like Lily. Changing sexual roles, using that little trick I had learned from Johnny, I would penetrate that springy flesh with the white plastic dildo from the rose velveteen box I kept at my bedside. "You're tryin' to turn me into a girl," one of them complained, just after I had licked, sucked, and penetrated his body in every way possible. As he leaned over to pull on his cowboy boots, I noticed his eyes were like long-lashed chocolates—*like Dwayne's,* I found myself thinking. It was amazing what beautiful eyes a criminal could have. "I don't need a mama—I already got one," he said, patting the switchblade knife in his front pocket, checking out his ducktail in my mirror before leaning over to stick his tongue into my mouth in a way that was decidedly not sonlike.

It was good, if it wasn't perfect, I wrote to Sherry, who, having fucked her way through New Orleans, had taken the money she had made in the law and had left for Los Angeles, where she complained that all the cowboys were gay. For ultimately, every man I got involved with—that is, slept with more than once—always ended up (even the boys in the black leather jackets) wanting me to leave whatever or whoever else I was doing to become the perfect mother to *him.*

Until finally, bloated by their pain, their misery, I would crave the salt-sweet piquancy of a woman. For polymorphous perverse as I was, I wanted women, too. And the rougher the man I'd been with, the more I'd want a woman's billowing softness—perfect mother love, Joan of Arc, an androgynous Christ (though a priest in skirts would do), someone strong enough for *me* to lean on. For one thing, they were pretty—a black woman had skin like melting chocolate, a vagina the color of fresh cherries; the youngest of the white girls had nipples of a pale shell pink. And some of them were mothers, too. "Who mothers mothers?" a woman lying beside me asked into the air, then passed the joint we were sharing. We lay silent, contemplating her question, our naked bellies extended beneath us like silvery deserts, covered in twin stretch marks.

Once, I lay in bed with a woman whose pregnant belly was delicious, promising, a hard, fat pear beneath my fingertips. The painting that rose out of that experience was one of my most controversial: an X-ray vision inside a woman's hugely pregnant uterus, her face completely covered by her long hair, her vagina filled by the oversized hand of the naked woman who leans over her, the tips of her breasts drooping to touch her lover's. It was part of a series begun during a period of minor influence by Magritte, the first of which was "The Amazon's Daughter," an image of a young woman amazingly like Lily, on her elbows above a girl her age, a silver-sequined waterfall rushing from her vagina into her friend's, a dozen tiny men flailing arms and legs, drowning in the rush of sparkling liquid.

Then there were the women who were discontent with their lot, who couldn't understand why I had given up what I did, who—had I been a man—would have wanted me to marry them, carry them off to the suburbs. Sophie, the transvestite who danced with a live python on Bourbon Street, told me mournfully in Johnny Matassis one 3:00 A.M. that she hoped someday to live in a little house in Metairie, maybe even have a washer and dryer; absently stroking the snake that still hung around her neck like a fur piece, she sipped her martini and told me that what seemed to me the heaven of the French Quarter had come to her to be like purgatory. The snake had an elegantly crisp black-and-beige design that looked out-of-place in our seedy surroundings; touching it, I had an odd sensation of muscle inside a cool, thin casing, constantly moving over a bony frame; it ate one white rabbit a month, she told me. Then she pulled up her skirt, and taking a bill from her stocking top, ordered our next round—"There was a gentleman who was particularly generous tonight." "Yeah, you'd make a perfect housewife," I said encouragingly, remembering how I had seen her the week before, sitting on top of a garbage can on St. Philip, her stockings torn, her legs spread, her dress hiked over her muscular thighs, revealing the tip of her dick.

And often, that assumption of tenderness, understanding, was false, especially if I chose the wrong kind of woman—the kind who, even more than Sophie or Iris, was really a man in disguise, whose motherly instincts were almost nonexistent— the kind who, shot through with as much testosterone as a man, driven crazy by years of being a weirdo yet courting that consensus through her male clothing, swaggered down the streets of the French Quarter, angrily deflecting the remarks of the sailors. No, those were worse than any of the men had been, shooting hot daggers at me if I wore a flower in my hair or spoke politely to a man in a restaurant. And however compliant I might be in bed, they could tell—as they twisted me into strange postures, clamped their mouths on my vagina while placing themselves above me in a way that almost forced me to do the same—that for me, the act of sex with them, what they wanted me do in exchange for their licking and probing, was an acquired taste akin to my taste for caviar, or even my whole life in the French Quarter. And that sleeping with them had more to do with what I didn't want to do—go back to the suburbs, be a wife—than something I did.

And through it all, there would still be a part of me, the neat, secret genitals, that didn't feel any of it, that was still the chaste wife and mother, more chaste even than I had been before I had met Wayne that day on the dirt road in the pickup—because now every carnal desire was satisfied.

Yes, my life was a dazzle of sequins, of satins, of purples and pinks and mauves, both on canvas and off. There was Mardi Gras in New Orleans, and visits to my jet-setter jazz-poet daughter in New York.

Sometimes I would follow the azalea season, flying from New Orleans to Atlanta to Charleston, visiting the friends I had made along the way. Occasionally, I would get into my old Alfa-Romeo and drive over to Baton Rouge to see Rose, where we would go to the Cotton Club and talk about scholarly things. Rose was still the picture of angelic purity, her snow-white complexion untouched by makeup, her long-lashed eyes bright with intellectual, rather than chemically or erotically induced, excitement, her primary interest still in books. In fact, Rose, widely read, would be the one to turn me on to Frida Kahlo: "Mother, I read about a Mexican artist, a woman—she reminds me a lot of you." At the same time, Rose kept me at arm's length; she couldn't bear mention, I noticed, of her siblings, and as often as not went to Musette's for holidays. At times, I would go there, too.

Address books—they were becoming the story of my life: Addresses for Lily. Addresses for Dwayne. Addresses for Rose.

Only Musette's address was always the same.

Driving along the Gulf on Interstate 10, through Gulfport, Biloxi, Pascagoula, toward South Alabama, I would remember the high hopes I had held on that honeymoon drive with Bobby, if not for the marriage, then for Dwayne and me together. The motel where we had stayed that first night was still there, but the letters on the neon sign were dark, broken, the buildings were stucco shells overgrown by vines.

As I drove into Southeast Mississippi, then into Alabama, I entered the country I had once hoped to escape forever—the cotton fields, thick with orange-white boles, the gray wood shacks where overalled blacks stood like sullen watching icons on falling-down porches. Passing the small white paint-peeling churches, like the one where I had sung the blood-filled hymns with Mama and Musette and Aunt Darlene, I held my breath for a moment, recalling with a rush of anxiety the power such a few people could hold, managing to control each other by fear of hellfire and damnation. And struck afresh by the miracle of my escape, I would shudder, tears of some strong emotion—it couldn't be longing, though at moments it felt like it—rising to my eyes. Or was it a grief for Mama and even Daddy, that they had been trapped there, forever?

If it hadn't been for Musette and for Dwayne, who was still living with Homerdessa, I would never have gone back there. Whenever I visited, Homerdessa appeared grayer, fatter, and more unkempt, her large print housedresses covered in more and more spots, every time I saw her. Sometimes, her mouth opened like a fish's, as though she wanted to say something. But Dwayne, a tall dark man, would be standing behind her in the doorway, looking menacing, waiting for me to take him somewhere—to buy him dinner, and give him money, as I always did. I had long since forgiven him for the night of the Terror of the Twirling Belt, the threats of arson against my and Johnny's condo in Atlanta. After all, he was my son, my blood. But still, I had learned to fear him, and for that reason as much as my guilt, I gave him what he asked.

My earlier worries about Lily appeared to have been unfounded. New York was made for Lily, and Lily was made for New York. She was seventeen, then eighteen, then twenty, and she and the Jazz Musician now lived in the West Village on Sullivan Street, in an apartment that cost more than twice what mine did, and while I never quite understood what they were doing for a living—"Oh, I'm working at a little café in Little

Italy, Mother," or "He still has that day job at Capezio's—
though I hope he can quit that soon, 'n do his music full time"—
they were getting by. She sometimes asked for a couple of
hundred dollars, and I would wire it to her; Bobby had called
to complain that she was asking the same from him. Because
she had chosen not to go to college, he felt exempt from any
need to help her further, he added bitterly, making it clear that
Lily had become a surrogate for his anger toward me. And
though I despised talking with him, I would cajole on her behalf, until he reluctantly agreed to send the money.

Lily was ravishing, a stalklike beauty, topped by a tumble
of dark auburn curls, a neck like the stem of the flower she was
named after. Striding up Fifth Avenue in Louis Jourdan pumps
(how had she afforded them?) at 4:00 A.M., wearing a narrow
miniskirt, a fox jacket (given her in lieu of a showroom modeling
fee, she said), insisting, over my fatigue, my objections, that I
hop a cab, go uptown with her, do more coke with her and
"some people I know," I couldn't help but admire her, this
amazing force of nature I had somehow—accidentally—created.

"It's the *style*, Mother," she would say, over my objections,
daubing my face with opaque pancake, then patting on white
talcum, painting on black-red lips, as though I were her doll—
was it because I looked so much older this way? When I slept
with a man she introduced me to in One University, a bar where
she and the Jazz Musician seemed to know everyone, she was
angry, and Lily's anger was something I was learning to avoid
if I could. "Do you want to know how I got these scabs?" she
screeched. Glancing down, I saw the rough brown patches on
her skinny knees through her beige pantyhose. "From giving
that same guy a blow-job on the stairwell of his building the
night before you got here!" she raged.

"Oh, Mother, I lo-o-ove you so much!" she would say the
next moment, covering my face in kisses, hugging me to her
skinny breasts, the bones in her chest feeling like a xylophone.
"Someday, I'm going to buy you a new Alfa—or maybe even a
Benz!" In New York, I was her child, the naive one, indulged
if hopelessly out-of-date. Boundaries were for Musette, for
Rose, not for her. At twenty-one, she lived in an open relation-

ship with her jazz artist, and also went out with men who wore gold chains, tight leather suits, bracelets spelling out their names in diamonds, men who hired limos and spent two hundred dollars on a bottle of wine. And how did she put that together with her poetry, her poetic self? I wondered, blind to the real reason for their attraction—the pockets full of white powder, the money to buy more when that was gone.

"Anteater nose, we call her," the Jazz Musician said sarcastically. "We have to be sure to get ours before Lily does, because if there's any coke left, she'll swoop it up."

But just as I had once hated anyone saying anything bad about Dwayne, I now hated anyone saying anything bad about Lily—especially the Jazz Musician.

The first time Lily visited me in the French Quarter, she lay on the balcony, sunbathing, her eyes covered with a silk scarf, her bikini top turned down until it was as narrow as ribbon, apparently oblivious to the men staring at her from the busy street below. Occasionally, she roused herself to come inside, lounge on the couch, flirt with whoever was visiting me. That night we boiled crayfish, arguing about how much crayfish boil to put in the pot, then went to Johnny Matassis, where, as "The House of the Rising Sun" played on the jukebox, she told me over our fifth drinks that she had been fucking Johnny whenever he came through New York. "I *always* had a crush on him, Mother—even way back when I was fourteen. He's so good-looking! And he *does* have a big prick, doesn't he?" she said, expecting me to understand. And I did—weren't we paper dolls, cut from the same page? But that night I got drunker than she did, and when we got back to the apartment, she and Ray, the lawyer she had picked up, a man I knew to be as corrupt as only a New Orleans lawyer can be, helped me up the stairs. Once inside the apartment, she tucked me in tenderly, giving both my breasts an affectionate squeeze as she kissed me good night.

The next time she visited, she was hyped up, shaky. As we sat in the bar at the Fairmont, a man in a business suit came straight over to her and asked, without preliminaries, whether she would like to "do business." She spoke dismissively, not even looking at him, but seemed to know without question what he meant.

I suddenly recalled how when Lily was fifteen, she, Johnny, and I had gone into the Lion's Head on Christopher Street in New York. It was hot, and Lily wore short shorts—with high-heeled pumps. Within minutes, she was surrounded by men. "They think she's a hooker," Johnny said crossly.

"What did that guy want?" I asked now. "Sh-h! Mo-ther! Be qui-et! There might be vice cops around here," she said sharply. When we went to Johnny Matassis, the man appeared again—had he followed us there?—and this time, Lily went off toward the ladies' room with him. She was back in fifteen minutes, and the man walked straight out the door. She wasn't ready to return to my apartment, she said. The next morning she explained that she'd gotten a ride with another man in his Mercedes, that he had given her fifty dollars for a blow-job. "I luv-v-v oral sex, Mother!" she enthused, dismissing my objections as if I had criticized her for eating potato chips rather than carrot sticks. Both she and Rose orgasmed easily, she told me (Rose had confided this in her, she said, though I had not even known that Rose had lost her virginity); sitting on the balcony of my apartment in my white silk wrapper, open to the pink tips of her tiny breasts, she explained to me how to do it without needing either my own hands or the man's.

That afternoon before she left for the airport, she handed me a folded hundred-dollar bill. "Put this in your billfold, Mother," she said. And I did, asking nothing.

She just liked giving me things, I told myself.

I didn't like the Jazz Musician, and I blamed him. "He's setting my poems to music, Mother," Lily said defensively during my next visit to New York. "He's going to play backup for me when I perform them. You just don't realize how talented he is."

That night, she was the little mother, her sweet self again, making homemade vegetable soup, corn bread, a chocolate layer cake. Her guests were a Canadian drummer who was passing through and two friends from the building: a depressed-looking blonde about Lily's age who said she wrote song lyrics but who dressed like a bag lady, and who I suspected was a prostitute; and a handsome baby-faced actor who looked about Lily's age—"My movie—*Big Where It Counts*—opens on Times Square this week!" he said proudly, as if it were an entry in the Cannes Film Festival. Lily stood behind him, trimming his hair, nodding in approval; then served us all big mugs of the soup— thick with carrots and potatoes and onions, as nutritious as what I had served back in Metairie—along with hunks of the corn bread. Then we sat around listening to the Jazz Musician's new songs, sharing a joint, eating the thick cake, scraping the Betty Crocker icing from our plates like children—like a family, I thought, marveling at the life my daughter had created for herself.

The next night, we drank straight Black Jack, and Lily ordered in Szechuan. As she, the Jazz Musician, the Canadian drummer, and I sat around in the living room where I was to sleep, she peeled off, first, her shirt, then the Jazz Musician's. Next, she unzipped his pants. "Look what a big prick he has, Mother," she said, grinning, holding out his erect penis, which did indeed appear to be oversized. The last thing I recall was him lying on top of me on the couch, its Indian spread, pumping in and out as Lily laughed in the background with the drummer, then the vague sounds of sex from the loft above us. When I woke near dawn, I saw the drummer sleeping on the rug beside the couch. ". . . at the Mudd Club . . ." he muttered when I asked where Lily was.

So what could I say about the Jazz Musician, or about her affair with Johnny, after that?

The next morning, I awoke Lily nervously, afraid of her reaction to what had happened the night before—had I hurt her irreparably? But when I went up to the loft bed and touched her shoulder, she only laughed, reaching up, in her affectionate way, to touch my breasts. That afternoon, we were to be photographed together nude by a world-famous Chinese photographer, a friend of Paula's; the least suggestive of the pictures were to appear in one of the better fashion magazines. I wore only a soft mauve angora scarf around my neck, to drape over my stretch marks, while Lily, totally naked, arched arrogantly before the camera, extending her thin body, poking out her bee-stung lower lip, jutting her perfect chin line accentuated by the Italian-boy haircut.

Someone in New York for one of my openings took the notion of using my paintings in her movie, the background for the obligatory chichi gallery scene. The woman director asked me to play myself, and when I heard that the scene would include a poetry reading, I suggested Lily: Thus she was able to read part of one of her best poems in a movie, if a low-budget one. Seeing my gorgeous daughter on film, the succulence seeming to spill from her very pores, I felt the way I had when she had been sixteen—that her beauty, her charisma, somehow made her larger than life, exempting her from ordinary pain.

It would be a long time before I would know about the suicide attempts—the pills, the wrists slashed at, the trips to Bellevue—that had taken place when I hadn't been around to see them. Yet how could I *not* have known—watching my worldly daughter read at the far end of a smoky jazz club; seeing her theatrically sad face, hearing her words full of grief, the poems that reflected back to those days in Metairie? For moments, once again, she was my three-year-old, murmuring "My moon, my moon," her plump arms around my neck, as we stood at the end of that driveway on that street of identical houses, looking up toward a radiant sky. And standing at the end of a long, smoke-filled room, I couldn't believe that some people within the haze of cigarette smoke were still drinking, talking, as my Lily poured out the pain of that childhood, couched in the metaphors of heterosex. Nor did she herself appear to take the sorrow of her poems that seriously. When she did a street performance in Washington Square Park with other poets from her group, "Southerners in Exile," the old and young men kept dealing. "It's just the way it is here, Mother," she laughed when I protested.

"Did you know your daughter has a serious drug problem?" the Chinese photographer asked me casually a few days after the shoot when he called to say the prints were ready. After we filmed the gallery scene, the director took me aside to ask the same question. And I hated both of them: The photographer

232

probably hadn't liked Lily's failure to succumb to the power of his penis; the woman director had probably been jealous of her beauty. And what did they know of my darling Lily anyway? Hadn't they seen the same gorgeous pictures of her I had, the pictures I believed in more than any evidence to the contrary?

Oh, I had to admit I liked those parts of it—seeing her image at the far end of a smoky room, hearing her husky voice, then the applause; or her image, larger than life, on the movie screen, or even on the cheap newsprint of *The East Village Other* or *The Soho Weekly News*—thinking that she was mine, that I had made her.

Thus, Lily and I colluded: We were allies, sisters, girlfriends, sharing the same fantasies of art and sex and freedom.

And though I didn't know it then, Oblivion.

CHAPTER TEN

BACK IN New Orleans, Ray and I were looking through a book of photographs. He was wearing black leather gloves, and he wanted me to wear them, too.

"You should do something like *this* in your work," he was saying, flipping through sleek pages of bored-looking girls about Lily's age, seated or standing inside elegant Louis XV interiors, convulsing mildly against black leather bonds, or else standing in stiletto heels, black hose, and garter belt, wielding a black leather riding crop.

I had wanted to become a Mary Cassatt, a recorder of domestic joy. Instead, I had become a female Francis Bacon, an artist of pain—even, some said, a woman pornographer.

"Now lean over that chair. But keep the heels and the gloves on," he was saying.

Now Ray's leather-clad palm was on my belly. And already, as he began, my vagina felt as though it might burst into sobs.

"This is quaint, but I guess I'm just a New Yorker at heart," Lily wrote from Los Angeles, on a card with a picture of the

Château Marmont. And I didn't want to ask why she was there, or who was paying her way.

How could I, when I, too, craved the places where the disaffected gathered, was more comfortable in a Guatemalan village, or a Costa Rican brothel, sitting at the bar talking to the whores, than I ever had been as a wife. In Panajachel, I hung out in the Blue Bird bar on a dirt road, danced at the Jaquar in the jungle, and slept with a lover and his woman lover in a two-dollar-a-night hotel. In San José, I painted from the live sex shows, held on the bar for my benefit, the pretty girls, often the mother of three by age eighteen, their Cesarean scars marking their rounded yet still childish bellies, sucking one another off for the benefit of the *norteamericanos* who hung out there. And I could see that they, too, yearned for tenderness: "I no lika the *machadas*, I lika *you*," said Marlena, a beautiful seventeen-year-old with long dark hair and a bad cold, wiping her nose with one hand while taking my own in her other hand, trying to persuade me to go upstairs with her.

"Mother, I'm in love with this guy, this playboy. His name is Dick, he's really weird, and does such funny things," Lily said over the phone: "Like when we're riding around in his limo, he has the chauffeur stop and run in and buy a whole box of Godiva chocolates. And he eats them right then and there. And he keeps boxes of them hidden all over his house. He's writing his memoirs, the papers are all over the floors in his bedroom— you have to walk over them to get around! . . .

"Mother, he's sending you an airline ticket so you can come up to spend New Year's," she went on. "And oh yes, he's really old, about seventy. . . ." In Lily's book, "old" was not a pejorative, but just another form of eccentricity; besides, it often meant "rich."

The day after Christmas, Lily and I were met at the door on Sutton Place by Edward the butler. "Edward's an intellectual, Mother, like Rose—he spends most of the time in library," Lily whispered to me. In fact, the portly man who led us up the broad curving staircase wearing coat and pleated pinstriped trousers was carrying two fat volumes under an arm. "Doesn't he make you think of the way she used to take her schoolbooks everywhere?" Lily giggled behind her hand. "This way, ladies," Edward said with a British accent, indicating a suite of rooms at the end of a hallway.

"My, my, my," said the Silver-Haired Playboy as Lily introduced me: "A lot of my girls say their mothers are pretty—but you *really* are!" Quick brown eyes met mine: Instead of the elderly roué I had expected to at least minimally object to, a still-handsome man with an unlined face sat on the king-sized bed against its padded-satin headboard, surrounded by a group of friends.

Still, how can I explain why that very night I ended up sharing the king-size bed with him and Lily, taking Lily's place beneath him as she rose early to bathe ("Maybe he'll marry *you*, Mother!")? Nor was I judgmental about the assortment of beautiful girls and boys, models and aspiring actors, who occupied the other bedrooms. Or that every night, all night, snowy white piles of processed cocaine were as available as scotch or vodka. One night the Jazz Musician came to play for us on the huge grand piano in the shabby, high-ceilinged living room. I was so out of it that I didn't realize that the Jazz Musician was the Playboy's dealer—that he had just brought a fresh supply. Instead, I took over the huge kitchen, sending out for every ingredient I wanted, making New Orleans–style gumbo and crayfish étouffée; Texas chili, jalapeño corn bread, and pecan pies; then slept with Lily and the Playboy from early morning till noon each day.

Each evening, we sat on a long couch in the den, watching old Joan Crawford or Irene Dunne movies, while Dick put his arms around my and Lily's shoulders, fondling both our breasts. One of the regulars was Janice, an ex-nun newly arrived from the Midwest, the flat map of Kansas; her ambition was to work at Andy Warhol's Factory, she confided. In the meantime, she was just hanging around, watching, or helping me dish up the food from the big kitchen, not doing the lines of coke or anything—someone the Silver-Haired Playboy had met somewhere and had taken a liking to. I supposed it was her short bouffant hairdo, her primly buttoned Peter Pan–collared shirtwaist, that protected her from becoming a candidate for his caresses. Having her sitting there with us was like having a resident religious, or the blessings of the heartland.

"Dick, this place needs redecorating! Look at those awful old chintz curtains! And you're *rich! Rich! RICH!*" Lily was screeching, her voice rising in decibel with every line of coke she did. And he laughed, just as he would laugh when she and I argued vehemently on New Year's Eve over the shade of lipstick I should wear: She wanted to cover my face once again with the pale pancake, powder it over with stark white talcum, outline my eyes in black, paint on the same blood-black lipstick she wore. I had already agreed to don the long-sleeved jet-brown beaded chiffon blouse without a brassiere, my nipples showing through like dark fat rosebuds.

By the time we went up the marble staircase, onto the mezzanine of the Big City Club, I was so high from the line of coke I'd done at Lily's behest that I didn't care anyway. The ceilings must have been at least fifty feet high—as high as the sky and as dizzying. Dressed in less than a nightgown, I sat chatting with women in their twenties and early thirties who wore heavy diamond bracelets and necklaces—a delicately beautiful blonde was dressed in a silver-beaded chemise, "an original from the twenties," she told us. Beautiful diamond-tiaraed or tuxedo-clad old people glided like a drugged dream around the dance floor. I could almost feel the heavy weight of the beaded fabrics rolling between my fingertips. The elderly women looked like old movie stars, the younger ones like *Vogue* models; they all appeared to be married or "engaged" to more silver-haired, tuxedoed men—even their heads of hair looked like sleek jewelry to me: Was this what Lily wanted for herself? I wondered.

As the Silver-Haired Playboy introduced us, I saw the men's eyes flash in interest—a mother and daughter: Was he sleeping with both of us? One of the women—her chunky wrists weighted by diamonds—was from Montgomery; I recognized her name as one I had seen in the Alabama newspapers; I knew she was that dowdy southern type from an old family. As she suspiciously asked me whom I knew in New Orleans, people I had only heard of, then about Johnny's "people," and learned of that connection, the corners of her lips raised in that stiff parentheses. Beneath the table, the Playboy had his hands on both Lily's thigh and mine. "Stop it, Dick!" I squealed as the woman turned pointedly away from us, toward her dinner partner.

Later, at Magic's, a man we had seen earlier in the evening from the window of the limo, dancing wildly through an intersection of Fifth Avenue, was now doing the same broad steps all over the dance floor. As Lily danced first with him, and then with one young man after another, Dick and I sat on the balcony, his arm around my shoulder, his hand lightly fondling my breast. "Will you talk to this girl?" the fiftyish man clad in leather suit and gold chains and seated next to me said of the sad-looking Raphael-delicate blonde at his side. "You look like a smart, mature woman—maybe you could explain to her that there's *no* way she could know whether she's gay at eighteen!"

Still later that night, there was a party given by a modeling agency, a basement full of young people so beautiful that I could think of nothing but a field full of kittens or flowers. "Easter!" cried Lily's old friend Trevor from across the room, rushing over to clasp my hand, look down into my eyes. "I have *so-o-o* much to tell you!" In his tux, he was even more classically handsome than I remembered. As he talked, I recalled his long, slender body, pale ivory against white hotel sheets, after we'd had tea at the Plaza. All the while, a smartly dressed brunette, the only other "older" woman there, watched me speculatively from across the room: the woman he now lived with, Trevor explained; she was gay—would I like to meet her?

As Mama used to say in her better days, I felt like I had died and gone to heaven. Sexual definitions were as vague, as heady, here as they were in the French Quarter. And I preferred not to look at the signs, just to think it was all okay. Like Lily, I wanted it to last forever.

"Buy your mother a little something," Dick said one afternoon, handing Lily his American Express card. We took a cab to an Upper East Side shop where we had to ring a bell to be admitted. Inside, Lily went wild, trying on clothes—a Chanel-like—or was it a *real* Chanel?—taupe bolero, trimmed in black

239

soutache braid, a tight, *tight* black leather skirt, then a black sequined one that barely covered her buttocks. She preened before the multiple mirrors, smoothing the textures over her bony frame. I bit my lip at mentioning her new thinness, a thinness that was even more extreme than it had been, but later I would think of it, what it must have meant.

She found so many things she liked that the saleswoman called Dick to okay the amount of the sale. He and Lily argued loudly over the phone, venom pouring from Lily's mouth as if she were a fire hydrant, and by the time she handed the receiver back to the clerk, he had given in. When we left, I wore a new five-hundred-dollar hot-pink angora sweater, cut in a deep V down my back. I thought its blouson shape made me look fat, but Lily kept saying impatiently—in the new, phony tone she now used sometimes—"No, Easter—it looks dee-vine! Take my word for it!" I was getting used to not arguing with Lily—it took too much energy, and she always won anyway. She had also taken to using my given name when we were out together. It was as though she wanted me to be a mother when she wished, and at other times an unfashionable peer over whom she lorded her powers.

In any case, I always hated that sweater and never wore it back in New Orleans—because of the weather, I told myself.

One night, the Silver-Haired Playboy confronted two young models who were sharing a flowered bedroom at the end of the long upstairs hall, telling them that they would have to leave the next day. Lily had told me the girls were lesbians, that Dick was only letting the prettier one's girlfriend stay there as a favor—they were both broke and couldn't afford an apartment—but that he was fed up because the one he liked wouldn't sleep with him.

That night, as Lily, the Playboy, and I lay in the king-size bed, I heard the sounds of china breaking, furniture being thrown. Someone battered the door into our suite, and Lily and I clutched one another, but the Playboy didn't even waken.

"Well, well, well—just a little scene from Currier and Ives," Edward said the next morning as he brought in our breakfast tray, smiling at the sight of the three of us. Wearing a gown like a peach satin slip, the strap falling down over a shoulder, Lily sat in the middle against the satin-padded headboard like our child; I had on a black lace teddy that barely concealed my breasts.

Edward went on to report the damage: "They pulled the kitchen door off the hinges, threw the everyday dishes from the cabinets, crashed the china vases in the upper hallway, and broke the lock to your rooms, sir, before the police finally arrived. . . ."

Dick seemed only mildly annoyed. "Call the locksmith, get estimates on the broken vases, call the insurance agent, order some new dishes from Bloomingdale's. . . ." he instructed in a bored voice, lifting his teacup from the bed table, barely looking away from *Good Morning America* while fondling Lily's upper thigh with his other hand. And that afternoon, I left my daughter in his ménage and flew back home to New Orleans.

Back in the French Quarter, I got fully into my sickness: sleeping with more and more younger men, men younger than Dwayne was now. Often, in one low-rent bar or another, I would look around the room, half fearing, half hoping to see him there. Would I somehow inadvertently pick up my own son, wake to see his head on the pillow beside me, the knife I knew he carried stuck into my headboard?

One afternoon, I read a novel by Pete Hamill about a young boxer from Brooklyn, his love affair with his mother. I read it, drinking Gallo chablis, for five solid hours when I should have been painting; then I went out to Johnny Matassis and got drunk on the fifty-cent martinis. That night, I cried my grief into my pillow.

Later, I consumed the novels of Earl Thompson, his stories of a boy's affair with his mother, and wondered with anguish why my own love for my son had been more damaging—was it *because* it had never been made flesh? Would incest have been better than what he saw as my rejection?

And what did this man I had made look like naked, how did his penis compare to the many I had seen? I knew that Dwayne shared my dead daddy's view of my sexuality as aberrant, as belonging legitimately only to him. And my awareness

241

of him—his dark good looks, his wiry muscularity, the way he stalked and moved around a room—led me to feel that he was right, that the guilt was mine.

It was like a ringworm going round and round, or the herpes zoster, running like fire up and down the nerve endings of one side of my body after the trip to Guatemala, something contracted in the two-dollar-a-night hotel.

There was only one good thing about my frustrated love for my son: I had suffered so much over him that I was immune to suffering over other men.

More than ever, Musette, Aunt Darlene, even Rose and Lily, wanted me to stay away from Dwayne.

But each time he came to New Orleans, I determined to have a "normal" visit with him. I would imagine us sitting around the apartment, chatting, laughing, getting into that crazy humor of ours. Instead, he would stride menacingly through my rooms, looking with disgust at my current paintings. "Why don't you paint some pictures with *animals* in it? Something like *cats* or *horses*?" he would ask. As I tried futilely to explain the evolution of my current images, he would flip on my answering machine, listen to my messages, looking dark when a man's voice filled the tape. Finally, I would become so aware of his sexuality, his rage, the Bowie knife on his belt, that I would suggest something, anything, to get out of the apartment: that we go to Bourbon Street to hear jazz or somewhere uptown to play the pinball machines. Once there, we would quickly get drunk on Kamikazes, and he would pressure me for money, or do drug deals so openly on the street that I would hurry home, and locking the guillotine door behind me, refuse to answer his 4:00 A.M. yells from the street below.

"Does he have a piece?" the man in bed with me asked, panicked, when Dwayne showed up unexpectedly one day. He pulled on his pants and, grabbing up his docksiders, rushed past Dwayne through the one door out.

Dwayne explained that he had come to see an oil-company tool-pusher about a job as a rigger. But instead of going out to check on it, he stayed inside the apartment for the rest of that day, hovering behind me as I painted the same small section of canvas over and over. There were predictions of a hurricane, and the sky above New Orleans was charcoal. That night, strong winds were blowing around the building, and in the middle of the night, unable to sleep, I walked into the darkened room where he slept on the couch, holding my cat, Moana, and the unsheathed Bowie knife on his lap. I noticed for the first time the heavy silver skull-and-crossbones ring glittering on his knuckle. His sticky dark brown hair drifted around his shoulders. And as I looked down on this man, my son, his fear seemed palpable—or was it mine? In any case, I could almost smell it, a strange pungent odor in the air, and my pity for him—for us both—pierced my heart.

By the next day, he had dropped all pretense of applying for the job. Sheets of gray rain fell throughout the morning; the radio announced hurricane warnings. Dwayne lay on the couch fondling the cat, his knife. That afternoon, the rain lightened, and I rushed out of the apartment before he could follow, calling back to him that I was going to the A&P. An hour later, I came back with a bag of groceries and with Sophie. As the three of us sat in the living room, the wind making the building creak, I served goblets of the Gallo chablis, and Sophie and I made strained conversation, chatting about Dwayne's chances of getting on with an offshore rig.

With a violent motion, Dwayne threw his glass down to the frayed Oriental carpet, breaking it. He stood over where I sat on a low ottoman, wielding his knife. "Get down on your knees, bitch!" he snarled, indicating that I should pick up the broken glass. My legs went weak, boneless, feeling like water as I crawled, collecting the jagged fragments.

The phone rang on a small table at my elbow, and I jumped up before Dwayne could stop me. Musette was on the line. "Is everything okay?" she asked anxiously. "That storm looks like it might be bad up your way." "No," I said, Dwayne standing close beside me with the knife. "What? you're *not* all right?" "*No!*" I said again. She paused. "Is Dwayne there?" "*Yes!*" I said before he pulled the receiver from my hand, slammed it down.

After the police came, I went to Sophie's with my telephone, checkbook, and credit cards in a brown paper bag, my

243

painting in progress in a green plastic trash bag; Sophie carried a stack of my finished paintings in another bag. If he burned down the building, at least I would have saved those. I would give him one day to leave, I had told him in the presence of the police officer—either that, or he could go for observation on the psychiatric floor at Charity. As we walked through heavy winds, Sophie began chattering: "I was so scared, so scared . . ." she said over and over. Along the streets, people were sealing windows with corrugated cardboard and masking tape. I strode stoically beside her, looking back occasionally to be sure he wasn't following. I was that Crazy Woman again, cushioned by a cocoon of numbness.

Two days later, the sun was shining. Homerdessa had wired me money to deliver to Dwayne, "so thet boy kin come on home." As I walked to meet him at Felix's, I envisioned him striding purposefully toward me, stabbing me with the Bowie knife. Instead, he joked as we lunched on soda crackers and oysters Rockefeller. He was taking the Greyhound back to South Alabama that afternoon, he told me pleasantly. Feeling guilty, I handed him another fifty, which he pocketed without comment. After all, he was my son, wasn't he? He had long since adopted my view that I had betrayed him, that I owed him. And he had confirmed mine: that he was someone I needed to fear.

"Mother, I've got this new friend, he's got a house out on Southampton, we'll go there 'n sit beside the pool!" Lily said over the phone the following August, sounding excited—*too* excited, I should have noticed. But I didn't. I had never been to Southampton, and I envisioned the two of us, cozy and chatting, doing one another's nails, sipping tall drinks, wearing broad-brimmed straw hats and raising our smiling faces to the sun. . . .

But first I had an opening at Paula's, and a PBS special on my work, for which Lily insisted on doing my makeup. I arrived late on a Tuesday, at the Gramercy Park Hotel, where I would be put up for the night. When Lily came to my room the next day, she looked wild-eyed, her own lengthening hair in disarray. Her hands were shaking, her usually perfect manicure was chipped; despite the August heat, she was wearing long sleeves. "I got in at four this morning, I just haven't had any coffee," she said irritably. It was two in the afternoon, and I was due to leave for the studio at three. Picking up the phone, I ordered coffee, juice, and a chicken sandwich, then sat as patiently as I could before the mirror as she laid out a huge array of cosmetics, trying one unflattering color after another. It was time for me to leave for the studio, and it was raining, which would make it harder to get a taxi. But when she began outlining my lips again with the blood-black shade I hated, I had to protest: "Lil-lee! I don't think that color will look very good on television. . . ." Angrily, she swept the makeup from the dresser top onto the floor and burst into tears.

I took her in my arms and squeezed her tight, feeling the incredible tension, like a wound spring, inside her thin body. "Just rest here until you feel calmed," I said soothingly. "Eat a sandwich, have some coffee—you'll feel better. . . ."

On the way to the studio, I sat rigid with my new fear. And that's all I remember—that, and posing stiffly before the camera as the interviewer discussed my "outrageous" paintings in a challenging voice. And thus began the ten days that would seem, in memory, like a Fellini movie, or, if I had heard of him then, a plot by David Lynch—a time during which I would become the Crazy Woman again, a controlled hysteria gripping me—controlled, because I knew anything else would drive Lily further from me.

We never did make it to Southampton. At the apartment on Sullivan Street the next day, the air was thick with a sweetish smoke. A dark girl I'd never seen before lounged on the couch where the Jazz Musician had fucked me. "Monet—I just moved in," she murmured, holding out her hand in a languid manner. "I'm a model." The phone rang every few minutes, and people knocked at the door, coming inside for a brief transaction with the Jazz Musician, who took them upstairs to the loft.

"It's called 'freebasing,' " Lily told me. Yes, I mumbled, trying to control my hysteria; I had just heard what had happened to Richard Pryor. Lily sat curled like a cat, or as if she were cold, on the couch beside Monet. She said she had two new boyfriends: the Mafia Man was rich, had the house at Southampton; he lived on the Upper East Side in an apartment overlooking the East River; his tongue had been cut all over by the Mafia, a hundred tiny scars, and he wore a bracelet spelling out his name in diamonds. The Baby-Faced Brit had recently come to the States from Amsterdam, "illegally," Lily said—*he* was the one she was in love with. She told me all this as though it were ordinary. And given my past acceptance of just about everything she had ever done, not to speak of my own rejection of conventional mores, didn't she have every reason to think that I would accept this, too?

Hadn't I given her, at nine, the cookbook with the drawings by Cocteau, the motto "Children and Artists Disobey"? Told her over and over that she didn't have to live like Mama or Aunt Darlene or Musette, or even the way I had, early on with Bobby?

And because of my own crimes, I hadn't seen her more deadly ones. But now all limits were gone. I sat on the couch feeling sick, the sweetish chemical smoke filling my nostrils— suddenly, frantically, trying to figure out how to save my daughter's life.

I had only one comforting thought: A mother couldn't lose two children, could she?

Every night, over dinner at Bradley's or One Fifth Avenue, dinner for which I paid and to which Lily wouldn't go without the Baby-Faced Brit, I begged her to leave New York, go back to the South with me. As I talked, cajoled, finally pled, the two of them would nuzzle and hold hands, giggling at whatever I said. Occasionally, her long lashes drooped to her cheek, as though she was very sleepy. Was what I was saying that boring? And why were she and this hateful boy with whom she was holding hands rolling in laughter at everything I said?

No, she didn't want to leave New York, she would finally answer, yawning. She was happy with her life—happier than she ever had been, she said, gazing meaningfully at the Baby-Faced Brit.

I had the same feeling I had had when Dwayne had begun sniffing the glue—that something was happening that I didn't understand and couldn't stop. And that powerlessness was turning me into the Crazy Woman, screeching and spinning out of control.

I flew back to Louisiana, feeling as if I had been wrestling alligators. For a week, I lay in the four-poster bed, unable to paint, floating amid images of sharp-finned piranhas, sharks with teeth like needles; of a dais on which Lily, still and white, eyes closed, hands folded over her small breasts, drifted farther and farther away, propelled by the underground tides, out to sea.

Two weeks later, Lily phoned, exuberant: She and the Mafia Man were getting married in a big wedding on Long Island. He would be taking her on tour around the country to perform her poetry: "He has the contacts, he'll pay for the whole thing, Mother!" What had happened to the Baby-Faced Brit? "Oh, Joey took care of *him*," she said blithely.

The following week, she called me in tears: The Mafia Man had gotten her a red kitten "just like Marmalade," but a hawk had swooped down from the East River, carrying it off. From the terrace, she had watched the bird carry it up, up, up, into the distance, the scruff of the kitten's neck in its talons, the tiny thing mewling piteously, its small body twisting, its little paws flailing.

The next week, she called again. This time, she was sobbing in great gulps. Monet had died of an overdose; she had just been to the funeral on Staten Island. "Can I still come home, Mama?" she cried. The Mafia Man got on the line. He would put her into a limo to Kennedy: "Your daughter's gettin' outta control, I can't handle 'er no more." So without her clothes or even a suitcase, she was on her way home to me in New Orleans.

At the airport gate, Lily chattered seductively to a tweed-jacketed, balding man. She looked thinner, more glamorous than ever. As she introduced me to her confused-looking companion, she cast a fluorescent smile from one of us to the other. "He has just been *fascinatin'* me all the way from Kennedy, Mother, telling me this 'n that about the insurance bid-ness!" she enthused, mocking his accent as he carried her small makeup case toward the terminal for her. "An' my mother—don't you think she's *be-oou-tiful? And* she's beautiful inside, too! *And* she a famous artist!" Her speech slurred as though she had had several drinks; the blusher stood out on her pale cheekbones. "Now you be sure to call me—we'll go out for that *dinner!*" she called out to him brightly, her lipsticked mouth stretched into a glistening fuchsia slash as we walked through the glass doors toward the short-term parking lot. As she frantically waved good-bye to the man, I glanced back to see him wilting, his narrow shoulders drooping, collapsed at the sudden withdrawal of her radiance.

Before we had gotten back to the French Quarter, she had wilted, her manic chatter turning to tears, her head laid weakly back against the car seat. That night, I held her as she writhed and cried out beside me in the four-poster bed, the sweat pouring from her wraithlike body.

And Crazy Woman that I was, I thought that this was the end of it, that in getting her out of New York and home to me, she had been saved.

I didn't know that soon I would be watching her carried off, caught in the claws of her addiction, as helpless as she had been watching her kitten carried off into space. That soon there would barely be enough images in the world—a smushed turtle on Airline Highway, a crippled pigeon facing a barking dog—to contain my pain.

Or that what was to come next would be as devastating to my hopes, my sanity, as Hurricane Camille had been to the coast of Louisiana—when graves had been dissolved, washed away, making it impossible to tell whether the bodies caught in the trees were those from the graves or of the newly dead.

CHAPTER ELEVEN

WHEN LILY *was nine, she especially liked a poem I read to her by William Carlos Williams, the one of apology to his wife for eating the plums she was saving for breakfast. "Why don't you write your own poem after that one?" I said to her. She bent her little head, hunched her plump shoulders, and in a few minutes handed me a piece of tablet paper:*

"*I am so sorry
I put your goldfish down the drain—
But they were so slippery they just kind of went down by themselves. . . .*"

I had gathered her up, hugged her, kissed her, until she protested, "Mama, you're bumpin' my glasses off!"

Goldfish down a drain. A kitten twisting out of reach. Graves shifting underground, drifting out to endless sea.

And now my Lily, carried off on a cloud of white powder, as slippery as talcum or kaolin—she just kind of disappeared by herself. . . .

Heroin—it was never among my worst nightmares. In fact, I knew little about it, had never given it much thought. It wasn't the sixties anymore—Jimi Hendrix, Janis Joplin, Mama Cass,

Jim Morrison, were long since dead. It was certainly not among the party drugs—the grass, the Quaaludes, the lines of coke—now so popular.

The moment I heard the word pronounced in the same sentence as her name, I assumed it to be a death sentence. The vision it conjured was as bad as leukemia or any other fatal wasting away—worse even, because along with it went some unimaginable degradation, a wasting of spirit along with flesh: a gaunt body lying in his or her own shit in some ghetto worse than I had ever seen.

I walked around the French Quarter, numbly trying to come up with words, thoughts, images, to comfort myself. There *are* junkies in the world, I thought: Yes, there are junkies, and why shouldn't she—Lily—be one of them? The question is not *why her?* but why *not* her? I told myself bravely, glaring at the people, the cars passing, all those who had escaped, whose children were *not* junkies. The boys with rings through their tits, the blacks lounging against storefronts, the ragged artists painting bad portraits at the edge of Jackson Square—those who courted life on the edge every day—let *them* be junkies, I thought meanly. And why *not* them? Why not *them* instead of my beautiful, white, oh-so-white, 110-pound daughter?

And then my neat row of thoughts would crumble, the pain coming at me full-fledged for as many moments as I could stand it before the numbness would mercifully descend again.

I already knew that bad things can and do happen, and that probably they would happen to me. But what I was learning now was that what the gods have in store is often not what one fears most, but something worse—horrors I had never even thought of: a demon's surprise, a cake full of snakes, just waiting to spring.

Heroin—Ray was the one who told me, using that word flat out. The sound falling from his lips flooded through me, a holocaust of the brain; and along with it, a frenzy of images, bumping into and falling over one another, of needles, wasting away, and death. "Haven't you noticed the track marks?"

Track marks?—I was spiraling out of control, nauseous with yet another image: red dots, purple pinpricks, blood-black scabs; my mind skidding back, back, back, to Rose and Lily at three and four, the vision of them sitting on the floor with their drawing books, following the dots with their crayons.

Paula had arranged an opening in Houston that night, and I dressed up, flew there, was photographed. Ray said he would stay with Lily and help me get her into a hospital the next day. During dinner with the gallery owner and his lover, I excused myself over the candles and chardonnay, the lamb fajitas and white-bean nachos, to call Ray from the pay phone in the back of the bistro. "She's got to have it, I've gotta take her somewhere, buy it—she's goin' crazy," he said. I left the pay phone reeling, not yet understanding that in the life of an addict, twenty-four hours is an eternity. Numbly, I put on fresh lipstick, checked out my fuchsia satin shirt and tight jeans in the mirror, pitched my purple felt cowboy hat at an angle, and went back to the table and smiled.

When I was painting, I had control within the parameters of the canvas. I created a world, and no matter how disturbing, wild, outrageous, that world became, I controlled it. And what I couldn't control I walked away from.

Until the day I found out that in New York Lily had been going to the shooting galleries. "They were like bombed-out buildings on the Lower East Side," she would tell me later. "Men—black men—stood up on the roof with rifles or machine guns, and John and I would get in the line that would wind around through the rubble. You had to stand in a line—the other people who were waiting looked rough, even though there were some who looked like they worked on Wall Street. First, you handed your money through this crumbly little hole in the wall, then the drugs were handed back through it—the men with the guns were watching all the time, 'n most everybody was sittin' around shootin' up right there in the dirt 'n plaster." She paused. "It was exciting, like going to a war zone. . . ."

Within days of her arrival in New Orleans, Lily had met a new Sugar Daddy, a rich silver-haired man who had had a penile implant, and who liked young women, particularly addicts. He lived with his elderly mother in a trailer park across the river, but he owned office buildings all over the city. He had rented Lily an apartment, nicer than mine, on Fourth Street off St. Charles. He had once been a well-known developer, he said, showing me the yellowed clipping from the *Times-Picayune*, before his "breakdown." And yes, there he was smiling, his face as lineless as though he had been airbrushed.

For our first meeting, Lily had dusted his pasty, sagging jowls with blusher, then talcum, and, as she explained, "just a hint of" navy eyeliner. "Doesn't he look cute, Mother?" she asked, in that same ingenuous tone in which she had asked me to admire the size of the Jazz Musician's penis. He smiled sheepishly, a plump old body leaning back in the armchair; I noticed the incongruously large lump lying against his leg beneath the corduroy trousers. He cleared his throat self-consciously, adjusting his silk ascot as we said good-bye. Then Lily and I went off to the first of hundreds of meetings. Ray had told me about the Program, and I suggested we go to one together, assuming, of course, that once I got her there, she would be saved.

Two weeks later, I took over the lease on the apartment the Sugar Daddy had rented for her, so she wouldn't be beholden to him. "You'll see, Mother, I'll get a job soon—I'll get off this stuff, go to meetings, I'll be fine," she assured me. At the meeting, she had already made new male friends, a regular cache of them. I had seen her eyes glittering as she looked around the smoke-filled room; and the eyes on *her*, her small breasts filling a formfitting long-sleeved T-shirt, her long, thin legs encased in tight jeans, her tangle of long hair held back by a bright red bandanna. The next day, feeling old and dowdy, I wrote out the check to the apartment manager for her next month's rent, then rode with the Sugar Daddy in his big silver Coup de Ville to the furniture-rental store, where I signed a paper, taking over his lease on the rental furniture.

"Why do you go after girls Lily's age?" I asked as he drove me back to the apartment. "Ah jes' cain't hep mahself," he mumbled, a look of unabashed sentimentality coming into his watery blue eyes. "Ah've always had to have me a purty young gull." And later, Lily would tell me how he got them, about the endless pocketfuls of Dilaudids, other prescription drugs.

* * *

Soon the files in my studio were stuffed with flyers on the new hospitals that were springing up everywhere; they were called treatment centers, and charged from $10,000 to $20,000 a month; "Six hundred and forty dollars a day—and she'll probably need to stay six weeks," said the counselor at one place I called. Suddenly, everyone in the world seemed to be in them—at least everyone who had insurance, which definitely didn't include Lily and me.

She had come to New Orleans in September. By November I had talked her into going into the detox ward at Charity, still certain that all she needed was to dry out and forget about her life with the Jazz Musician. The next day, I took her flowers, books, a basket of fruit, as though this were an ordinary illness. "Why, you look as fresh as a flower!" the nurse said, opening the double-locked door to admit me. As I sat with Lily on the torn plastic couch in the visiting area, my arm around her thin shoulders, I wondered at the looks the staff gave me.

Later, I would understand: I thought this was the end; they knew it was just the beginning. That Lily would be back time after time—that by the fourth time, the fifth, I would walk wearily across the by-then-familiar parking lot, carrying only what she needed.

But the first time, I assumed it would be the last—that by getting her there, in that refuge, behind locked doors with nurses attending her needs, I had saved her. That finally, the nightmare was over, that she was about to be healed, passing as she was into the hands of the Experts—Experts who knew everything about her disease, who would care for, would cure her. And Lily seemed to feel the same way: "This is the *last* time, Mother," she said, hugging me to her as though I were the one being hospitalized.

Hope—it was the cruelest thing. And regardless of what I had once believed, having read T. S. Eliot didn't help at all.

By the week before Christmas, I was desperate again. After many phone calls, I was put in touch with a man who worked with one of the new treatment centers, and who told me about something called "intervention." Then I called Bobby, who, I could tell, didn't like hearing about any of this, and who wanted to do as little for Lily as he could get away with.

As we sat in a living room filled with overstuffed furniture, decorated much like Big Bobby and Miss Lisa's house had been, the man—who had ruddy cheeks and silvery waves like Lily's Sugar Daddy—told us the story of how he had once been a down-and-out alcoholic lawyer but was now dedicating his life to "heppin' others." As he spoke, his plump blue-haired wife served us coffee from a silver service. "Naow, if y'all want a *reel* drank, yuh kin have one," the man said convivially. "Jes' 'cause *ah* don' drank don't mean I don' keep it for mah friends. A li'l Black Jack, Wild Turkey—I got it right ovah in that li'l ole bar ovah there. . . ."

When I had called Bobby, I had wished for the first time that I still had my old sexual power over him. But I could see that bringing him here had been right: The man was an alumnus of Tulane, of Bobby's own fraternity, ATO, and there was no way Bobby would shame himself by refusing to sign the papers that would commit him to paying for at least part of Lily's treatment. Despite his desire to do as little for Lily as possible, his good-ole-boy bonding would win out.

The "inner-venshun," the man continued gravely, would be an event during which we would confront Lily with the reality of her disease, our love and concern for her—could Musette fly in from Alabama? He would be there to smooth the way, to offer to her the treatment plan, which would include a stay at the treatment center he worked for, then six months at a halfway house. While he talked, a thought nagged at me— how much of a cut did he get? But I could see from Bobby's face that he was completely taken in by his fraternity brother's oily spiel. Besides, whom else did I have to turn to?

I had recently read in Alice Miller that 70 percent of all prostitutes, 80 percent of female drug addicts, have a history of sexual abuse as children. But I didn't think Bobby had ever touched her that way—only that he was a drip, who, since her early childhood, had turned on her, using her as my emotional stand-in.

* * *

The next day at her apartment, big tears rolled down Lily's face; she looked stricken, stunned by seeing Bobby, Musette, this strange man, and me in her little living room, sitting on the white rental couch; and she readily agreed to the treatment plan. The rest of the afternoon was spent driving to the treatment center, a one-story building off Highway 10, signing papers, then taking Lily on to the Hotel Dieu Hospital, where it had been decided that she would spend three days in the psychiatric ward, detoxing prior to admission.

"This is an unus-yal case, a *very* unus-yal case," I heard the man telling the admitting doctor on the floor as we waited. "A beautiful young gull, a divorce, a mother who is not quite, well, shall we say, *conven-shunal*, an *aht-ist*, the chile's father says. . . ." As he talked, he cut his eyes toward me, as though it was obvious where the blame lay. I had dressed conservatively that day, my long hair pulled back, a pleated navy midiskirt; but beneath the wool, the tattoo on my groin burned like neon.

On Christmas Eve, I planned to visit Lily early the next morning before flying to Montgomery to meet Rose, who would be arriving from Baton Rouge to drive with me by rental car down to Musette's for her annual Christmas dinner. I had gifts for her, silvery-wrapped packages from Musette, Rose, and me.

On Christmas morning, as I lay in the grips of a dream from my more sensual days, the phone rang. "Mother, come get me, I'm leaving this place!" Lily shrilled. "Well, I'm getting out anyway," she said stridently when I refused. "It's *Christmas*, Lily. If you're going to leave the hospital, won't you at least fly to Montgomery, go down to Musette's with me? Rose will be there, it'll be so much fun. . . ." I pleaded weakly. "No *way*," she said determinedly. "I'm gettin' outta here 'n coppin'!"

I left the wrapped gifts on my bed, the silver ribbons, the cerise tissues, as bright and wrong as a clown's face.

That evening during the old-fashioned Christmas dinner Musette had prepared—the turkey with the separate pans of corn-bread dressing and giblet gravy, the sticky-sweet boiled cranberries and the orange halves stuffed with candied sweet potatoes, then topped with a dark toasted marshmallow—I wanted to cling to Rose, but I knew she wouldn't like it.

Somewhere near the end of her sophomore year at Baton Rouge, like a cloud over the sun, Rose had become angry. She had brought home a boyfriend from her karate class who had never tasted an avocado and didn't know who Vincent Van Gogh was. When I didn't react, she began to hang out with a gay dorm mate who shaved her head, telling me, "I know you won't be able to accept this, Mother, but I think I'm gay." Disappointed in my lack of response, she rented a shack off campus with an Arab male student. When I visited her in Baton Rouge, she drank double scotches at the Cotton Club, complaining to the bartender of their weakness, her angelic face fierce with righteous anger and looking delicately feminine despite her work boots, her denims, and her rage. As we sat at the bar, she ranted about materialism, saying that she wanted nothing more than to break the plate-glass windows in shopping centers. Once, she almost got into a fistfight with a man, she told me— four policemen had been sent in to break up the argument, and one had had the nerve to ask her out. And then it was all over, a brief storm on a sunny day.

Later she would learn to break up molecules instead of plate glass, to daily chop the heads from rats and mice on a tiny guillotine, to churn the brain cells in a centrifuge. Then, looking at the nucleus through a microscope, breaking it open like a seed that contains the world, she would feel she was coming close to finding the key to everything: "I'll find everything there is to know about the brain someday, Mother—you'll see!" And secretly, I believed it was because she had been born on Sunday, that she was my magical child.

But as Musette's husband, Ned, said the long blessing, I shuddered: What if Rose had been taken? Then that would have been all of them: three out of three. As he carved the turkey, I noticed that despite his polyester pants and Sears Roebuck dress shirt, he seemed more filled out and less of a nerd than he had in high school—in fact, biceps bulged through his sleeves, and his belly looked washboard flat. During dinner, Musette's kids chattered excitedly about new clothes and dates and football games; Ned played his favorite Willie Nelson album, and though Rose gave me a look, not one of their kids said, "Ugh, how corny!"

Nobody asked about Lily, or about Dwayne, who hadn't been invited. I guessed Musette had coached them, hoping to spare me. But instead, I felt as if they were dead, ghosts whom only I grieved, seated at the table among us.

Back in New Orleans, I talked Bobby into helping me put Lily into a treatment center with a locked ward—if we could find her. We went downtown, got the court order, then drove out around the Quarter, looking for her.

As Bobby talked on and on about his problems with his new wife and stepchildren, with his salesmen on the car lot, I wore my phony smile, the one I had rarely needed since I had left him. For Lily's sake, I would be "nice," freezing my face in an unfamiliar expression of humility, drawing him out and buttering him up, just as I had when we had been married.

Then he began on me. And wasn't it only right that I should be punished? After all, hadn't I had more freedom than any woman had a right to? And worse, hadn't I, a high school dropout and unwed mother, dared leave him, a respectable man and a Tulane graduate? But all I could think of was how ugly he was, with his thinning hair and thick glasses, how his scowl made me glad I no longer lived with him. "If it wasn't for you, your *lifestyle*," he ranted, "she'd never have gotten these ideas. . . ." "Or maybe she took after *your* mama, Celanese," I murmured mildly after a while, but he went on as though he hadn't heard, the acid rhetoric pouring from his mouth.

When we finally found Lily, she was sitting in a dingy bar, watching a small black-and-white television set. She looked shocked at seeing Bobby and me together; and when Bobby held out the court order, which meant she would be picked up by the Sheriff's Department and taken to the state hospital at Mandeville, she nodded almost meekly.

As we rode back, I held Lily's sweating, small-boned fingers tightly, and Bobby talked about how she was going to have to straighten up or else. This time he would only pay half of her hospital care, he said as he turned into the curved drive toward the two-story building half-hidden by magnolia and mimosa trees. He knew I lived in a little apartment on Royal Street, while he lived in a big house on Lake Pontchartrain. But he also knew that he had me, for there was no way I would not help Lily.

And every other Friday for the next eight weeks, I wrote out the checks, to be paid in advance, for twenty-five-hundred dollars a week, then eighty dollars a day for the quarter-hour she spent with the psychiatrist. When my small savings ran out, I began writing checks against my Mastercard. Every other week, I wrote them out, until, taking an elevator down along with a visitor, disappearing, Lily ran away again.

"If she doesn't want to stay, there's nothing more we can do," the hospital administrator told me adamantly, her stout arms crossed across her large bosom. "We're just not equipped for such hard-core cases." I could see that it would be no use to protest that they might have told me earlier, before I had written all those checks.

"Let's just drive down this way, Mother," she said, directing me.

I had just picked her up at the Holiday Inn on Dauphine— by now, I knew better than to ask what she was doing there. Then we had stopped at a pawnshop, where I paid to get her Hermes portable out of hock.

Then, as though mesmerized, I followed her directions, turning into an area where the houses became more and more ramshackle, where more and more muscular blacks lounged against storefronts.

When I paused for a Stop sign, she jumped from the car. "Just wait here, Mother," she called back, and glancing around apprehensively, I realized that I would: Otherwise, I would be leaving her stranded. I looked over to where she stood talking to two blacks. She seemed to be trying to be ingratiating, to coax them into something. Finally, one strode into a nearby shack, and when he came back, he and Lily touched palms; then she was back in the car.

"I asked for some 'boy,' " she said casually. " 'Boy' is heroin, 'girl' is cocaine. But first I had to convince him that I wasn't a cop," she explained in that matter-of-fact manner she some-times used, as though I were her child or her student, and this was information that I might find informative.

And in a way I was: As usual, stunned by Lily's daring, I was too numbed to say anything. If I thought I had led a wild life, had successfully escaped domestication, sexual repression, a nine-to-five life—I was a puritan, a slacker, a pale shadow, next to Lily. And for a moment, I admit it: I admired her in the same way I had Dwayne.

Yet the peril of her life on the streets made my stomach cramp. For a while, she camped out on Esplanade in a rooming house filled with transient oil riggers, whores, and a family of five who were from Texas: "He lays around in his cowboy boots, and the wife cooks pot roasts on the heat register," she told me. "I've got to write a short story about this place! I'll call it 'Sifting Down to the Dregs, or How I got to the Very Bottom of Things.'" Inside her oversized purse, Lily always carried her bulky makeup case, the pristine cellophane-packaged syringes, the bright yellow condoms she favored for her trade, several dog-eared, compulsively kept journals, composition books full of notes for her new work; one wall of my studio was stacked with them. For by now, I was once again accepting the unaccept-able: my daughter the junkie. I would rather be with her on those terms than never see her at all.

Besides, she had the right to kill herself in any fashion she wished, didn't she? It was called the American Way.

Sometimes I would even meet her after "work" at a bar in the French Quarter, just as I once had met Sophie. I told myself that her lifestyle was her business, that she was a separate person from me. And when she walked into the place, despite every-thing, my world lit up. Overwhelmed by her beauty, my love for her, I would put my arm around her skinny shoulders, clasp her to my breasts until she would pull away, embarrassed. "*Eeeas*-ter!" she would protest, calling me the name she now used in public, not wanting people to think we were lesbians.

"Can I wear these, Mama?" Lily asked, dangling a piece of my mama's costume jewelry through her fingers.

I had brought the shoe box full of it back to New Orleans with me after her funeral. BAKER'S, FOR BEAUTIFUL SHOES it read at one end. It was full of the kinds of doodads that Mama had liked to wear when she worked at the truck stop: earbobs with glittering multicolored glass stones, long ropes of beads, tinny bangle bracelets, and strands of fake pearls. As Lily held up some rose glass balls, I admired their radiance against her ivory pallor, her smut-colored lashes; and I was struck afresh by how much she looked as Mama had back then—Mama, with her obvious pleasure in her own girlish beauty. For the first time, I noticed that Lily had plucked her brows into the same narrow line Mama had favored.

But the wrist of the hand that dripped the beads was thickly bandaged with adhesive. The night before, I had taken Lily to the emergency room at Charity: She had called from the room on Esplanade to say weakly that she had cut her wrist, that the blood was everywhere. And that bright white also called up Mama's wound, the one from which she had never recovered, the way she had crippled herself trying to save me—just as I was doing, trying to save Lily?

And worse: Would Mama's costume jewelry—those same fat rose balls, that same glass—drip from Lily's ears, her arched throat, the next time she went upstairs with a customer at the House of the Rising Sun?

Like a boomerang, Lily was back, living with me again. When I would leave to go to teach, she would be sitting at the kitchen table or the worktable in my studio, her notebooks before her, her hair hanging around her chalky face: "I'm going to make some calls today. I heard about a job—they want some-body to write copy over at Maison Blanche. . . ." she would call out. Once as I came home from the Royal Street A&P with juices, fruits, soups, salad greens—anything to make her healthy again, I saw a black man leaving the building. "No, Mother, there wasn't anyone here while you were gone," she lied sleepily, surreptitiously holding closed the cuff button of her long-sleeved blouse as I came through the guillotine door. The burnt bent spoon, the used disposable hypodermic, I would find later—stuck inside a roll of paper towels, or a bowl of fruit, behind my rolled canvases, among the twisted tubes of acrylic. The sordid glamour of her life as an addict had turned my life shabby and mundane. I was merely the keeper now, the tool in her drive to obtain drugs.

And thus came the end of the years of the Glittering, of easy sex and good times.

The rose velveteen box full of sexual devices—beads, bulbs, vibrating phalluses—under the edge of my four-poster bed was covered in dust. The novels of sensuality and existentialist decadence once stacked on the small oval table beside it had been replaced with a litter of self-help books.

The sex I had known seemed far away, as did my pals at Johnny Matassis and Lafitte's Blacksmith (in fact, Matassis, like several of my favorite hangouts, had closed). Instead, I lay reading earnest first-person accounts by people who had saved their children through something called "Tough Love," which sounded to me like standing by while watching someone commit suicide. R. D. Laing, Abraham Maslow, Norman O. Brown, Alan Watts—all my gurus of the sixties, early seventies— seemed far away, too. Had they all been living in a dream, or had I been?

Oh, for a while, I tried to keep up my old life, my pleasures. Balzac had insisted on eating well even in prison, I reminded myself. Or was that Oscar Wilde? I couldn't remember anymore. All I knew was what had appeared harmless—a little drinking, a little drugging, and fucking whom I pleased—now looked different in light of the extremes to which Lily was taking them. As soon as one man or another had left, I put on a peignoir, poured a straight Black Jack, tried to lull myself to sleep by repeating my new mantras, reading the self-help books. Again, as during Dwayne's crack-up, I was drinking not for fun, but to ease pain.

"You drink too much, stay out too late—all those bars with that cigarette smoke!"

I had chosen a woman doctor in order to be supportive of women. But I wished I hadn't chosen this puritanical, makeup-free bitch.

261

"It wipes out your vitamin B. How much *do* you drink?"

"Oh, a half-bottle of good wine a night," I lied.

"That's too much," she said severely. "And no wonder your eyes are inflamed, with all this blue gunk around them. . . ."

It was easier just to see just one man, an Army Sergeant, to wait for his visits from Fort Polk, the rest of the time sleeping alone but for my cat, Moana, her small, hot animal back pressed against mine in the four-poster bed.

The sergeant and I had met a few months before Lily came back: Sophie, dressed in high fairy, and I were close-dancing to the jukebox in Johnny Matassis, and some redneck hassled us, making remarks about Sophie's gender. The bronzed Sergeant suddenly loomed large, rebuking our heckler, then taking me in his arms to finish the dance himself. As he held me, my face near his weathered throat, I inhaled a pleasant masculine scent, a mixture of Camels and musk. And though I hadn't even known that I was afraid, I suddenly felt safer than I had in a long while, his strong shoulders comforting me as we danced.

That first night, he ran his callused fingers tenderly over the stretch marks on my belly, now silvery, near-disappeared, but as much a permanent part of me as Dwayne, Rose, and Lily. He listened without comment as I talked about them, the tears rolling down my cheeks, just as he had listened as I talked about my work while we tugged the quivering oysters from their shells at a table in Felix's.

And he would turn out to be *right*—strong enough to keep me safe from Dwayne; to look away mildly when Lily walked naked around the apartment, the poison pouring from her forked tongue ("I think your *boy*friend *likes* me, Mother"). Or to wordlessly remove her hand when, angry with me, she reached for his penis.

For the first time, I took commercial jobs, courtroom illustrating or magazine work. Paula hated it, said I was wasting my talent, so I began keeping such jobs secret from her. After all, what did she know about what it was to have kids like mine —she, with her perfectly angled haircuts from Kenneth's, reclining in designer comfort in her swank Central Park South apartment with its all-white walls, it huge art collection, its interior photographed time after time for *The New York Times* or *Architectural Digest?*

All I knew was that I needed the money, and that pictures took time, a focused mind. Mine, these days, was scattered. I wasn't even dreaming much. Now that I was a moralist, a guard, a keeper, I felt constricted in my work for the first time. On my worst days, it seemed effete, useless. Yet I painted, and technically my painting grew better. I was doing tight little pictures of snakes and needles trapped in boxes. "I'm not sure about this new direction you're taking," Paula said over the phone after receiving the first of them.

I did have the visions, but they were fragmented, jagged— too painful for me even to put down on canvas. I sketched them out lightly, in order to preserve them, but without committing them to color—which at that point would have to have been all red. For a while, I found myself compulsively sketching syringes injecting gorgeous juicy flowers—orchids, lilies, irises—which browned and wilted in the next frame.

Then the breakthrough came, like a torrent: It started with animals like cave markings—fanged creatures with fiery eyes, lolling red tongues, claws and teeth like needles, apes with hairy biceps, snakes heavy with muscle and malevolence, forked tongues glittering a hypodermic silver. At first they were the only images that even came close to the power of the drug's hold on Lily, her very body.

Next came my obsession with *tracks*—that nibbling away of the flesh, that purpling up on a forearm, an ankle, even the neck: signs of death, of mutilation. I dreamed of them, line after line, covered entire canvases with them, aubergine pinpricks, curling in on, crossing and recrossing, themselves: small scabs of paint on a pale, pale background.

My paintings became silver streaked with blood, blood streaks on white linen. Blood drops. Bruised inner elbows. The shades of infection, of hematoma. I wanted my pictures to scream out that pristine, needlelike pain.

"These are among your finest works," Paula said over the phone. I could hear the awe in her voice, and her pleasure was like a poultice to me, the first sign of anything good to come from all this.

There were other things she was less happy about. "They're like rock stars these days," she said of her newer clients. "None of the warmth, the community, of the past. And the demands they make!" As she spoke, I thought of Johnny's icy eyes, Madeleine's jealousy, of Hannah and Kissy and Harold.

Neither of us yet knew that many of our old friends were already dying from the new Virus. Or that before long, Paula would be fading from it, too.

I gave Lily a natural burlap blouse embroidered with flowers in thick bright-colored yarn at the yoke. I had bought it during my last trip to Mexico, and still under the delusion that something as simple as a pretty blouse might deter her from her chosen destiny, I left it for her at the current treatment center.

During my next visit, a fat, homely woman walked with Lily into the waiting room. "This is LaRue, Mother," Lily said, introducing us. The woman, her lank dark hair draped around her flat face, was stuffed like a sausage into the gathered cotton that I had imagined hanging gracefully from Lily's slender shoulders, her delicate collarbone. Next to LaRue's pallid skin, the colors looked garish rather than cheerful. "I knew you wouldn't mind, Mother," Lily whispered to me as the woman left the room. "She needed it more than I did."

I didn't yet know the role clothes were to play in Lily's madness. Or that during the course of her disease, she would carelessly—time after time—shed whole wardrobes to emerge overnight with new ones bought for her by lovers or pimps, the sleek outfits as bright, as evil, as a snake's new skin.

When I left her, I was so desperate that I ripped an inspirational article out of a dog-eared issue of *Guideposts* on the waiting-room table. That night, I sat before the TV, drinking Black Jack, crying and watching *The 700 Club*. Once I even started to dial the 800 number, to ask the smarmy-looking man on the screen, his handmaiden in her flowered-print dress, high heels, smut-colored lashes, to pray for me, to pray for Lily.

Sophie, a lapsed Catholic, had recently gone back to the Church. Wearing pleated pants and tuxedo shirts, a cross hanging around her neck, she went to mass early each morning, and to confession on Saturdays. "Saint Dymphna, the patron of the mentally ill," she explained earnestly, handing me a brightly colored plasticized card as we sat in Port 'O Call, sipping martinis. It featured a young blonde draped in sky blue, gazing heavenward; the story on the back said that the girl had gone to her death rather than submit to sex with her father.

"That's definitely not me!" I laughed. But in order not to hurt Sophie's feelings, I put the card inside my purse.

I had always wondered how people could be dumb enough to believe in faith healers, and now I was becoming one of them. I quickly poured myself another drink. "Why cain't yuh jes' buh-li-*eeve* thet a good God loves yuh?" the smarmy-looking man, now walking through a garden of fake flowers, asked plaintively from the screen.

Why indeed?

No longer did the French Quarter feel like a refuge. Instead, as for Sophie, it had turned to purgatory.

Suddenly, uncharacteristically, the sleazy streets I loved were filled with touring *families*—suburban mothers and fathers with 2.6 children, shining slicked back nine- and eleven-year-olds—sent like a vision to haunt me.

In the courtyard beneath my apartment, I glimpsed a mother cat nursing her half-grown kittens under the mimosa tree. The younger cats nudged heads between her spread thighs, kneading her skinny body with big paws. As she lay back, resigned, indulgent, I turned away in nausea.

Crippled pigeons, their feathers thinning piteously, pecked at the trash in the gutters. The boys, once so sexy in their black leather jackets, wore studded metal, razor blades on chains, and hair that looked hacked instead of cut. At night, I heard doors and bodies slammed, women being beaten, glass breaking.

Had it always been this way, and I hadn't noticed?

GLOBAL SEARCH: *We can find anyone*—whenever Lily disappeared, the ads for private detectives, the 800 numbers, jumped out at me from the newspaper, the Yellow Pages. *Dr. Edith Fiore*—whoever the hell she was—*claims that possession is responsi-*

ble for over 89% of all illnesses, declared a cheap New Age flyer. I had all the common fantasies: of finding a priest to do the exorcism; of chaining her to her bed and standing watch; of taking her out to a locked cabin in the middle of the bayou, hiring an armed guard to keep her there. . . .

I would lie on my bed, the mad birds beating inside my brainpan—trying as hard not to pick up the phone, start searching for her, as she would have had to try, shaking and shivering, to stay off the drug for another hour. . . .

And after giving in, "saving" her again, I would drive home singing "My baby and me, just my baby and me. . . ." Back in the apartment, I would undress, still singing to myself. In the kitchen, I would add extra cheese, green olives, jalapeño peppers, to a frozen pizza, stick it into the oven; and fix myself the drink—Black Jack, seltzer, lemon juice, Sweet 'n Low—I had been craving all evening. And only as I lay in the four-poster bed, drinking, eating, reading, would my frenzy begin to subside. . . .

I was crazy with love—oh, not for any man, but for my sick junkie daughter. She had become my drug, just as surely as heroin was hers.

Later, I would see that the three of us—Dwayne, Lily, me— were not that different, that we were each, in our way, obsessed by a personal myth from which nothing could deter us. For Dwayne, it was his savage rage, his sense of betrayal. For Lily, it was the drug, blotting out even her poetry. For me, it was my passion for *them*—a passion running even deeper than my drive to art.

Only Rose, the scientist, was safe.

PART THREE

The Ashes of Love on My Forehead

"Perhaps everything terrible is in its deepest being something helpless that wants help from us."
    —Rainer Maria Rilke, *Letters to a Young Poet*

"It is in the midst of evil circumstance that grace is most clearly perceived."
                    —Flannery O'Connor

"It is only through the senses that the soul can be cured."
                    —Oscar Wilde

CHAPTER TWELVE

HORSE—IT was Dwayne's passion, too.

I couldn't help but think that when I heard from Homerdessa that Dwayne, back in South Alabama, was working in a
stable, cleaning the stalls of horses. I remembered how, as a
boy, anything about animals had moved him. He read *White
Fang* and *The Black Stallion* over and over. Though I had deliv-
ered him from the wilds of Alabama, I would see something in
his eyes that craved leaves, brush, trees. I always thought it was
the Seminole in him, the way he had begged me, at eight or
nine, to stop the car when we passed a pasture of ponies, how
he would plead to stand beside the fence and try to lure them
to his outstretched little brown hand. And then there had been
his obsession at ten with searching woods and creek beds, when
we visited Musette and her family, for the bones of the single-
toed sloth, the saber-toothed tiger, which he had learned in
school had once lived in South Alabama. Even when he had
been in New Orleans, threatening me the year before, he had
stopped on the street to tenderly pick up a wounded pigeon,
cradle it inside his arm before cutting its throat with his Bowie
knife, "to put it out of its misery," he had said. As the bird

staggered off, its neck spurting blood, I thought of Mama wringing the chicken's neck for our dinner—it had seemed that natural.

Whenever Dwayne had a job of any kind, my hopes would flare briefly, like a match in a dark room. He had had a job for a few months in a shrimp-processing plant, but one day had suddenly quit—because his dog, a ragged hound he had found in the woods, had been hit by a car; Homerdessa wouldn't take proper care of it, he claimed. Once I had encouraged him to apply for a basic education grant to a vocational school near where he lived; his high school equivalency test had revealed what I knew already—that he had a high IQ. When he received the grant, I sent him the money for registration. Later I learned that he had never gone to the first class. According to Homerdessa, he slept until three or four each afternoon, then left the house about nine o'clock at night and stayed out until three or four in the morning. "I'm gonna be a painter—like *you*," he said when I complained. "You didn't go to school, did you?"

The next time I visited South Alabama, he took Musette and me into a back room to show us his "studio." "It's exactly like *your* studio in New Orleans!" Musette exclaimed as we left, and, yes, his arrangement of easel, paints, and narrow daybed with the faded pink spread thrown over it was almost like mine. I had also seen the five-by-seven photo of me on newsprint, framed in what looked like a tin frame from Woolworth's, the stamp collection, and all the books on birds and fish I'd given him over the years.

His paintings showed that divided world; there was a logic to them, the logic of madness. Some had strange words scrawled on them in large letters—"Neologisms—typical of psychosis," Rose told me years later. And he did have a bizarre capacity for color, for a wild kind of figurativeness, huge whirls of reds and yellows across a canvas, almost like the convolutions of fire. Horses galloped through the fire, fish swam underground beneath their hooves, just as fish swam within the lava rock of Montana, Wyoming—but how had he known that?

Recently, he had appeared at the guillotine door in New Orleans: "Do you need me to look for her?" he asked without preliminary, as if he were a tracker. I had just been on the

phone to the New Orleans Police Department: Lily was missing
again.

With a chill, I remembered what I had heard on one of the
talk shows I was watching these days: "An eerie study," the
doctor guest said. "Children at play act out their parents'
dreams: Heads are chopped off, planes crash. . . ."

And currently, these were my nightmares: Dwayne sees my
picture in the paper, sneaks into the gallery opening where I
stand in my long dress among reviewers, men in tux, women in
crepe and black sequins. He shows up in his patched jeans, his
old fishing cap, his dark sideburns, literally mad, revealing, by
his presence, who I am—the *mala mujer*, the bad mother. . . .

Or I have on a beautiful skirt of flame chiffon, am twirling,
twirling, blue sparks going off in the air around me. And then
I see them, my partner sees them—the small Dwaynes and Lilys,
clinging to the fragile hem of my designer dress, hanging like
clumps of shit, pulling me down, finally squishing beneath my
high-heeled sandals, the stink of dung, of *merde*, exploding in
the air: revealing to the world the stinking abcess, the rotting
lime-hole sink of my violent South Alabama past.

With Dwayne, I had had to go it alone. Now there was the
Program.

The regulars at Al-Anon, at Nar-Anon, reminded me of
Miss Lisa or the church ladies at the Church of God back in
South Alabama. Or Muslim women, in constant purdah. Each
carried a little blue book as thick as a Bible or the Koran, a
ribbon marking the meditation of the day—usually something
exhorting passivity, patience, and long-suffering love. Some
had even needlepointed covers for their books. They wore girdles and heavy bras, and talked about God and self-denial.
Their lips turned thin as the alcoholics and addicts came—
laughing and flirting—out of their meeting room across the
hall, none willing to admit that our excitement came from the
Bad Ones. And now, sans the girdle, I was one of them.

"Sounds like a juke joint in hell," shuddered a plump-faced
woman with a droopy white bow tied beneath her double chin
when a newcomer mentioned being in my old hangout, Johnny
Matassis, with her lover. I thought of the good times I had had

271

there, the sense of heightened pleasure brought on by several martinis, of dancing on the tiny wooden floor before the juke-box with a man whom I had never met before but with whom I would soon be in bed.

When I said I was angry, that Lily's addiction had inter-fered with my "work," that my perfect, sensual life had been disrupted by the young woman I'd left prowling my apartment like a caged panther, they looked at me mildly, like disapprov-ing cows. Apparently anger was as taboo here as it had been for anyone (and especially women) back at the Church of God— except, of course, for the preacher, whose rage came straight from above.

Didn't any of them want anything for themselves? I won-dered. Hadn't I escaped the prison of marriage, of conven-tion—to lead a life *they*—these dumb women—never dared dream of? Indeed, wasn't that why I had become an artist—so I could have some control, at least more control than Mama and Aunt Darlene had had—over my feelings, or a piece of canvas if nothing else?

Yet if that was true, what was I doing sitting here in this dreary church basement back in the dreary suburb of Metairie, two blocks from where I had lived my dreary life with Bobby?

The worst thing was admitting that there was something in me like them, something ensnared, like a rabbit in a trap; maybe even more so, because I had known something else. Despite all my struggles to escape, here I was in exactly the same place as any woman down in South Alabama, praying for some no-good man or, in my case, a daughter gone wrong.

Some of the passive ones argued that having a strung-out child was no different from having an alcoholic husband, but I didn't believe that. Beginning with Daddy, I had found men easy to leave. But Lily and Dwayne were different. No matter how many affairs, one-night stands, no matter how much recog-nition for my work, they had been born from me, and the hole that was my love for them was still there.

Just as Dwayne had filled my life with his craziness, Lily now colored it with her disease, a nauseous shade filling the canvas to its very edges. ("It's *her* life," the counselors would say. I felt as if it were mine. I had made her, hadn't I?)

272

"Let go and let God . . . One day at a time . . . You didn't cause it, you can't control it, and you can't cure it," the Church Ladies intoned. They had sayings for everything, mottoes shaped by thirty years of living with a crazy person, and from something called the Big Book. It was like a form of self-hypnosis, a gang of female Jobs praising God for their infirmities.

"You're as sick as your secrets," they would say, and we would all sit around waiting for someone to tell us something juicy about "my alcoholic" or "my addict," as we called them. At other times, we were forbidden to speak of the Bad Ones, on the premise that doing so exacerbated our condition.

Yet we knew that across the hall, *they* were talking about *us*, that they even had a saying for it: *"They're the sick ones,"* the Bad Ones would joke, laughing and motioning with their cigarettes, indicating our meeting as though it were an intensive-care ward.

What I hated most was when someone tearily testified about "just how sick I am," as though the Bad One she was living with had nothing to do with it at all. At first I wanted to put my hands over my ears.

But that was when I still believed it would be over soon— a *short* war, as they would say of the Middle East: when I was still in what they called *denial*.

Later I would cave in and would need them. Like a prisoner breaking down under torture, I would break into sobs of grief and receive strokes for "showing my feelings . . . moving through pain to peace." Then the slogans would lap around my head like white sound.

There was another Program, one for grown people whose parents had been Bad Ones and who didn't want to remain among the Church Ladies. "Find your family of choice," the people in that program said. "When I get well, I'm going to stick with winners," they asserted, and I would wonder who those healthy people were—*as though you could escape the blood.*

No matter how brutal their fathers had been, they all blamed their mothers: "Daddy may have been a drunk, beat us, but it was *Mother* I hated," they declared. I would think of Mama in her wheelchair. Mama, who had saved me from paralysis or death, by taking it on herself.

My own desire for excitement was explained away as an aberration, a response to growing up among the Bad Ones. But what about Vincent and Frida and Colette and all the others? I wanted to ask. And where did that leave the foreign correspondents, mountain climbers, slack rappelers, race-car drivers . . . ?

I started to cite some research I had read—that rodeo riders were among the happiest people. But by now, I was too brainwashed to argue.

Mental health—how I hated it!

Soon I was going to meetings four nights out of seven, and was spending my weekends at conferences and retreats. I, who believed in Art and the Unconscious, was an information junkie, my head full of statistics, quotes, aphorisms, even prayers.

I would sit on an uncomfortable folding chair in an institutional-green concrete-block room in the basement of a hospital or church, listening to a lecture in which some Expert, usually a doctor or minister who first testified about once being a skid-row drunk or junkie—used a pointer to indicate the areas of the brain on a huge white-beaded screen: First came the drawing of the skull and the talk about the hypothalamus—the old brain, with its insatiable hungers; then the huge cells like amoeba-shaped blobs; and next the synapses presented in primary colors.

". . . Once the cell has tasted its drug of choice, it craves it forever . . . the synapses collapse, the endorphins are gone, down a drain . . . this one wants Hawaiian Gold, this one wants Valium, this one Dilaudid . . ." he would drone, moving the stick about. It was almost as though the cells knew the drugs by brand name; for a moment, I wondered if generics could be substituted.

"Imagine being at a feast with a table loaded with food, and you're starving to death," the man went on somberly. "But to eat the food laid out before you would kill you—well, that's what addiction is like. . . ." Here, I squirmed on the metal chair, imagining Lily dying of starvation, or worse, thirst. . . .

Sometimes there were graphics of wasting body parts, the effects on the various organs. At the same time, it was a spiritual disease, the Expert would say, adding to my confusion, a condi-

274

tion only a belief in something called a Higher Power could cure. But always, the message was dire.

Afterward we all drank bad coffee and munched store-bought cookies. At first I cruised the sexier men leaving the adjacent A.A. or N.A. meeting. I would stop at Port O' Call or Lafitte's Blacksmith on the way home, what I had heard making me want to flee to the nearest bar as soon as possible.

But now I was beyond that, too—there was even a saying for it: "It ruins your drinking." And, they could have added, fucking.

The System—I had never given it much thought before, but now, like every poor person desperate for help, I became entangled in it. And the System in the state of Louisiana and the city of New Orleans was a many-headed snake, a sea serpent, a boa constrictor, writhing this way and that; at times slipping out of reach, at other moments locking me, throat, heart, and brain, in its brawny grip. But it was all I—who hated rules, bureaucracy—had left to me.

Just getting the information, over the telephone, was hard; and usually, by the time I needed it—after another suicide call or note—I was desperate, my fingers trembling over the wavering black lines of the Greater New Orleans phone book. How could anyone with an IQ of less than 140 even find the right number, much less the right agency? Was there a conspiracy against the dissemination of such information?

By the time I finally reached someone, the receiver would be slick in my hands. At first I would speak reasonably, explaining and explaining to some slow-talking twenty-five-year-old or, worse, even a former art student of mine. Then, barely controlling my hysteria, I would begin to plead, to babble, begging for someone to help me save my daughter's life.

I would hang up suffused with shame: Despite my sophistication, despite having shown my paintings in New York and L.A., that I had read Ivan Illich and Thomas Szasz, I was just another hysterical mother, writing letters, making calls, visiting offices where I tried to sit with the humility of the supplicant, with proper gratitude for any help that *was* given.

Against my will, I was learning about waiting, about the welfare agencies, and about the Feminization of Poverty. I may have been a successful artist, but as Jacqueline Bisset says in the movie *Rich and Famous*, "A *lot* of people who have their pictures in *Newsweek* are broke."

There were moments when it seemed that money would have solved everything; at times, I even blamed my painting: If I had used my talent in another, more commercial direction—advertising, magazine work, even the movies—if I had not taken the vows of poverty, of Pure Art—could I have saved her? Paid the posh hospitals, however many weeks, months, years, it took? Gone with her to Amsterdam or London, where she could have lived as a legal addict?

Until finally I had to face it: It was not the System or my lack of resources I was battling, but Lily's own will to self-destruct.

Lily, it turned out, could deal better with the monolith than I did: food stamps, SSI, Medicaid—she knew how to do it all. Charity Hospital was, often as not, her mother now, the one she turned to for help with the infections raging inside her perpetually bruised elbow, the sexually transmitted diseases, the tests for the Virus. And every day, she went to another clinic for the methadone.

"Methadone was invented by Hitler," one of the counselors who earned his living by dispensing it said casually. "It gets into the marrow, the long bones of the body, has an afterlife of eight to nine months." It was one of the facts I stored in my brain, along with how cocaine embeds itself in the hair follicles. "The percentage of successful withdrawals is far less than from heroin. . . ."

So there *was* something worse than the smack. Some people were dying of cancer, or had a retarded child, and I had a daughter with methadone eating out her skeleton. As the counselor spoke, I could see the wiry, tenacious filaments clawing into her tissue, through the permeable calcium, still porous despite the perfect meals, the thousands of quarts of milk I had poured into her.

"I'm just going to stay on it a *little* while, Mama—just till I can get myself together, get a job," Lily said, squeezing my

276

hand. "Then I'll do a gradual detox, five milligrams a week. Go to a meeting every day. *And* start takin' mega B vitamins!" As she spoke, I thought of what Sophie had said—that Lily was the only junkie she knew who was also a health-food freak.

The methadone clinic was like purgatory, a stream of ravaged-looking people arriving on foot, or driving up in ragged cars. They stood in line smoking, chewing gum, cracking jokes, waiting to pay the three dollars, drink the paper cup of pink liquid that would hopefully keep them off the streets, street drugs, for the next twenty-four hours. After a while, I began to hate giving Lily a ride there, for by that time of morning she was shaking, a manic wreck until she got into the clinic, got her dose. Then, over a period of two hours, her nervousness subsided—until the next morning. Even if she was only screeching at me over the phone, I could feel the cords standing out in her thin neck. I learned to avoid talking to her during that time of day.

The worst relapses were the ones Lily had on top of the methadone.

Her thick, rich auburn hair appeared to be the only healthy, living thing about her. The rest of her body shuddered, shivered, sweated, screeched, emitting a vile language that, coming from her beautiful lipsticked mouth, seemed like nothing less than possession. Seeing her wild-eyed, wild-haired, on the street was like seeing another person inhabiting her thin body. The cords in her neck stood out, her heart-shaped face turned cerise with rage—she became my Crazy Woman personified. All *my* rage—at Daddy, at Dwayne, at Bobby, at Johnny—poured from her arched throat like bile.

And I, standing by like the observer at an accident, would turn numb with grief again.

Once, during a relapse, I looked for her outside the methadone clinic on Tulane; I knew it was the one place she was certain to appear, whatever she was doing. Even if she had been down in the projects, she would be there to get her legal fix.

I hadn't seen her for days: Her hair was wild, a tangle, and worse, her eyes were, too—the eyes of a wild animal, out of control. When she saw me, she began running. For that was the time when I was using any means to contain her, to lock her in yet another hospital.

A useless gesture, since once she was there, her evil powers would surface again. While the other patients shuffled the hallways half-drugged, Lily worked out in the weight room, fixed her hair, and put on makeup, preparing for her next getaway. It was a gorgeousness I had come to dread, seeing already the snakes wrapping her slender body, the forked tongue emerging from her full lips, the emitting of a notorious charm, a manipulativeness recognizable, I later realized, only by other addicts. "Calling your daughter charming is like calling water wet," someone had said of her in New York. At the time, I had been flattered. But in fact, it was her most finely honed skill, the skill every junkie needs most.

The counselors always gave her a choice. After her first relapse, I begged her not to get back on it. After her third, I begged her not to get off it.

But the worst part was the tests for the Virus, especially the inaccurate ones, the repeats. The idea of it was constantly clawing at the base of my brain. What would happen; would I be able to stand it? "See that girl?" Lily would say, pointing out a skinny woman in a striped jersey, her thin brown hair plastered by the hot New Orleans rain, standing in a bar front on Bourbon Street. "She's got it. . . . Remember that girl who always wore that orange Dynel wig? The one who worked right up until she was nine months pregnant last year?" she would ask. "Well, she died last week. And her baby has it, too. . . ." I remembered her: She had looked all of fourteen.

Suddenly, my bank card was gone. When Lily stole my one piece of good jewelry, a gold necklace with a single emerald that had belonged to Johnny's Philadelphia grandmother, I slapped her face for the first time and did what the counselor at the drug clinic suggested: I had my own daughter arrested.

At the police department, the detective explained to me that each charge was a felony count, that every check she had written would be an additional one, that they added up to twelve. As he talked, he sat on the edge of his desk, his gun jutting sexily at his muscular thigh, and I remembered: Hadn't

278

I picked him up one night at Tipitina's, even gone home with him? Shame suffused me as I bent to sign the paper, my long hair covering the side of my face.

That afternoon, when the buzzer sounded at my apartment, Lily's head jerked up from her notebook. "Mother, don't answer it!" she begged as I pressed the downstairs door open, unlocked the guillotine door. When she finally came out of the bathroom where she had locked herself in, the detective and his colleague asked her to empty her purse to show that she had no weapons. "The handcuffs are just a formality," the Tom Selleck lookalike said kindly, guiding her by an elbow. "Mama! . . ." she cried, looking back at me.

There was a small story that night in the *Times-Picayune*: WELL-KNOWN NEW ORLEANS ARTIST CHARGES DAUGHTER WITH FELONY. The next morning, I found Lily's suicide note, the cache of pills, under the paper flowers on the bed table on her side of the bed.

Twice a week, I visited her at the Community Correction Center on Gravier Street. First, I gave the matron the *chames*— the cash I brought to be held in trust for her for Cokes, candy bars, and cigarettes; then maybe some underwear, which could be only opened, new, and regulation white cotton, or a pair of slippers or tennis shoes. Since gifts of books were forbidden, I contributed poetry collections to the "library," hoping she would find the Adrienne Rich, the Sharon Olds, among the Harlequin Romances.

The blacks in the waiting room were dressed up, like women at a disco, or army wives visiting their husbands. Learning about the longest-lasting mascara and where to buy cheap bangles, I waited among them as they chattered, admiring each other's earrings, rearranging one another's hair, until finally Lily's name was called.

Then I would go into the hallway to sit before one of six smeared Plexiglas double windows and gingerly pick up the sticky telephone receiver. Lily, in ugly green cotton pajamas, would be sitting on the other side inside a small, narrow room. We talked about nothing much—mostly what she needed or how she was feeling. She would complain—lethargically, because of the Thorazine or Benadryl the addicts were routinely given—about the food, the roaches, the rats. The worst part was that I couldn't hold her skinny body against mine.

One day, the inmate next to her was talking loudly to her visitor. "Please be quiet—I can't hear my mother!" Lily said abruptly to the woman. "You white bitch!" the inmate screeched, turning on Lily as two other blacks joined her. Suddenly, they were beating Lily down beneath the level of the Plexiglas with the telephone receivers, their fists. The guards rushed into the narrow space, grabbing the snarling women by their biceps, dragging all of them away. A half hour later, Lily was brought out again, a bandage on her forehead, so that I could see that she was still alive.

"Hey, lady, I like your earrings!" a young cop called out to me as I left—did he think I would be feeling flirtatious after seeing my daughter almost beaten to death?

"Your mother is just trying to save your life, young lady!" the judge said sternly as Lily stood at the dock. Musette, who had come up from Alabama, sat beside me, gloved hands in her lap. Lily had on the arsenic-green pajamas. Beneath the courtroom lights, her powdered face looked chalky, her lips a garish red-black. But with her heavily lashed eyes, her head held high on her slender neck, she looked like an orchid stuck into a ugly vase. Already she was outside society, the System, and she knew it, standing like a beautiful woman going, defiant, to her hanging. And her pride, her small attempts at glamor, stabbed at me more than surrender would have: Like me, she couldn't resist trying to look good, even—*especially*—in the worst of circumstances.

Ironically, she was often more beautiful these days than she had ever been. Even when she had been hit by a boyfriend or a trick, the purplish hue of the bruise, the way her cheekbones stood out now, almost added to her exoticism. But that was the worst for me, even worse than her addiction, the needles that she stuck into her arm: knowing that she had been hit by a man.

While Lily was in jail in New Orleans, Dwayne was in jail in South Alabama.

Homerdessa had had him arrested for shooting off a gun inside the house, then she had fled, despite her blood clots, her high blood pressure, to the Swan Motel near Pascagoula, and on to the Live Oak Trailer Park, which had no phones, outside Biloxi.

A few weeks before, she had called me, saying that while she had been napping on the couch, he had come into the room and tried to put her in handcuffs. "Gimme that phone, Granny!" he said, apparently grabbing it from her. I couldn't call her back, because he had changed the number to an unlisted one without letting her know what it was. "I think something's wrong with my son," I said over the phone to the probate judge in that county. "Thet buoy jes' needs to come up against the law!" he advised. When I called Adult Protective Services in his county, Dwayne phoned me back in a rage: "You sent that social-worker bitch here, stickin' her nose in my business!" "Well, yay-ess—ev'rythang's fine here," Homerdessa said, getting back on the line, her aging voice quavery.

The night of Lily's court appearance, he called me collect from the jail in South Alabama. He had been beaten by the cops, he said angrily; as he spoke, I suspected, with a sinking heart, that it was true.

"Somebody just oughta come over there 'n put a bullet through your brain!" he concluded, slamming down the receiver.

I wasn't surprised. Wasn't that what *I* was feeling about myself?

On the eve of the fourth Christmas of Lily's addiction, I was visiting Rose in New York, at the little apartment on Bedford Street where she was living as a graduate student at New York University.

When the collect call came from Lily in jail, she said that a woman was screaming—I could hear the wail rising and falling above the chaos behind her—that she was going to kill her daughter's boyfriend: "She's tearing a magazine into tiny bits, having a nervous breakdown, like somebody in a Tennessee Williams play. . . ." For Christmas, each inmate had received a Salvation Army package, she said: talcum powder, shampoo, and conditioner. They had had ham for lunch, "but it had a lot of fat on it, and all the bread is white." No gifts from outside were allowed, so I hadn't been able to give her anything. "It's not getting through the next *year*, Mama," she moaned when I tried to comfort her: "It's getting through the next *hour*. . . ." Her body was aching, her hair falling out, she had a pain down the side of her leg—she was certain she had the Virus.

Rose didn't want to get on the line. "She's just going through withdrawal," she said dismissively. "Like any addict, she has a constant low-grade infection, plus a low pain threshold and, as a result, has become a hypochondriac."

And one other thing was certain, I thought as I hung up: As long as there were jails and mental hospitals (and, I would later realize, wars), AT&T would be making money.

"And just when do you hope to see her again?" a doctor who had done life-after-death research asked me at a cocktail party in the Garden District.

I had circles beneath my eyes that looked engraved there— I had seen them in the mirror as I had dressed in the wine panne-velvet bodysuit with the sweetheart neckline. The reflection showed a dissipated if still beautiful woman. If Lily had wanted to age me, she had succeeded, without the aid of the blood-black lipstick, the white talcum. But at the moment, I didn't care about my looks or about men—just my daughter and the fact that she had disappeared again, this time from the rehab center to which the judge had remanded her. I knew I was obsessed, but I couldn't help myself.

The doctor's brown eyes bore down into mine as he held my hand in his. "In this life—or the next one?" he asked. His palm was damp; his enlarged irises swam: He obviously didn't think Lily's addiction was that serious, since death wasn't such a bad thing anyway.

His gaze finally settled on the rise of my breasts, which he seemed to find pleasing. "By the way, would you like to go out onto the balcony, try some Ecstasy? Maybe we could make contact with her that way. . . ."

* * *

In Malibu, I curled in an eggshell velour chair, watching the tide of the Pacific go out through the big window. Absently, I listened to Sherry, now totally celibate and tediously New Age.

Moving back and forth behind the breakfast bar in crinkled cotton pajamas, spreading something healthy onto something wholegrain, she described the seven chakras of the body, how they are red, orange, green, yellow, violet, indigo, each vibrating to a different sound, each representing one of the seven ages and seven stages. Now she was talking about how we choose our own reality, our own parents, even if that meant being born a lower-caste woman in India, or raped or murdered. . . .

I looked down at the beach, the crowds of overfed, mostly blond, young, healthy flesh oozing through skimpy tees, deliberately frayed jeans as they jumped up and down after a volleyball—the rich sons and daughters of rich directors and producers, the kids who, when they had a problem, got sent to some thousand-dollar-a-day treatment center in Hawaii. . . .

"Do you have a pain here?" Sherry murmured, coming up behind my chair, massaging the area just above my breasts. "Your heart chakra—all your pain is right here, in this hard knot. . . ." Her small palm was poultice against my breastbone; and yes, as she rubbed, I felt something—suddenly fevered, like clotted milk, a pressure so constant I had grown used to it— melting, melting beneath the Vicks Vaporub of her fingertips. "Think of a candle burning—the hot wax is your grief. . . ."

That night, believing I was healed, I giggled with her over the sole, the white wine. But as she talked about how wonderful her life was, about what the gurus, the nutritionists, the personal trainer—the whole movement—were doing for her, I remembered the photo I had seen of her and her family, just after her twelve-year-old son's death from a brain tumor. She was standing stiffly beside her business-suited husband, dressed in proper southern-lady style—a navy dress with white lace collar, white gloves, a small veiled pillbox atop her gold curls—a woman on the edge of a nervous breakdown.

And the next morning I could feel my heart chakra again, as hard, as solid, as a cyst, a calcium deposit.

* * *

"Eeeas-ter! You look like a concentration-camp victim!" Musette exclaimed, coming into the room while I was changing into jeans and western shirt. "Don't you wanna put on a skirt 'n go to church with us?" I shook my head, cringing at the thought.

More and more often, some sick magnet was drawing me back to South Alabama. I would lie in the back bedroom at Musette's, reading books like *Codependency No More*, eating Hershey Kisses, rolling the silver paper into little pills between my fingertips, and drinking Black Jack from a flask hidden beneath the pillow. Despite the chocolate, the booze, I was concave, shadowed. Except for my breasts, which still ironically jutted like a teenager's, the rest of me was thin, even wasting.

Musette's hulky kids milled through the rest of the house, fighting over who would get the Feed and Seed pickup truck to go down to the local Dairy Queen. Watching them, so healthy and ignorant of evil, was excruciating, but I needed to be with my sister. Musette was making art pieces, dried flowers on crushed velvet, which she painted with acrylic and sprinkled with glitter. There was something sweet about the pieces that I liked, the product of an ordered, peaceful mind, small and satisfying—utterly different from my own bloody surrealism.

This time, I was free of the need to visit Dwayne; he was in Costa Rica, on some mission that Homerdessa, her voice quavery, couldn't quite explain. The men with the guns and the chains were coming, he had predicted; he had to get out of town *fast*—so she had once again handed over her cash and her credit cards.

This time, I didn't try to convince her that he was sick. Dwayne was a southern male, with that southern male sense of entitlement, even unto keeping the woman in his life hostage. Hadn't Daddy done the same thing to Mama, and would have done it to me if I had let him? It was hard to know how much was craziness, and how much was a cultural form of insanity, one that Dwayne simply carried to an extreme.

Take Cudden Jones: Aunt Darlene would have turned over in her grave if she could have seen him. Despite her pretensions, her son had coarsened into a man who, according to Musette's whisper, took an ax to his ex-wife's head, "jes' as like she wuz a chicken out in the chicken yard," and, acquitted, roared in drunk every night from the local roadhouse. Just to see his broad, pock-marked face, the eyelids perpetually at half-mast, the sideburns that looked like graying pubic hair, sickened me. His ugly slitted gaze said as eloquently as words, *Don't yuh git on yuh high horse, gull. We don' keer if yore pitcher has been in the paper. We know whut yuh are down hyah—jes' another slut who couldn't keep 'er britches on. . . .*

I knew that the people at the Church of God had their own ideas about why two of my "chirren had gone bad"—that I hadn't beaten them enough, that I hadn't been Saved, that I lived in "N'Awlins." "But she has thet nice sister," they would say. "All *her* chirren turned out *fine. . . .*"

Being there made me glad to be driving back toward the evil that was New Orleans. Until I saw first one, then another, funeral cortege—shiny black cars on the lonesome overhung two-lane. As the second one passed, I shivered. A shabby rural grammar school stood next to a small graveyard, a garage full of the bodies of rusted autos. The day was overcast, ominous. I thought of a white jazz funeral. Somebody was walking over my grave. Or was it Lily's?

I couldn't even tell anymore.

There was nothing left to me but art, and a sterile, stainless-steel goodness, as pristine and concise as Lily's needles. But if it took being good to save her, I would be good. I remembered the promises I had made to God when Dwayne had been hurt in the accident in the red convertible, and how I had broken and broken them.

I had my long hair cut and crimped into curls that had to be held aloft with quantities of stiff—"highly flammable," the label warned—spray from a white can. Giving up on my Mastercard entirely, I ran up bills at Maison Blanche, browsing for outfits proper enough for a PTA meeting. Almost contentedly, I grazed the counters, looking for the perfect button earrings. And back in my studio, I began a series of pictures in which women cowered in corners, the accoutrements of their trade, housewife or hooker, flying through the air around them: electric irons and skillets, mascara wands and garter belts. "Safe House" I named one of them; "Dramamine Dreams" I called another, after the over-the-counter pills I was taking sometimes to help me sleep.

For the first time, I began having my nails done: Every two weeks, I sat before a fat, perspiring girl who sanded the base of my nail near the cuticle with a little machine that left the nerves beneath it quivering with a gratifying pain. She buffed and coated and glued and baked on an acrylic gel with a special lamp. Then came the choice of color, my excitement for the week; there was something soothing in the boredom of the process, in the way she first carefully stroked on the clear base coat, then the thick strokes of mauve or vermilion or hot pink; and, finally, the glistening top coat. All the while, I talked about Lily, her problems, as the girl nodded in empathy.

"Be careful now! Don't touch anything for thirty minutes!" she would finally interrupt to warn me, waving her own fingers in demonstration. And I would promise, feeling the stiff projections weighting my fingertips. Then, almost as an afterthought, she would call after me.

"Oh, I meant to ask you—has she tried Christ?"

The worse things were, the more perfect I wanted to be. I talked to a plastic surgeon about having my tattoo removed. I had the fat zapped from beneath my throat, snipped from beneath my eyes. The bloodiness, the stitches, the actual flesh sliced from my flesh seemed only right. I took little brown pills to make sure my cells were plumped by estrogen; but not until after I had punished myself further by letting another doctor snip little bits from the inside of my uterus sans anesthesia, while I lay half-drunk, listening to Tina Turner at top decibel on the headphones of my Walkman. Ignoring the muffulettas, the oysters Rockefeller of the Quarter, I ate low-fat everything. The only thing I didn't do was try to get rid of the stretch marks, the signs of childbirth still engraved on my rounded belly.

"You look so *glamorous*," old friends would say, seeing me on the street. Sophie, who yearned for middle-class life, liked the way I looked. And for a moment, I saw the lust rising again in Bobby's eyes when we met to talk about what to do next about Lily. The Army Sergeant was the one the least impressed by my transformation. But wasn't I only doing what women have always done—waiting for Dwayne and Lily to get well, waiting for the Army Sergeant to visit from Fort Polk, waiting for my life to begin again? Television and manicures, girdles and crimped hair and clamped thighs and kaffeeklatsches—wasn't this just how women had always dealt with their pain? Giving up what one *knew* was wonderful—sex and the life of the senses?

Yet nothing I did could stop the jagged edges, the razor blades, from coming up through my sleep at night. Booze didn't work anymore, and with what I knew about addiction, I wouldn't allow myself the pills, other than an occasional Dramamine. When I heard of a woman who committed suicide, leaving behind a perfect house full of perfect closets full of perfect outfits, I understood.

I, who had not even had a TV during the first delicious days of my decadence, now lived for talk shows. I kept a small set in my studio; otherwise I might miss, say, *Sally Jessy Raphaël* on the day she hosted the mother and her daughter who was an addict and pregnant for the sixth time by age twenty-five. Or *Geraldo*, when he pulled two weary-looking young hookers off Times Square and into the studio to tell a shocked audience from suburbia about their habits.

Or *Oprah*, on the day Jaid Barrymore sat next to her daughter, Drew, revealing to the world that almost everybody in the Barrymore family was an addict, including Drew's father, John, who was always calling to ask for money for his next fix.

On *Oprah*, I also learned about "the Emotional Incest Syndrome: When a Parent's Love Rules Your Life." Yes, for the past five years, my love had ruled Lily's life, just as it had ruled Dwayne's, but now a Dr. Love pointed out my guilt toward Rose as well: "For a child to be perfect is not normal, either."

Everywhere I looked, even at the movies, I saw addiction, Even Audrey, the plant that fed on human blood in *The Little Shop of Horrors*, demanding "feed me, feed me. . . ." seemed to be calling out for drugs, for my Lily's blood. . . .

On *A Current Affair* in August 1989—a rerun, Maury Povich was on vacation, I remember that—a mother from Albuquerque talked about having seen a photo after two years of her missing twenty-year-old daughter, bound and gagged in the back of a panel truck. "People say how can I be happy, seeing a picture of her like that—but I am: I know she's alive!"

And that was the way I felt about Lily. Just so long as she was alive. My hopes had sunk that low—beneath sea level, like the whole of New Orleans.

How old are they? acquaintances would ask, puzzled, thinking I was talking about teenagers. When I would tell their ages— Lily was twenty-two, twenty-three, then twenty-five and twenty-six; Dwayne twenty-seven, then twenty-nine—they would look at me strangely, as though to ask, aren't they adults then?

Sometimes I would pick up the white leatherette Bible Mama had given Lily, finger the fake gold lettering, *Lily Monique Bowers*. Or I would pick up one of the photograph albums I had made when they were children, my fingertips recalling a curve of shoulder, the soft spot on a skull, and along with my desire to reach inside the pictures, lift each miniature child, warm and wriggling, to my breasts, I would be filled with a piercing keening, a cry that would escape involuntarily from my mouth, at last subsiding into a crooning of the words to the Mickey Mouse Club theme song.

Vaguely, I recalled how men had called out to me in bed: "Baby, baby . . ." they had cried out like supplicants. But now I cruised children rather than cock. Instead of a hard biceps, an ass in tight jeans, I craved the smell of innocent perspiration, of talc, even of ammonia.

On Royal Street, a small black boy walking barefoot behind his mother looked down seriously as the rosy taupe pink of his soles slapped the brick street. "Git up on thet banquette, buoy!" his mother yelled when she saw me looking at him.

"Nicholas—he's three months old," the girl in the Laundromat answered perfunctorily, looking up from her paperback. Her baby rose on her lap, dark-eyed, muscular, a statue I could almost feel, the very model of the little man Dwayne had been.

"Ry-*yun*!" a woman said in Felix's, looking down crossly at her nine-month-old as she tried to pry the oysters she had ordered from their shells. Until the woman looked up, I gazed at him hungrily: He was already a little person, his red hair receding; his pale-lashed eyes cramped closed, he sucked desperately at a fake nipple, clutched a brown monkey made from a sock: determined to live, regardless of how inconvenient he might be.

The weak, the dependent. Yes, everyone wanted them—*I did.* . . .

> *You are to blame if you care too much*
> *you are to blame if you don't care enough*
> *you are to blame for every childhood thing.* . . .

a huge Expert, a woman who looked like Aunt Darlene and wore long gold earrings, chanted two inches from my face as I woke. . . .

I was in yet another group, Mothers Who Love Too Much. Every one of us had been accused by the experts—"How have *you* wanted secretly to be an addict, a prostitute?" my most recent therapist had asked. Yet they never thought to put the *real* question, the one that kept us each awake at night: Had we wanted to have children at all? I would read, say, a novel by Mary Gordon, in which she heaped blame, through the persona of an art historian doing research on the artist's work, on a woman painter whose son sat outside her studio, crying as she worked.

And then that guilt would come on me, the guilt I hadn't yet learned to stomp, like a cockroach—until I read the biography of some male painter, a Picasso or Pollock: some man who had been waited on hand and foot, served by the hapless woman in his life; a woman who, like Pollock's wife, Lee Krasner, often as not had set aside her own work to do so—as long-suffering as Mama had ever been. Worse, a woman artist driven mad by it, as Camille Claudel had been by Rodin. . . .

Or that of some childless woman, Georgia O'Keeffe, or my early idol, Mary Cassatt, who had painted children beautifully without being driven mad by them. And Frida Kahlo—what if she had had even one child? Or two of *mine*? . . .

We agreed that the worst thing about being a mother was that everything we did for ourselves affected somebody else. Was it our desires for something beside the ordinary that made our love like cyanide? "Doesn't it seem like the children you love most are the ones who cause you the most pain?" asked Camille, echoing all our thoughts.

And it was true—we were an odd lot: Camille had been tried as a witch in her church. Charlotte was a novelist who, years before, had rejected the Junior League and, worse, refused to help plan the krewes' balls.

A West End actress I had met through Sherry wrote from London, where she was starring in a Tom Stoppard play: Her daughter was strung out and was blaming her. On the other hand, David Lynch wanted her for his films—did he see the same thing in her that her daughter did? She felt she could write to me, she said. But for most people, it was like the Holocaust. They didn't want to hear too much about it.

I sat at the kitchen table, drinking bourbon and watching TV, while Moana wound herself about my ankles. I was used to weeping now—it was just a part of my life, the overflow of a grief that even if I had wanted to, I couldn't have put a stop to. At times, I even courted it—sitting before the TV, drinking shot after shot of Black Jack, watching the maudlin shows while I thought maudlin thoughts. . . .

I remembered walking down the aisle with Bobby, wearing the cream-colored nylon dress with matching slip that Aunt Darlene had bought for me at Sears Roebuck, excited about the honeymoon trip I would soon be making with Dwayne on my lap—about the pristine new life I foolishly assumed I would have control over.

Instead, I had these two wounds, these two blood spots, as permanent as the red-black menstrual stains on the back of the washed-out Mexican wedding dress that I wore when the Army Sergeant wasn't around. I had bought identical gowns for Rose and Lily, and while Rose still had hers, Lily had quickly lost hers or given it away, at some hospital, rooming house, or jail. . . .

Now the faceless narrator on the PBS special was talking about the lynx, the dangers of its life in the wilds: ". . . But whatever happens to her kittens, the mother *will* survive," he said. "It's called the survival of the species. . . ."

Was that what I was to become, the mother of the lynx, destined to outlive her young? And if so, how would I bear my grief, my unending grief?

CHAPTER THIRTEEN

RAPHAEL, ANGEL—the very name, I had read, meant healing. It was what Lily named him before he was even born.

One night she called and asked me to meet her at the Humming Bird Hotel and Grill on St. Charles. When I arrived, she introduced me to Brett, a man about her age with curly light red hair, clear blue eyes, freckles across the bridge of his short Irish nose. He was a former New Orleans cop, a cabdriver now, she said: Lily knew many cabdrivers; I suspected they helped her get tricks. As we talked, her long lashes occasionally drooped to her cheek. I was so glad to see her that my heart ached. I hadn't seen her in weeks, hadn't known where she was or how to get in touch with her.

"She's got a bad habit," Brett said when she went to the ladies' room, as though he were telling me something new. "Two hundred dollars a day, minimum. . . ." I still couldn't comprehend the finances of it: How did one get that kind cash every day, plus money for food, for a room? I wondered if she'd been staying in one of the SROs upstairs. "She hasn't had a place for a while. I've been tryin' to get her to stay with me— but you know how hardheaded she is. . . ."

"Yeah—and, Mother, he's got the cutest apartment over on Barracks Street!" Lily said, coming back to the table. "Three cats, and candles instead of electricity!" She used the same tone she had used to describe the Silver-Haired Playboy, the Jazz Musician, and the Sugar Daddy.

But that wasn't what she had called me there to tell me. What she wanted to say was that she was pregnant again. "Got to go now," she said, pushing back her chair. I noticed that she hadn't touched her country-fried steak. "I've got to get to work. So why don't you go on back to the apartment." I knew what she meant—she didn't want me to see her turning a trick.

She didn't know how many weeks pregnant she was. At the clinic, I wrote out a check for the sonogram required before such an abortion. Brett and I sat in the waiting room, and he told me a little about himself. He had been working on his master's in psychology at Tulane. Then he had become a cop; and now he was driving—not for United, the best company in town, but one of the low-rent, sleazy ones. . . .

Lily came out of the counselor's office, looking determined. "I'm not having this abortion, Mother. I saw his little hands and feet."

"*Lil-lee*," I pleaded outside on the steps of the clinic. Brett sat in his cab, watching us dejectedly. "You're twenty-five years old, you're homeless, you're a heroin addict. . . ."

"I don't care. I'm not killing this little baby, Mother," she said stubbornly, her mouth set.

"You have no way to take care of it—you don't know how much *more* painful it will be if you have to give the baby up after it's born. . . ." I felt as if I were in a movie, arguing for her life. What was it about women—*southern* women—that made them like lemmings, dashing into the sea? The concrete steps, the iron railing, felt cool, unreal, an extension of my body. "If you think having an *abortion* will be painful, think—just *think*—of giving up that baby! . . ."

Watching the scene from the sidelines, I wondered at the ineffectual woman playing me. Lily's performance was by far the more powerful one. "Even if I have to give him up for adoption, I'm *still* havin' this baby, Mother." She took a Kent out of her purse, slammed the clasp shut, lit up. "I'll go into another hospital, withdraw if I have to. . . ."

My heart sank like a stone in someone else's body. For her sake, for *my* sake, I wanted her to have an abortion, not to have this baby who would be another person I would have to either lose or save.

But once again, I had to admit it: In all her dazzling self-destructive glory, I had to admire my daughter, her guts. . . .

A few nights later, she called me from the Bridge on Camp Street, a shelter where only the most down-and-out alcoholics and addicts crashed. Two nights after that, she called to say she had gotten into a car with two blacks who had taken her into the basement at a house in a strange neighborhood, raped her at gunpoint. They had taken her leather jacket, ripped a gold necklace from her throat. "I thought they were going to kill me, Mother."

"But it wasn't that bad," she added quickly when she heard my gasp. "It's probably worse for you, hearing about it," she told me later. "After all, I was *medicated*."

She didn't know about my own built-in anesthesia, about the Crazy Woman and the way she took over, pervading me with her cold numbness. But first, there were always those moments when I was still myself, when there was no way for me to stop the images screaming and screaming down the needlelike corridors of my brain.

Lily did go back to Charity to withdraw. But the doctors, saying withdrawal could cause her to miscarry, put her back on the methadone.

When she got out, she moved in with Brett and lived off welfare. "We get under the covers, and the cats keep us warm!"

The baby wasn't Brett's: In fact, she had no idea whose it was. Later she would say to me hesitantly, "Mother, he may be black—I don't know." Seven months pregnant, she brought up the subject again: "Mother, I've got something to tell you—he might not be black *or* white—he may be Chicano. See, there were these Chicano guys who all lived together in this apartment. . . ." I laughed. By then, there was nothing Lily could possibly say to shock me. The worst thing about it was that through an attorney she had found in the Yellow Pages, she had picked the adoptive couple—a young white engineer and his wife from Shreveport, and they might not want him if he turned out to be colored. She had picked them because she wanted her baby to have *conservative*, middle-class parents, letting me know for the first time that what I had tried to give her had not been what she had wanted at all.

"We're resting, Mother," she said one day when I called her when she was over eight months. For weeks, she had had false labor. Because she was an addict, her pain threshold was low. I knew she had signed the papers with the attorney, but I wondered whether she would be able to go through with it.

At nine months, she felt well enough to put the kittens born to Brett's cat into a cardboard box; to stand, her belly resplendent, near a corner where she had once hooked, giving the mewling things away.

Brett took pictures of us that day, leaning against his cab. We had just been out to a cheap café with country cooking—as a taxi driver, Brett knew these little-known places—where Lily had eaten two platefuls of fried chicken, butter beans, sweet potatoes, and corn bread at $2.95 a plate, plus fifty cents for each tall glass of iced tea with lemon. In the photos, she looks adorably pregnant in her full smock and jeans, her face radiant, freshly scrubbed, her long hair in a ponytail—much as I had looked at nineteen with her inside me. But despite my low-cut sundress, my sexy sandals, my hair that was growing out, long and soft and red again, I have that anxious look worn throughout the ages by women when they know too much—a look I had seen on Mama's face, on Aunt Darlene's, and the women's at the Church of God. No amount of worldliness, and none of my efforts to escape, had saved me from claiming it for my own.

Lily's insides were scarred from the gonorrhea. Her low tolerance to pain would make the birth difficult. She had been in labor for over thirty hours when I went to pick Rose up at the airport. We had just arrived at the apartment on Royal Street with her luggage when the phone rang. "She's threatenin' to leave the hospital, get some heroin—she can't stand the pain. She's screamin', her face is all red! . . ." Brett said frantically. When Rose and I arrived in the labor room, Lily tried tremulously to smile; they had finally given her some medication, she said. A monitor beside her bed was describing the contractions in sharply peaked arcs. The leather straps they had used to restrain her had been thrown into the corner of the room. "They might have to do a Caesarean, Mama—they say that the methadone's slowin' down the labor."

In the basement cafeteria, Rose and I ate bad chicken-salad sandwiches; then, on the tenth floor, in the waiting room, I resumed my reading of yet another true account of a woman who had saved her child through Tough Love, while Rose fooled with her camcorder, getting ready to document whatever might happen next.

GOOD-bye, HAP-pee-ness . . . an elderly black man sitting across from us in the waiting room sang out loudly, nodding and grinning at us when my name was announced over the loudspeaker. Raphael had been born by Caesarean while Rose and I had lingered over coffee.

Then I saw the nurse walking down the hall, carrying him, wrapped in a blanket, his tiny pointed head covered by a knitted beanie. *Like blood calling out to blood*—I knew him before she even approached us.

Rose and I looked hard at the scrinched little face and then at each other. "Do you think he's black?" we both asked as the nurse walked away. Later, in the nursery, we realized that his color had been merely a newborn's natural swarth; the black infants around him lay like fat caramels in the surrounding cribs. I drank in his tiny cleft chin, the dimples sucked deep in his cheeks as he tugged on his thumb, just the way Dwayne had done.

In the recovery room, I tried to tell Lily how beautiful he was, but she lay on her side, moaning, her now-long hair tangled and damp, her dark lashes at half-mast across her pale cheeks. "Yeah, like a cat in diapers!" Rose said, already recording Lily as she lay there, twisting and turning.

With her camcorder, Rose took movies of Lily, Raphael, and me in the nursery, in the hospital room. Later she showed them to me as evidence—as we argued over the right way to diaper him, or whom he really looked like—of just how sick my relationship with Lily was.

When Bobby finally came to the hospital, I commented how like the cleft in his chin Raphael's was. "Yeah—well, *we* looked good when *we* were born, too," he said meanly.

That night, Rose and I went to Lafitte's, where we sat drinking, planning a trip to Nicaragua. We would carry guns, she said, and go dancing in bombed-out hotels. It was like the old days, drinking with her at the Cotton Club. The next morning, the phone rang. "Mother! I changed his diaper!" Lily said elatedly, as though she wasn't giving him up at all.

Had she imagined for one moment, that day back on the steps of the abortion clinic, that I would end up giving in, taking him to raise? If so, she had another think coming—she had underestimated my own drive to survive, my selfishness. I knew she wanted me to play the long-suffering Theo to her dazzling Vincent, but I was an artist myself.

I was clinging to the thin vision of my own freedom like a drowning woman clinging to a life raft.

"I felt it when they cut me, Mother," Lily said the week after the birth. We were in the Alfa, and I was driving her to pick up her food stamps. "The doctor said it wouldn't hurt— that it *couldn't* hurt with the spinal block—I kept tryin' to tell them that it was wearin' off, but they wouldn't listen. . . ." It was hot, and she was still weak, but she had just been to the Happiness Salon on Iberville to have her long hair washed and styled. Her peach crinkled-cotton wraparound skirt concealed the slight thickening of her waist, and she was wearing high-heeled sandals. It was hard to believe that she was a woman who had just had a child.

"That's where it was, Mother—where those two black guys held the gun on me and raped me," she said, bursting into tears as she pointed out a small frame house on Terpsichore. She spoke bitterly, as though I should somehow have saved her. "I thought they were going to *kill* me, Mother—didn't you *know* that?"

Every time she told me yet another way she had been

wounded, I felt a blade in my own gut. But I also knew that she needed someone to blame for what was about to be her loss— just as I had needed to blame someone, anyone, for what had happened to her and to Dwayne.

There are moments in life—or at least there have been in mine—when one can imagine what it was like to walk to the guillotine during the French Revolution. Or to be a mother going to the death of her own child, as I had read had happened during a televised public execution in a huge stadium of a Salvadoran guerrilla in San Miguel: "His mother was there to see him killed," wrote the reporter.

Taking Dwayne to Mandeville that first time, then Lily to the detox at Charity—not to speak of the day I stood by and watched her handcuffed, arrested—had been among such moments for me. And now, another was imminent.

Raphael was held in the nursery at Charity for thirty days, to make certain he had withdrawn from the methadone. When the month was up, Lily and I took a tiny little blue knitted outfit to the hospital. Lily had to go sign some papers, leaving me alone with him for a few minutes. I didn't want to cover him up, his belly with its still-healing umbilical scab, the miniature penis and balls; my hands dragged as I pulled the small white undershirt over his head, then the blue jumper. When Lily came back, she lifted him in her arms; his head was still wobbly, but he looked around with an alert, serious expression. As Lily carried him down in the hospital elevator, Raphael's jet eyes fixed on her own. "A baby's mama is the mos' *important* thang in the worl' to him," a black woman standing near us said approvingly.

Outside, he squinted unflinchingly against the hot breeze, seeing sunlight for the first time. Lily handed him to me, and he looked up at me with blind trust. As Lily drove through the crosstown rush-hour traffic, he leaned into me peacefully. I held him and fed him from the bottle of Similac—watching him pull at the acrylic nipple, then turned him over my shoulder as he burped, falling against me like a sack of warm, passive weight, recalling to my very cells, it seemed, the times I had held *them*—Dwayne, Rose, Lily—in just that same way. Then, as he sat still in my lap, lying warmly against me, I brushed his Indian mane with my hand, letting my face fall to his hair. Now he wiggled a bit, like a puppy or a kitten. "Wiggle worm," I murmured, remembering what I had called Dwayne. The sounds of afternoon downtown traffic were all around us— horns honking, the squeal of tires—yet I felt suspended in a moment, a bubble, of pure happiness.

Lily parked in the pay lot on Poydras Street, locked her side of the car, and came around and took him from me. Striding deliberately across the parking lot toward the lawyer's office in the high-heeled sandals and wrapped skirt, a cigarette dangling from her other hand, she looked like any purposeful young mother.

"Oh God, he's so beautiful!" gasped a round-faced blue-eyed man dressed in tie and blue blazer, coming up beside us on the sidewalk. He put his hand to his eyes as though to shield them from the sight. I knew from the way Lily greeted him that he was Jimmy, the adoptive father. He carried a Styrofoam cup in his hand, the Coca-Cola he had gone out to get for his wife, he said. "*Please*—take as much time as you need," he added reverently, then walked up the staircase ahead of us.

On the sidewalk, outside the building, we took turns holding Raphael, taking pictures with the camera Sophie had loaned us. Later it would turn out that Lily had put the film in incorrectly. I was learning that that was the way it was with addicts— even the simplest things go wrong.

Inside the lawyer's office, a stout black woman attorney, attired, despite the heat, in her dress-for-success suit, presided behind her broad desk. We all sat in large swivel chairs, politely discussing the better parts of each of our families' heritage. The new parents, Jimmy, a crew-cut mechanical engineer, and Caroline, a pretty thirtyish housewife, were radiant—eager, I could tell, for us to leave, so they could have Raphael to themselves, so they could undress him and consume his perfect body with their eyes. They had already had the result of his test for the Virus, the doctor's assessment of his withdrawal from the methadone. They were Christians, they told us, devout Baptists, and had been unable to have a child of their own. They had with them a bright blue plastic infant carrier, fat packages of

Pampers, a blue stuffed dog with floppy ears, a yellow cat with a permanent smile embroidered on its face, and had already changed his name to James Junior. Jimmy held Raphael—now James—tenderly to his chest, just as I had done inside the Alfa. "You're goin' to be the happies' li'l boy in the world," Caroline crooned, staring at him as though she couldn't get enough; "Sugah, you're gonna have *toys* 'n ever'thang you evah want. . . ." I could see the tears of happiness glittering in the corners of her eyes; she discreetly dabbed at the softening mascara with a tissue. She had worn the perfect dress for a young mother, a full-skirted cotton sprigged with tiny flowers. She was skinny, and already I imagined her running down a driveway in the suburbs, much like our driveway in Airline Park, pushing the stroller, racing after balls and tricycles.

Lily had on the peach crinkled-cotton skirt, even more wrinkled by the heat, and as she always did when she was under stress, had applied too much black eye makeup. For once, she almost looked the addict she was, jaded and harsh and washed out—far from the pretty pregnant girl she had been a month ago. I had worn black cotton that day, a dull skirt and shirt, and felt older, older than I ever had, and disheveled from the July New Orleans heat. "New Orleans in summer is like walking through hot water," a friend had once said, and that irrelevant thought came into my head. Or was it because I felt as if I were drowning?

Now Lily and I were standing, each kissing Raphael one last time on the cheek. Lily was handing Caroline the letter she had written to be given him when he was eighteen, and Caroline was unenthusiastically accepting it.

A few days later, the lawyer sent the letter back to Lily, saying the couple had forgotten it, giving her their address in order to send it on to them herself. "I know who they are, Mother, James and Caroline Johnson," she told me over the phone, her voice trembling. "It wouldn't be right to try to contact him before he's grown," I said. But I drew hearts around their name and address, fat babies and birds floating, and put it inside my safety-deposit box.

And what was it like to say good-bye to my grandson forever that morning? Fortunately, the numbness descended like a fog or a veil. I could depend on it. It was the Crazy Woman's one virtue.

Everything was silvery, white, light, floating, just the way I imagined death to be.

. . . Dark brown birds, their feathers like silky jet hair, their large eyes as melting as chocolate, flap glistening silver wings, flying off into the distance—beautiful birds that I know are mine, but which I can never reach or lay claim to. . . .

I'm smiling, floating effortlessly atop my cross, my arms outstretched on the boards, Raphael lying facedown, relaxed on my chest, trusting me as we fly through the light sweet air, up, up, up, toward the silvery clouds. . . .

Once, driving back from South Alabama, three small jet animals suddenly slithered out of a wooded area off Interstate 10, up onto the embankment—silvery minks or ferrets, moving as gracefully, as mysteriously, as mercury, pausing at the edge of the road, then gliding just as quickly back into the trees. For a moment, I laughed out loud with the surprise. They were the most beautiful, graceful things I had ever seen. Small, slippery animals seen briefly, creatures I could never hold on to, other than in memory.

And after a while, the brown-feathered, silver-winged birds, the silky, sinuous jet animals, each with the dark eyes of Raphael, began to appear in my paintings, perched or seated on a shoulder, or as a small foreground detail. A part of my imagery forever, along with the pang I would feel whenever I saw a little brown-eyed man like that.

Lily had been swollen at first, casually showering in front of Rose and me at the hospital, her belly extended, the scar red, livid, as loud as her complaints to the nurses about how much pain she was in, how in need of medication she was. Rose, with sibling vindictiveness, had wanted to video her as she stood before us, unselfconsciously naked, not even beautiful for once. But Lily had waved her away.

And now, six weeks after the Caesarean, her stomach was as flat as a boy's again, the only sign that she had given birth the small still-crimson incision line at the top of her pubic hair.

She had received a Visa card in the mail just after the birth with a credit limit of a thousand dollars and had spent it over the limit within a week—not for drugs, she had the methadone every day—but for clothes, having her hair done, and going out to bars with or without Brett. She looked as glamorous as I had ever seen her. And the day after she gave Raphael up, the relapse began.

A week later, she checked herself into another hospital, this time a swank one she had gotten into on the strength of her Medicaid. That night when I visited, she had carefully applied a dramatic makeup, birdlike wings rising at the corners of her dark eyes; her auburn hair tumbled long and curly around her thin shoulders. Seeing her so deliberately beautiful, my heart sank. I could almost see the snakes wrapping themselves around her slender body; her tongue, when she spoke, was forked.

The next night, she belted the pale green cotton hospital gown tightly at the waist like a minidress and put on the pair of high heels borrowed from another patient. Walking down the steep hill to the street, she got onto a bus without a cent, convincing the driver to let her ride free and getting off at the Pontchartrain Hotel on St. Charles. In the bar, she ordered a double gin-and-tonic, then picked up a well-off young couple, who paid for all the drinks. She went to their house on Lake Pontchartrain, where they ordered out for heroin and shared coke with her until it arrived, the three of them swimming nude in the pool. When she wouldn't swing in their particular way, they had kicked her out. . . .

Brett repeated all this to me as we cruised in his taxi along Magazine, then around the projects, searching for her. He had called me at dawn: Lily had gone by their apartment, leaving an eleven-page suicide note. We went first to the methadone clinic to alert them—"that would be the one place she *would* go. . . ."

For the rest of the morning, we drove through sections where for miles and miles no white face was to be seen. These were the areas, Brett assured me, where she would go to buy the heroin—the parts of town where blacks lounged during the day against the sides of liquor stores fitted out with iron grids, where one paid through a slot beneath Plexiglas as thick as that

301

in the jail visiting room. Before I had known of Lily's habit, I had shivered driving near these neighborhoods. Sometimes I had glimpsed a lone white girl, often a long-haired dirty-blonde, and wondered what she was doing there. Now I imagined a desperate Lily—striding purposefully, fearlessly, as I knew she would—to do whatever it took to get her fix.

"Some of the cab companies won't even drive into these areas," Brett was saying. "Hardly any of 'em will at night." He pointed out a concrete-block liquor store where several muscular men leaned, eyes half-closed. "That's where she usually cops."

Once, in New York, deep in dreams of a new painting, thinking I was getting off near a friend's apartment overlooking the Hudson on 110th Street, I had gotten off a bus in the wrong place. Instead of at the park running along the Hudson River, I stood deep in Spanish Harlem. I had just been to the offices of *Harper's Bazaar* to talk with an editor about an illustration; I wore the false lashes I had had glued on individually at Sak's, a red linen sheath, scarlet sandals with high gold-lamé heels. Twilight was falling, and the men leaning against the storefronts were eyeing me speculatively. Every woman or child I asked for directions spoke a liquid language I couldn't understand. "Where you from, girl—the South? Don't you know what we do to white girls up here?" teased the middle-aged couple who finally saved me, refusing the money I gratefully tried to thrust into their hands as they guided me onto the right bus.

I remembered my terror that day. And I thought of Lily, walking these streets alone, approaching these blacks who looked like huge cats, reclining in the bright sunlight, ready to spring.

At the emergency room at Charity, a drag queen with one broken high heel, her upswept blond wig bedraggled, staggered toward us. It was Sunday morning in New Orleans, and Lily lay loosely tied by her wrists to a gurney. I had rushed down there as fast as I could when Brett had called, saying he had found her. She had been given medication, Brett said. As her head lolled toward me, her wide-open eyes falling on me vaguely, she looked like a stunned, beautiful animal, a doe or a rabbit.

When the attendant said it would be an hour or more before she could be seen, Brett and I took the elevator downstairs for coffee.

When we came back, we were told Lily had slipped from her bonds, escaped: "Your daughter is very sick," an intern who looked about twenty-two said sternly.

Back at Brett's apartment on Barracks Street, we found her, curled in a fetal position on the mattress on the floor, sucking her thumb, clutching one of the cats to her breasts.

". . . when I lost my baby," she would murmur later, referring to that time.

A woman knows where her daughter is broken. Why she is drawn to certain men, the men who would break her. Among my nightmares was that she and Dwayne would meet one night on the dark streets of New Orleans, that not recognizing one another, they would be drawn together, and that he would hurt her, his own sister. For hadn't she been brought up to be magnetized by men like him?

And Brett with his red hair and freckles, his choirboy sweetness, was turning out to have his mean side, too. More than once, I went to their apartment, fearing I would find one of them dead, fatally wounded by the .38 Brett carried in his cab. Instead, I would find them lying stunned, each wearing black eyes, bruises, cigarette burns. "It was because he was sexually abused as a child," Lily would explain to me when she was no longer mad at him. That would be on the days when she was making him special little dishes, inventing recipes for new kinds of meat loaf—"Just taste this, Mother! Chili loaf with pinto beans mashed up in it, and grated cheddar cheese. And try one of these jalapeño muffins!"—as domestic, as much a young housewife, as I had ever been.

And more than once, she and Brett were at Charity at the same time, hospitalized with infections in their arms. At first I hadn't realized Brett was an addict, too. "Why do you think he's not a cop anymore, why he works for that sleazy cab company, was sellin' his blood over on St. Claude Street? Why he lives in that dump 'n uses candles 'n doesn't even have electricity?" Lily said, incredulous. "It's because he spends all his money on speedballs," she added, as bitter as any wife with a no-good husband.

Showing the first, pale-as-watercolor signs of turning out as pious, as prim, as any woman back at the Church of God in South Alabama, Lily had begun reading the Bible. One afternoon, after she had read it and read it ("for at least three hours a day, Mother!"), she suddenly got dressed up—"it was like something came over me, I couldn't help it"—and walked over to the bar at the Monteleone, where she promptly picked up a trick. Brett had come in, tried to drag her out by her hair, and when he didn't succeed had gone back to the apartment, made a bonfire in the courtyard from her clothes, her notebooks: "That was the worst part—they had a lot of my new poems, my new religious ones, in them." She told me all this when she came into Lafitte's Blacksmith, wearing a chic black-and-white outfit, part of a whole new wardrobe the trick had bought her at Maison Blanche. "But it's okay, Mother," she said, putting her arm around my shoulders as though I were the one in need of comfort. In fact, she looked like a high-fashion model, while I was distraught, disheveled from searching for her all day.

Before Lily got better, she got worse.
On the fifth Christmas Eve of her disease, she lay on the mattress on the floor of Brett's tiny apartment with a fever of 104. I had brought soup—she didn't like the kind, Campbell's chicken noodle; "I wanted hot and sour!" she screeched. Getting up from the mattress, wearing a thin cotton wrapper, she raced around the apartment hysterically. "Where is my methadone? Where is my methadone? *Did Brett cop it again?*" "He wouldn't do that, would he?" I asked, trying to soothe her. Yet I raced around looking, too, infected by her desperation. "You *always* side with him, don't you, Mother!" she yelled, turning on me, her face crimson. "Oh, *here* it is!" she said at last, jerking the small paper cup from behind a milk bottle inside the refrigerator, tearing off the silver paper cap, then gulping the pink liquid.

"See these piles of clothes?" she said, indicating two huge

mounds filling the small room beside the mattress, next to the tiny black-and-white TV. "I've *got* to go to the Laundromat, wash them to*day!*" "But Lily, you've got a fever of a hundred and three—you've got the flu; last night, you were afraid you had meningitis, and wanted to go to the emergency room. . . ." "And these filthy rugs, too!" she went on. Nothing I could say would deter her. Finally, to protect her from going out into the cold air, I began dragging the garbage-bagged clothes to the trunk of the Alfa, while she followed, lugging the rugs. I could see how hard it was for her to breathe, and she wore only an unbuttoned cardigan over a thin cotton Indian shirt. "Lily!" I protested, "you'll die of pneumonia! . . ." "Mother, *when* are you going to stop *caretaking* me?" she shrieked hoarsely, stashing a big straw bag full of papers inside the car. "What's that?" I asked. "My song lyrics—I want to work on them while the clothes are washing!" she snapped, tugging a Salem from a pack and lighting it. "Oh damn, my last cigarette! Will you stop at that Seven-Eleven over there? Will you please just do what I say, Mother? Pull in right there? Park right *there!*" She jumped from the car, agitated; I went in behind her to see if she needed any quarters for the Laundromat. The man at the counter looked confused as Lily snapped at him, asking first for one brand of cigarettes, then another. As we rode the remaining half-mile to the Laundromat, Lily screamed about how I didn't like to hear her feelings, how I always sided with Brett against her, and how I didn't really listen when she talked. As her face grew redder, her voice more hoarse, I became silent, stony. At the Laundromat, I sat without moving as she feverishly lugged the clothes, the rugs, the big bag full of papers, from the trunk of the car. Then she got back into the front seat and burst into tears. "I'm so sorry, Mother," she said, throwing her arms around my neck. She would say it again, the next day, on Christmas, when she called me at Musette's to let me know, her voice cracking, that she had lost all her song lyrics.

I felt something hardening inside me. I still cared whether she lived or died. But did I have any control over it? For a long time, I had been like one of those mothers who holds her child out of the sea after the shipwreck, until her arms become so numb that the child finally slips away. Or one in the death camps—by the time her child is ripped from her, she is already too weakened to resist.

Now I was beginning to accept it; I had begun planning Lily's funeral in my mind. If only I believed in an afterlife. As the life-after-death doctor had suggested, meeting her in another incarnation could be soon enough.

Now she, like Dwayne, blamed me for everything.

"You ruined my life when you took me out of private school. . . . when you took me to New York, to all those art galleries . . . when you left me at home with Johnny while you went out to teach. . . .

"You were competitive with me about men. . . . I felt like you wanted to overshadow me, my psychiatrist said so. . . .

"You're so *perfect*, Mother," she finally snarled. It was her worst epithet, the one she always saved till last. Sitting outside at the Café du Monde, stirring the thick chicoried coffee, making the powdered sugar fly as she waved her beignet at me for emphasis, she dumped the blame on my head like acid, then yelled at me because of my silence: "You've *always* been like that, Mother—tuning out, disassociating! . . ." I opened my mouth, trying to explain the Crazy Woman, how she had helped me survive.

Lily's decibel increased to a pitch, drowning me out, segueing into sobs. As the tourists around us looked on, curious, I hugged her thin body to mine, her hot tears falling on my silk blouse. In the movies, I would have burst into tears, too, dissolving the pain between us in one damp scene. But instead, as she fell against my chest, I felt something as pervasive, as deadening, as Novocain.

The next day, she called me full of forgiveness: "You're just like Christina Crawford, Mom. I just saw her on *Oprah*—she was abused by *her* mom—Joan Crawford, a movie star way back when *you* were young?—and she can't respond emotionally, either. . . ." She made kissing sounds over the phone: "I just want to kiss you and kiss you, Mother, for all the wonderful things you've done for me! You're the very best mother in the world!"

She added that she was going into therapy to deal with "incest issues," that she was joining a group to deal with her relationship with Bobby. "It's not that he ever really touched me, Mother. It's just that when he was mad at you, he would take it out on me. Or treat me like a little wife, wanting me to take care of *him*, his needs. It's called 'emotional incest.' "

"Don't get your hopes up, Mother," Rose said when I told her about the changes that Lily was going through.

"It's a time-ended disease," she went on. "The latest research on alcoholism and addiction shows that it lasts *about* fifteen to twenty years"—I counted back in my mind: Lily had started the drugs at fourteen; she was twenty-eight now—"and when people start going to A.A., it's because it's already waning. But I don't think her time's up yet."

"I have a father now. My father is God. Our Father in heaven takes the place of my parents. He forgives everything that ever happened in the past. With *Him*, there *is* no past or future. . . . I forgive you, Mother. I love you. . . ." Lily's voice brimmed, filling the tape of my answering machine, a palpable vibrance.

When she called me now, it was with visions, exaltation, exhilaration, a bedazzlement of insights. What she had once medicated with drugs had become a saint's full-blown monomania of intensity, religiosity. As it had for me, something had flooded her brain at childbirth, bathing it, making it burst with images, brilliant white lights, meteorites that, when she could capture them, became the fragments of new poems. Going off at random, running away with her poems, filling them with religious images, making them not only unpublishable, but unreadable. Yet while I had always been able to control my bursts, surges, pictures, she seemed unable to do so.

"It's biochemical, Mother," Rose said, explaining how, if one portion of the brain is pressed, a person will be be filled with religiosity, how if another is, he or she is driven by the desire to write, to keep journals: "It's her PMS plus the addiction plus a bit of manic depression. Some research shows that bipolar disorder may be similar in some ways to epilepsy, that there's an effect called 'kindling'—a kind of spontaneous sparking of seizures or mania in both; also that in families with bipolar disorder, there's also a higher rate of creativity. *That's* probably why you're an artist, Mother!"

"Just let me die! Let me get a fifth of liquor and some dope 'n die!" Lily sobbed over the phone. It was not that she wanted to die, she said; it was that she didn't want to live as an addict anymore. "I guess that's up to you," I replied nonchalantly. I had seen her suffer so much that at this point I would have given her the gun or the pills to kill herself if I could have.

It was the way I had been feeling ever since I had hardened my heart against her and begun planning her funeral. I wished I had gone ahead and bought a black pillbox with a little veil. I didn't want people looking at my face after she died. I did have a good black crepe dress—if I pinned it at the deep V neckline and wore a black slip to obscure the slit.

It wasn't that I didn't care anymore. It was just that I had run out of things to do. "It's a circular rug, Mother," Rose said, encouraging me in detaching. A spiral, a pattern going in circles, and nowhere—like those rag throw rugs Aunt Darlene had filled her house with, saying they complemented her fake maple "Early American" furniture. Running down her hall to get away from Cudden Jones, I would always slip on them, losing my balance.

Or like the follow-the-dot drawing books Lily and Rose had had as children: Lily would sometimes connect her dots at random, creating monsters. A pattern was there, a simple one. But she couldn't seem to find it. I always praised her for those drawings, believing them a sign of her specialness. Now I saw that refusal to connect the dots in an orderly way as a part of her incredible drive to chaos.

Even though she lived in New Orleans less than a mile from me, I didn't see her more than a few times during the next year. I avoided the streets where she might be working, never drove near the projects. Being separated from her turned my heart leaden. If this was what detachment was, I hated it. But seeing her as she was was worse, a knife.

Oh, she would call every once and a while, telling me that she had checked herself into this treatment center or that, or worse, that she was in jail again; that she and Brett were split up, or back together again; that they were going to meetings and were evangelically clean, or that they were back at Charity with infections.

"I feel so guilty when I go to the meetings, Mother, knowing I'm still on a drug," she said, meaning the methadone. The people in A.A. and N.A. were hard core about that, she said. One of her worst relapses had happened after she had gradually—and successfully—withdrawn from the methadone. "Five milligrams a week, Mother—it took five months. And even that was *hard*." And then someone at a meeting had criticized her for the lithium, the Prozac a doctor had prescribed. She had gone cold turkey that night, and a week later was a raving junkie again, more strung out than she ever had been. So now I blamed the people in the Program, too: It was hard to know who was ally or enemy.

Yet gradually, there was a difference: "It's not the drugs, or anything else. It's something inside *me*, Mother—something inside *me* that makes me fuck up everything. . . ." Her voice was almost too calm as she said it; it was the first time I had ever heard her say such a thing. "I'm just 'sick 'n tired of bein' sick 'n tired,' " she said, using an expression from the Program. "It would make you *sick* to know what I did for four cigarettes the last time I was in CCC. . . ." She was doing the Twelve Steps again, she said tiredly; and this time, she hoped to make amends for all the wrongs she had done me. . . .

But I had been through too much: I didn't believe a word she said.

Patterns, repetitive patterns—they were on my mind these days. A nurse told me of seeing a breast lopped off during surgery—"a perfect breast, nipple and all—just thrown into a pan like a piece of raw meat." When she said that, I was struck by the image; it emerged in one of my paintings, a perfect breast, bloody and dripping, shorn from its fleshly moorings, repeated over the entire canvas. *Triage* was what I named it, and that was the way I was feeling then.

In another painting in that series, a self-portrait stands to one side of the canvas; in it, I wear a simple white gown, my hands hanging at my side, loosely tied by what looks like an umbilical cord. In my chest, where my heart should be, is a cavern, torn blood vessels hanging out like roots; the rest of the picture is simply a repetitive image of clinically realistic hearts, dripping over the whole picture. I want to reach out, reclaim one, but I can't—my hands are immobilized.

The Mother of the Lynx, I named this one.

After all the hospitals, posh and public, it was finally in the most severe circumstances that Lily was able to escape the methadone.

"She's kickin' in lockdown, 'n she's got a bad jones for a smoke," a woman named Rocky said, calling collect from the Community Correction Center. It turned out that Lily and Brett had been arrested for creating a public disturbance in front of his apartment on Barracks Street.

A few days later, Lily called. I could almost hear her shivering against the background of the screaming women in the day room. "I would kill myself if I could. But there's no way to do it." She had refused the Thorazine, had received just one Benadryl to relieve her discomfort. They were holding her in the urine-scented lockdown with one scratchy blanket; she hadn't been able to have the cigarettes I had sent over because the woman who inspected packages was off for a four-day weekend. But she didn't ask to be bonded out. "Pray for me, Mother," she said weakly. And that night I got on my knees just in case.

Nine months later, she was still like a woman with the flu, but her bones were aching just a little less, she told me. For a while, she drank to ease the anxiety. "It's just that I have a lifelong history of medicating any pain, Mother," she explained wearily. Then she stopped doing even that. Despite her discomfort, she clung to life in the same way she had clung to her addiction. What had been the serpents of her disease, their muscular strength, gave her a tenacity. She had left Brett after

310

getting out of jail, and was living in a terrible little room, her only income the disability she received because of her manic depression. She was trying to work on her poems again, but her back ached when she sat before the Hermes too long, and her wrists and fingers hurt when she held the pen. She told me these things without a trace of self-pity, but with a tiredness that made her seem like an adult woman to me for the first time.

Once, when I went to her room, I saw her body, long and pale beneath her old chenille robe. She looked as I imagined I had looked, grief-stricken over Dwayne at twenty-eight. Deep circles etched themselves beneath her long-lashed eyes; for the first time, her appearance seemed not to concern her. She went to meetings, to the grocery store, wearing running shoes, an old gray jogging suit. Some days she looked too tired to comb her hair.

For the first time, I saw what the drugs had masked, a sadness that had surfaced only when I had stopped trying to stand between her and her pain. A woman's sadness that she had never let me see before. A woman with grief for her own life.

Gradually, Lily began to look pretty again. She was writing greeting-card verse, verses on demand and adorned with hand-done calligraphy, tiny water-colored flowers, which she sold to a shop in the Quarter. With her new religiosity had come a forced sunniness, and people liked them.

Then she called to say she was selling dry-cleaning certificates door-to-door in Metairie. None of the other jobs—the greeting cards, the phone soliciting—had earned her enough money to live even minimally. "That sounds *hard*," I said, trying not to think of her, arrogant and gorgeous, stalking up Fifth Avenue at 4:00 A.M. in high heels and fur jacket six years before.

It was like watching a dazzling but destructive comet dying out.

A plague besides the plague of drugs, of the new crack cocaine, was raging through the Quarter. Every day, I heard about somebody who had it, or had just died from it.

Lily had been tested and retested, and miraculously was

still negative. But that didn't mean she was safe. And it was only my obsession with saving her life rather than mine that had restrained me enough, during the last few years, to keep me minimally chaste—one could even say, ironically, that I owed my life to her addiction. "For men, the incubation period for the disease is ten years, for women a little longer—eleven or twelve years," a researcher working at Tulane told me at the Bombay Club, disseminating information in the usual manner of the French Quarter.

In New York, it was Paula, and her husband, and several of her clients. It was Harold and Kissy—I remembered how they had wanted to have a ménage à trois with Johnny and me, and how my jealousy, which had enraged Johnny and brought on fresh accusations of bourgeois rigidity, had kept us from it. And Trevor, male-model gorgeous Trevor, with his beautiful curls, his long, pale body so languid on the sheets that day long ago after tea at the Plaza—he was fading fast.

Two days before Sophie's test results were due, two rednecks threw a full beer can at her from their pickup, hitting her hard on the leg, drenching her with hot, sour liquid that smelled more like piss than malt. Wearing her usual high fairy—the ruffled-front tuxedo shirt and full trousers, the cross around her neck—she had been walking away from the Bridge on Camp Street, where she now worked as a volunteer.

I put my arm around her muscular shoulders and felt her shuddering as I had when Cudden Jones had shown me the starfish. To cheer herself, she was wearing a jaunty denim jacket, on its lapel a brooch shaped like a seagull, enameled bright blue and silver, with sparkling rhinestone eyes. We were walking to Charity to pick up the results of her blood work, and she *knew* the test was positive, she said—she had known the moment she was hit by that sour beer. I thought of the years she had saved for the sex-change operation, of her dreams of going to the clinic in Baton Rouge; of the pennies pinched from the low-paying jobs she had held since she had given up stripping.

The encounter had occurred, she went on, around the time of her return to the Church, the first mortal sin she had had to confess. "And I didn't even want to go to bed with him that much—I was drunk, he was a new queen in town, just was hangin' around the Quarter. And a year later, he was dead. . . ."

As three years from that moment, Sophie would be—but not before the months of seeming good health, then the brave fading days with a cane, of sitting out, thinner and thinner still, on the balcony of her tiny apartment over Decatur Street.

Other than what she saw on CNN, my baby sister Musette knew nothing of these things.

More and more often she came to New Orleans, armed with her credit cards, to shop at Maison Blanche, or just to visit. Over cups of thick dark coffee at the patisserie on Chartres Street, she would enthuse over my life in the Quarter—"I declare, I don't know *how* you stan' the excitemen' of bein' here *all* the time," she would say, waving her hand toward Jackson Square, where we—she dressed in pumps and stockings, I in faded cotton skirt and sandals not that different from what I had worn back on the farm—had just walked past the blues band playing at 11:00 A.M. on a Tuesday, the painted clowns making animals out of balloons, the drunks sleeping it off on the benches, the tourists milling about drinking Hurricanes from tall glasses.

As I fed bits of my brioche to the fat, yellow-breasted sparrows that filled the courtyard, she talked about the achievements of her healthy, handsome young: little Darlene's upcoming wedding—"the biggest event in the county, *ev'*rybody's goin' to be there!," Ned Junior's grades at Tulane—" 'n he's pledgin' ATO, jes' like yore ex"—and the fact that they had successfully nipped Eugenia's tendencies to wildness in the bud, getting her safely into nursing school.

Later, when Ned Junior became a law student at Tulane, I would see them together, Musette, in her size-14 Linda Faye dress, leaning against his broad shoulder, and would feel a pang, remembering that quote from Freud, that the most perfect relationship is that between mother and son. And at Ned's wedding to a debutante from Mobile, I would see Musette dancing in his arms, a bit plump in her designer dress, a little heavy on her feet, but as excited, as radiant, as I had been at my first gallery opening.

Among the gay men in the Quarter, it was a point of honor—at least among those who evaded the Virus and had avoided becoming alcoholics—to go back to wherever one had come from—Natchez or Memphis—in order to care for one's ill or aging mother until the end of her life. And I envied Musette that, having a strong son to lean on.

"Sometimes I almost wish I had another one," Musette said wistfully, reminding me that sensitivity wasn't my sister's strong point. She rarely asked about Lily or Dwayne anymore, probably preferring, like Rose, that I forget all about them. "I don't know," I said meanly. "It could have been crazy or a drug addict, like one of mine."

I knew that Musette was revising history these days—that she didn't want to remember what Daddy had done to me or to Mama, even though she had been sitting right there, banging away in her high chair. My baby sister, Musette—she hadn't changed that much from the person she had been back then, arranging her dolls in a little row, the only sign of her anxiety the way she sucked at her thumb while Daddy did things to me, or half killed Mama.

She had had a family genealogy done; bound in maroon leather, THE O'BRIAN FAMILY embossed with gold letters, it lay on her mahogany coffee table, right next to the grand piano that they had bought for Darlene's piano lessons. Atop the piano perched gold-framed portraits of Mama and Daddy, just as if they had been normal. But then, how could I fault her? Didn't I have framed pictures of Lily, of Dwayne, all over my apartment?

And really, I enjoyed my sister's ability to recreate history, to be satisfied with the neatly framed quality of her life—the ikebana flower arrangements, the little paintings on crushed velvet. I had grown up with such efforts—Mama's picture-smeared linoleum, the stories of Grandmama's hand-painted China teacups: It was like a small, well-defended foreign country to me. I soaked up my sister's accomplishments, the insignificance of her problems, in the same way I absorbed novels about nuns still behind the wall, or Barbara Pym stories of maiden ladies hopelessly in love with the vicar.

For if Musette had ever had a secret life, I didn't know it.

314

Oh, sometimes she would giggle over some movie star, glimpsed for a moment in the Bombay Club on Dumaine Street—say, "that sexy Dennis Quaid," in town to make *The Big Easy*, or later, Kevin Costner or Oliver Stone, in the city to film an account of the Kennedy assassination.

I never told her about the boys in the black leather jackets, the switchblades stuck into the headboard of my bed, the tattoos of panthers or 'gators quivering just above my face. They were among the many things I knew of, things of which my baby sister was totally innocent, and at this point in her life always would be, like one of those southern mothers who never could quite believe that *her* sweet boy, now middle-aged, was, well, one of those *sodomists*.

And now that I was dashed down, broken, I saw what Hannah and the others in New York so many years before hadn't liked about me—my naïveté, and the arrogance that went along with it. Because I could see it now in my own sister. When Aunt Darlene had died, she had stepped right into Musette's rangy if well-padded body. The scraggly youths (who could have been Dwayne) eating out of garbage cans; the fading girls (who could have been Lily) lounging against the bar fronts; the gay boys (who could have been Sophie) piercing and distorting themselves in every way possible—they were all *Other*, a part of another species.

But I also knew that anything else would have frightened Musette too much.

"He's a lot like Dwayne, Mama," Lily told me of her new lover, an over-the-road truck driver she had met at the Program. "No, Mama—he's *sweet*, like Dwayne was when he was a little boy," she added, seeing the fear in my eyes. "And he even looks like him—that beautiful olive skin, that dark Indian look. . . ."

That Pete had been hospitalized after Vietnam, had been in prison for armed robbery, and had a drinking problem didn't seem to worry her. When I tried to talk to her about it, she wore the same self-satisfied smirk she had when she was first strung out and was still romanticizing the high. So I knew her old compulsivity was there, alive and thriving beneath her new exterior.

I packed up my self-help books, all the flyers for the Twelve Step groups, put the boxes into the backseat of the Alfa, and took them over to the little house she and Pete had rented in Metairie. "This is really great, Mother. These will be wonderful for my library, to loan out to people when the groups meet here." The house had a little yard, a kitchen with a dishwasher, three bedrooms, one bathroom. I could hear the traffic on Interstate 10 rushing by, but Lily was thrilled: "Now I can have a *life*, Mama!"

Walking through the rooms, I shivered, feeling as if I were walking through my own life: "Don't you remember, Lily? This is just like the little house we lived in when you were born." But it was a little different, too: Lily already had the old Hermes manual I had bequeathed her out on the dinette table; books littered the floor. She was writing inspirational poems, and notes for her lectures to the Twelve Step groups. Her thick auburn hair was in a ponytail, the sleeves of her chambray work shirt rolled up as she unpacked, and the scars of the track marks, like small purple dots, or periods made by a ballpoint, were visible just beneath her pale skin.

As she turned away to make coffee, I picked up a clipped sheaf of yellowing second sheets from the dinette table beside the typewriter and flipped through it. "Oh that—that's just something I wrote a long time ago. I got it out, might turn it into a story someday," she said, turning back to me with the coffeepot. As she did so, I slipped the manuscript into my purse.

She poured me a cup of the coffee and set a plate of muffins, oozing fruit and nuts, on the table. "Here, Mama, you've got to try one of these—orange-marmalade-pecan! . . ."

When I got back into the car to drive back to town, I felt the tears gathering behind my eyelids.

So Lily, my Lily, had done what every woman I had ever known had done, what I had done, and probably Mama before me: She had struggled with all her strength and for half a lifetime—almost killing herself in the process—to become as different from me as possible.

And in the end, had turned out just the same.

CHAPTER FOURTEEN

The Things I Did to Please My Mother by Lily Monique Bowers, aged fourteen.

The first time I really knew what I wanted in life was one day when I was ten, looking at one of Mother's Vogue *magazines—on the cover was a beautiful lady, dressed in beautiful clothes, her arms and neck covered in diamond and gold jewelries.*

I knew then what I wanted to do when I grew up: be rich, live in a rich house, surrounded by expensive things, wearing expensive clothes, my arms and neck covered in those diamond and gold jewelries.

"But what were you doing in your fantasy?" Mother asked when I told her about it. Mother is great on doing things—she one of those people called a "high-acheever." So she didn't understand when I explained that I wasn't doing anything at all—that was the point!

"And what about your poems?" she kept on. "Wouldn't you still want to be writing your poems, even if you had on those clothes? And just think about it—maybe if you were, you'd be having so much fun writing them that you would forget about what you had on, and it wouldn't matter anyway!"

I could tell she didn't really like the fact that I wanted to be rich, that what I wanted cost money. Because besides being a high acheever,

Mother is what is called non-materialistik. She's an artist, and our whole house in Algiers is messy. One time she was having her art class over, and Marmalade shit on the mantel piece over the living room fireplace, and she didn't even care, she just laughed, saying something like, "Well, the one thing most artists need is a little more shit in their lives!" even though her students, these women who looked like regular mothers, were looking around like they didn't know whether to laugh or what.

She was always making us eat carrot sticks and dried apricots instead of candy—the more fights she and Daddy had, the later they argued over their drinks before dinner, till my sister and me were just about starving. And the house is piled up with books, and because it's hot down here in Louisiana, the roaches eat the color off the backs of them—and there are papers and canvases and paint smears and old palettes full of dried-up blobs every color in the rainbow everywhere (though mostly red colors because those are her favorite) and the house is falling apart while Mother stands there at her easel—that's what Daddy says, and he always sounds mad when he says it.

"Mama, last night I dreamed the house was on fire, but you were standing there painting and wouldn't save me!" I told her one morning at breakfast—we were having our usual, wheat germ and prune juice, and I think I was about nine. Every morning, she wanted us to tell her our dreams—that was another thing she liked. We already had a family therapist—that was something else she believed in; later, when my sister, Rose, read a book called Primal Scream Therapy, *she told Mother that if she couldn't have primal scream therapy by the time she was 16, she had just as well commit suicide. I think she was about 14 then, but by the time she was 16, she had forgotten about it.*

Anyway, I had what our family therapist, Henry, called school phobia, and it seemed like she would have cared, but she didn't—she just said "talk to Henry about it—he'll tell you what to do." Even when I told her that Rose had said she would cut my forehead with a piece of a broken Welch's jelly jar if I didn't do what she said when we were playing Barbie. She just told Rose not to talk to me that way, but I could tell she was kind of smiling, too. She thought everything about me was cute—I was sort of roly-poly then, that was about the time she was always hugging me and calling me her "sweet roly-poly bug," like that kind of bug that rolls into a ball and rolls around when it rains. So there were a lot of things I couldn't come out and tell her, like the funny way Daddy looked at me sometime, and later, the way I felt about her different husband, Johnny.

Anyway, the thing called school phobia that made me not want to go to school because I might come home and she might be gone. It had started when she started going out sometimes in the daytime without us, and she and Daddy started fighting about this man called Martin, and then she took us all—even Dwayne—out to his house one day—it was way out somewhere and he had funny red hair growing on his face, and even inside his ears a little bit, and the inside of his house was filled up with paints and things, just like ours, but really all over the place, and we went for a walk in the woods, and Mama started crying. Well, at least he let us have Mallamars, big marshmallow cookies covered in this shiny chocolate, and for once Mama didn't say anything. And we never went there again, but every day I was afraid Mama would go back there, and never come home again. Because Daddy talked about that every night when they were drinking the Wild Turkey—I liked that picture on the side of the bottle, and for a long time, until I asked Rose and she told me, I thought it was the juice from a turkey, boiled up and turned into a drink. And they wouldn't stop until Mama was crying again. And Dwayne would look funny. The whole time, Dwayne would look funny, like he understood what they were talking about, and it bothered him.

That was when I left her the note with the drawing of my Pitiful Pearl doll, a plastic tear rolling down her plastic cheek—with a poem coming out of her mouth in one of those balloons like in a cartoon, saying "Please love me/better than your boots made of white vinel/ better than a pie in the sky with a white meringue/ better than clouds floating by/ please, Mother, love me and keep the hot rain/ from falling out of my eyes." I wrote it in red and pink ink, because I thought she would like that. Then she cried some more and hugged me and said she liked my little card, my drawing and my message, and that she would always love me—that I didn't have to worry about that.

Well, that was part of it: She liked what I wrote or drew so much. She would have liked for me to say I wanted to struggle like her and be a writer or an artist—it seemed like it was just about the only things she cared about. She didn't understand how somebody could just want to be rich and wear pretty clothes. It was because she didn't like that, that I wanted to do it—even if it seemed like not doing anything to her. Besides, I didn't want to live in a messy house like her, and sit a long

319

time writing my poems, or stand all day in front of an easel, getting paint all over myself, and have an ugly husband I had arguments with, and want to go to New York and not get to go, even if people always said how great I was, and put my poems in the newspaper.

Then there was the smell of the cat box, and the baby box, where Lulu has her kittens, and the dirty laundry—I wet my bed for the longest time, and so did my brother, almost up until the time he went crazy, talking mean and running after Mother with the butcher knife. And every day at school, I would worry: Would she be alive when Rose and I got home? There was a girl who waited at the bus stop: Her brother had killed her mom. She didn't speak to anyone, it was like her face was frozen. I was afraid I would be like that.

But even the bed-wetting didn't seem to bother Mother. She didn't mind what she called an "earthy" smell, and that's one of the things, but just a little one of the things, that she and Daddy fight about—he wants our house to be as clean as my grandmother, Miss Lisa's; and wants Mother not to dress so much like a hippie. And I had to admit it—she didn't look like a regular mother. In the daytime, instead of skirts or Bermuda shorts, she wore cotton shirts and ole blue jeans with paint all over them. And when she dressed up, she wore white vinel go-go boots, just like mine and Rose's, and she had a dress with a mini-skirt, striped in all kinds of sickadelic colors, like Joseph's coat in the Bible. She said that colors were good, even colors that everybody knew didn't go together, like pink and orange. She bought Rose and me hot pink and orange mini-dresses, oranger than Marmalade's fur, that looked as bright as Christmas tree lights, and said they looked good, even when we said we hated them.

The one thing that could bother her was my brother Dwayne. When he started going crazy, I would hear her crying and walking around in the middle of the night—not just arguing with Daddy like she usually did. It seemed like it was all she could think about, like Rose and me didn't even live there. But then one night in the middle of the night, they took him away to a hospital—we had to have that fat ole baby-sitter, that awful one who would tell us what would happen to us if we didn't get saved, how we would burn up, our skin turning to blisters, then melting; and about what boys can do to girls if we were not careful, how they would stick big things up us and hurt us. . . .

And then the next thing happened was that Rose started flopping around and babbling while we were watching "Outer Limits" one night.

320

And afterwards, she couldn't remember anything about it. I thought for certain she was possessed by aliens, but when it happened again, Mother took her some hospital where she had to stay for about a week to get "tests." And then it was like all Mother would think about was Rose, just like before, all she could think about was Dwayne. And the whole time Rose was gone, I didn't have anybody to sleep with, and I was worried that something mean I had thought about Rose had caused her to get like that—even though it turned out it was just some silly ole thing Mother called "epilepsy" that Rose started taking some little white pills for, and then she was her usual ole self again. . . .

It was around that time that I saw the Vogue *magazine. That I decided I wanted a life as different from Mother's as I could get it. That I wanted to be taken to some other place, some other planet. And for a long time, it seemed like that place was New York, a place where I would wear those beautiful clothes.*

Though there was already something that had made me feel that way. I had felt that way once before, when Mother took me to the dentist's office, telling me that it wouldn't hurt. And she was right: The man put something over my face, and I smelled something strange, then felt like I was floating, that I was somewhere else, on that other, perfect planet. "You are funny!" Mother said, kissing me on the forehead, when I asked her earnestly in the car going home: "Can't we go back there soon, Mama?" It was a little like the feeling I got sometimes, when Rose and I went around and around when we were little, or when we drank the bottoms out of Mama and Daddy's drinks after they set them down. Or later, when she and her other husband, Johnny, had cocktail parties and she would let us help her—I would love to see all the different colored bottles there, standing right out on the table, like we were rich, and in a movie—and Rose and I would drink and drink until we would start laughing and laughing and acting crazy, sticking our fingers in the steak tarter—it was something awful Johnny made out of raw hamburger, mixing it all up with a raw egg and stuff—then letting Marmalade lick it off under the table, then sticking his germs back into the gooshy meat. Or seeing how much caviar we could swallow without gagging, while the other one said, "Fish eggs! Fish eggs!" And finally, we would get so crazy that we would go into the bedroom so she wouldn't know. It was sort of like that. But the gas was better. Just like it would be better later, when I would find out about something else, even better, and that was dope, any kind of dope. I would go out in the woods at recess, and smoke it with the boys. And I didn't mind if they wanted to touch my boobies after we smoked, because it turned out that despite what that ole Willadene said, I liked that, too.

It was like a dream—like I was already away, away—far away. It was like I was already there, in New York, wearing those beautiful clothes and those jewelries. . . .

Notes, 1987:

Reading back over what I wrote back then makes me feel sad, and repentant. I can't believe how shallow I was, how much I thought I could be saved by things. *Well, I had the Louis Jourdan pumps, and the rich men, and they didn't work at all.*

So I went to substances—*whatever I could put into my body, and more and more of them—dope, coke, speed, ludes, smack, methadone. And none of it ever satisfied that yearning I couldn't yet name, the yearning for God and for light.*

But being a junkie—that was just a part of it. I was like Caravaggio, that painter from way back Mother told me about: " 'Why did you paint the flesh so green?' asked his bishop-patron. 'Because I've been ill all summer, Your Excellency,' he replied. 'And art?' the old man questioned. 'This is not art, this is life,' he said. Mother said he was about 18 at the time. And that story stuck in my head, the sick arsenic green of his desires.

" 'No hope. And where there is no hope, there is no fear,' " she said he had engraved on his knife.

And people, so-called normal *people, want to know what it's like to be a junkie, to stick a needle into your arm and sell your body for a fix. To be with blacks, when you're a white southern woman. To live off the streets, your ass—every day to have to come up with the money for the Man, for your dose. People always want to know such things, the details of the worst that can happen—as though if they do, they'll be safe, it won't happen to them or their kids. . . .*

But I don't tell them any of that. I just say it was fun for a while and then it wasn't fun. That I'm like the woman I read about who survived the death camps—who said it was like a dream to her: that if it wasn't for the tattoo on her wrist, she wouldn't believe it. (Mother probably remembers more about it than I do. That's why, in the Program, the Al-Anons sit weeping on one side, while on the other, we sit laughing and smoking: We recall nothing, they recall everything.)

What they don't understand is that for me, the main thing has been that voice calling, calling me toward death. That's what I've been running toward my whole life; the drugs were just a means to it. "A dual diagnosis—the depression predated the addiction," says my current psychiatrist, a handsome Jew who reminds me of Johnny. In the past, I would have felt driven to seduce him. But now all I care about is ridding my soul of the sick arsenic green of my desires—those desires, engraved, it turned out, into my very genes.

For Aunt Darlene finally told us that my grandmother Monique had died of an overdose of the pills—those pills that she had been taking for years, since the accident that had happened before I was even born. The pills I would sneak into and steal from, as many as I could get away with, whenever we went to visit.

Then Aunt Darlene told something else—that my grandmother had been that way, crying one week and laughing the next, for her whole life, ever since they had been girls together, not just since the accident. That she had once had to hold Monique back from jumping into a rock quarry and drowning, another time from setting herself on fire from the fireplace. That that notion to kill herself would just come on her sometimes.

All those years, people—Mother, Aunt Musette—had been telling me how beautiful my grandmother was, how much I looked like her. And when I found out that she had killed herself, her grief seemed to rush right into me, jumping over Mother and my sister, Rose, both of whom always seemed to have some kind of steel inside them.

And I had thought it was just Mother, ballooning up inside of me and smothering me, that it had been her love I was running from. But all along, it had been both of them, Mother and her mother, Monique, splitting me down the middle, like somebody drawn and quartered, way back in the Middle Ages—one side pulling me toward the Abyss, the other toward Art and Life. . . .

The whole time I was strung out, Mother was afraid I would die. But really, it was later, when I got clean for the first time—when the center of my bones had almost stopped aching— that was when I felt like jumping out of a window or running in front of a streetcar on Canal Street. It was something I literally had to hold myself back from, as strong as the desire for drugs had ever been. . . .

Once, Mother and I were talking about Anne Sexton, how she thought she could do nothing but become a prostitute; but instead, at her doctor's suggestion, had started writing poetry, and ten years later had won the Pulitzer Prize. About how I had always *known I could write poetry— that was* easy—*so I had become a junkie and a hooker instead.*

What I didn't say to Mother that day was that the poetry didn't stop Anne from killing herself, from finally going into her garage and doing it, wearing her *mother's old fur coat. Because what Mother doesn't know is that I can still imagine doing that—wrapped up in something of hers—maybe that old Mexican wedding dress with the spots on it—that that could be my final comfort, the smell of her on the washed-out cotton. . . .*

"Where there's hope there's life," Mother is fond of saying. But it's her *hope she means when she says that.*

And though I've gotten it together—thank the Lord and lithium, and all the people hanging on to my every word—the people I help, let crash on my couch, calling out to me for soup and for comfort—I know how fragile, how precious, life is.

All I have to do to be grateful is to think, like an endless roll call, of the suffering people I've known in the hospitals, the jails—that pretty girl with Tourette's syndrome, the one who wanted so much to be loved but who couldn't stop the curses from falling from her mouth, or the one whose temporal-lobe surgery meant she had to be kept locked up because of her uncontrollable desires. . . .

And then, there's my husband, Pete: that he's sick comforts me, keeps my mind off the voice, my grief. The miracle of my recovery—it's that I'm still alive. But I know there are no guarantees on that.

And I wonder: Will it ever become too strong, as it did for for my grandmother Monique or for Anne—that siren's song that my mother, Easter, has never known or heard, except through her *mother, my brother Dwayne, and me? . . .*

CHAPTER FIFTEEN

" 'EVERYTHING THAT'S dropped must be picked up,' " I said to Rose, describing to her my sense of presentiment, even knowing how she hated it when I quoted Jung, or anything she categorized as "hocus-pocus."

I knew that others considered me a risk-taker, a wild woman. And it was true—rough men, real peril, had little impact on me. I had learned about those back in our little tenant-farm house in South Alabama. I could look at the most cruel images with immunity, the way some people can look at blood or the sun.

But for a long time, I had been afraid. Indeed, the whole time I had lived in New Orleans, I had dreamed of the water above and around and below me: of the city, six feet beneath sea level; of my whole world—my studio, the art galleries, the restaurants and the bars I frequented—kept afloat only by the grace of something monstrous and volatile. At such times, I felt dangerously perched there, the levee shimmying like Jell-O beneath my feet—ready for the earth to melt at any moment, turn to a child's nightmare of quicksand.

And for a long time—a lifetime?—I hadn't let the reason

surface. All I knew was that as my obsession with Lily waned, my fear of Dwayne rose, full blown. That it was because of him that I was still on shaky ground.

When I had moved back to New Orleans, to the apartment on Royal Street, I kept my address from him. For a long time, I didn't have a phone, then I had an unlisted, old-fashioned black one that sat on the carpet beside the four-poster bed.

"I know where you are," he said through the receiver when I picked it up one 3:00 A.M.

" 'How doth the little crocodile . . .' " a distorted voice snarled a few weeks later, ending with an ugly laugh before the caller hung up.

After I bought the answering machine, I had a recurrent message: the sound of taped birdsong, heavy breathing, then nothing.

When I did relent, accepting his collect calls, he said that I had spirited Homerdessa away to get his inheritance, which I had hidden in a Swiss bank account; that he knew I had sicced the FBI, the CIA, on him. That his daddy Wayne was not really dead, but had had plastic surgery and was in Gulfport, dealing drugs. . . .

"I knew . . . that voice . . . the minute I heard it . . ." a woman on *Donahue* said a few weeks later of the son she had given up for adoption. As she stared out from the television screen, it seemed as though her words were meant just for me.

Suddenly, violence all around and inside me. It resonated through my body, a constant hum. The words and pictures to it swam in my brain like underwater monsters, picked up from every newspaper and television program.

John Hinckley shot the president.

John Lennon was shot by a fan.

Movie starlet and Hugh Hefner protegée Dorothy Stratton was tortured and murdered by her jealous ex-husband.

Joan Didion's niece was murdered by a spurned lover.

And then there was my own passion for it, lying in wait since before I could remember. I searched out stills of B-movie bit-player Susan Cabot, taken early in her movie career in the fifties, long before she was murdered by her twenty-year-old dwarf son after years of force-feeding on steroids, in the isolated house they shared in the Hollywood Hills. I followed trials and did paintings from what seemed to me to be mythological crimes: a woman in Fort Lauderdale, charged with mental child abuse in the suicide of her topless-dancer teenage daughter whom she had charged fifteen hundred dollars a month for her bedroom in their two-bedroom apartment. The man in Philadelphia who kidnapped women and kept them chained in his filthy basement, torturing and murdering them. In the middle of the night, my toothed sleep, I would think of Richard Speck and the nine nurses.

I was fascinated by psychopaths. "Arrogant, smirky . . . that's the way Ted Bundy was," the father of one of his victims said on *Geraldo*. "An evil grin on his mug," Geraldo commented of another murderer. Mass murderers are usually "a white male, in his thirties, unemployed," testified an expert, describing my son perfectly.

There are about a hundred serial killers wandering the country at all times, I read somewhere. And worse were their childhood symptoms: bed-wetting, fire-setting, cruelty to animals—and the most frightening one, *head injury*. As the words leapt out at me, I was in the red convertible again, Dwayne still and quiet beside me, the blood smeared across the white dogwood, his pale child's face. . . .

In every crime, I saw Dwayne's face superimposed on the killer's, mine or Lily's over the victim's. On a television special on the insanity plea for murder, bitterness flooded the faces of the male defendants as they stood at the table or dock. I could see Dwayne on trial for *my* death—and read his justified expression.

But worse, I understood. I understood just as actress Dorothy Stratton did, going—in answer to her disturbed ex-husband's pleas—to his apartment to soothe him, to offer seven thousand dollars in atonement; then dropping her car keys and going back inside for them, only to be tortured and murdered on the wheel device he had especially designed for the occasion. Those keys had become symbolic to me of the one slip I might make that would cost me my life.

Had it been five years later, I would have been chilled by hearing a would-have-been victim of Jeffrey Dahmer quote what the killer had tenderly said to him: "You'll never leave me. You'll be a part of me, and I'll be a part of you forever." Because that was the way I thought Dwayne felt about me.

For a while, the terror got so bad that if I had any kind of sign—if my watch stopped, or I lost the beautiful silver bracelet that Sophie had given me for Christmas—I felt my time had come. And sometimes I felt I should just give in, let him kill me—that it was my destiny.

Yes, he was mine, this terrorist stalking me. And both of us knew who was the guilty one.

The homeless mentally ill were everywhere now. The streets of New Orleans, like the rest of America, were full of them, these people who couldn't afford an SRO, or even a meal.

The Prosperous Ones had trained themselves in detachment, become perfect acolytes of the Program, which had spread into every strata of society; ignoring the cardboard signs begging for money or for food, they stepped easily over the crippled, the homeless. As some people work for biceps, I was struggling for that imperviousness: to become—like my sister— a woman of selective vision.

Instead, I was handing out money left and right and thinking how every one of them was somebody's child. Sally Jessy Raphael did a show on children whose skin slides off like waxed paper at a touch. And I was like that—porous, my defenses as fragile as dried leaf.

One day, I pressed a five into the dirty, long-nailed palm of a man about Dwayne's age, darkly handsome, but bearded, grimy, wearing a filthy wool battle jacket, his feet in painfully cracked shoes. It was July, the mercury at 102. He looked at me with a surprised snarl. And when I saw him again, creeping into a darkened doorway beneath a No Trespassing sign, I yearned to follow; to lie down, hold him amid the debris. After that, it seemed that he was everywhere, beside me as I walked along Magazine Street, entering the double doors of St. Louis Cathedral, as if we were chained and moving in tandem.

When a kitten with only one eye was born in a litter in my courtyard, I couldn't look into the empty pink wet socket, his innocent one-eyed gaze; stroke the tiny extra ear given as though in compensation, or the seam up the other side of his fat little black-and-white face—a welt as neat as though made by a seamstress, reminding me of the scar that still ridged my son's scalp.

It was around that time that I saw the photograph on the front page of the *Times-Picayune*: a defiant twenty-year-old black, being led away in handcuffs, after having been talked by his mother—the distraught woman trailing behind him in a flowered print dress and orthopedic shoes—into turning himself in after shooting a policeman. D.A. TO SEEK DEATH PENALTY, the headlines read the next day. Always, I felt a little *ping*, like a shot to the heart, at the sight of a tan sheriff's car, the wire mesh separating the armed driver and some woman's son, shackled like a calf being taken to the gelding. And now I felt it for that poor mother, doing what she assumed was right, trusting in the goodwill of the "authorities" while delivering the child she had borne over to those who would kill him.

She became the first of the women in my series of paintings *Mothers of Murderers*—my fantasy of a voluptuous, whorish Mrs. Manson; a deliberately lurid interpretation of the bleached-out, fake-lashed, alcoholic, and bloated Susan Cabot; the tiny, wraithlike Mrs. Bundy standing in her tacky kitchen, clutching her son, Ted's, Boy Scout uniform to her; the sleek Mrs. John Edgar Wideman—wife of the renowned writer, mother of the sixteen-year-old who stabbed his roommate on a very middle-class camping trip, only to confess to yet another murder a year earlier—staring down her detractors: women universally crucified, blamed by the media from *Vanity Fair* to the *National Enquirer* for the crimes their children had committed. . . .

I sat in on such trials when I could, sketching the mothers' faces, agonized like the ones in the drawings of Käthe Kollwitz. And however calm they seemed, I recognized their torment. The faces of those mothers, and my nightmares of myself on trial, caused me to wake at four in the morning in the four-poster bed, my heart pounding. But nonetheless, I continued drawing the most excruciating portraits that I could.

* * *

Whenever the police whom I had met through Lily visited, they admired my paintings, set out to dry around the walls of my studio. They liked the craziness, the violence, in them. They were my pals now, and would have been lovers were it not for the Army Sergeant. I liked the way their biceps pushed at the sleeves of their uniforms, the guns jutted at their flat waists, the frank cynicism with which they viewed the world. I needed people around me who had seen terrible things, to whom my little family was not that unusual. "Have you known other people like him?" I would ask casually as we sat on my balcony, sipping coffee and chicory or Irish whisky, only to be reassured that, in their worlds, they met people like Dwayne every day.

In fact, I was beginning to believe that the whole idea of middle-class life—of civility, suburbia, safety—was a facade, an overlay, something made up by Madison Avenue, that the *real* world was that underclass the rest tried so hard not to know about, except via the movies. And when I would read about the hypocrisy, the lies on Wall Street, in the White House, even in the art world, it would even seem to me that Lily and Dwayne and those like them might be saints who had just not been able to learn to lie and compartmentalize, to adapt to what we called society, like that pilot who had gone mad after dropping the bomb on Hiroshima, or the men who came back from Vietnam strung out and crazy.

"These are great—hot! They'll really sell! Violence is *in* right now!" my new dealer exclaimed over the phone from New York when he saw my new pictures. He was a fey boy half my age whose picture was often in the back of *Vanity Fair*, amid the snaps of the right people at the right parties. "Somebody big just might pick these up, do a feature! You know how big Frida is these days!"

Later, it seemed ironic when Madonna, queen of bustiers and sadomasochistic imagery, bought the rights to Frida's story in order to play her, and also bought one of my most graphic paintings. For much of her life, Frida wore a bustierlike body cast, painted with flowers and other images; she had been artist of pain—portraying in bloody tableaus the lifetime of suffering resulting from the streetcar accident that had occurred when she was sixteen: A metal rod had pierced her uterus, emerging through her vagina; gold dust from a painter's bag in a rack overhead had scattered down on her torn, naked body—"it was then that I lost my virginity," she said. And I was an artist of pain of another kind, expressed in an equally violent imagery.

But at the moment, as my dealer spoke, I shivered in shame and dread, flashing my paintings, my guts, my terror, on the walls of people who led civilized lives in civilized places—hanging in elegant apartments in Manhattan or architectual tour de forces on the sides of the mountains above Malibu, while I went on making more of them, in my crumbling apartment down in New Orleans.

Homerdessa had had two strokes and was in a nursing home. She had abandoned her house and everything in it, just to escape him. "He beat her so bad that she's blind in one eye," her sister told me. When I repeated this to him, he just got madder: "Thet ole bitch—she doesn't know what she's talkin' about!"

But that didn't mean he had food. I was sending him UPS parcels, canned and dried food. When I visited South Alabama, I would get Ned, or Musette's hulking son to go with me, and take him bags of groceries.

Because I knew about the System now, I applied for SSI payments for him. To begin them, he had to be seen by a psychiatrist, who I told him was an administrator, also that the funds that he would receive would be based on his daddy Wayne's Social Security. When I picked him up for the interview, he came out wearing ragged jeans, his usual good-ole-boy cap, his graying hair swagged back in a ponytail; he carried the "important papers" he now never went anywhere without in a large plastic garbage bag. His eyes, as he got into the Alfa, burned with a light that seemed focused somewhere inside him. It hurt to see him looking so skinny, so ravaged.

After he had been seen by the doctor, the man called me into his office. "I think your son is doing the best he can," he said, looking at me kindly, after asking me a few questions about Dwayne's history. I remembered another doctor, another interview room, way back when Dwayne had been thirteen. But

331

this man didn't use the words *mental illness*, or recommend any treatment at all.

"That guy was a shrink, wasn't he?" Dwayne said as we drove away. I expected another diatribe about my "collaborating with the enemy." But that was all he said, and soon he started receiving the monthly payments that would buy his groceries.

But still, over the phone, I heard the breathing, the birdsong.

At moments, I was drawn into Homerdessa's belief that we were the only ones in the world who loved him. That it was the two of us and Dwayne against the world, as it had once been Dwayne and me in my painting, after his accident. "Did he look good for his interview? It's so important to look *good*," she said when I visited her at the nursing home to talk her about making a will on his behalf. "When Dwayne is hisself, he is the *sweetes'* thang," she went on, ignoring my entreaties. "Why, it's an a-*bom*-mination unto the Laird fur thet boy to be in need lak thet. . . ."

I didn't argue with her, and I had given up my rage at all those years she had kept him from any kind of treatment. After all, she was an old lady, an old lady who was dying. Years later I would read a news story—*A woman beaten so severely that she forgot the son who attacked her . . . visited him in jail and said he seemed like a nice person. . . .* And I would think of Homerdessa. Apparently, she had forgotten about the handcuffs, the meat fork piercing the pillow beside her face, even lying in her own back bedroom with her face bruised, the door chained shut.

"Oh, save him, *save* him from the cold, cold *hearts* of in-*stee-too-shunal* pity," she mumbled weakly, her voice rising and falling like a line from a hymn at the Church of God, the unexpected poetry of her words chilling me as she reached out her veined, splotched hand to me. Chilling me because her blind love for him made me realize how like her I was.

And then Homerdessa died, and he was mine again.

"I don't see the harm—he's been callin' 'n callin', wantin' you to come over. If you wait till I finish this piecrust, I'll go with you," Musette said after I drove in from New Orleans one afternoon.

He let us in through double locks; I saw a small wooden barrier nailed in the floor before the door as if to trip whoever might enter. As we entered the dark, heavily draped living room, the miasma of cat shit, he locked the door behind us, turning two different keys, which he stuck back into the pocket of his jeans. I couldn't tell whether Musette had seen it or not, and was afraid to say anything. He began playing a demented music, then showing us paintings that were full of satanic-looking symbols and more of the neologisms, plus jagged volcanic red peaks spewing threats and weapons, all the while ranting of the wrongs I and others had done him. Terrified, his six cats hid beneath the furniture. As he stopped and restarted a tape, searching for a song he insisted we hear, I heard the sounds of the birdsong I had heard over my answering machine. "Come back 'n talk to me while I change," he demanded, finally calmed a bit; he had finally agreed to leave the house with us—to *let* us leave—if we would drive him where he wanted to go: an art supply store in a nearby town. In his filthy, disordered room, I saw the knife stuck into the closet door quiver as he opened it, the words AND THE EVIL SHALL PERISH scrawled across the wall. I glimpsed my picture everywhere. As he pulled off one shirt, reached into the closet for another, I wondered if he was reaching for a gun—if these were the last moments of my life.

"Whew! I was scared outta my wits!" Musette said after we finally deposited him at the art supply store. "I was lookin' all around for somethin' to hit that boy over the head with. And the only thing I could see was an ole lamp!" For once she didn't object when I suggested we stop at a bar before driving back to her house. I didn't stop trembling inside until I had downed three shots of straight Black Jack, and Musette, usually a teetotaler, had two, gulping them down like medicine despite the fact that she shuddered each time she did so.

For the next half hour, we just sat there and looked at each other. There was no denying it: My son wasn't just good-ole-boy mean, he was crazy.

"Shoot!" Musette exclaimed, shuddering again. "I'm *never*

goin' back there again!" But then she had that option. He wasn't her beloved son. He was mine.

To see that Dwayne got the treatment he needed, the Army Sergeant and I took him to a Pancake House where we drew him out about the FBI agent who he claimed spoke to him through a loudspeaker in the middle of the night; then we swore to his state of mind in a probate judge's office. That same day, we got the news that Homerdessa's sister had had him evicted. That night, the deputies broke down the door and took him away in leg chains.

A few weeks later, I had to testify about his crimes at a long table of Experts; all the while, he was sitting right there looking at me. Musette, who had come with me for support, held my elbow as we walked back out into the corridor to await the verdict. "Now remember, no matter what happens, I'm not gittin' into the car with him," Musette said, seeing me glance toward Dwayne. He milled restlessly at the other end of the hall, held loosely in place by his male caseworker, his court-appointed attorney beside him. Every few seconds, he glared at me. He had on a white T-shirt, the sleeves rolled to his shoulder, his Camels pack stuck inside one of them, and a good-ole-boy cap from which someone had picked out the letters but I could still read the motto: UP AGAINST THE WALL, REDNECK MOTHER. His sideburns curled long and unkempt down his thin, swarthy cheeks.

The social worker stood between us like a stout SS guard. "If he's not committed, are you prepared to move, change your phone number, so he won't come and kill you?" she asked harshly. As she spoke, I felt she was speaking not of my son, but of a snake or a spider. Her mouth was a red slash, barely moving in her doughy face. "At first we thought he was manic-depressive, but now we think it's schizophrenia—perhaps paranoid schizophrenia. The drugs we use to treat it are sometimes successful, sometimes not. And there are side effects." So *that* was what had been wrong with him all those years. Walking from the building in my funereal black outfit, I felt as light, as porous, as ash or a piece of old bone, adrift within this new knowledge.

The next week, the Army Sergeant and I went down to pack his things and put them in storage—the books on wildlife and nature and painting techniques I had sent him; his easel, paints, brushes, and palette. His guitar. His tools. His boots, jeans, shirts, and his black leather jacket.

It was then that I found the lingerie, the scrawled writings, the handcuffs and chains. And the pictures of me, and my letters to him—the stacks of them. Like love letters, in my pink envelopes.

When I visited Dwayne in the hospital, the tears rose in my eyes, rolled down my cheeks at the sight of him, calmed for the first time by the medication. "Your tears are like diamonds, Mama," he said tenderly, wiping one away with a finger.

Mickey Mouse was big again that year. On a flight from Houston to New Orleans, the stewardess had given out cardboard Mickey Mouse ears to people with children. I had gotten a pair for Dwayne—after all, he was only thirty-three.

"I've been wonderin' whether your eyes are blue or brown," he said as we sat in the noisy dayroom. I was still clutching the Mickey Mouse ears, which he hadn't seemed to want after all. "And your hands—they're so *small*," he added wonderingly, turning my palm over in his, making me drop the wrinkled cardboard into my lap. "She was so pretty, in a country sort of way—pretty to me, anyway. Almost as pretty as you, Mama," he said of a girl he had met at a hospital dance. He seemed to have forgotten his anger at my signing the commitment papers.

"Thy-ar is a *ti-em* to be *borned*—'n a *ti-em* to *die*. . . ." A young woman sat nearby reading loudly from the Bible, the same verse over and over from the book of Ecclesiastes. A man of about sixty sat on another man's lap, his arm draped affectionately around his shoulders. Occasionally, he leaned over and kissed his friend's balding forehead. "Miss Bee-oo-tee-ful!" they called out in unison as a fat black woman in a short print rayon skirt and fuzzy dirty-pink bedroom slippers sashayed by. A youth with intense blue eyes stared at me unblinkingly from across the room. "Thet's a purty blouse," he said in an intimate voice, still unblinking, when Dwayne got up to get us Pepsis from a machine.

"Bye, Mama," Dwayne said sweetly when our time was up, reverting again to his baby name for me and kissing me on the cheek.

"He was like a little boy again, calling me Mama. . . ." As my fear abated, my love flooded back in.

"And how did that make *you* feel?" asked the stout SS guard, indicating something malevolent, a hook. "All of us like to be flattered. It's more likely to be his pathology—that he was just trying to manipulate you," she went on, implying that any warmth, any spark of love, he showed me was sick. "Now do you think that's *normal*—an *appropriate* way for a son to talk to his mother?" Did that mean that she regarded my visiting him as the equivalent of visiting a reptile in a zoo?

On the bad days, Dwayne wore his Camels inside one white sock, meanly dispensing them from his ankle to the less fortunate at ten cents each. He wore the billed cap over his scraggly graying ponytail, his sideburns; the shirt hanging out, the cowboy boots, gave him a nervous confidence. He spit on the floor in the same way my daddy, Patrick, had. Talking with him then was like trying to communicate with a shark—a shark who was also my son.

"It's about time you got your butt over here!" he would snarl. He complained that "they" had stolen the twenty one-dollar bills I had sent him in an envelope, per his instructions. That he had been so angry, he had torn up the accompanying money order.

"They say I'm gambling."

"Well, are you?"

"Not that much—but will you send me two decks of Bicycles with the small numbers?"

Whenever Daddy had made any money, he had gone down to the roadhouse, to come back empty-handed, and Mama would cry. The memory washed through me like a picture show.

"If you can just think of him as a beautiful tiger in a cage. You can look at him from a distance, admire him. But you wouldn't want to pet him," said the gentler social worker. "Your goal has to be to take care of *yourself*. Not accepting collect calls is not enough. You're a part of his delusional system, and always will be. . . ." Randy was plump and blond and kind, the type that burns out fast. Over the years, I had watched them come and go.

"As long as he stays on his medication—the problem is, when people start feeling better, they think they don't need it anymore," he told me just before Dwayne was released.

I didn't want to hear it when the Experts warned me. But I knew that his plan had been to find me and punish me. Thus, if I was to stay alive, I had to do what I had done with Lily— turn from someone I still loved.

That afternoon, I started packing to go to Costa Rica. I would do the dangerous things I had only thought about be- fore—fly a single-engine plane over the jungle; visit the border, the remaining Contras. . . .

I picked up the phone to call Lacsa airline. Instead I dialed Rose's number in Baltimore, then a number Sherry had given me.

"It's out of your hands now, Mother," Rose said calmly after I told her the diagnosis.

Rose had gotten her Ph.D. in neuroscience, completed her postdoctoral years in San Francisco, and was working in a lab in Baltimore. I didn't see how she could stand it, it was so ugly, after growing up in New Orleans. But she didn't want to live too close to the South, she said. I knew she was afraid of getting stuck on the flypaper of my troubles: "Face it, Mother, it's like a cancer, running through your family," she would say some- times, as though we weren't even related.

Somewhere along the way, Rose had picked up a hand- some, well-read carpenter. At home in her town house in Balti- more with her lover, she prepared gourmet meals from Craig Claiborne, read *The New York Times*, watched foreign-language videos, studied, and wrote papers. On Saturdays, they antiqued, looking for pieces he finished. It was the civilized, intellectual lifestyle I had imagined, but that nobody in our family had ever lived.

Every day at her laboratory, doing research funded by the NIDA or NIAAA, she and her lab techs decapitated white mice

337

or rats on a tiny guillotine, churned and separated the nucleus of the brain cells in a centrifuge, studied the cells, then gave or published reports unfathomable (to me) on the results.

And now she, my Daughter the Doctor, was the Expert I turned to: from the near-unintelligible papers she sent me on "Molecular Genetic Studies of Schizophrenia" or "Schizophrenia: The Cellular Basis of a Functional Psychosis," I learned about the temporal lobes, about how certain dopamine neurons go wild, flooding the brain; and about the "anomaly that is probably genetic in most cases and affects brain development during the third trimester. . . ."

"The lack of insight is *part* of the delusion," Rose said when I puzzled over how Dwayne could so firmly believe things that weren't true. "It's all in the genes, the *biochemistry*, Mother!" she went on, exasperated. "And in his case, maybe minor brain damage."

Periodically nowadays, Rose gave me these little lectures, contradicting all my years of belief in the psychological underpinnings of everything—even Rose, still under my influence back then, had been a true believer in primal-scream therapy; at sixteen, she had spent her summer-job money being Rolfed. "It's been statistically proven that the drugs work better than psychotherapy, even with simple neurosis—that's why the psychologists are so worried." She claimed that dreams—sacred territory to me as an artist—were simply detritus, the trash of the day. She scorned the self-help books, the Twelve Step programs, the currently popular gurus of dysfunction. Indeed, she believed that Lily's new evangelism was simply a manifestation of her addictive personality. "Read sociobiology, Mother!" she would exclaim, as though talking to an illiterate. And I had to admit it: If there was one organ the "Let Go and Let God" people seemed against using, it was the brain.

"The brain is the source of *every*thing," she said unequivocably. "For example, if a certain area is stimulated, one becomes idealistic, possibly religious, wants to keep journals—like Dostoyevski: He had temporal-lobe epilepsy, and he wrote those voluminous journals. Van Gogh's syphilis affected *his* brain; he became obsessed at St. Rémy with the poor, the homeless. . . ."

Art history was another of Rose's interests, the one that would lead her to become my official biographer. As she spoke, I thought of Vincent, the paintings left at the hospital after his death, to be used as targets for bow-and-arrow practice. And what of me, Frida, Käthe Kollwitz—had we all just suffered from pressure at a certain point in the brain? Was that what my painting was all about?

"Epilepsy, addiction, mental illness, creativity—they all appear in some families. And yours is like that, Mother."

Rose also believed that a scientific paradigm would someday be found for psychology, much as DNA and molecular biology were now the paradigm for biology—that this paradigm would provide the key, bringing together environmental influences, genetics, and biochemistry. When she told me this, I felt hope rise, a small, rainbow-colored bubble: If only she, my special child, could find it—the key to all of it, the history of our grief. I flashed her standing before a podium, wearing the crisp kind of skirt and shirt she favored; her navy eyes shining, her pristine, unmade-up face, curtained by her dark silky page-boy, filled with certainty as she spoke.

But whatever the truth might be, Rose—without even knowing it, thinking all the while she had escaped—had devoted her whole life to healing our little family.

My Rose—I loved her for that.

"I will help you," he said in his thick European accent.

The last therapist was about my age, his blond Danish face, his stubble of a beard, appealing; yet I found I could sit across from him without thinking of sex. But then, he wasn't my type anyway, dressed as he was in pinstriped shirt, coat, and dark tie on which I saw a mustard stain. And I had seen him drive up to the building in a metallic-gray Chrevrolet sedan, a Lutheran symbol on its rear window.

"The images you have of your life, of the past—I will help you change, soften them." A small flame of hope, just a lick of it, flickered inside me. I thought of the others, the ones who had blamed me.

"You are very, very tired; you have suffered," he said,

kicking off his tassel loafers. I noticed that his feet in the navy socks were small and arched. "You have to let yourself feel the grief, the loss. This is real, your *reality*. . . ."

Post-Traumatic Stress syndrome, he called it: "You needn't have been on the battlefield to have it, you know." At first the flashbacks had come at night, almost every night. But now they came in his office. My thoughts were grabbling, sliding, moving through solid matter. I wanted to break through the walls, or run from the room screaming.

He only loosened his tie, waited patiently. At last the pain crashed in like a tidal wave. I babbled about how I had watched two of my children taken away in handcuffs, my grandson handed over to strangers. How I seen them become wards of the state, those children I had wanted to fly, fly—via art, books, bohemianism, above "the frozen tundra of bourgeois emotion," as Norman Mailer had put it. How instead they had become two of the disenfranchised, the pariahs of an affluent society, among those the Prosperous Ones would have sprayed with a fungicide if they could have. How, in the face of this, one can collapse, lean on friends—friends who inevitably grow weary—or go on. How none of it helps anyway. . . .

"I've never run away from any man," I objected during the next session, when he suggested mildly that perhaps I should listen to those who had advised that I stay away from Dwayne, even move, keep my address secret from him.

"What of your father? Didn't you leave your home at sixteen to escape him? Don't you think it is your anger with your father, your denied grief for him, that holds you in thrall to your son? . . ."

His words penetrated, a small blade. "Have you seen the movie *Fatal Attraction*?" he persisted. "Haven't *you* ever wanted somebody you couldn't have, somebody you wanted so bad you could taste it?" He was missing the point. Dwayne wasn't a *man*—he was my son. "There's a logic, a system, to what he feels and believes. And part of that is that he's your spurned lover."

I looked down at the garish gold carpet. He was saying something I had known all along but at the same time had not known, an ugly puzzle piece falling into place.

"I wouldn't be surprised if he took that bit of money, went

out, and bought something related to his fantasy of you," he said, referring to the small sums I had mentioned sending to Dwayne since his hospitalization.

"Would you let any other man treat you this way? Just what *do* you hope to get out of this relationship?" he went on, suddenly a detective bent on confession.

"A son, someone to love, enjoy, be supportive of. To love unconditionally. To go to concerts with . . ." I answered lamely, recalling how Musette had gone with Ned Junior to hear Asleep at the Wheel when she had been in New Orleans last.

"And are you getting any of those things?"

I cried, my hands over my face. He didn't try to get me to deny my love, as the others had. "Dwayne is a person with an illness: He feels he has been hurt, that he must now hurt others before they can hurt him. But he is still your son. And you can love him without loving the sickness. . . ."

"But what of *my* sins?" I mumbled one day.

"You're too hard on yourself—you torture yourself. You survived, didn't you? You, that little girl, survived. Your pity, your inability to rage on your own behalf—*that* has been your downfall."

I had always thought of how I had betrayed others. Now I thought of how I had been betrayed. *The ways I betrayed myself. The ways I, as a woman, was betrayed.*

The Crazy Woman had learned to numb herself. Now she had to learn to feel. First came the jagged teeth, rocks breaking, sharp-edged, shattering inside me; or barbed wire, untangled, set free to rake my chest cavity, my throat, my very brain cells. Not just what I had done to *them*, but what they had done to *me*. . . .

First came the anger, then the grief. When I would think of my losses, of theirs, my two wounded children, my breasts would ache, a ghostly milk coming down. The tears I cried then were like postmenopausal blood—dark and bitter and reluctant. For a time, bereft of my obsession, I was so lonely that I wanted the tourists on the streets of the French Quarter to stop me, ask for directions. . . .

At last he let me tell the things I had done wrong, how I had put my art and my own life before them. He asked me to say, first to Dwayne, then to Lily, as they sat on the empty couch before me: "I made some choices. They didn't work out the way I hoped. I'm sorry. I did the best I could. . . ."

The image of a smiling four-year-old Dwayne, a plump Lily on his lap, was as clear as though they were there in flesh, and I could reach out my hand to them. . . .

For several minutes, the tears washed down my cheeks. By now I didn't care if he saw me crying, or how I looked. "I wish— I just wish—I could have them back again, do it all over again!" I gasped.

"I know what you mean," he said gently. If, as he said, trauma was cellular, so was healing. I felt whole planes moving, portions of my very brain shifting. I recalled how the ones in the Program had spoken of spirituality, how it had sounded foreign to me, like some African dialect. "Where my power stops, my prayer starts," they would say. I remembered the women who had had dead children, how they sat silently, hands folded in their laps, like mutes or saints. The ones who had lost their Bad Ones to drugs, then went on to lose their Good Ones to accidents or illness. And now I wondered if there really *was* something called *faith*. Or was it just acceptance? . . .

"What are you thinking of?" he asked on that last day.

"Something that I read in Freud—or was it Fromm—that 'a man cannot die without a mother's love.' "

"*Do* you love him?"

"Yes."

"*So—he will not die without a mother's love.*"

So it hadn't been meanness after all, but a simple biochemical disease: When Dwayne's brain was out of whack, he became afraid, and when he became afraid, he reacted.

He wasn't at fault, I wasn't at fault—nobody was, as schizophrenia specialist Dr. E. Fuller Torrey confirmed on *Donahue*: "It has nothing to do with anything your mother said to you," he emphasized, thus informing me that my twenty years of self-recrimination, of guilt, had been useless.

At a lecture on "Violence and Mental Illness," I heard another Expert talk about the fact that many who make violent gestures or threats during psychosis go on for the rest of their lives without repeating that behavior. "My son got better as the years went on," a kindly graying woman told me afterward.

I thought of those poor Mothers of Murderers, of the women in my Mothers Who Love Too Much group, of how we had raked ourselves over the coals of every peanut-butter-and-jelly sandwich that went unmade, every less-than-sensitive remark. And of course, since I had never followed the rules, I had had more to blame myself for than most.

Yet I was finding out that I, with my liberal ways, my bohemian inclinations, hadn't been the cause of it at all; in fact, that mothers who sent their children to schools where they wore little uniforms, who served perfect, nutritionally correct suppers—one meat, one starch, two green vegetables, and Jell-O pudding—promptly, à la Donna Reed at five-thirty each afternoon; mothers who had early selected as husbands men destined to law and accounting, men who looked born with starched white shirts, those little black shoes on; mothers who had never had, or had successfully, beat down any aspirations they might have had for themselves—still could have had children done in. People who could never have imagined such things, way back in the fifties, had children in jail or among the homeless.

"This is your brain on drugs," the public-service announcements reminded TV viewers ten times a day in the South's remotest hamlets, an actor breaking and sizzling an egg on a hot skillet to demonstrate. In New Orleans, a heroin city if there ever was one, red banners over the streets read DOPE IS DEATH. *Does your adolescent have problems?* newspapers in small towns all over America, advertising the "treatment centers" charging twenty thousand dollars a month, ask, then go on to list the symptoms: *Bed-wetting? Anger and defiance? Stealing? Fire-setting? Cruelty to animals? Loss of interest in usual activities?* Magazines like *Woman's Day* informed just about everybody that PCP can trip psychosis. Indeed, all this was now common knowledge—as though mental illness and drug addiction were only slightly more serious than, and as ubiquitous as, the usual measles and chicken pox.

Every Sunday and some week nights, a Dr. John Bradshaw filled the PBS screen, exhorting in the rhythms of a suck-back preacher, about "the shame of the shame . . ." (meaning the guilt about feeling guilty about being victimized—the whole thing had gotten that crazy) to audiences who looked as rapt— and as ashamed—as the folks in Jimmy Swaggart's audience, or those in the Church of God when I was a child (indeed, some of those very preachers were now on trial for their sexual sins). And I knew that those women in his audiences—always, such audiences are mostly women—were educated, some of them even with Ph.D.s in psychology, yet were no different, really, from Mama, and those women back in Alabama who believed their men were drunks because they hadn't prayed enough for their salvation. (And even then, the praying didn't work: "I'm the only hell my Mama ever raised," goes a Johnny Paycheck song from a few years back, describing a hapless woman who undoubtedly had been at the First Baptist Church praying every time the doors opened.) And then at the bottom of the heap were the painted hussies, the women who didn't even *want* to do right, the actual sinners like me, who, God knows, deserved what they got.

But I was learning that what had happened to Dwayne had had little to do with me at all. My son had turned out to be just another man with a treatable biochemical disease, an illness best managed, not with my self-immolating love, but through the simple ingestion into his body of a missing chemical element. That if he was ever able, after all these years, to lead anything like a near-normal life, it would be because of that chemical, not because of anything I had done or not done.

And I was grateful, simply grateful, that I was not one of them, those Mothers of Murderers, the mothers of my dreams, of my nightmares. . . .

How my daughter Lily had tried to break from my love: by using me on behalf of her addiction—lying to me, stealing from me, manipulating me, even sleeping with my lovers; but worst, almost destroying the mind and body I had given her.

And Dwayne, my son—for a season, I had lived in fear of him for my very life.

Yet I would forgive either of them in a moment. In fact, I already had.

CHAPTER SIXTEEN

A FEW YEARS after I started showing paintings, Jacques Dupree invited me to a private opening at his apartment: He was hanging the works of Delicia, woman a bit younger than I was who had been living in a shack without electricity on the edge of the bayou for five years, in a place near where she had grown up. She was pretty in that pale, wispy way of some white-trash southern women, a redneck Cajun with apricot curls down her skinny back. Her pictures were good, Jacques said, though not as good as mine. She was a primitive, and he wanted to help her. So, already, I was a bit jealous.

Then, the day before her opening, her father murdered her mother in a nearby trailer park. But Delicia went on with the party anyway, a slightly hysterical smile on her full red lips as she worked the room perched on stiletto heels—being toasted with cheap champagne, meeting New Orleans's more fashionable dilettantes.

As the evening went on and the news worked its way around the room, I heard the whispers—"How *could* she, with her mother just dead!" As they spoke, they cut their eyes at her cheap, too-tight tank top, the sleazy rayon-velvet skirt.

345

But I understood perfectly. Delicia was one of my kind, the kind I had been since the end of my dreams of a happy family life.

There is a rule: *Chaos multiplies.* It's never just one thing.
Take that girl in Musette's class in high school: At seventeen, she married a boy from around there, lived with him and their three children right next door to her parents and down the road from his, for all of their married life. It took her ten years, but she got her teaching certificate, worked at the local grade school; they were making ends meet, even building on a Florida room.

That was when he ran away with "this white-trash blonde" who worked at the 7-Eleven down the road the other way, where he went every night to buy his six-pack. "I was just gettin' ovah *that* a bit," she told Musette, when her beautiful teenaged son turned paraplegic in a head-on car wreck out on Highway 10.

So now the rest of her life is cut out for her—not for her the breezy single's life, the men and travel she had imagined, but the care, along with her aging parents' help, of a crippled, embittered man-child.

The best she can do nowadays is to go over to the Holiday Inn in the next town; sit in the bar, hoping to meet some married man for a one-night stand.

"I used to think your sister, Eastah, was wild," she told Musette, "but now I understand why she did the things she did."

"I have to celebrate life a *little* bit," Evelyn said defensively, lighting up a joint back at my studio after dinner in the Quarter; I noticed how her manicured fingers trembled. "After Beau died, I stayed at our condo on the beach for six months and smoked dope. I just couldn't do anything else. It was a kinda nervous breakdown, ah guess. . . ."

Evelyn's only child O.D.'d in a rooming house in Atlanta while she was at the theater in London, watching *Cats.* A rich Montgomery matron, she had flown here from Alabama to buy one of my paintings: "They say what's in mah haht—all that blood 'n *agony*. . . ."

When she left, I found that she'd stolen a favorite piece of costume jewelry from my dresser top—a red heart paved with fake rubies, given to me by Sophie.

But all she would have had to have done was to ask: I would have given her *anything*, so fortunate was I that my Lily, my Dwayne, were alive.

Indeed, it was an age of miracles of sorts.

The cat with one eye, his other socket sealed over like a little pink seam, was now my favorite—One-Eyed Jack, I called him. I loved the way he knew nothing of his deformity, prancing before me sideways, or digging in the dirt beneath the elephant ears. When I went down into the courtyard, he rubbed against my leg purring, his uneven black-and-white fur moving up and down. I would reach down, caress the extra ear, scratch him along the welt on his fat little face, not thinking of my son's scar at all.

And there was Dwayne, joking, jostling with the other ex-cons at an opening of his paintings at the Abstract Café. During a time off his medication, he had come to New Orleans, where he had been in a shoot-out with a SWAT team; arrested, he had been sent first to East Louisiana Forensics over at Jackson, and then had served a year in prison.

But he had survived, and the real miracle was his paintings: a world of myth and mystery, of silvery burnished egrets, alligators, fish, barely seen through shimmery water or bayou brush. His new caseworker was a Vietnam vet and an Audubon member who shared his interest in wild things—they talked, he said, about the woods, about birds, about fish. One painting, which I envied, was of trout swimming beneath water, their pastel silvery colors barely visible.

When he sometimes turned bitter—"I'm an ex–*mental* patient, Mother," he would say when I voiced some hope for him, Pollyanna to the end, "and an ex-con. And I'll *always* be those things"—he would look for a moment like the aging hippie that he is, a sad-eyed graying man in need of dental work, a scraggly beard covering his concave cheeks. He who never had anything feels he has lost everything. Along the way, like many of his kind, he has been beaten and robbed; with his acceptance of his disease, a depression has set in.

347

"I have this anger inside me all the time. Even on the medication, I have it," he says. It is impossible for me to convince him that his paintings are better now that he's sane. And the truth is, I'm not too sure of that myself. His anger was his energy, he claims, along with his sexuality, which goes dead, like a battery, on the medicine. And then there was that stigma, like the mark on Cain's forehead, of those labeled mentally ill.

So his choice is feeling dead or feeling insane. And isn't that the choice a lot of us had to make? That I had made over and over in his and Lily's favor?

And then there is Lily: Shuffling the pots and pans in her hot little kitchen in Metairie, a fine sweat on her pretty brow, hurrying with the cooking, the cleanup, in order to get off to speak at some church basement, one of the meetings where she's becoming known for what she considers her divinely inspired metaphors, her power to raise drunks and dopers from the gutters of New Orleans. She has a following among the molelike groups that gather in those drab meeting rooms—there's even been talk of a television show.

I've seen her in those rooms, and if I thought she had the power to enthrall back in those smoky New York jazz clubs, that was nothing to what she has today, a charisma that almost drips from her, oozing from her very pores, speaking as she does of the depths to which she has personally descended, to rise again, healed. Few in the Program around New Orleans can match it. Nor is she above calling on the same resources she used back then—her looks as gorgeous, if more lush, than in her first drug days, mesmerizing from the podium with huge long-lashed eyes skillfully outlined in black, the rich red-brown froth of a mane that whips about her small, heart-shaped face when a point is to be made. And afterward, there is always a crowd around her, supplicants drawn to the sun of her radiance. And in those moments, she is someone I've never even met before. Instead of the poet I dreamed—my own answer to Rilke's call for the great women poets to come—my daughter is a tough small-time evangelist of sorts, filled with a fiery, quasi-religious fervor.

"*These* are my people," she told me. "*These*, not *you*, Mother."

I can tell that she doesn't totally approve of me or my lifestyle. For one thing, I don't believe that the Bible is the Word of God. For another, I still hang out with cross-dressers and assorted crazies, as well as the social workers, cops, and whores I had the good fortune to meet through her and Dwayne's auspices.

I'm also wearing sexy clothes again—swing skirts and low-necked blouses, high-heeled sandals and dangling earrings. And always, my toenails painted vermilion—the writer Colette and I are alike in that. My body is fuller now, with a fullness that feels solid; my breasts beginning, though only slightly, to droop a bit like white peaches; with the help of an underwire bra, they give me a luxurious cleavage.

I've stopped watching TV and going to meetings, and have gone back to hanging out at bars, preferring places like the Bombay Club on Dumaine, where everyone is reasonably well dressed, near middle-aged, like me; and where, though the martinis are served in huge glasses, I more often than not drink "designer water," looking for all the world like Stolichnaya with a twist. Without meaning to, I've become—like Jacques Dupree, the flaming Iris, Sophie before she died—what's known as a French Quarter character.

My work is still considered aberrant; I have a cult following. But I'm no longer the *enfant terrible* of the Deep South. I suspect that, like Frida, I will have few major shows in my lifetime.

Yet more and more often, the young, the aspiring ones, seek me out. "Was it worth it?" one will ask, thinking she is speaking of the struggle to paint, rather than the pain of those years. But it's a moot question, isn't it? I don't see that there was a choice—it was all as inevitable as the hot rain on an August afternoon in New Orleans.

Sometimes I visit Lily in her little house in Metairie, scattered throughout with flyers and books and her friends from the Program.

Or we meet for coffee at the patisserie on Chartres Street. One day I had received a clipping from *The Village Voice* in the mail. *Whatever happened to the jazz poet Lillee Bowers—that beauty with the husky voice who, for a while, was filling clubs all over lower*

Manhattan? it asked. *She got married, got religion, got kids, down in old New Orleans*, the columnist wrote, answering his own question.

"Oh yeah, *that*," she said when I showed it to her; "Somebody at a meeting had a copy of it—talk about days of decadence! . . . Speaking of decadence, did you hear about Johnny Thunders—that guy who played with the New York Dolls, hung out with the Sex Pistols, Sid and Nancy 'n that crowd? Well, he O.D.'d last week in a room over on St. Peter. Some people just *never* learn. . . ."

It was Raphael's third birthday, but she didn't mention it, so I didn't, either. She was seven months pregnant, and on her way to shop for baby clothes. She had to get to the bank before 2:00 P.M. to cash the paycheck Pete had given her—to deduct his road money and the cash for household expenses before he left town again.

As she stood to leave, I noticed that she had gained more weight than just that of her pregnancy, that she was filled out at breast, belly, thighs. I thought of the skinny girl I had seen the week before in New York. She was dancing nude at the opening of a new restaurant, a former coffee shop at Sheridan Square where I had been taken by a young woman half my age, the art reviewer from *Interview*. Near a stove where lobsters were grilling, arrogant-looking young *GQ* types around the bar at her bare feet, the girl gyrated feverishly atop a chopping block, twisting breasts that were barely there, a belly between hipbones that looked like a Holocaust victim's. She was the entertainment for the evening, and looking up almost reluctantly, I glimpsed the misery in the girl's eyes, a girl so much like Lily had been.

Now I thought of her, and her mother, and was grateful. For Lily, this Lily, looked happy, bending to kiss me perfunctorily, in a hurry to be off into her real life.

But isn't that the way it is with kids? They never know, can never know, until they have done it themselves, *the sacrifice*.

Since Dwayne had gotten out of Jackson, he had been working in the shop behind the Abstract Café on Magazine Street,

across Canal—a coffeehouse-cum-art-gallery in a bad neighborhood, right across the corner of Thalia, where Lily once tricked
me into driving her to cop drugs. A local judge had started the
café and the shop to give jobs and a meeting place to ex-cons
and others of the disenfranchised.

It was the first time I had visited the café, and Dwayne was
working in the kitchen, fixing the omelet I had ordered for
breakfast. "Here's the jelly," he said unceremoniously, plopping
down a sticky, institutional-size jar of Welch's grape.

He was living with a fat woman on disability in a rented
house trailer in a trailer park outside the city. He was driving a
broken-down gray Chevy with rusted fenders these days, and
had started doing paintings of people's pets. But that was just
a way to make extra money, he said.

"How do you like the mural we did all over the outside?"
he asked, referring to the huge, jubilant primary-colored beasts
dancing along the exterior of the one-story stucco building.
Getting out of the Alfa, I had seen a bunch of skinny cats eating
leftover red rice and fried chicken, dumped right out on the
sidewalk for them.

The small room was full of bookshelves, the walls covered
in a manic art done by ex-cons and other clientele. A poster on
the wall announced Dwayne's upcoming one-man show: *Duane
Davis, Artist of the Earth*—it was what he had changed his name
to while he was in prison. "*Du*-ane," he told me adamantly, as
though he thought I might protest. "Du-ane Davis—that's the
name I want to go by from now on." I wondered if it embar-
rasses him for his mother, the Famous Artist, to come by, say
"hey."

I knew that Dwayne still didn't believe that I had ever
loved him. That was the worst thing, his feeling that I caused
everything bad that ever happened to him. That he still hated
and blamed me, despite the control the medication gave him
over his damaged biochemistry, the short circuits in his brain;
also that he might once again decide to go off it, that that hate
could blossom once more, giving him notions of conspiracies, a
lifetime spent plotting against him.

And I remembered the day he said to me, mentioning a

young local theater actress, "She looks so much like you did, Mama." For a moment, I saw that look in his eyes; and was afraid again—afraid of his obsessive love and his rage.

But then, a lot of kids hate their parents, don't they? I'm just grateful for this, this life he has. So only once in a while do I dial his number, just to hear his voice. For I know to be careful, not to activate his illness, the hurt or lust that may or may not be lurking there.

But isn't that the way it is with kids—no matter what you've done for them, or gone through with them?

"Don't you know it doesn't work that way?" Sophie said to me over and over through the years. "In the movies, is the mother *ever* the main character? . . .

"Do you think *I* cared when *my* mama cried over what I was? Or that it changed me one iota?"

Nowadays I hear the impatience in Lily's voice when I call: She has things to do, doesn't want her mother clinging, a millstone—even an "interesting" mother like me.

When I call Rose at her lab in Baltimore, one of her techs usually answers. "Dr. Bowers is in the middle of an experiment right now," an efficient young male voice will say. And even when Rose calls back, she sounds preoccupied.

But isn't that just the way kids are?

Last week, driving down Claiborne, I veered a bit to avoid a young girl, about twelve, bicycling in sweater, calf-length skirt. It struck me how vulnerable she was, how vulnerable a girl-child is. How vulnerable Lily was, how vulnerable I was.

By now, I know too much to assume that it's all over. I know something vital has been zapped from my son, my daughter. I think of Bing Crosby's son, Dennis, suicided after ten years of sobriety; of Primo Levi, the Italian writer who survived Auschwitz only to leap over a stairwell forty years later. And though Lily's still clean, there is always the possibility of a relapse, even the Virus.

Sophie and her python, which had long since lost its sheen and was by then spending its days coiled at her balcony door, the one shaft of sunlight in her apartment, both died during my last trip to Mexico. The snake went mad at the end, eating the kittens that lived in her courtyard. I heard that the Sugar Daddy blew out his brains in a motel room where he lay with another sad, strung-out girl, his perpetual hard-on. Bobby had a heart attack, which seemed right: His heart never seemed big enough to let the blood through anyway. Rose called to tell me that he was having an angiogram, that his new girlfriend was taking care of him, and that he didn't want to see Rose or Lily. The Army Sergeant went first to Panama, then to the deserts of Arabia, and then he was gone, that comforting bronzed body disappeared in "friendly fire"—one of the few who didn't come back in what most agreed, after all the yellow ribbons, the parades, was mostly a useless war.

So now it's usually just an aging Moana and me, her hot back against me in the four-poster bed. The radio turned on low, the lights of the Quarter flickering through the gauze curtains, I dream of dead men, artists and visionaries—Matisse, Theo and Vincent, Carl Jung, and Joseph Campbell—just as I once dreamed of sex and New Orleans.

What was that clinging to life all about? I sometimes wonder as I lie there. Watching people drift away—Sophie, Paula, the Army Sergeant—and in their own way, Dwayne and Lily: Each has made it easier to let go of the next. And it *is* a kind of death, not having to struggle anymore.

"Remember what we used to think?" Sophie asked a few months before she died.

"Well, we were *wrong*," she said when I nodded.

I didn't need to ask what she meant. But I didn't really agree.

Sophie still felt guilty about her former small and miserable pleasures, and not just because of her disease. "But you don't under*stand*," she would say almost proudly of the guilt that went along with being Catholic. "It's a pre*requisite*."

My own joy started again as she and I stood on Royal Street on a Monday morning about 11:00 A.M. Around us stumbled the early morning drunks; a ruddy-faced young man in his twenties wore atop his tumble of red curls one of the pastel-beribboned flower tiaras from his cart of souvenirs. On the other side of the street, a woman about Lily's age sat on the sidewalk in black T-shirt and jeans, drinking a beer from a plastic cup. One eye was blacked; I could see darkness where some of her teeth should have been.

We were on our way to Charity for Sophie's AZT treatment, but we had stopped to listen to the jazz band that had set up right in the middle of the avenue—a bright yellow upright piano, a bass fiddle, a steel guitar, a set of drums. Now a skinny girl in a skimpy black crepe cocktail dress was banging away at the yellow piano. A boy in a red bandanna was leaning sensuously into the guitar, making it cry out. The young man on the drums closed his eyes as though in ecstasy, a cigarette hanging from the corner of his voluptuous lips.

Across the street, the girl in the black T-shirt stood up and began to dance, eyes closed, smiling to herself; the beer cup held aloft like a tambourine. I saw just how bad her teeth were, how deep purple the bruise beneath her eyes; that rather than close to Lily's age, she was probably not more than twenty-two or twenty-three. But I also saw how strong she looked, how her dark brown ringlets shone, alive and sparkling, in the New Orleans late morning sunlight.

"I think I'm the happiest I've ever been, right in this moment," Sophie said, smiling at me with a sudden radiance.

"Yeah—I know what you mean," I said, leaning against my dying friend.

It was the first time I decided to live. And I would decide it again and again:

Scratching One-Eyed Jack's fat, scuffed tomcat's jaw.

Seeing the homeless man who had followed me licking a vanilla ice-cream cone in Jackson Square.

Dancing with the whores in San José at that little bar where they liked to go after work.

Or looking into the center of the flower on my kitchen table: Right where the sunlight strikes the table's white-painted top, I have a purple gloxinia with petals so velvety, so lush, that to gaze into its quivering center takes my breath away.

* * *

That flower makes me think of the paintings Musette is doing now, reminding me that I wanted to help her get a little show somewhere.

When we were girls, Musette and I bought little lizards at the county fair, wearing them chained—living bits of jewelry—to our cheap sweaters, waiting impatiently for them to change color.

Just as these days, we both perch in beauty salons crowned by globs of foam, waiting for the pigment to change in our hair. Since mine is brown, the gray turns to blonde streaks. But Musette, darker-haired, complains of her "roots," their stubbornness. "I swan, I always think you're talking about Mama and Daddy, our life back on the farm, when you use that word!" I say when she says that. And she laughs, hearing me revert to one of the phrases we used back then.

We've also had chemical peels, turning our faces first bright pink, then leaving us with complexions as fresh, for a while, as two thirty-year-olds. But strangely, Musette has deep lines across her forehead, indentations like parentheses at the sides of her mouth—as though *my* pain is engraved on *her* face. Every six months she comes to New Orleans to have them injected with a tiny needle full of collagen. Then, her face plumped again, she comes to my apartment, collapses on the chaise longue, while I feed her rum juleps to take away the sting.

"I declare, you've had twice as much fun as me, and have half as many lines!" she exclaims, exasperated at the procedure. Really, I don't know why she bothers, because it's only Ned and her kids and the people at her church to see them. But I guess it's that southern-woman thing—it's our duty, really, to be beautiful—at least as beautiful as we *can* be—and whether it *hurts* or not isn't a factor.

Then we go out to dinner somewhere—the G & D Patio Grill or the Bombay Club—to show off her new look. It's strange to me the way to Musette I represent freedom. After all my grief, I still see the flicker of envy in her eyes as I say that instead of hanging around for the family dinner at her house—the dinner that still takes her a week to prepare—I'm going to Amsterdam this Christmas, or to Mexico again.

355

"You! You're *always* off somewhere!" she says, as though my life has been one long glamorous event. And in fact, I tend to agree with her: Boredom, for some people—people like *me*—is possibly the worst hell of all.

In Berlin these days, women dye their hair the color of Mercurochrome, and everything else is chartreuse.

Here, addiction is on the increase—heroin and cocaine dealers have rushed into the east part of the city to capture the market. I've heard that in Romania—or is it Czechoslovakia?—there is a homemade substitute heroin addicts prepare for the equivalent of pennies in their own kitchens, that the homeless, Virus-infected young fill the streets. On my way here, I saw the legal addicts of Amsterdam, hovering in the vacant buildings near the Hauptbahnhof; the hashish and marijuana shops, the clean-needle and methadone buses, reminding me of how, before I knew better, I thought Lily could possibly go there or to London to live out her life.

I came here to see the works of Käthe Kollwitz, a mother and an artist whose vision was even darker than mine, living as she did through two world wars, the Holocaust, losing a precious son in the first, a grandson in the second, leaving her wishing only to forever use shades of gray in her pictures. Three stories of them in a quiet gray building on Fassanstrasse: ". . . the last third of life remains only work. It alone is always stimulating, rejuvenating, exciting and satisfying," she wrote of her dark art.

My own work, its horror—what seems so shocking in America, where "nice" boys in New Jersey are raping retarded girls with miniature baseball bats, and black boys, in Central Park out wilding, are smashing women to the ground and ravishing them—is ordinary here. On the street near the Hauptbahnhof, I rifle through vivid thin paper posters a skinny boy with a pink Mohawk is selling for five DM each: The two I buy are of an agonized-looking robin, ten-penny nails sticking out of its bleeding shoulders where wings should have been—I can't read the writing, which looks like Polish. The other is titled "*L'Esprit de la Géometrie*," by René Magritte: in it, an oversized baby dressed like a grown woman holds in its arms an infant-sized adult woman.

Looking at it, I recalled the two hulking black boys, no, men, really, I had seen in New Orleans the week before—carrying grocery bags, pushing a woman who must have been their mother in a wheelchair. *Good boys*, I thought, realizing in that moment I would probably never be taken care of in that way by any child of mine—unless Lily with her strong arms decided to do so. No, I had had to be the strong one, and now they mostly hated me for it.

Instead, I'm a born expatriate—if expatriates are those for whom ordinary life has not worked out; or as the joke goes, those who *are* wanted back home, or who aren't. Car bombs, terrorists, none are as worth running from as one's own past. I'm like someone who had always lived surrounded by emotional gunshot—a Beirut or Israel of the spirit. I may have said I wanted peace, but when the gunshot stopped, everything was too quiet.

And Rose has turned out to be the same way. "Mother, I just saw a building blown up by the IRA," she says excitedly, calling me from halfway around the world. In a photo of her taken in Moscow, where she had gone just before the coup for a seminar, I am amazed and pleased at how like me she looks, the differences in our coloring obscured by the black-and-white print. Sometimes I fly to see her, to meet her abroad at some international conference. It's hard to believe that this stern, respected scientist, author of indecipherable papers, speaker of several languages, not to mention my future biographer, is any one of mine. But then there will be a moment when I know it, when I glimpse that little girl again. Once she turned to me suddenly in Florence: "When will it be *my* turn to go crazy, Mama?" she said in the same voice she had used so long ago, asking whether she was about to die. Then she quickly rearranged her face, becoming her adult self, the *doctor*, once more. And going along with her recomposure, I commented on a book we had both been reading—*Why the Reckless Survive*, by Melvin Konner, I think it was: The possibility of ever losing Rose is one I don't allow myself to contemplate.

And ultimately, Rose will keep running—as a Fulbright scholar, then a visiting scientist in first England, then France—from her family, from the Deep South, until she is living more often than not on another continent. And finally, my children—those children I dreamed I couldn't live without—will all be living separated by land masses and even oceans.

Still, sometimes I wake from a dream in which Dwayne and Rose and Lily are all with me again—leaning up against me in a field of bright flowers, smiling, showing me this rock or that blossom. Even Raphael is there, with his dark eyes, his eager face. We are all the same age, the same size, in these moments, and it is as if the door to heaven has opened.

But at other times the dream I wake from is one in which Dwayne is lying on a hot sidewalk, writhing in his own blood; Lily, bound by pieces of once-white sheet, is being stabbed and stabbed by the trick rising above her; or little Raphael is crying—tied to a chair in a closet somewhere, the painted masks ripped from the fiendish faces of his adoptive parents. . . .

And it is in those moments that I think that this whole happy ending is a fiction, fabricated to keep myself from going insane; that this white, white space I find myself in is the walls of an infinite prison or hospital, the very limitations of my own brain. . . .

And then I awake; the day begins.

Strange, isn't it, how we spend our whole lives suffering over family, our children, and whom do we end up with—sharing our meals or our bed? Someone we met last week in a bar or at a dinner party. Someone who sat beside us on a plane.

Funny, too, how sometimes the myths we live our whole lives by turn out not to be true at all.

For so many years, I dreamed of the graves around New Orleans, shifting beneath my very feet: of Lily's grave, and of Dwayne's, floating, floating out to sea, and me unable to stop them. Yet the whole thing turned out to be a myth—a tale Bobby had made up to scare me? One he had heard as a child? "No! No!" laughed a woman who was researching a guidebook to the city when I told her. "That's a nice story—where did you hear it?—but that's not the way the tombs work at all. The bodies *are* layered on top of one another inside the family vaults. But the top one disintegrates, is only bone and dust, falling to join the bone and dust below, by the time the next body replaces it in the crypt. . . ."

The other night, outside Lily's little house in Metairie, I saw lightning bugs for the first time in years. I remembered how she and Rose had laughed, chasing them as they dipped, rose, levitated; of how Dwayne would appear, show his prize— the caviar of tadpole eggs in a Mason jar.

I thought that lightning bugs had disappeared, like those evenings with them, my children, had. But it was not them, just us, who had gone.

And that night, with their perfect grace, the lightning bugs make me think of little Latin dancers; of the liquid sway of hips, thighs, calves, feet, moving to a mariachi band.

Will there be lightning bugs in Mexico?

I'm thinking of leaving New Orleans behind, moving south of the border, possibly to San Miguel de Allende. To go on with my painting there, to live among a group of handsomely aging *norteamericanos*.

I know how it will be in Mexico: At first I will keep in touch, fly back and forth. But after a while, I will stop doing even that. I will sometimes wonder how Lily is, whether she will ever go back to her poetry; whether she is pregnant again; and what kind of mother she is. I will occasionally think of Dwayne: Is he in the country, surrounded by the animals he loves, or still caught in the grime of New Orleans? Are his mood swings less violent, is he less afraid? Or the worst—is he still alive? And Rose—is she well on her way past her first Fulbright, working toward some major prize? Even the Nobel—if women begin receiving the recognition in science that they deserve—wouldn't really surprise me, not that I would be around to see it.

Yes, I will think and wonder about these things. But mainly, I will sit on the tiled verandah, looking out over the bougainvillea, the lush green, sipping the freshly made margarita brought out for me by Manuela: the lime juice too perfectly pungent, sharp; the bougainvillea, the azaleas, the tiger lilies, too bright to allow for regrets.

Or I will sit with a silver-haired friend, drinking mescal straight from the bottle, peeling a perfect *aguacate*, offering a piece to my visitor, sucking a lime between bites. Manuela will serve the soup, the gray swirls of *cuitlacoche*, the melting fungus that grows on the rotting husks of corn, marbling the creamy pool of pale fresh yellow. And my friend and I will be eating and drinking and talking, the moments dissolving like the cotton candy I had once begged Mama to buy me at the county fair. And then I will hardly wonder at all.

This friend will be a traveled man, one who has suffered as well: He will speak of his brain-damaged adult daughter, of the wives he has had—the second of whom died terribly of cancer; of the girl he had later in Africa, before the onset of the Virus. Of the best kind of salmon for gravlax, or the music of Jean-Michel Jarre, and the bars, restaurants, and museums of Berlin or of Amsterdam. Yes, we are so lucky, we will say, sitting here in this beautiful little town in South Mexico, drinking this mescal, eating this soup—"food of the gods," he will comment, this man I met only last month.

And the whole time we are talking, I will think of the smell of him, of what is to come—small white sparks dancing in my groin, for now, closer to death, it has come back to me, even if muted and silvery—the desire I first felt back on that dirt road in South Alabama. . . .

I will tell him of how I had lived a long time ago in a unique Norte American city that existed six feet below sea level, of how that image had tormented me; of how I had read of an experiment in which rats, allowed to drown, thrashed about frantically, in terror, up to the very moment of their deaths.

"Oh, I don't know," he will say mildly, this man who spent many years at sea. "I don't think drowning's so bad. . . ."

A bright white light seems to fill my brain these days as I stand at my easel.

The series I'm working on now is of rooms, beautiful, big, high-ceilinged rooms: a bright white kitchen, a living room filled with colors and flowers, bedrooms with beds so high that sunlight filters through the filmy white curtains, right up under them to the other side, shining off the hardwood floors. The main color is a buttery, healing sunlight. The rooms are filled with this yellow glow and cut flowers and chaise lounges and pillows, plus egg shapes as comforting as Ovaltine, reminiscent of when I was still fertile; and everyone I have ever loved— Mama, Daddy, Dwayne, Rose, Lily, Raphael—is moving, floating, gracefully in and out of them. I'm in the pictures, too, and in some rooms we flow together in a fluid embrace. *Rooms, or the Comfort of Enclosed Spaces*, I call them.

In one of the pictures, Dwayne floats before an easel, several tamed wild animals—a lynx, an iguana, an opossum—at his feet. Lily, in the kitchen, is mixing something in a big blue bowl, babies floating around her head. In a bedroom, Mama is pulling on a beautiful sexy dress, her body as shapely as Betty Grable's, spraying cologne around her hair, her beautiful hair, which turns into an aura of many-colored light. In another room, Rose is suspended over strange machines, laboratory test tubes; books and symbols fill the air around her. Musette is floating free of the butter beans she had been shelling, rising right up through the top of the house, which has no roof. And Daddy—Daddy is smiling, as sweet, as protective, as the Daddy of my dreams, a little me, plump and safe, sitting on his welcoming lap.

Superimposed in the foreground of one picture is a perfect purple gloxinia. I thought of connecting a sound track to the back of one of the canvases, playing that hymn from my childhood: *Love LIFT-ed me . . . Oh, love LIFT-ed me. . . . I was SINK-ing DEEP in sin . . . FAR from the PEACE-ful shore . . . when He CAME and took me in. . . . Love LIFT-ed me. . . .*

That's what rings through my mind as I paint. I can hear it almost as though it were yesterday, the one near-cheerful hymn we sang at the Church of God. The words I grew up with as a girl back in South Alabama now reverberate in my dreams.

Oh, I know what the critics will say—too much Matisse, and where is her usual blood? What they once criticized me for they've come to expect. But this floatiness is what I want now, what I dream at night. The best one is Mama and Daddy and me in a field of bright flowers: We're all the same height, the same age, and the flowers are as tall as we are; our smiling faces are shining, raised right up toward the sun. . . .

This, these pictures, are my dream come true—all of us together in a beautiful house of many rooms.

"How did you die?" I ask Dwayne. He is sitting in my bedroom, friendly and smiling. A tall lifesize puppet of him hangs within one side of my armoire, the door of which is open, so I can see it. It, too, seems a friendly presence.

I want to know how he died, to know that it was easy, peaceful, not painful. His smile is reassuring. So he hasn't had to die without a mother's love after all; nor, worse, have I without his. Now that he's dead, I'm able to love him, be embraced by him, even to make love with him if I wish—to love him as I never have been able to do in life, I realize, taking his warm hand in my own. . . .

And this is my beloved son, with whom I am well pleased.

From *Notes for a Biography of Easter O'Brian* by Dr. Rose Bowers

Dearest Rose, my daughter and my friend:

. . . . You wrote to ask whether I have regrets.

Looking back, I see that there were three things I wanted in life, and that I was driven toward them equally—sex, you three children, and Art. I was obsessed by each, and at times they seemed to war inside my very soul. . . .

But we *norteamericanos* think we can be happy despite everything, and I'm no exception. About my kids, I've "accepted reality" (with you, of course, this has been easy). I'm careful in my choices of men. I haven't been murdered, committed suicide, contracted the Virus, or turned alcoholic—all of which, for an artist, borders on the slightly miraculous. . . .

I do know how driven we are by biology—I credit *you* with that, Rose; a personal myth engraved onto our genes: a myth that, deterred for a moment, turns us crazed, aberrant. . . .

Jargon can't say what it's about, that mystery. But the body knows—the body is imprinted. And now it all seems to have been as inevitable as the seasons, or death: in its own strange way beautiful, a blood-black leaf twisting on an endless breeze. . . .

"Take what you want, and pay for it"—isn't that what the Spanish proverb advises?

And I have, Rose—I *have*.

San Miguel de Allende, 1995